"You're here now and apparently I can't do anything about that.

"But let me make one thing very clear. I don't want your sympathy, Alexis. I'm all sympathized out."

"I can see that," she said. Her voice was dry and calm but he could see the shadows in her dark chocolate brown eyes and he knew he'd hurt her.

He closed his own eyes briefly and dragged in a leveling breath. He hadn't meant to be so harsh, but it was his default setting these days. "I'm going for a shower," he said tightly and left.

He'd fought against this happening. He'd known, logically, that one day his defenses would be worn down. He just never imagined those defenses would be stormed by the one woman in the whole world he'd hoped never to see again and yet still craved with a hunger he could never assuage.

* * *

Wanting What She Can't Have
is part of The Master Vinters series:
Tangled vines, tangled lives

WANTING WHAT
SHE CAN'T HAVE

BY
YVONNE LINDSAY

Published in Great Britain 2014
by Mills & Boon, an imprint of Harlequin (UK) Limited,
Eton House, 18-24 Paradise Road, Richmond, Surrey, TW9 1SR

© 2014 Dolce Vita Trust

ISBN: 978 0 263 91464 1

51-0414

Harlequin (UK) Limited's policy is to use papers that are natural, renewable and recyclable products and made from wood grown in sustainable forests. The logging and manufacturing processes conform to the legal environmental regulations of the country of origin.

Printed and bound in Spain
by Blackprint CPI, Barcelona

New Zealand born, to Dutch immigrant parents, **Yvonne Lindsay** became an avid romance reader at the age of thirteen. Now, married to her "blind date" and with two fabulous children, she remains a firm believer in the power of romance. Yvonne feels privileged to be able to bring to her readers the stories of her heart. In her spare time, when not writing, she can be found with her nose firmly in a book, reliving the power of love in all walks of life. She can be contacted via her website, www.yvonnelindsay.com.

This book is for you, Soraya Lane—
the most awesome sprint buddy a writer
could ever want. Without you this story would have
been so much harder to write. Thank you!

One

Alexis watched him from the doorway to the winery. Late afternoon sun slanted through the windows at the end of the room, illuminating tiny dust motes that floated on air redolent with the scent of fermented grapes. But she was oblivious to the artistic beauty of the setting—her focus solely on the man who worked on, unaware of her presence.

He'd changed. God, how he'd changed. He was thinner, gaunt even, and his signature well-groomed appearance had given way to a self-executed haircut, a stretched and faded T-shirt and torn jeans. His face obviously hadn't seen a razor in several days. But then grief was bound to do that to a man—to diminish the importance of the everyday tasks he'd done automatically and replace them with indifference.

How could she help a man who was clearly long past any interest in helping himself?

The weight of what she'd agreed to do felt heavy and uncomfortable on her shoulders. She, the one who always willingly stepped up to the plate when everything went pear-shaped, was now thinking that perhaps this time she'd bitten off more than she could chew.

Straightening her shoulders, she shook off her doubts. Bree had turned to her in her time of need—had written a letter that begged Alexis to take care of her husband and the child she'd been on the verge of delivering should something happen to her, as if she'd known what lay ahead. While her best friend had died before Alexis could give her that promise, in her heart she knew she couldn't refuse—couldn't walk away. Even if keeping that promise meant putting her heart back in firing range from the man she'd been magnetically drawn to from the moment she'd first met him.

Raoul stilled in his actions. His attention shifted from the table of wine samples before him, his pen dropping from his hand to the clipboard covered in hand-scrawled notes that lay on the stark white tablecloth. He lifted his head and turned toward her, his face registering a brief flash of surprise together with something else she couldn't quite put her finger on. It was gone in an instant, replaced by a tight mask of aloofness.

"Alexis," he said, accompanied by a tight nod.

"I came as soon as I heard. I'm sorry it took so long. I…" Her voice trailed away. How did you tell a man that it had taken almost a year to hear about the birth of his daughter and the death of the love of his life because you'd severed ties with his wife, your best friend since kindergarten, when it became too painful to see her happiness with him? That you'd "forgotten" to give her your new email address or the number to the cell phone you bought when your work started requiring more international travel because you couldn't bear to hear any more about how perfect they were together? Because you had coveted him for yourself?

Because you still did.

She took a deep breath and swallowed against the lump of raw grief that swelled in her throat.

"I've been traveling for a while, ever since my business…" The words died at the expression on his face. Clearly Raoul could not care less about the success she'd been enjoying ever since her clothing line finally started taking off. "Bree's letter caught up with me at my father's house. It must have been following me around the world for the past year."

"Bree's letter?"

"To tell me about her pregnancy."

Should she tell him also that Bree had begged her to watch out for her husband and her, at that time, as yet unborn child? That she'd somehow known that the aortic aneurysm she'd kept secret from her family would take her life in childbirth? One look at his face confirmed he hadn't known of his wife's correspondence to her.

"So, you're back."

Finally. The unspoken word hung on the air between them, both an accusation and an acknowledgment at the same time.

"My mother was ill. I made it back a few weeks before she died at Christmas."

"I'm sorry."

The platitude fell automatically from his lips but she sensed his shields go up even stronger. He didn't want to know, not really. Not when he was still locked tight in his own sorrow, his own grief.

"I only got Bree's letter last week and rang her mom straightaway. I'm here to help with Ruby."

"The child already has a carer, her grandmother."

"Yes, but Catherine needs surgery, Raoul. She can't keep putting her knee replacement off, especially now that Ruby is getting more active."

"I told her to find a nanny if she needed to."

"And I understand you rejected every résumé she presented to you. That you wouldn't even agree to interview any of the applicants."

He shrugged. "They weren't good enough."

Alexis felt her temper begin to rise. Catherine had been beside herself with worry over what to do. The osteoarthritis in her knee caused constant pain and made looking after a small child more difficult every day. She needed the surgery as soon as possible, but that meant Ruby absolutely had to have a new caretaker. By refusing to look at the résumés, Raoul was ignoring his responsibilities—to his daughter, to her grandmother and to Bree's memory. He looked at her again, harder this time. What on earth was going on behind those hazel eyes of his?

"And what about me? Am I good enough?"

"No," he answered emphatically. "Definitely not."

She pushed aside the hurt his blunt refusal triggered.

"Why? You know I'm qualified—I have experience caring for little ones."

"You're a dressmaker now, though, aren't you? Hardly what the child needs."

Wow, he was really on form with the insults, wasn't he, she thought. Dressmaker? Well, yes, she still made some of her signature designs but for the most part she outsourced the work now. She'd trained as a nanny when she'd left school, and had completed a full year intensive academic and practical experience program because her parents had been opposed to her trying to make a career following her artistic talent alone. But three years ago, when her last contract had finished, she'd realized it was time to follow her dream. That dream was now coming to fruition with her clothing label being distributed to high-end boutiques around the country and in various hot spots around the world. But Raoul didn't care about any of that.

"I've arranged cover for my business," she said, sending a silent prayer of thanks to her half sister, Tamsyn, for stepping into the breach. "Catherine's already hired me, Raoul."

"I'm unhiring you."

Alexis sighed. Bree's mom had said he might be difficult. She hadn't been kidding.

"Don't you think it's better that Ruby be cared for by someone who knew her mother, who knows her family, rather than by a total stranger?"

"I don't care."

His words struck at her heart but she knew them for a lie. The truth was he cared too much.

"Catherine is packing Ruby's things up now and bringing them over. She thought it best if she settled here from tonight rather than having me pick up Ruby in the morning."

Raoul's face visibly paled. "I said no, dammit! No to you as her nanny, and definitely no to either of you living here."

"Her surgery is scheduled for tomorrow afternoon. Ruby can't stay at her grandmother's house any longer. She needs to be home, with you."

Raoul pushed shaking fingers through hair cut close to his scalp—shorter than she'd ever seen it before. His hand dropped back down again and she watched as he gathered himself together, his fingers curling into tight fists as if he was holding on by a thread.

"Just keep her away from me."

Alexis blinked in shock. Catherine had said Raoul had little to do with his nine-month-old daughter aside from meeting the financial requirements of her care. But despite the warning, Alexis couldn't come to terms with what she'd been told. Ruby had been born out of love between two wonderful people who'd had the world at their feet when they'd married only two and a half years ago. She'd attended their wedding herself. Seen with her own eyes how much they'd adored one another and, to her shame, had been stricken with envy. That Raoul virtually ignored Ruby's existence was so terribly sad. Did he blame the little girl for her mother's death? Or could he just not bear the constant reminder of how he had lost the love he and Bree had shared?

Alexis forced herself to nod in response to his demand and started back up the unsealed lane from the winery toward the house—a large multiroomed masterpiece that sprawled across the top of the hill. Catherine had already given her a key along with a hefty supply of groceries and baby products. She'd need to put everything away before Catherine arrived with Ruby.

Ruby. A sharp pain lanced through her when she thought of the baby's cherubic face. A happy, healthy and contented child, she was obviously closely bonded with Bree's mom. To look at her, one would never guess that she had faced so much trouble in her short life.

After a slightly early arrival, exacerbated by a post-natal infection, Ruby had spent the first few weeks of her life in an incubator, crying for the mother she would never be able to meet. Catherine had shared with Alexis her theory that the pitiful cries, piled on top of his own grief, had been too much for Raoul to bear. He'd withdrawn from his newborn daughter, leaving her care to his mother-in-law. Catherine had been Ruby's sole caregiver ever since.

Transplanting her to her father's house and into the care of someone else would have its challenges. Getting Raoul to acknowledge and interact with his daughter would be the hardest—and the most necessary.

They needed each other, Alexis was certain of that. Even though she could do nothing else for Bree, she'd make sure that Raoul stepped up to his responsibilities to his late wife's memory and to the child she'd borne him.

She was here. He'd known that one day she'd come and he'd dreaded every second. Seeing her had cracked open the bubble of isolation he'd built for himself, leaving him feeling raw and exposed. He was unaccustomed to having to share this place with anyone but Bree—or, for the past year, Bree's memory.

Two years ago, returning with Bree after their marriage to his roots here in Akaroa, on the Banks Peninsula of New Zealand's South Island, had felt natural and right. He'd bought out his father's boutique vineyard operation, allowing his parents to finally fulfill their lifelong dream of traveling through the wine-growing districts of Europe and South America, and allowing himself to settle in to what he'd seen as an enjoyable new stage in his career.

At the time, it had been a fun and exciting change of pace. Raoul had gone as far as he could go as Nate Hunter-Jackson's second in charge at Jackson Importers up in Auckland. While he'd loved every minute of the challenges working in the wine purveyance and distribution network built up over two generations, his heart had always been locked in at the source of the wine.

After settling in following the wedding, Raoul had dedicated himself to the vines. Meanwhile, Bree had project managed the building of their new home, seeing to the finishing details even as Ruby's anticipated arrival had drawn near.

At the start of his marriage, what he did here, wrapped in the science of blending his boutique wines, had been an adventure, almost a game. His work had been filled with the same exuberant hopes for the future as his marriage.

Losing Bree had shaken the ground under his feet, and his work had gone from a pastime to an obsession. Life was filled with twists and turns that were beyond his abilities to predict, but this…this was something he could control. He was working with known quantities, with wines that had been made in the stainless-steel vats behind him from the very grapes grown on vines that snaked down the hillsides to the harbor—*terroir* that had become as much a part of him as breathing. Work was stable, steadying. And when he'd finished for the day and returned to the house, he could sink back into his memories and his mourning. He'd never shared this home with anyone but Bree—and now he shared it with her ghost.

Alexis's arrival changed all that. She was so vibrantly alive and in the moment that she made living in the past impossible. Even their brief conversation had been enough to make him feel self-consciously alert, keenly aware of the disheveled appearance he usually couldn't be bothered to notice.

And aware of *her* in a way that filled him with shame. He hadn't been the husband Bree had deserved, not entirely, not when—even though he'd kept it fully under wraps—he'd desired her best friend. Was it infidelity when a person only thought about another? He'd loved Bree, there'd been no doubt about that. Adored her, idolized her. Cherished her. But deep down inside, there'd been a primitive part of him that had craved Alexis Fabrini on a level so base he'd had to jam it down deep inside.

He'd been relieved when he'd heard Alexis had headed overseas—how, after her last contract as a nanny had neared completion, she'd changed career direction and had begun pouring herself into fashion design. Some of Alexis's designs still hung in Bree's closet. Bree had been so excited for her, albeit a little hurt and puzzled when Alexis let contact drop between them.

Living with Alexis would be hell. He gave a humorless laugh. What else was new? Just living was hell. Each day a torture. Each day a reminder that he'd failed in that most basic tenet of keeping his wife safe. Of ensuring her needs were put before his own.

He'd never made it a secret that he'd wanted a large family—and because he'd been so outspoken, so determined in his plans for the future she'd felt the need to keep a secret that would have made him change his mind. Given a choice between a family and Bree, he'd have chosen Bree every time. Yet she'd hidden the news about the aneurysm that killed her until it was too late, putting the baby's life ahead of her own.

Ruby. He could barely think about her without being reminded of failure yet again. Drowning in his own grief, he hadn't been able to bear the weak sound of her cries—or the bone-deep certainty that he would lose her, too. She'd been so ill at birth... It was better this way, he'd decided. To keep his distance and not risk the pain that would come if he got too used to having her in his life.

Raoul turned back to the table, to the wines he'd been sampling and assessing for what was his favorite part of wine production—the blending. He forced himself to settle back down in his chair, to study his notes and then to reach for another glass of wine.

Sour. He grimaced and took a sip of water, rinsing the bitter tang from his mouth before reaching for another glass. Again, sour. He threw himself against the back of his chair in disgust. He knew the flavor of the wine had little to do with his skills as a vintner and far more to do with his current state of mind. Whether he wanted to admit it or not, his working day was over—which left, what exactly? Time to go up to the house to reminisce about old times with Alexis?

His gut twisted at the very thought. Even so, he pushed himself upright and cleared away his work, neatly filing away his notes for tomorrow and rinsing out all the glasses, leaving them to drain on the rack before he started up the lane.

Alexis was in the kitchen when he got into the house. He could hear her moving around, opening and closing cupboard doors, humming in an off-key tone. It sounded so domestic and normal for a second he allowed himself to hope, to dream that it was Bree there in the kitchen.

But the second Alexis's curvy frame came into the doorway the illusion was shattered.

"I can see why Catherine sent me up here with all this food. You had hardly anything in the pantry at all, and the fridge just about echoes it's so empty. What on earth have you been living on? Thin air?"

He knew she was trying to be friendly but he armored himself against the attempt.

"I get by. I didn't ask you to come here and criticize how I live."

"No, you didn't," she said with a rueful twist of lush lips that were made for long, hot, hungry kisses.

Viciously he slammed a lid down on the thought. He wasn't going there. Ever.

"By the way," she continued blithely, "while I found Ruby's room easily enough, I'm not sure which room you wanted me in. I went into one of the spare rooms but it looked like your things were in there."

He hadn't been able to bear returning to the master bedroom, not with all its memories of Bree.

"Take the room nearest the nursery."

"But isn't that the master suite?"

"I don't use it, aside from storing a few clothes. I'll take the last of them out of there for you."

"Okay, do you need a hand? Maybe I could—"

"Look, I don't want you here, and I certainly don't need your help. Catherine's decided you should take care of Ruby, but that's all you're here to do. Let's just agree to stay out of one another's way and everything will be just fine."

He ground out the last word as if his life depended on it.

"Raoul—!"

"Don't," he said putting up a hand. "You're here now and apparently I can't do anything about that. But let me make one thing very clear. I don't want your sympathy, Alexis. I'm all sympathied out."

"I can see that," she said. Her voice was dry and calm but he could see the shadows in her dark chocolate-brown eyes and he knew he'd hurt her.

He closed his own eyes briefly and dragged in a leveling breath. He hadn't meant to be so harsh but it was his default setting these days. Living alone didn't make one the best conversationalist, that was for sure.

The sound of a car outside heralded the arrival of his mother-in-law and, from the shriek and gurgle of laughter that followed the sound of a car door opening, the baby. His blood ran cold. His chest tightened making it hard to breathe.

"I'm going for a shower," he said tightly, and left before Alexis could move to let Catherine and Ruby into the house.

He strode to his room and slammed the door behind him before moving to his bathroom and locking the door. He disrobed with a minimum of movement and stepped into the shower stall even as he turned on the faucets. The water, when it hit him, was chilling—painful—but that was nothing compared to the pain of the gaping hole inside him. Nothing at all.

He'd fought against this happening, having the baby here under the same roof, and he'd won the battle for so long. The nursery, so lovingly decorated by Bree, had never been used. He'd known, logically, that one day his defenses would be worn down, that he'd have to step up to his responsibilities as a father. He just never imagined those defenses would be stormed by the one woman in the whole world he'd hoped never to see again and yet still craved with a hunger he could never assuage.

Two

Alexis held little Ruby's weight against her, relishing the solid warmth of the child's small body and inhaling the special baby scent of her hair and skin. So far, so good, she thought as they watched Catherine drive away. The older woman had been torn, clearly reluctant to leave Ruby behind, but Alexis had hastened to assure her that she was doing the right thing, for them all, but most of all for herself. She was already nervous enough about her upcoming surgery, she didn't need the added worry of wondering how well Ruby would settle into her father's home.

A light breeze lifted a tuft of Ruby's fine auburn hair and brushed against Alexis's cheek, the touch as soft and delicate as fingertips tracing lightly across her skin. A sudden pang for Bree cut her to the quick. The realization that she would never see her friend again, never share a bottle of wine and silly laughter over happy remembrances. Never again squabble over who was the more handsome out of the Hemsworth brothers.

Her hold on the baby in her arms, the child her friend never got to see outside of a sonogram, tightened and Ruby squawked in protest.

"I'm sorry, precious girl," Alexis murmured into the baby's soft fuzz of hair.

She fought back the burn of tears that threatened to cascade down her face and made a silent vow. *I will look after your daughter, Bree, I promise. And I will love her and care for her and keep you alive in her heart forever.*

Stepping back indoors, Alexis noticed that Raoul was nowhere to be seen inside the house. A good thing perhaps? Alexis couldn't be certain. She popped Ruby on the floor with a few of the toys that Catherine had brought over with the baby and sat down with her. She seemed a placid enough child now, although Alexis knew from Ruby's grandmother that she'd been very ill and demanding as a newborn. Understandable, given her start in life, she rationalized as she watched the little girl reach for a multicolored teddy and pull it to her, cuddling it as she popped her thumb in her mouth. Her big blue eyes stared back solemnly at Alexis.

Somewhere in the house a door slammed shut and Ruby and Alexis both jumped. Alexis laughed softly.

"Goodness," she said rolling onto her belly on the floor and tickling the baby on one of her delightfully pudgy feet. "That was loud, wasn't it?"

She was rewarded with a shy smile that exposed four perfect pearl-like teeth and she felt her heart twist in response. While Ruby's coloring was exactly that of her mother's, her smile was all Raoul.

"You're going to be quite the heartbreaker, aren't you, young lady?"

The baby's chin began to wrinkle and her lower lip to quiver. Her thumb fell from her mouth and she let rip with a wail, her blue eyes filling with tears as she stared past Alexis.

"Oh, dear, was it something I said?"

Alexis pushed herself up into a sitting position and pulled the baby into her lap, rubbing her back in an attempt to soothe her but to no avail. A prickle of awareness up her spine made her realize they were no longer alone.

She swiveled her head and saw Raoul standing there behind them, frozen to the spot. His usually tan face was a sickly shade of gray.

"What's wrong with her? Why's she crying?" he demanded, his voice harsh and setting Ruby to cry even harder.

"Raoul, are you okay?" she asked, lithely getting to her feet and holding the baby against her.

His eyes were clamped on Ruby who buried her face into Alexis's chest and continued to cry.

"I'm fine," he said tightly, looking anything but. "Why's she crying like that?"

"I assume it's because she got a bit of a fright when you came into the room. Plus, this is all strange to her, isn't it? Being here, missing Catherine, having me around."

He nodded. "Please, can't you do something to calm her?"

Alexis gave him a rueful smile. "I'm doing my best," she said, jiggling Ruby gently. "Perhaps you could soften your tone a little?"

He made a dismissive gesture with one hand. "I'd prefer you keep the child confined to her room while I'm in the house."

"But this is her home. You are kidding me, right?" Alexis said incredulously.

His eyes dragged from Ruby's sobbing form to Alexis's face.

"No. I'm not."

He turned to walk out of the living room, but Alexis would have none of it.

"Stop right there," she said with as much authority as she could muster. "You act like Ruby is an unwanted stranger here. She's your daughter for goodness' sake."

Raoul turned around slowly. "It wasn't my wish for her to come here and her presence is disruptive. As her nanny, your role is to confine your skills and your opinions to her care and her care alone. Is that understood?"

Alexis didn't recognize the man in front of her. Sure, he mostly looked like the same Raoul Benoit she'd been introduced to shortly before he married her best friend, and he sounded the same. Her body certainly still had the same response to his presence, that unsettling thrill of awareness that buzzed along her nerve endings whenever she was near him. But the words... They weren't the words of a bereaved husband or a caring father. And he *did* care—whether he wanted to admit it or not. So why was he trying so hard to distance himself from Ruby?

"Is that understood?" he repeated. "Your charge is distressed. I suggest you do whatever it is that you need to do to calm her and do it quickly."

He tried to sound aloof but she could see the lines of strain around his eyes. It pulled at his heart to hear his little girl cry. She knew it as sure as she knew the reflection of her own face in the mirror each morning.

"Here, you take her for me and I'll go and get her dinner ready. It's time for her evening meal, anyway."

He took a rapid step back and looked as her as if she'd suggested he tip vinegar into a barrel of his finest wine.

"Are you telling me you're incapable of fulfilling your duties as a nanny?"

"No," she said as patiently as she could. "Of course not. I thought you might like to hold your daughter to distract her, while I prepare her something to eat before her bath."

"I don't pay you to hand the baby over to me, Alexis," he said bluntly before spinning around and leaving the room as silently as he'd entered it.

Ruby lifted her little head to peer around Alexis carefully, putting her thumb firmly back in her mouth when she was satisfied her father had departed.

"Well, that didn't go quite as well as I expected," Alexis said softly to the little girl. "I thought your grandmother might be exaggerating when she said that your daddy didn't have anything to do with you. Looks like we have our work cut out for us, hmm?"

She kissed the top of Ruby's head and, adjusting her a little higher on her hip, took her through to the kitchen. Grabbing a paper towel, she moistened it under the faucet and gently wiped tear tracks from two chubby little cheeks. Ruby clearly wasn't a fan of paper towels and Alexis made a mental note to search out the muslin squares she'd seen amongst the baby's things in the nursery. She popped Ruby into her high chair and gave her a plain cookie to chew on—who said you couldn't start dinner with dessert every now and again?—while she scanned Catherine's comprehensive notes on Ruby's diet and sleeping times. The baby was still napping twice in a day and, after a 250 ml bottle at bedtime, pretty much slept through the night except for when she was cutting a tooth.

It all looked very straightforward. Alexis sighed and looked at the little girl. How could Raoul not want to be a part of her care? The very idea was almost impossible to contemplate. If she hadn't heard him just a few moments ago she would have denied that he could possibly be so cold.

But was he really cold? There'd been something flickering in his hazel eyes that she hadn't quite been able to identify. Thinking back on it, could it have been fear? Could he be afraid of his own daughter?

Ruby chose that moment to wearily rub at her eyes with cookie-goop-covered hands, galvanizing Alexis back into action. If she was going to get a dinner inside the tot she needed to feed her now before she fell asleep in her high chair. After coaxing Ruby through her meal of reheated soft-cooked ravioli, which Catherine had thoughtfully made and supplied for tonight, she held Ruby carefully over the kitchen sink and turned on the cold tap, letting her clap her little hands in the stream as the water washed away the food residue.

"I think you're wearing about as much food as you've eaten." Alexis laughed as she used a clean tea towel to dry their hands and give Ruby's face a quick wipe before whisking her back through the house to the nursery.

After a bath and a new diaper, fresh pajamas, and a bottle, Ruby was down in her crib. Alexis rubbed her back for a little while, concerned she might not settle in what were obviously strange surroundings, but it seemed her earlier upset had worn Ruby out and she was asleep in no time. After Alexis checked to ensure the baby monitor was on, she clipped its partner to the loop of her jeans and left the room.

Outside in the hall she came to a halt. She really didn't know what to do next. Should she seek out Raoul and press him for more explanation over his behavior earlier, or simply carry on as if nothing had happened? She worried at her lower lip with her teeth. Until she'd seen him again today she would have done the former of the two—without question. But after that stilted, almost hostile, encounter, she was reluctant to muddy the waters between them any more than they already were.

She still needed to unpack her things, so she went into the master bedroom where she'd put her suitcase earlier on. The door to the walk-in wardrobe stood open and she gravitated toward it. One side was completely bare of anything but naked hangers, the other still filled with women's clothing. Her heart stuttered in her chest as she reached out and touched a few of the things hanging there, as a hint of Bree's favorite scent wafted out.

That awful sense of emptiness filled her again along with a renewed feeling of deep sympathy for the man who hadn't yet been able to bring himself to pack his dead wife's things away. She stepped out of the wardrobe and closed the door behind her, turning instead to the native rimu tallboy that stood proud against one wall. The drawers were empty, so she filled them with her things, then shoved her now-redundant case into the wardrobe without looking again at the silent memorial that still hung there.

A knock at her door make her start.

"Yes?" she called out.

The door opened and Raoul filled the frame. Instantly her senses sprang to life. Her body hummed with that almost electric responsiveness to his proximity—her eyes roaming over him, taking in the way his clothing hung just a little too loosely on his rangy frame. It was hard to believe he was the same man as before. But then again, he wasn't, was he? He'd been through hell and she needed to remember that as she tackled her new role. To perhaps be a little less judgmental.

For all the differences—from subtle to striking—in

his appearance and in his manner, there was no doubting the instant effect he had on her equilibrium. Even now she could feel her heart beat that little bit faster, her breathing become a little more shallow. She dug her fingernails into her palms in an attempt to distract herself from her reaction to him.

"I just wanted to make sure you'd settled in okay," he said stiffly, not quite meeting her eyes.

She nodded, unsure of what to say about Bree's things. Or even if she should say anything about them at all.

"The baby's quiet now. Is she all right?"

"Ruby's down for the night. Catherine tells me she usually goes through until about six-thirty, or seven, so as long as she isn't unsettled by sleeping somewhere unfamiliar, you shouldn't hear from her again until morning."

"How do you know she's okay? You're not with her right now."

Alexis tapped the monitor on her belt loop. "I have the monitor. As soon as she stirs I'll know, trust me."

"Hmm, are you sure it's working?"

"It looked pretty new when I removed it from the packaging and I put fresh batteries in this unit myself before Ruby arrived."

He flinched slightly and Alexis took a moment to realize why. Of course, he and Bree would have bought all the things in the nursery in readiness for when they brought their infant home for the first time. Bree was likely the last person to have touched that monitor before Alexis.

"They might be old. I'll get you new ones. Make sure you change them immediately."

Alexis fought the urge to salute at his command. Instead she merely inclined her head. He was showing concern, which was a good thing even if she wished it came with a less imperious tone.

"Is there anything else? I thought I might start getting our evening meal ready. Ruby obviously ate earlier but now I have time to put something together for us. Will you be joining me?"

"No." His response was emphatic. "I'll see to myself."

"It's no bother. I may as well cook for two adults as for one. I'll leave your meal warming in the oven."

His body sagged, as if he was giving up in this battle—perhaps choosing to shore up his strength for another time. "Thank you."

"If you change your mind about eating with me, feel free. It'd be nice to catch up. Or, if you'd rather, have breakfast with Ruby and me in the morning. It'd be good for her to spend more time with her dad, and good for you, too."

Raoul sighed and swiped one hand across his face. She saw his jaw clench before he spoke again.

"Look, I know you're determined to do what you think is the right thing, but you and the baby being here is a complication I can do without. Don't make it any harder for me than it already has to be."

"But—"

"No buts, Alexis. I mean it. If there had been any other alternative to this, believe me, I would have chosen it. Once Catherine is mobile again I expect things to return to normal."

"Normal? But this isn't normal, is it? Not by any stretch of the imagination," Alexis protested. "Bree wouldn't have wanted you to be so distant from your own flesh and blood."

He paled as if he'd been dealt a mortal blow. "Don't," he said brokenly, shaking his head and backing toward the door. "Don't throw that at me. You have no idea—"

He shook his head once more. "Just do what you were hired to do, Alexis. End of topic."

He was gone in an instant and Alexis wrapped her arms around herself in a vain attempt to provide some comfort for herself where there was none. So, it seemed she couldn't even mention her best friend without making Raoul run. That he'd loved her deeply was patently obvious. But how could that love not extend to their little girl?

Three

Raoul lay in bed unable to sleep any longer. It was time he rose anyway, time to escape to the winery before Alexis and Ruby took over the house. No longer was his home the quiet sanctuary contained by the boundaries of his property. No longer was coming to the house a peaceful pilgrimage to the past. No longer was it his safe place where he could be alone with his memories.

They'd been here a week—a hellishly long time, in his estimation—and since Alexis's and the baby's arrival he spent as little time as humanly possible in the house. And since he still wasn't ready to face the world at large, that meant he spent as much time as he could in the winery where he wasn't constantly being distracted by the presence of two very unsettling females.

Just yesterday he'd caught Alexis shifting things in the sitting room—raising the tide line, she'd called it—because Ruby was pulling herself up on the furniture and starting to walk around things, grabbing for whatever she could reach. While he understood the necessity of keeping Ruby safe, the idea of changing anything from the way Bree had left it was profoundly unsettling.

He yawned widely. Sleep had been as elusive last night as it had been since Alexis's accusation of his behavior being abnormal. Her words had stung. She had no idea what he went through every time he looked at Ruby. Every time he saw a miniature Bree seated before him. He'd almost managed to bring the shock of pain under control, but the echoing empty loss that came hard on its heels unraveled him in ways he didn't even want to begin to acknowledge.

And then there was the fear—an awful irrational beast that built up in his chest and threatened to consume him. What if Ruby got sick, or was hurt? What if he didn't know what to do, or didn't react fast enough? It was an almost unbearable sense of responsibility lessened only slightly by knowing Alexis was here shouldering the bulk of it. Raoul shoved aside his bedcovers and got out of bed, yanking his pajama bottoms up higher on his hips. Everything slid off him these days. It hadn't mattered when he was here alone but now, with his privacy totally invaded, he had to be a little more circumspect. Even locked in his antisocial bubble he could see that.

Suddenly his senses went on full alert, his skin awash with a chill of terror as he heard a muted thump come from the nursery followed by a sharp cry from the baby. For a second he was frozen, but another cry followed hard on the heels of the first, sending him flying down the hallway toward God only knew what disaster. His heart felt too big in his chest, its beat too rapid, and he fought to drag in a shuddering breath as he reached the doorway, almost too afraid to open the door and look inside.

Ruby's howls had increased several decibels. Where the hell was Alexis? The child's care was her job. Reluctantly, he turned the handle and pushed open the door. He winced as Ruby let out another earsplitting yell. Something had to be horribly wrong, he was sure. Fine tremors racked his body as he visually examined the red-faced infant standing up in her crib, howling her throat out.

His eyes flew over her, searching for some visible cause for her distress. She was so small—miniature everything from the tiny feet tipped with even tinier toes to the top of her auburn fuzzed head—all except for the sound bellowing from her lungs.

Clearly nothing wrong with those.

There was absolutely nothing he could see that could be responsible for her upset. Nothing external, anyway. Fear twisted in his stomach as he took a step into the room. It was always what you couldn't see that was the most dangerous.

One pudgy little hand gripped the top rail of the side of her crib, the other reached out helplessly...toward what? Looking around, he spotted a toy on the floor. From its position, he'd guess that it had been in the crib with her and she'd flung it across the room. And still she screamed.

Was that all this was about? A stupid toy?

He gingerly picked up the mangled black-and-white zebra and handed it to her, avoiding actual physical contact. The sobs ceased for a moment—but only a moment before she hurled it back to the floor, plonked herself down on her bottom on her mattress and began once more to howl.

"Oh, dear, so it's going to be one of those days, is it?"

Alexis bustled past him and toward the crib.

"Where the hell have you been? She's been crying

for ages," Raoul demanded, pushing one hand through his hair.

"About a minute, actually, but yes, I agree, it feels like forever when she's upset."

She competently lifted Ruby from the crib and hugged her to her body. Raoul became instantly aware of how the child snuggled against Alexis's scantily clad form—in particular Alexis's full, unbound breasts that were barely covered by a faded singlet. She wore it over pajama shorts that, heaven help him, rode low on her softly curved hips and high on her tanned legs.

A surge of heat slowly rolled through his body, making his skin feel tight—uncomfortable with recognition of her lush femininity. But then he became aware of something else.

"What is that god-awful smell?"

"Probably the reason why she's awake earlier than normal. She needs a clean diaper and she's very fussy about that. It's good really, it'll make potty training so much easier later on. Some kids are absolutely oblivious."

Raoul backed out of the room. "Are you sure that's all? Maybe she ought to see the doctor and get checked out."

Alexis just laughed. The sound washed over him like a gentle caress—its touch too much, too intimate.

"I see nothing to laugh about. She might be sick," he said, his body rigid with anxiety.

"Oh, no. Nothing like that," Alexis replied, her back to him as she laid Ruby down on her change table.

With one hand gently on the baby's tummy, she reached for a packet of wipes, the movement making the already short hemline of her pajama shorts ride even higher and exposing the curve of one buttock. The warmth that had previously invaded his body now ignited to an instant inferno. He turned away from the scene before him, as much to hide his stirring erection as to avoid watching the diaper change.

He turned back a minute later, almost under complete control once more, as Alexis dropped the soiled packet into the diaper bin, one Raoul distinctly remembered Bree ordering in a flurry of nursery accessory buying the day they discovered she was pregnant. He didn't even remember when it had arrived or who had put it in here. He should probably have given it to Catherine but here it was, being used in a nursery he'd never imagined being used at all after Bree's death.

"Raoul? Are you okay?"

Alexis's voice interrupted his thoughts, dragging him back into the here and now as she always did.

"I'm fine," he asserted firmly, as if saying the words could actually make them true.

"Good, then please hold Ruby while I go and wash my hands."

Before he could protest, she'd thrust the baby against his chest. Instinctively he put out his arms, regretting the movement the instant his hands closed around the little girl's tiny form. His stomach lurched and he felt physically ill with fear. He'd never held her before. Ever. What if he did something wrong, or hurt her? What if she started crying again? He looked down into the blue eyes of his daughter, eyes that were so like her mother's. Her dark brown lashes were spiked together with tears and to his horror he saw her eyes begin to fill again, saw her lip begin to wobble. He couldn't do this, he really couldn't do this.

"Thanks, Raoul, I can take her back now if you like?"

Relief swamped him at Alexis's return and he passed the baby back to her with lightning speed. But the moment his arms were empty something weird happened.

It was as if he actually missed the slight weight in his arms, the feel of that little body up against his own, the sensation of the rapidly drawn breaths in her tiny chest, the warmth of her skin.

He took one step back, then another. No, he couldn't feel this way. He couldn't afford to love and lose another person the way he'd lost Bree. Ruby was still small, so much could go wrong. He forced himself to ignore the tug in his chest and the emptiness in his arms and dragged his gaze from the little girl now staring back at him, wide-eyed as she bent her head into Alexis's chest, the fingers of one hand twirling in Alexis's shoulder-length honey-blond hair.

"Are you absolutely certain she's all right?" he asked gruffly.

Alexis smiled. "Of course, she's fine, although she might be a bit cranky later this morning and need a longer nap than normal thanks to this early start today."

"Don't hesitate to take her to the doctor if you're worried."

"I won't, I promise."

Her voice softened and his eyes caught with hers. Was it pity he saw there reflected in their dark brown depths? He felt his defenses fly back up around him. He needed no one's pity. Not for anything. He was doing just fine by himself, thank you very much. And that was just the way he preferred it.

Except he wasn't by himself anymore, was he? He had Ruby and Alexis to contend with, and goodness only knew they both affected him on entirely different levels. Feeling overwhelmed he turned around and strode from the room, determined to keep as much distance between himself and them as possible.

* * *

Alexis watched him go, unable to stop herself from enjoying the view, finally letting out a sigh and turning away when he hitched up his pajama bottoms before they dipped any lower. He'd always been a beautiful man and it had almost hurt her eyes to see him nearly naked like that. His weight loss had only given his muscled strength more definition, particularly the long lean line that ran from his hip down under the waistband of his pants. Oh, yes, he still pinged every single one of her feminine receptors—big time.

She'd been glad for the distraction of settling Ruby or she might have done something stupid—like reach out and touch him. She might have followed that line to see what lay beneath it. To see whether she'd imagined his reaction to her own body before he'd so valiantly controlled it back into submission. Her mouth dried and her fingertips tingled at the thought. She closed her eyes briefly in an attempt to force the visual memory of him from her mind but it only served to imprint him even deeper.

No, acting on her ridiculous impulses would only complicate things beyond control. Her attraction to him was just as pointless as it had always been, and dwelling on it wouldn't do either one of them any good. She was here to do a job and she was doing it well—no matter how often he'd already managed to suggest otherwise in the short time she'd been here.

She'd taken a risk making him hold Ruby like that but it had given her the answer to a question she'd been asking herself all week. And just as she'd suspected, big, strong, successful Raoul Benoit was scared. Terrified, to be exact. Not so much of his own daughter—although, there was something of that, too—but *for* her.

Alexis hummed as she collected a few toys for Ruby

to play with while she took the baby to her room so she could get dressed for the day. As she did so, her mind turned over her discovery. It all began to make sense. His reluctance to be in the same room as Ruby, to hold her or to interact with her in any way. His near obsession with her safety. Obviously he'd felt she was secure in her grandmother's care, somewhere where he could ensure she was out of sight and out of mind. Someone else's problem.

But when she was close enough for him to hear her cries, all his fears took over. His instincts as a father had clearly propelled him into Ruby's room when she had woken this morning, but once there he had hardly any idea of what to do with them. She could help with that, could teach him—if he'd let her.

"Bree, it's going to be a hard road getting him back but I think we've made the first step," she said out loud to the photo of her friend that she'd put on the bedside table in her room.

Warmth bloomed in her chest and it was almost as if she felt her friend's approval slide through her before disappearing again. Dismissing the thought as being fanciful, Alexis quickly dressed for the day and scooped Ruby back up off the floor.

"C'mon, munchkin. Let's go find us some breakfast!"

She spun around, the movement making Ruby chuckle in delight. Yes, everything was going to be all right. She just had to keep believing it was possible.

Over the next few days Raoul remained pretty scarce, which served as a source of major frustration. Alexis wanted to gently include him in more of Ruby's routine here and there, but he always managed to duck away before she had a chance. On the bright side, the brief interaction Ruby had shared with her father seemed to have piqued her curiosity about the stern-faced man who hung around the fringes of her little world. Instead of crying every time she saw him she was more inclined to drop everything and barrel forward on all fours toward him if he so much as made a step into her periphery.

It was both highly amusing to see him realize that Ruby had fixated on him, and a bit sad, as well, that he distanced himself from her again so effectively afterward.

One step forward at a time, Alexis reminded herself. She and Ruby fell into an easy daily routine, helped in no small part by the fact that Catherine had enrolled the baby into a playgroup down in town where she happily interacted with other children her age and slightly older. It was good for both of them to get out of the house and interact with other people. Despite having been born a little early, Ruby was only marginally behind her peers when it came to developmental markers, Alexis observed.

One of the young mothers came over to Alexis and sat down beside her.

"Hi, I'm Laura," she said with a bright smile. "That's my little tyke, Jason, over there." She pointed to a little boy in denim jeans and brightly colored suspenders busily commando crawling toward the sandpit.

"Alexis, pleased to meet you," Alexis replied with a smile.

"Have you heard how Catherine is doing? We all have been wondering but didn't want to be a nuisance."

"The surgery went well. She's at her sister's home in Cashmere, recuperating. If you're heading into Christchurch at all, I'm sure she'd love it if you called by to visit."

"Oh, thanks, that's good to know."

Laura sat back and watched the kids playing for a

while. Alexis sensed she was trying to drum up the courage to say something but was perhaps figuring out the best way around it. Eventually, though, she seemed to come to a decision.

"We were surprised when we heard that Ruby was staying with her dad. Especially given…" Her voice trailed off and she looked uncomfortable. "Look, I don't want you to think I'm prying but is everything okay at the house? We were, most of us, friends with Bree during our pregnancies and our partners and Raoul all got along pretty well. We had our own little social group going. Aside from missing Bree, we really miss Raoul, too. All the guys have tried to reach out to him since Bree died, but he's just cut ties with everyone."

Alexis nodded. It was hard to come up with what to say, when it wasn't really her place to say anything.

"Things are going well at the house. We've settled in to a good routine," she hedged.

The fact that routine didn't include Ruby's father went unsaid. Raoul continued to spend the better part of most days in the winery. He'd made his displeasure clear on the few occasions when, at the beginning, Alexis and Ruby had walked down to bring him his lunch.

"Oh, oh, that's good," Laura said with a relieved smile. "Better than I expected to hear, anyway. You were friends with Bree, weren't you?"

"Since kindergarten," Alexis said, swallowing against the bitter taste of guilt that rose in her throat. "We went through school together near Blenheim and kind of drifted apart a bit when she went up to Auckland for university. We used to catch up whenever she was home, though, and stayed in touch until she married and I went overseas."

Even as she said the words, she was reminded again of

how she'd jumped on the opportunity to leave the country rather than remain and witness her friend's happiness. Shame shafted a spear through her chest, making her breath hitch and a sudden wash of tears spring to her eyes.

"We all miss her so much," Laura said, misunderstanding the reason behind Alexis's distress.

Laura reached for her hand and gave it a gentle squeeze. Alexis felt like a fraud accepting the other woman's sympathy. She hardly deserved it when she'd been the one to abandon Bree. She hadn't been here, hadn't even known what was going on, when her friend had needed her most—and all because she hadn't been able to keep her wretched hormones under control. She owed Bree a debt. It was why she was here now, and why she would stay as long as Ruby needed her, no matter what Raoul chose to throw at her.

Laura continued on. "Look, weather permitting, the playgroup is having a family lunch at the beach this Sunday afternoon. We're not planning to swim or anything, it's far too cold already this autumn, but there are barbecues and a playground and tables and it's so much easier to clean up afterward with the little ones. You and Ruby should come. And bring Raoul along, too, it'll do him good to mix with his mates again."

"I—I'm not sure. Can I confirm with you later on?"

It was one thing to accept an invitation for herself and Ruby, but quite another to do so for a man who'd clearly chosen to remove himself from his social circle.

"Sure," Laura said with an enthusiastic smile. She gave Alexis her cell number. "Just fire me a text if you're coming."

When Alexis got back home, Ruby was already asleep in her car seat. She carefully lifted the sleeping infant and transferred her into her crib, taking a moment to watch

her. Her heart broke for the wee thing. No mother, barely
a father, either. Alexis's hands gripped the side rail of
the crib, her knuckles whitening. She had to try harder.
Somehow, she had to get Raoul to open his life, to open
his heart again. If she didn't she would have failed everyone, but most of all this precious wee scrap sleeping
so innocently in front of her.

Four

Sunday dawned bright and clear. Raoul eyed the cloudless sky with a scowl. He'd been adamantly opposed to attending this thing today. Adamantly. Yet Alexis had barreled on as if he hadn't said no. In fact, when he thought about it, she hadn't so much *asked* him if he would go along, she pretty much *told* him he was going.

For a fleeting moment he considered disappearing to the winery, or even farther into his vineyards. Not that there'd be many places to hide there as the vines headed into their seasonal slumber, the leaves already turning and falling away. It was a shame it was still too early to start pruning. He could have lied and said that the work absolutely had to be done and right away, but he knew Alexis had grown up on a vineyard, too. She'd have known he wasn't telling the truth the instant he opened his mouth.

His stomach tied in knots. He really couldn't do this.

Couldn't face the well-meaning looks and the sympathetic phrases people trotted out—as if any of it would change the past. And he really didn't need to be within fifty meters of Alexis Fabrini for the better part of an afternoon.

Each day she was here he was reminded anew of how his body had reacted to her ever since the first time he'd seen her. About how his wife might now be dead and gone but his own needs and desires certainly weren't. After losing Bree, he'd believed that part of himself to be dormant to the point of extinction, until the second Alexis had walked into his winery. The discovery that all his body parts still worked just fine was a major, and often uncomfortable, inconvenience.

"Oh, good, you're ready!"

Alexis's ever-cheerful voice came from behind him. Instantly, every cell in his body leaped to aching life. Since that incident in the nursery the other day, he'd struggled to maintain a semblance of physical control. Even now the vision of her long legs and the curve of her pert bottom filled his mind. He slowly turned around.

Ruby was in Alexis's arms. Dressed in pink denim dungarees with a candy-striped long-sleeve knit shirt underneath and with a pale pink beret on her little head, she was the epitome of baby chic. She ducked her head into the curve of Alexis's neck, then shyly looked back at him, a tentative smile curving her rosebud mouth and exposing the tiny teeth she had in front.

His heart gave an uncomfortable tug. God, she was so beautiful, so like her mother. Ruby's smile widened and he felt his own mouth twist in response before he clamped it back into a straight line once more.

"Should we take your car or mine?" Alexis asked breezily.

His eyes whipped up to her face. She looked slightly smug, as if she'd just achieved some personal goal.

"I—I'm not sure if I'm going—I need to check something in the winery," he hedged. "How about you go ahead and I'll join you later in my own car if I have time."

Alexis's lips firmed and he saw the disappointment mixed with determination in her eyes. Eyes that reminded him of melted dark chocolate, complete with all the decadence and promise that brought with it.

"You're chickening out, aren't you?" she said, her voice flat. "You don't want to go."

Ruby picked up on her change of mood and gave a little whimper.

Chickening out? He instinctively bristled, programmed to instantly deny her accusation, but he had to admit she was right about him not wanting to go. If she insisted on putting it that way then sure, he was chickening out. Personally, he preferred to think of it as more of a strategic avoidance of a situation that would only bring him pain. Only a fool sought pain at every juncture, right?

"No, I don't."

"Fine," Alexis said with a sigh. "We'll go on our own. I just thought you were a better man than that."

"Better man? What do you mean?" he retorted, his pride pricked by her words.

"Well, I know you've been busily wallowing in your solitary world for at least nine months now, but you weren't the only person to lose Bree. I'm sorry to be this blunt, but you have to remember, all your friends lost her, too, and it was a double whammy for them when you shut them all out at the same time. I know they miss you and they're *your* friends, too, Raoul."

"I didn't…"

He let his voice trail off. He wanted to refute what

she'd said but he knew she told the truth. He had cut all ties deliberately. At the time, he hadn't wanted platitudes or sympathy or help, particularly from people who would advise him to "move on" or "embrace life again" when he had just wanted to be left alone with his memories and his regrets. And that hadn't changed.

Or had it? He missed the camaraderie of his mates—the beers and insults shared over a game of rugby, the discussion between fellow wine enthusiasts over one varietal trend or another. But he wasn't ready to get back out there, to reconnect with people…was he?

The idea was pretty terrifying. He'd been insular for so long now. Even if he could muster the energy to try, would his old friends even want to talk to him again? He had been outright rude on occasions. When he'd surfaced from abject grief he'd been filled with resentment instead, especially that their lives could go on unsullied while his had fallen into an abyss. And once he'd fallen, it had become easier to remain deep down inside the abyss rather than to claw his way back out and into the light.

Clearly Alexis had had enough of his excuses because she picked up the picnic bag she'd obviously packed earlier and headed to the door. He stood there, frozen to the spot as she blithely walked away.

"Wait!"

The sound was more of a croak than a word. She stopped in her tracks and half turned toward him.

"We'll take the Range Rover," he said, stepping forward and reaching to take the picnic bag from her.

The bag was heavy and made him realize just how strong she was. She'd already shouldered the baby's diaper bag as well, and had Ruby on her hip. It seemed to simply be Alexis's way. To do whatever needed to be done—to bear whatever burden had to be borne without resentment or complaint. He almost envied her the simplicity of that.

"Thanks, I'll transfer Ruby's seat over from mine."

"No, it's okay. There's a spare still in its box in the garage. I'll get that."

Alexis gave him a nod of acceptance and he was grateful she'd said nothing about his change of mind.

Twenty minutes later, as they approached the picnic area at the local beach, he felt his stomach clench into a knot and a cold wash of fear rushed through his veins. He started as Alexis laid her hand on his forearm.

"It'll be okay, Raoul, I promise. They won't bite. They're your friends, and they understand how hard this is for you."

Understand? He doubted it but he forced his thoughts away from Bree and to the here and now. To the vista before him, peppered with people he knew. People who knew him. And then, to the woman who sat beside him in the passenger's seat. The woman whose hand still rested warmly on his arm. A woman who'd put her own life and, he knew, her career on hold so she could look after Bree's daughter.

His gaze flicked to the rearview mirror. His daughter.

The sensation in his gut wound up another notch and he hissed out a breath.

"C'mon, let's get this over with."

He pushed open his door and turned away from Alexis, letting her hand drop. He stalked around to the back of his SUV and lifted the hatch, purposefully grabbing the diaper bag and the picnic bag out before lifting out the stroller. He tugged at the handles to try to unfold the thing but it remained solidly shut.

"I'll do that if you like," Alexis said, coming around the car with Ruby.

She pushed the baby at him, much like she'd done the other day. Stiffly, he accepted the child's weight into his arms. Ruby looked at him with solemn blue eyes and then reached up to pat him gently on the cheek. Alexis had the stroller up in two seconds flat and she put the diaper bag in the basket on the underside before placing the picnic bag in the seat.

"Shouldn't she go there?" Raoul asked.

"Nope, she's fine right where she is. Aren't you, precious?"

She reached out to tickle Ruby under her chin and was rewarded with a little chuckle. The delightful sound made Raoul's heart do a flip-flop in his chest and ignited an ember of warmth deep inside. He rapidly quashed the sensation. He couldn't afford to soften, it just laid you open to so much pain. He wasn't going there again. Not ever.

"No," he said emphatically, reaching for the picnic bag and putting it on the ground before buckling Ruby firmly into her stroller. "She's safer here," he said, once he was satisfied she was secure.

"She was fine with you, you know, Raoul."

"I know what you're trying to do, Alexis. It's not going to happen. You can't make me fit into the mold you want to squeeze me into."

Heat flashed in her eyes and her lips drew into a straight line. Something he'd noticed she did whenever she was annoyed with him—which was pretty darn often come to think of it.

"Is that what you think I'm trying to do? Squeeze you into a mold? For what it's worth, I'm not attempting to do any such thing. You're Ruby's father and it's about time you stepped up to your responsibilities." She softened her tone slightly as she continued. "Look, I know you miss

Bree, I know how much you loved her. But rejecting your child isn't going to bring Bree back. If anything it's only pushing her memory further away."

The permanent ache that resided deep within him grew stronger and he dragged in a breath.

"I'm dealing with this the only way I know how. The only way *I* can," he said quietly. "Just leave me be, okay?"

With that he picked up the picnic bag and walked toward the gathering group. This was hard enough as it was without fighting with Alexis every step of the way at the same time. Deep down he knew she had a point. Bree wouldn't have wanted this, wouldn't have been happy that he'd left Ruby with Catherine. After the amount of time the baby had spent in hospital, he was terrified to even hold her and it had seemed that Catherine needed her daughter's baby about as much as Ruby had needed a confident and loving touch. It had appeared to be the best choice for everyone for him to withdraw, to confine his contact with his daughter to financially providing for her care. After all, what did he know about babies? What if he did something wrong or missed some vital clue that could lead to illness or, even worse, death? Wasn't it better for him to take the time to mourn in his own way, safely alone where there was no one he could hurt—and no one who could hurt him?

Better or not, Alexis was dragging him out of the dark, and he wasn't happy about it. Her presence alone had been enough to spark a part of him to life he'd thought would be dead and gone forever. Basic human instinct, human need, had unfurled from where he'd locked it down, hard. She had a way about her—a warmth, a casual touch here and there—that had begun to thaw out the emotions he'd denied himself and that he knew he no longer deserved.

Emotions were messy things. They insidiously wrapped themselves around your mind and your heart and then when everything went to hell in a handbasket they squeezed so tight you could barely draw breath. He wasn't ready to risk that again. Not for anyone. The pain of loss was just too much. It was much easier to simply lock it all out, to prevent it happening.

He lifted a hand in greeting as one of the guys over by the barbecue area shouted a hello and began to walk toward him. Raoul steeled himself for what he anticipated would be an awkward reunion, but to his surprise he found himself relaxing under the onslaught of his friend's warm and simple greeting.

"Good to see you, mate," his friend Matt said, clapping his back in a man hug. "We've missed you."

Raoul murmured something appropriate in response and accepted the icy bottle of beer being thrust in his hand. Before long others joined them and, to his immense relief, no one mentioned Bree or his absence from their circle over the past nine months. He was just beginning to relax when one of the guys gestured over to where Alexis was sitting with the other women and the little ones.

"New nanny? Nice piece of work there, buddy," the guy said approvingly. His voice was full of innuendo as he continued. "Good around the house, is she?"

Raoul felt his hackles rise. Alexis *was* good around the house and great with Ruby, but he knew that wasn't what this guy was aiming at.

"Alexis is an old friend of Bree's. Ruby's lucky to have her. Besides, it's only temporary, until Catherine's back on her feet again."

His mention of Bree froze over the conversation as effectively as if he'd tipped a bucket of cold water over the guy.

"Hey man, my apologies, I didn't mean anything by it."

"That's fine, then," Raoul uttered tightly.

Anger still simmered beneath the surface for a while over the dismissive way the other man had talked about Alexis. She deserved more respect than that. While he might not necessarily have been warm or friendly toward her himself, he could certainly ensure she received the respect she deserved from others. He didn't stop for a minute to consider why that was so important to him and he missed the look exchanged between his friends behind his back as his gaze remained locked on his daughter's nanny.

Alexis felt a familiar prickle in between her shoulder blades as if she was under scrutiny. She turned and caught Raoul's gaze fastened firmly on her, a serious expression on his face. The moment their eyes met he turned his attention back to the group of men gathered around the barbecue where, by the smells of things, they were making a sacrificial offering of the meat as only a large group of guys could.

Despite the fact he was no longer looking at her, she still felt the impression of his gaze and a flush of heat stained her cheeks and chest in response. What had he been thinking to have such a somber visage? she wondered. Whatever it had been, he'd obviously pushed it to the back of his mind as he now appeared to be laughing at something someone else had said.

The sight of him laughing like that sent a thrill of joy all the way to her heart. He needed to laugh more often, deserved to. The way he'd hidden himself away, devoid of all company and support, had been wrong on so many levels she couldn't even begin to enumerate them. She knew everyone coped differently with grief, but he'd become a slave to his, and that hadn't done anyone any favors—not Raoul and certainly not Ruby.

She watched him a moment longer, relishing the warm sensation that coursed through her as she looked her fill. Laughter suited him. Happiness suited him. And somehow she had to make sure he had his fair share of both back in his world. He reached for another drink from the cooler, a can of soda this time, and she watched the play of muscles along his shoulders beneath the fine knit of his lightweight sweater.

Warmth soon became something more complicated as she felt her body react in a far more visceral way, her breathing quickening and a pull of desire working its way from her core to her extremities.

"He's easy on the eye, isn't he?" Laura's voice intruded from right next to her.

"What? Oh…um, yes." Alexis felt her cheeks flame in embarrassment at being caught out staring at the man who was essentially her boss.

"Don't worry," Laura said with a gentle smile. "Your secret's safe with me."

"Secret?"

Alexis deliberately played dumb, only to be on the receiving end of a gentle smile and a painfully understanding look.

"How long have you felt this way about him?"

Alexis sighed, the other woman's compassion breaking down any barrier she had thought to erect.

"A few years now," Alexis admitted, shocked that she'd given up her secret at the first sign of empathy from another person.

For so long she'd held the truth to her chest, fearful that anyone would find out how she felt and judge her for it. You didn't get attracted to your best friend's partner—it just wasn't done—and you certainly didn't act on it. That was a no-go area in every aspect.

It was terrifying to know that her secret was now out. Not even her parents had known how she felt about Raoul Benoit and, here, a virtual stranger had plucked it from her as easily as if it was a piece of lint on her sweater.

"You…you won't say anything, will you?" she hastened to add in an undertone.

"Of course not, Alexis. To be honest, I'm glad."

"Glad?" Alexis was confused.

"Maybe you're exactly what he needs now, hmm? To mourn someone is one thing, but he's been hiding away from *living* for far too long," Laura said, reaching out to give Alexis's hand a squeeze. "We all deserve a bit of happiness, right?"

"Right," Alexis agreed numbly.

Happiness. Could she bring that elusive ingredient back into Raoul's life? While her aim had been to reunite father and daughter, could he find room in his broken heart to consider love again?

She pushed the thought away. If he could accept Ruby into his life, she'd be satisfied. She had no right to hope for anything more.

Five

After everyone had eaten, the group of adults sat around watching their kids at play. Alexis kept her eye on Ruby as she crawled a couple of meters across the grass toward the playground where Laura and some of the other parents had taken their babies for a turn on the swings. The grass would be hell on those pink dungarees, she thought ruefully, but it was good for Ruby to be out in the fresh air and interacting with everyone else. It wouldn't be long before tiredness would set in—she was already overdue for her nap—but Alexis wanted to prolong the fun for as long as possible.

A cry of anguish from behind her dragged her attention off the little girl, distracting her for the moment it took to return a clearly much-loved piece of tatty muslin to its stroller-bound owner. She turned her eyes back to where Ruby had been, only to feel her stomach drop. She lurched to her feet, her eyes anxiously scanning the crowd for the little splotch of pink. Her feet were already moving, taking her over the grass and toward the playground. Ah, there she was. Relief flooded Alexis with the force of a tidal wave and she covered the short distance between them as quickly as she could.

Ruby sat on her little padded butt, chewing on something she'd picked up from the ground. A small stick by the looks of it, Alexis thought as she reached her.

"What's that she's got?"

Raoul appeared beside them to stand over his daughter, an expression of distaste on his face as he reached down and extricated the twig from Ruby's fingers. The baby voiced her disagreement with his action, loudly.

"I thought you were supposed to be watching her," he accused, holding the stick out for Alexis to see it.

"I was. I—"

"Not closely enough, it seems. God only knows what else she could have picked up and put in her mouth while you weren't looking."

"Raoul, you're overreacting. It's just a twig, and off a nontoxic plant at that. Babies learn by putting things in their mouths. Don't worry, she's fine."

"And if it had been a toxic plant? Or if she'd toppled over and the stick had gone into her throat? What then? Would she learn that you can die from something like that?"

There was a note of harsh censure to his voice that made her blood run cold in her veins. She should have kept a closer eye on Ruby, she knew that. It still hurt to hear Raoul speak that way to her. She reached down and gathered the little girl close to her, taking comfort from Ruby's closeness as she soothed the baby's cries, rubbing her back and automatically rocking gently from one foot to the other until she settled. Raoul threw the offending twig onto the ground with a sound of disgust.

"I knew this was a mistake. We're leaving now," he said, and turned on his heel to stride away before Alexis could answer.

"Are you okay?" Laura said as she came up beside Alexis. "I don't mean to pry but I couldn't help overhearing. Protective, much?"

"Yeah, he's right, though. I should have been keeping a closer eye on Ruby."

"He's paranoid about losing her, isn't he? I mean, we're all a bit off the scale when it comes to our own kids, but with him it's more, isn't it?"

Alexis sighed as she watched Raoul say goodbye to his buddies and then gather their picnic bag and Ruby's diaper bag together. His movements were short and jerky, a clear indication of his foul temper.

"Yeah, it's definitely more."

"He'll come around. Y'know, we all thought that maybe he didn't, or couldn't, love Ruby after Bree died. That maybe he blamed her somehow. But after seeing that, I think he possibly loves her too much—that he's afraid he'll lose her, too."

"I was thinking the same," Alexis agreed. "Hey, thanks for asking us along today. Sorry it kind of ended on a sour note."

"Don't worry about it. We're just glad you managed to talk him into coming. Maybe we can all get together again sometime soon."

Alexis gave her a thin smile and said her goodbyes to the others before joining Raoul over by the picnic table where he waited with ill-concealed impatience.

"We need to talk," he said as she drew nearer.

"When we get home," Alexis conceded.

Yes, they did need to talk, but she had the feeling that Raoul wasn't going to listen to her opinions no matter what she said. She flicked a glance at his stony face, lingering on the pain that reflected in his eyes. Pain that made her heart twist with longing to put things right for him. But she couldn't do it on her own. He had to meet her halfway.

As they drove back to his house she stared blindly out the side window doubting, for the first time since she'd come here, her decision to try and help out. She was in way over her head with this situation and she lacked the objectivity she needed to get through it.

How on earth could she be objective when all she wanted to do every time she saw him was to obliterate his grief with sensation, with her love?

Raoul turned the Range Rover into the driveway at home with a measure of relief. Ruby had fretted the entire journey home, making it seem a lot longer than the twenty-minute drive it really was. He was glad to have gotten her home, but the relief didn't compare to the fury that simmered through his body. Alexis had one job to do—look after Ruby. That was it. Except it wasn't.

Life was so much simpler before she came along. He'd relished his time alone. Life was lonely, yes, but predictable. Safe. Now, every day was a challenge and he rose each morning not knowing what he'd face. It used to be that he'd relish a challenge like that, but not anymore. Not when each challenge came with a new emotional twist that he'd thought he'd never feel again.

He pulled the SUV to a halt outside the house and got out, going around to the rear of the vehicle to extricate the bags and the stroller while Alexis took Ruby from her car seat.

"I'll just give her a bottle to calm her and get her settled for a sleep."

He responded with a curt nod. "I'll wait for you in the study."

While he waited he paced, and then he paced some more. He didn't know how to handle this, how to handle Alexis, but he knew he wanted her gone. Everything had blown up into larger-than-life proportions since her arrival, and he desperately wanted to fit everything back into its neat little boxes all over again—boxes he could keep closed or open at will.

It was nearly half an hour before he heard her quiet knock on his study door. She let herself in without awaiting his acknowledgment—a suitable simile to how she behaved with him on a daily basis, he realized with a rare flash of bleak humor.

"She was a bit difficult to settle, but she's out for the count now," Alexis said by way of explanation as she came in and crossed the room to take a seat.

As she walked, he couldn't help but notice that her jeans stretched tight across her hips, accentuating her very female curves. Curves that he had no business looking at, he reminded himself sternly. Except he couldn't quite bring himself to look away. Even after she sat down in the chair opposite his desk, he remained mesmerized by the fade pattern on the denim, by the all-too-perfect fit around her thighs.

Oblivious to the battle going on in his mind, Alexis blithely continued. "She was definitely overtired, after today, but I checked her gums and she's cutting more teeth, too, so that was probably part of the problem."

Raoul grunted something in response before taking the chair behind the desk. He needed the physical barrier between them. Scrambling to get his thoughts together, he drew in a deep breath.

"About today—" he started, only to be cut off by Alexis speaking over him, her words chasing one after the other in a rush.

"Look, I apologize. What happened was all my fault. I took my eyes off Ruby for a few seconds and she went out of my line of vision. I shouldn't have done it and it was wrong and I'm deeply sorry."

"Sorry isn't enough, Alexis. I don't think you're the right person for the job of caring for Ruby."

Raoul forced himself to look at a spot just past her, so he could pretend that he didn't see the flare of distress that suddenly crossed her features. A hank of her honey-blond hair had worked its way loose from her ponytail and she absently shoved it back behind one ear.

"Don't you think that's a bit of an overreaction?" she said, her voice shaking just a little.

"You're here to mind her. You didn't."

"Raoul, it's not like you weren't there along with several other adults who could see her."

She pushed up to her feet and leaned forward on the desk, the deep V-neck of her T-shirt gaping and affording him a breathtaking view of her breasts cupped in the palest pink lace. Flames of heat seared along his veins, taking the words he was about to utter and reducing them to ash in his mouth. He rapidly lifted his gaze to her face. Bad idea.

A flush of color stained her cheeks and her eyes shimmered with moisture making them look bigger and even more vulnerable than ever.

"Look, I admit I made a mistake," she said fervently, her voice even more wobbly now, "but no harm came of it and I promise you I will be far more vigilant from now on. She won't move an inch without me being on her shadow."

"I don't know," he said, shaking his head and fighting back the growing physical need to reach for her that rose inexorably from deep within him.

"She needs a nanny. If not me, then who else is there, Raoul? Catherine's not even two weeks out of surgery and she won't be home from her sister's for a couple of weeks yet. She couldn't possibly be capable of chasing and looking after an active child at that point—she'll barely be able to care for herself. Ruby could very well be walking by then, if the past few days are any indication. Who else can look after her? You?"

A cold dash of terror quelled the heat of his desire. There was no way he was assuming sole responsibility for Ruby. He simply couldn't. If Alexis, a trained nanny, could make a mistake like today, what hope did he have?

Alexis continued with her tirade. "I suppose you could always put her into day care but is that really what Bree would have wanted? Wasn't it always her wish to have her children raised at home? Can't you at least respect her wishes in that? You lock yourself up in this house as if you want to bury yourself in her memory, but don't you know how furious she'd be with you for pushing everyone away?"

"Enough!" he all but shouted back. "You've made your point. You have one more chance. But that's it, Alexis."

"What's the matter, Raoul?" she goaded. "You don't like to hear the truth?"

"Don't," he warned. "Don't mess with what you know nothing about."

"I know Bree would have hated to see you like this. So cold and closed down that you can't even show love or care to your own daughter!" Alexis persisted.

Raoul flew out of his chair and around the desk, grabbing her by her upper arms and swinging her around to face him.

"You think I don't feel? That I'm cold and don't care? Let me show you just how wrong you are."

Without thinking, he lowered his mouth to hers, his lips laying claim to hers with a sense of purpose that drove him to take and to plunder with little care for the consequences. She uttered a tiny moan, her arms coming up around his shoulders, her fingers pushing into his hair and holding him. Even now she sought to comfort him, it seemed.

But comfort was the last thing on his mind.

He softened his onslaught as he took the time to luxuriate in the soft plumpness of her lips, to taste the sweetly intoxicating flavor of her mouth and to—just for this moment—lose himself in sensation.

A shudder racked his body and he pulled her in closer to him, molding her body along the length of his own. Her hips tilted gently against the growing ridge of his erection, sending a spear of want through him that threatened to make his legs weaken beneath him.

His hands reached for her waist, for the hem of her shirt. He lifted the thin fabric, groaning against her as he felt the soft delicate heat of her skin. He stroked his hands upward until they came into contact with the rasp of her lacy bra. Beneath the lace her nipples jutted out, tight beads of flesh. He brushed his thumbs over them, once, twice. Oh, what he wouldn't give to take them, one by one, into his mouth right now. To tease her and taste her. To discover every last secret of this woman who'd remained a shadow in the back of his mind from the day he'd first met her.

The thought was as sobering now as it had been back

then. Reluctantly Raoul dragged his hands out from beneath her top and reached up to disengage her arms from around his neck. As he gently pushed her back his eyes met hers.

Desire reflected back at him, magnifying the demand that still surged and swelled inside him. Her lips were slightly swollen, glistening with temptation.

Raoul let her go and took a step back.

"Trust me, I feel," he said, his breath coming in heavy puffs. *"Too damn much."*

Six

Alexis stood in the study, watching Raoul's retreating form with a stunned expression on her face. What the hell had just happened? Well, okay, realistically she knew exactly what had just happened—but why?

One second they'd been arguing, the next… She raised a shaking hand to her lips, lips that still felt the searing heat of his possession. Her entire body pulsated with energy. Energy that begged for release. She slowly shook her head in disbelief. She'd always been attracted to him, she'd known that, but this…this reaction went way further than simple attraction. This went bone deep, soul deep. And it left her wanting so much more.

Physically, she'd always been incredibly drawn to Raoul—not only to his body and his mind, but to his heart. He'd been a fabulous husband to Bree and it was his devotion to her friend and their obvious love for one another that had made their happiness together all the

more bittersweet for her to witness. Seeing how they'd
felt about one another was a reminder to herself that she
never wanted to settle for anything less. She wanted the
kind of love that Raoul and Bree had had—the same kind
of enduring love that her parents had enjoyed through
multiple trials and tribulations in their marriage.

Most recently, all through her mother's rapidly ad-
vancing early-onset dementia, Alexis's dad had stuck
by her—caring for her at home by himself, since Alexis
had been overseas, until he was forced to see her admitted to hospital. Even then, he'd barely moved from her
side until her death almost four months ago.

Alexis wanted that kind of devotion in a relationship.
She was prepared to give it and she believed she deserved
it in return. But none of the men she'd dated had ever
shown that capacity for love. Then she'd met Raoul, the
handsomest man she'd ever met *and* someone who loved
so fully and deeply that it took her breath away. Was it
any wonder she'd fallen for him in a matter of moments?

But what were his feelings toward her? After the blis-
teringly hot kiss, she knew attraction was part of it…but
was that the extent of it for him? Was he capable of feeling anything more for her? She knew it was still early
days for Raoul, that the pain of Bree's death was still a
simmering thing lying on the surface of his every day.

She was caught between a rock and a hard place. Did
she keep gently pushing him to expose the attraction she
knew he felt for her any further? Or did she wait and see
what happened next after today's kiss?

Bree would forever be a part of their lives. Ruby was
full testimony to that, not to mention the fact that true
love, like energy, could never be destroyed. But she also
knew that love, *if* it existed between two people, could

grow and become enriched in even the worst of situations. Her parents were the perfect example of that.

The question was, however, could Raoul Benoit give that to her? Would he ever take down the barriers he kept so firmly erected between them again?

Did she even have the right to ask him to?

Her first month caring for Ruby had passed in a blur of time, Alexis realized as she watched a fun educational DVD with Ruby, clapping hands with her and jiggling along with the music. She'd lifted Ruby to her feet and was holding her hands as the baby pumped her thighs in time to the beat. She couldn't help laughing at the happy energy the little girl exuded as she squealed and danced.

"Someone sounds happy. She's got her mother's sense of rhythm, I see."

Alexis turned to see Raoul standing in the doorway, a look on his face that was half quizzical and half humorous.

"Dad-dad-dad-dad!" Ruby shrieked as she saw her father.

Alexis bit her lip. Over the past few days the baby had gone from curiosity about Raoul, to grim determination to make him acknowledge her. Ruby plopped down onto her padded bottom and Alexis let her hands go, only to see the child pull herself up using the coffee table beside them and take at first one, then two, then more tentative steps toward her father.

"Oh, my God, she's walking. She's actually walking!" Alexis cried.

"Should she be doing that already?" Raoul said, his eyes fixed on his daughter's tiny form as it teetered toward him on the carpeted floor.

"Well, she's a little early at ten months, but she's been

showing signs of wanting to get onto her feet properly for a couple of weeks now. Oops, there she goes."

Ruby lost her balance but before she could hit the carpet, Raoul was right there. His large hands hooked under her tiny armpits and swung her up into an arc that made her release a gurgling laugh of sheer joy.

Alexis felt a pang in her chest at the sight. This was how it should have been all along. Father and daughter sharing special moments like this one.

"Dad-dad," Ruby said again, her little hand patting Raoul on the face.

"That's right, Ruby," Alexis said from her position on the floor. "That's your daddy. Good girl."

"She can't really understand I'm her father," Raoul said, putting Ruby back down on the floor.

He was forced to reluctantly hold her hands as she tugged herself up onto her feet again and continued to want to walk, this time with him bent over, holding her hands as she tottled toward Alexis.

"Why not?" Alexis asked, feeling her joy at seeing them together dim a little at his lack of pleasure in Ruby's behavior. "You are her father and she ought to know that, don't you think?"

"It would be no different if she called me Raoul. She only mimics what she hears you say," he said repressively.

Provoked, Alexis returned with, "I prefer to think she knows you are her dad. I think she deserves that, don't you? Or would you rather she grow up calling you Raoul? As if you were some stranger who just happened to live alongside her?"

He waited until Ruby was closer to Alexis before extricating his fingers from the baby's clutches. Beaming a toothy smile, Ruby continued to take steps unaided. Alexis opened her arms and Ruby walked straight into them.

"Look at you, you clever girl!" she laughed as she hugged the child and smothered her neck with kisses, eliciting yet more baby giggles. "I'm seriously going to have to keep my eye on you now, aren't I?"

She looked up and caught the expression in Raoul's eye. Was that longing she saw there? Did he wish he could express the same spontaneous love for his daughter that she did? Alexis gave Ruby another cuddle before setting her loose. Bit by bit she felt as if she was beginning to break through the shell he'd built around himself when it came to Ruby. The thought brought her to an idea that she wanted to suggest to Raoul.

Drawing on a liberal dose of courage, and buoyed by the fact that he'd stayed in the room rather than withdrawing again quickly as he was in the habit of doing, she launched into speech.

"Raoul, I've been thinking. Catherine is due home this weekend and I thought since it also ties in with Bree's birthday, the first time dealing with that date for both of you since she's gone, that it might be nice to have a bit of a get-together here—you know, invite a few of your friends, make it a potluck dinner kind of thing. I think it would be nice—partly to celebrate Catherine's recovery to date and partly to remember Bree."

"I don't need a gathering to remember her. It's not a good idea."

"I was afraid you'd say that," she said, dragging in another deep breath and refusing to be cowed by his rejection, "which is why I kind of went ahead and organized it anyway. Catherine was really eager to participate and she's just aching to see Ruby again, and Laura and Matt and the others were equally keen."

"You had no right to do that," Raoul said, a sharp edge to his voice that all but sliced through the air between them.

"Look, I know you're still struggling to get back to normal—"

"Normal? Normal died along with Bree. I don't think you quite understand just what that has meant to me."

His voice was quiet, yet filled with emotion and anger. Sensing the change in mood in the room, Ruby crawled onto Alexis's lap, turned her face into her chest and uttered a whine of protest.

"Which is exactly why we should honor her memory and have a get-together in remembrance of her. Catherine needs it, your friends need it. I truly believe you need it, too, and you'd agree with me if you could just let yourself believe that you don't have to face all your grief alone."

His hazel eyes narrowed as he stared down at her. The air between them thickened, filled with his unspoken words and met by her equally silent but no less adamant challenge.

"Fine," he uttered through clenched teeth. "But don't expect me to be involved."

"Just be there, it's all I ask."

"Sometimes, Alexis Fabrini, you ask too damn much."

He left the room, taking her heart with him. It was hard to feel a sense of victory when she knew how much this was hurting him.

"Dad-dad?" Ruby said, lifting her face away from Alexis and looking around the room.

"He's gone off again, poppet. But he'll be back. Bit by bit, he'll be back."

At least she sure hoped so.

Raoul looked around the gathering in his house. This was exactly the kind of thing Bree would have loved to have organized for her birthday. All their closest friends, her mother, some of his cousins who lived locally, Alexis…people he knew and should feel comfortable with. And yet, he felt like an outsider. A stranger in his own house. Sure, he went through the motions—made sure everyone had a drink, asked some opinions on his latest blend—but he felt as if he didn't belong. As if he was a mere onlooker, not a participant.

Conversations swirled around him, things he would normally have been a part of but as he overheard snippets from here and there he became increasingly aware of how life had continued for all of them. It seemed wrong to resent them for it, but he did—fiercely. The uninterrupted way their lives had moved on after Bree only made his empty world so much more hollow—the void in his heart echo that much more.

He looked to Catherine to see how she was coping. This had to be hard for her, too, but she appeared to be taking it all in her stride—not afraid to shed a tear or two over a shared memory or a hearty laugh at some reminiscence, and eager to hear everyone's news after her monthlong absence from the playgroup. She looked up and caught his gaze and he could see the concern reflected in her eyes—eyes that were very like Ruby's and reminded him so much of Bree.

And there it was again—the pain, the loss, the anger at having all that perfection torn away from him. Having choice removed from his hands. Losing Bree from his life, forever. Catherine pushed herself to her feet and, adeptly using one crutch, crossed the short distance between them. She laid one hand on his shoulder.

"She'd have loved this, wouldn't she? Alexis has done a great job."

"Everyone contributed," he said abruptly.

"But Alexis brought us all together. We needed that. It's been long overdue. I know I'm always going to miss her, it would be impossible not to, but I feel better today, y'know?"

He nodded because it seemed to be the response she expected, but inside he was screaming. No, he didn't know what the hell she was talking about. This was all too hard. He couldn't find it in him to allow himself to enjoy the company of everyone here today. He needed space, silence, solitude. The moment Catherine's attention was taken by one of the guests he slipped out the room and toward the front door. Once he had it open he walked through the entrance and kept going into the night—down the unsealed lane that led to the winery, past the winery and on down the hill until he could go no farther unless he wanted to swim the inky dark waters of the harbor.

He waited until the moon was high in the sky before he clambered back up the hill. The cold air had filtered through his clothing, his long-sleeved cotton shirt—fine in the centrally heated interior of the house—was totally unsuited to the outdoors. Initially he'd barely noticed it. Now, however, he was frozen through and through.

The outside lights were still on at the house when he got back but, he noted with relief, the large parking bay outside was devoid of cars. He slipped back inside and decided to go directly to his room. He had no wish to see Alexis and face her silent or, more likely, not-so-silent recriminations for ditching the party this evening. He just wanted to be alone. Couldn't anyone understand that?

"Raoul? Is that you?"

Alexis, dish towel still in hand, stepped out of the kitchen and into the hallway. He halted in his tracks—frozen like a possum in the headlights of an oncoming vehicle. She was the last person he wanted to face right now.

"Are you okay?"

He gave a bitter laugh. "Okay? No, Alexis, I'm not okay."

He turned to head to his room but heard her rapid footfall on the carpeted floor behind him. She put out a hand to arrest his progress.

"I'm sorry, Raoul. Maybe organizing today wasn't such a good idea," she said as she drew nearer.

He wheeled around. "You think?"

He could see his response stung her but he wasn't into mouthing platitudes so others could just blithely go on doing what they did without consideration for how it made anyone else feel.

"I told you that you asked too much," he growled.

"I know—now, at least. And I am sorry, Raoul. Everyone understood, though, especially today with it being Bree's birthday. It was bound to be hard. Even for me. Look, I know how you feel—"

"Do you?" he said incredulously. "Do you really? I don't think so. I don't think that for a minute you could *ever* understand how I feel so don't presume to try."

"You weren't the only one who lost her," she said, her voice small.

"She was my *wife!*" His voice shook, with fury and with something more that rolled and swirled inside him—filling his mind with a black emptiness that threatened to consume him. "She was my world," he whispered fiercely before striding the short distance to his room where he slammed the door solidly behind him, uncaring as to whether or not he disturbed Ruby.

He stood in the darkened room, hardly daring to breathe or move in case the angry monster that he could feel growing stronger inside him broke free. The monster that wanted to rail at the world for the unfairness that took Bree from him. The monster that was full of anger toward Bree herself, even though he could never openly express it, because she'd taken the choice of family or her away from him.

The monster that held the untold disgust he had with himself because, despite everything—the love he'd borne for Bree being paramount in his life—he still lusted for her friend, now more than ever before.

Seven

Alexis went through the motions of getting ready for bed but she was so wired right now she knew sleep would be impossible. Today had gone off well, if you discounted how it had left Raoul feeling. No one had seemed to mind when he'd cut and run from the gathering, not even Catherine who'd seemed to understand his need to be alone. The party had gone very pleasantly, even if she hadn't been able to enjoy it, too aware of Raoul's absence.

She'd not long thrown herself against the fine cotton sheets of her king-size bed and switched off her light when there was a gentle knock at the bedroom door. There was only one person that could be. She slid from the bed and walked quickly toward the door.

"Raoul?" she asked, as she turned the knob and opened the door wide.

His eyes flew across her, taking in her silk nightgown—one of her few indulgences from her time in Italy last year—and her bare feet in one sweep.

"I'm sorry, I shouldn't have disturbed you."

He went to walk away but she put out a hand to stop him.

"It's okay. Did you need me for something?"

He looked at her in the dark, and through the sheen of moonlight that filtered into her room she saw the glitter of his eyes. His face was pale, his whiskers a dark shadow on his cheeks and jaw. He'd never before looked so dangerous, or so appealing to her. She took an involuntary step back and saw the look of chagrin that crossed his face.

"I shouldn't have spoken to you like that."

"You're hurting. I—" She stopped herself before she could repeat her earlier words of understanding.

He'd been right. She couldn't possibly know or understand what he'd been through. Bree had been her friend for years, but the last two years of Bree's life she'd barely even spoken to her, battling with envy, then guilt, after Bree and Raoul had gotten together. Now, even though she desperately missed her friend, those bitter emotions were all still there. The envy that, even in death, her friend could command such unceasing love—and the guilt that she continued to not only want that for herself, but that she wanted it from the very same man.

She drew in a breath. "There's no need to apologize, Raoul. I should have been more sensitive to your needs."

"My needs? I don't even know what they are anymore. Sometimes I feel as if I don't know anything anymore."

She made a sound of sympathy and reached up to cup his face with one hand. "You've been through hell. You're still there. It's okay. I'll back off with the social stuff. You obviously need more time."

He lifted a hand to press against hers and she felt the heat of his palm on one side, the rasp of his unshaven jaw on the other. The mingled sensations sent a tingle of longing up her arm and she was appalled that even as the man was visibly struggling with a devastating loss, she couldn't hold her attraction back. That her body, having a recalcitrant mind of its own, was right now warming to his very presence. Her nipples were beading against the sheer fabric of her nightgown and she felt a long slow pull of hunger dragging from her core.

"Time is something I have too much of. Time to think. I don't want to think anymore, Alexis. For once, I just want to feel."

"Feel…?"

"Yes, feel. Something, anything other than the pain inside. I want the emptiness to go away."

He turned his head so that his lips were now pressing against her palm. If he'd seared her skin with a branding iron it couldn't have had a more overwhelming effect. She gasped at the jolt of electricity that shuddered through her hand and down her arm. When he bent his head to hers and his hot dry lips captured her own she felt her knees buckle beneath her. Momentarily she gave an inward groan at how clichéd her reaction was, but it was only seconds before awareness of clichés, or anything else other than this man and how he made her feel, fled from her consciousness.

All there was right now was scalding heat, flames of need licking up through her body as she clung to Raoul, as she anchored herself to his strength and poured all her years of forbidden longing into returning his kiss. When he lifted his mouth from hers she just stood there, dazed by the power of her feelings for him and by the emotion he aroused in her.

"Come with me, to my room," he rasped. "I can't do this in here."

She nodded, letting him draw her down the hallway and into his room. The bedroom door snicked closed behind them and he led her to his bed.

She tumbled into the sheets, Raoul following close behind. As the weight of his body settled against hers she flexed upward against him, pressing against the hard evidence of his arousal. He groaned against her throat, his unshaven jaw scraping softly against her skin, and she relished every sensation, every touch. It felt as if she'd put her whole life on hold for this very moment and she was going to savor every second of it.

Alexis fought open the buttons on Raoul's shirt, her fingertips eagerly skimming along the ridged muscles of his abdomen as she worked the garment away from his body and then off entirely. She wanted to touch every inch of him and then to taste every inch in turn. She trailed a gentle line down his neck and then skimmed over the strength of his shoulders before tracing the definition of his chest. Beneath her touch she felt him respond with tiny tremors, especially when she circled his nipples with the pad of her thumb then lifted her head to kiss him there.

He shifted, bearing his weight on one arm as he manacled her wrists with his free hand.

"But I want to touch you," she protested on a whispered breath.

"Too much," he said succinctly in reply before restraining her hands above her head.

She knew she could have pulled free at any time but there was something so decadently wonderful about being laid open to him like this. About giving him her trust, total and unquestioning.

He kissed along the line of her jaw, down her neck, making her squirm and arch her back, pushing herself upward, supplicant, toward him. And then, his mouth was at her breasts. Through the fine fabric of her nightgown she felt the warmth of his lips, his breath and then, oh, God, his tongue as he suckled on her.

His whole body shook with restraint as he lingered over each aching tip, sending shock waves of sensation tumbling over her and winding up the tension in her lower belly to near excruciating tautness. He let go of her hands to grab at the hem of her nighty and sweep it off her body, laying her bare to his scrutiny in the moonlit room.

A sense of unreality hit her, as if she was watching a black-and-white movie starring strangers coming together for the very first time. In a sense, that was exactly what was happening. Not for them a normal period of courtship. They'd been acquaintances, at best, when she'd run off overseas. Combatants since her return. For all that Alexis was falling in love with him, she barely knew him—not in all the ways that counted.

One thing she did know, though, was that in his time of need tonight, he'd turned *to* her rather than away. She would do whatever he wanted, give him whatever he needed of her, and along the way she'd receive a slice of what she had always wanted in return.

She moaned as Raoul continued his sensual onslaught on her body, his fingers and his tongue tracing a magical dance across the skin of her belly, and lower. When his tongue flicked across her center she all but jerked off the bed. It was as if every nerve in her body had congregated on that one point. It took bare seconds before she flew over the precipice and into the rolling swells of a climax so intense, so exquisite, that tears leaked from her eyes and down the sides of her face.

She was still riding the crest when she felt him shove his trousers off and move between her legs. With a gut-

tural cry, he entered her still-spasming body. She felt
herself stretch to accommodate his length, felt her inner
muscles contract and squeeze against him, welcoming
him into her heat, her heart. He thrust against her, deep
and strong. She'd barely recovered from her first orgasm
when she was in the throes of a second.

Through the rolling, intoxicating fog of pleasure she
was aware of his body growing taut, of him surging into
her once, twice more until with another cry he spent himself within her. He collapsed onto her, his body racked
with paroxysms that mirrored her own. Alexis closed
her arms around him, holding him to her, relishing the
ragged sound of his breathing, the involuntary shudder of
his hips against hers as he rode his climax to completion.

Raoul could barely breathe, much less think. He rolled
off Alexis and sank into the mattress beside her as the
perspiration on his body cooled. As the realization of
what he'd just done slowly sank in.

Deep down he'd always known that sex with Alexis
would be explosive. It was exactly why he'd stayed well
away from her. Guilt slammed into him, chasing the buzz
of physical satisfaction into oblivion. By doing what he'd
just done, by seeking and taking pleasure, he'd just betrayed the one woman he'd pledged to remain faithful to.

Tears burned at the back of his eyes as recrimination
filled him, making his mouth taste bitter, making each
breath a painful necessity. He didn't deserve to seek re-
spite. He certainly didn't deserve to find pleasure and
most especially not in the arms of Alexis Fabrini.

He could feel her, lying silently beside him. Her
breathing was still quick and shallow. The warmth of her
body extended across the short distance between them,

offering him succor. Support and comfort he didn't deserve.

He screwed his eyes shut tight. He was so wrong to have done this. He should have just stayed in his room, alone with the bottle of brandy and the snifter he'd taken from his study with the idea of finding oblivion in alcohol's potent depths.

Alexis reached across the sheets and took his hand in hers, squeezing silently. Even now she offered him reassurance. He felt the mattress shift slightly as she rolled onto her side to face him but he couldn't bring himself to open his eyes and meet her gaze.

He tensed, waiting for her to say something, but instead she reached out a hand and stroked his chest. The light circular movements of her hand soothed him, when he didn't want to be soothed. He wanted her to yell at him, to demand to know what he'd been thinking when he'd come to her room, when he'd all but dragged her back to his. When he'd given in to the clamoring demand of his body and taken her without thought, without care.

Without protection.

His heart hammered in his chest even as her hand worked its way lower, over his rib cage and to his abdomen. Despite the horrifying realization that had just dawned on him, his body continued to respond to her touch—to be soothed and ignited, both at the same time. His flesh begin to stir again, the thrum of desire beat through his veins.

"No!" he said abruptly, gripping her hand and halting it on its inexorable journey down his body. "We didn't use protection," he said grimly.

"It's okay," Alexis said. "I'm on the Pill."

He gave her a considering look. Was she telling the truth? She had no reason to lie. Through the gloom, she met his gaze full on and he saw enough there to relax just a little.

Alexis rose onto her knees, then straddled him, gently pulling her hand free from his grasp.

"So, I guess it's yes?" she whispered softly back to him. "Please, Raoul. Let me love you."

"This isn't love," he said bluntly, hating the fact he couldn't control his growing response to her.

He felt her flinch a little at his words and heard the sharply indrawn breath.

"Then let me enjoy you, let yourself enjoy me," she coaxed, bending her head to kiss him.

Her tongue swept along his lower lip before she sucked it between her teeth. He fought the rising tide of desire that continued to swell inside him—but made no effort to pull away. He could feel the heat of her core as she hovered over his belly, felt his penis twitch in response. Exactly when he surrendered to her will and became an active participant he wasn't entirely sure, but all of a sudden his hands were cupping her head and his fingers were tangled in the honeyed strands of her hair as he kissed her back with all the pent-up longing and despair that had tormented him these past ten months.

When she broke away he would have protested, but her small deft hands massaged and stroked him, gliding along his shoulders, down his chest, over his belly and finally, finally, reached his aching erection. He felt her fingers close around his length, felt her squeeze gently as she stroked him up and down. His hands fisted at his sides as he felt himself harden even more. When she shifted and bent to take him in her mouth he almost lost it right then and there. The slick moist texture of her lips and tongue against the smooth swollen head of his penis sent jolts of pleasure radiating through his body.

There was no room for any more thought, no room
for right or wrong, there was only space for sensation
and its inevitable, relentless buildup. With a final lave
of her tongue Alexis released him from the hot cavern
of her mouth and realigned her body so she was poised
over him. He held his breath as her darkened silhouette
slowly lowered over him, as he entered the silky hot wet-
ness of her body.

She gave a moan of pure delight as she took him deep
inside her, tilting her pelvis and rocking against him.
He felt her inner muscles clench and hold him. Pressure
built inside him until it became a demand he could no
longer ignore.

His hands found her hips and he used the leverage
to move beneath her as she set up a rhythm designed to
send them both screaming into a molten mess of fulfill-
ment. She grabbed at his wrists, pulling his hands free
from her hips and guided them to the lush fullness of her
breasts. He cupped and held them, his fingers massaging
their softness until his fingertips caught tightly beaded
nipples between them and squeezed.

"Oh, yes," she breathed, her hips grinding into him.
She pressed her breasts more firmly into his touch, so
much so that he bore most of her weight now on his arms.
She was magnificent. Her hair in disarray around her
head, her slender throat arched and her shoulders thrown
back. His climax built inside him, demanding release, but
he held back, gritting his teeth and fighting for control,
and then he had no need to hold on a moment longer. A
thin keening sound escaped Alexis's throat and he felt her
entire body shudder. His shaft was gripped by a silken
fist that squeezed and released until he, too, tipped over
into heady addictive gratification.

Alexis slumped against him, and he drew her close,

her breasts now squashed against his chest, strands of her hair caught on his whiskered jaw. She shifted her legs to be more comfortable but they remained joined together and somehow it felt right. For now at least.

Refusing to question it a moment longer, Raoul allowed himself to drift into a slumber of sheer exhaustion, his arms still locked tight around her waist. Tomorrow would be soon enough to face the recriminations that would undoubtedly meet him in the mirror in the morning.

Eight

Alexis felt the cool sheets beside her and knew he'd gone, withdrawn from her again in every sense of the word. She'd hoped they'd stay together the whole night but she was realistic enough to know he had to be dealing with some serious personal demons about now.

She opened her eyes, searching for where he'd thrown her nightgown, understanding that it would probably be best if she returned to her room.

It was still semidark. A sound over by the floor-length window caught her attention. Raoul stood there, naked, framed in the window. His gaze was fixed on something in the distance, his body caressed by the silver hint of moonlight. She slipped from the bed and came up behind him. Her arms slid around his waist as she leaned against his back.

Still he didn't move, or acknowledge her presence. It was as if she was hugging a statue.

"Are you okay?" she asked softly, pressing a kiss between his shoulder blades.

She felt his body tense, then his rib cage expand as he drew in a breath.

"Yes…and no."

"Talk to me, Raoul," she coaxed. "I'm right here."

"What we did. It was wrong. I shouldn't have come to you last night."

"Raoul, I'm glad you did. We needed each other. What we took from one another, what we gave, we did that honestly. There's no reason for shame between us."

He remained silent for a while but she could still feel the conflict that coiled and strained inside him. Eventually he shook his head.

"I can't do this—"

He gestured futilely with one hand. Alexis loosened her arms and stepped back.

"It's okay," she said, even though she felt as if she might fracture apart.

It took all of her strength to hold her emotions together. Last night had been deeply special to her and, she'd hoped, special to Raoul, too. Apparently hoping that had been premature. So they were simply going to have to take this step by baby step. If she could give him his space now, perhaps it would allow him to realize that he deserved happiness, too.

"No, it's not okay. I have done nothing to earn your understanding. I've used you, Alexis, can't you see that? Don't you think you deserve better than that?"

She fought not to flinch at the harsh words. "Of course I do. We both do. But don't you think I got to use you, too? You're not alone in this, Raoul, no matter how isolated you feel, no matter how alone you try to be. I'm here…for you."

He faced her and she could see the scowl that twisted his handsome face into a mask of displeasure.

"Can't you even allow me to apologize for what I did?"

She shook her head vehemently. "You have nothing to apologize for. Nothing!" she repeated with even more emphasis than before. "Did you feel me try to push you away? Did I ask you to leave or did I turn my head away when you kissed me? No. I welcomed your touch, Raoul. I welcomed *you*. We all need help sometimes. Trouble is, you're too afraid to ask for it and if you do, you see it as some kind of weakness, something to be sorry about."

"I still shouldn't—"

"Oh, please." Alexis rolled her eyes. "Stop it. You were man enough to reach out to me last night. Just accept that I am woman enough to want to grasp hold of you, to be there for you. I don't do anything I don't want to, Raoul. Or anyone. So get over it."

Wrapping her bravado around her like a shield, Alexis walked away from him and found her nightgown on the floor. She dragged it on over her head and all but ran back to her room and into the en suite bathroom. She flipped on the shower and fought to take in a leveling breath as the water warmed. It was still early, at least another hour until sunrise and Ruby's usual time for waking, but there was little point in going back to bed. No way would she get any more sleep now. She stripped off her nightgown and stepped into the luxuriously tiled shower stall and closed her eyes against the stream of water, blindly reaching for the bar of soap she'd put there yesterday. Her eyes flew open when she encountered warm wet male instead.

Raoul's gaze was intense, his jaw a rigid line and his lips pressed firmly together as he stood there, water from the dual jets cascading over his hair and down his neck and shoulders.

He reached for the bar of soap and lathered it up in his hands before gently turning her around to face the shower wall. His hands were firm as he began to massage her shoulders with the scented foam, his thumbs working into knots she didn't know she had. He worked his way down the center of her spine, easing away any residual stiffness she had from her unaccustomed sleeping position during the night.

By the time his hands caressed her buttocks she was all but melting. Her breasts felt full and heavy, aching for his touch, her nipples ruched into tight nubs. She squeezed her thighs together to relieve some of the pressure that built at their apex but it only served to increase her hunger for more of his touch.

His hands left her for a minute, only to return, relathered and on a determined path around her body. She felt his erection pressing against her buttocks as he reached around her, cupping her breasts and gently massaging them. One hand began to track down her body, pressing her back against him. She widened her legs, felt him bend his knees and position himself at her aching center. She waited for his possession but he seemed comfortable just biding his time while his fingers teased and played with her, coaxing her flesh a little wider, grazing her clitoris with firm sweeps of his thumb.

Alexis's legs trembled as she felt her orgasm begin to build and build, the pressure almost too much to bear. When he finally slid inside her, he touched off something deep within. Something with more intensity, more complexity than anything she'd felt before.

She rose to the tips of her toes as Raoul drove into her body. She could feel the roughness of the hair on his legs against the backs of her thighs, the firmness of his belly against her buttocks. When he came, he came hard and

so did she. Pleasure didn't just come in waves, it rico-
cheted through her again and again.

His head fell onto her shoulder and his arms wrapped
around her until she didn't know who was supporting
whom to stay upright anymore. Eventually their breathing slowed and Alexis felt strength return to her limbs.
Hot water still pounded them both as Raoul withdrew
from her. He slicked a hand with soap and gently washed
then rinsed her clean. She was glad of the attention as,
while she was regaining control of her limbs, her consciousness was still under question.

"Keep taking your pill," Raoul said in the shell of her
ear, and then he was gone.

By the time she looked around, he'd swiped one of the
towels from the heated rail and had left the bathroom.
Steam filled the air, leaving her to almost wonder if she
hadn't just dreamed the entire sequence of events. The
racing of her heart, and the tendrils of satisfaction that
still ebbed and flowed through her, confirmed it had been
very, very real. She thought about what he'd said, as well
as what she'd told him about being on the Pill.

Technically, she was, but since she'd been here she'd
been less than fully careful about taking the contraceptive. In the past, she'd always been a stickler for taking
her tablet on time, but with the adjustment to a whole
new routine this past month she'd been a little lax. That
was something that was going to have to change if they
were going to continue with this…this…whatever it was.
Clearly he had reached some personal decision about the
two of them. One that involved their mutual pleasure, if
nothing else.

She turned off the showerheads and stepped from the
stall, drying her sensitized skin with a large bath sheet.
Could she settle for that? The pursuit of physical release

with none of the messy emotional stuff that usually came with it?

A while ago she'd have said a flat-out no. She had always wanted a relationship she could pledge herself to, fully and completely, and know that that pledge was returned. But Raoul had made it perfectly clear that he couldn't give her that. Could she settle for less than love from him?

A little aftershock of pleasure thrilled through her body again. Maybe she'd just have to give it a try and see what happened. At best, the ice around his heart may begin to thaw. At worst, well, she didn't even want to think about that just yet.

In the bedroom she grabbed her handbag and pulled her contraceptive strip from the side pocket. She'd missed three tablets in this cycle but not consecutively. Hopefully she'd still be safe. To avoid further memory lapses she added a new alarm to her cell phone, reminding her to take her pill each morning. To be doubly safe, she'd visit a pharmacy in town and consult with them about the morning-after pill, as well.

Sounds came through the baby monitor that Alexis kept on the bedside cabinet. Ruby was stirring. She quickly dressed and went through to the baby's room to start her working day—except somewhere along the line it had ceased to be work and was becoming something else instead. And as she lifted the little girl for a good-morning cuddle she realized that being needed was something she'd craved all her life.

Her parents had been sufficient to one another while she was growing up. And that was exactly as it should have been, she reminded herself as she changed and dressed Ruby. They'd always loved her, been there for her, but no one had ever truly needed her before. Not the way Ruby did now. Not the way she began to hope Raoul did, also.

A tiny flame of optimism flickered to life deep in her belly. This could work. They could become a family. She had to keep believing it was possible…because the alternative didn't even bear thinking about. Despite everything, despite her determination not to completely give her heart to anyone unless she was certain those feelings were returned, Alexis knew she was falling deeper and deeper into love with Raoul Benoit.

Only time would tell if he could feel the same way about her. She hoped against hope that he could, because if not, walking away from Raoul, walking away from Ruby, would be the hardest thing she'd ever had to do in her entire life.

She'd done something similar once before—distanced herself from him before she could let her feelings grow, knowing them to be futile when he loved Bree and was loved so passionately in return. But things were different now, so very painfully different, and it was going to be a difficult road ahead.

It had been a week and still he couldn't get her out of his mind. What on earth had possessed him to visit her room that night? Worse, what had made him take her back to his and then, in the morning, tell her in no uncertain terms to keep taking her pill? He'd had no right to any of that, a fact he'd reminded himself of constantly these past seven days as he'd forced himself to keep his distance. It hadn't stopped him wanting her, though, or remembering in excruciatingly vivid detail their night— and morning—together.

From his vantage point out in the garden he watched her sleeping in the window seat of the family room. She had a sketch pad on her lap and an array of colored pens spilled across the cushion she lay on. Her hair lay in a swathe across one cheek. Hair he knew was silky soft and carried a scent he found unique to her.

In sleep she looked peaceful, as if she no longer bore the weight of the world on her capable shoulders. His fingers tingled as he remembered how her skin had felt beneath them. How smooth and warm. She was so alive, so giving. Try as he might, he could not help but be pulled into her magnetic sphere.

She'd become a part of his every day in ways he had never imagined. Ways he never wanted or expected to imagine. But more, he now found himself wanting her to become a part of his nights, as well. Just one night with her had been nowhere near enough. He'd barely slept ever since for the memories of her in his arms, in his bed, crowding his thoughts. Replaying, time and again, the exquisite sensation of sliding into her body, feeling her welcoming heat, watching her shatter from the pleasure of his touch.

There'd been no recriminations from her. Not even when he'd treated her so bluntly these past few days. Ill-tempered and filled with mounting frustration, his fuse had been short and he hadn't been afraid to show it or to use it to push her away. She wasn't a fool, she'd read the signals. As a result, he'd noticed that she and Ruby had spent a lot of time away from the house and, dammit, he'd missed them—both of them.

As if Alexis sensed his observation of her, she stirred. A few of her pens slid off the cushion and onto the floor. They must have made some noise because she startled awake and moved to grab her pad from following in the same path. The sketch pad reminded him that she'd put her life on hold to come here.

He'd never have asked her to do that—to simply walk away from her growing business to look after a child who would have been fine with a different nanny, and a man who was perfectly capable of looking after himself. Things had been rolling along just fine here before her arrival—at least that's what he'd tried to convince himself. He knew, though, in all honesty, they hadn't.

What made someone do what she had done? he wondered. Simply shelve, at least for a little while, their own dreams and goals to help out someone else. Was it a lack of self-respect or belief? No, he knew she had self-respect, but she also had a big and giving heart. He'd seen it in the way she'd so quickly grown attached to Ruby.

He continued to watch as Alexis stood up and stretched, the movement pulling her long sleeved T-shirt upward, exposing the soft skin of her belly. In answer, his flesh stirred, reminding him that he'd been trapped in this awkward state of semiarousal this past week. He wanted her, but he didn't want the complicated hang-ups that came along with having her. And if he knew anything about Alexis Fabrini it was that she had a power of emotion stored up in that enticing body of hers. She deserved someone who could match her, physically and emotionally.

He had no space left in his heart for emotion.

He turned and pushed through the edges of the garden and strode out toward the winery. Somehow he had to find a release for all the pent-up energy having sex with Alexis had created. Somehow, he didn't think finishing labeling the wine bottles he was ready to put down would be enough.

Nine

Several hours later he was surprised at the sense of satisfaction he felt while recording the number of bottles of Pinot Noir he'd spent the better part of the day labeling. This wine was his best yet. While he was probably only looking at four hundred cases in total, he was sure that they would be integral in helping to establish his Benoit Wines label. If he could continue to ensure the same quality, and better, year after year, his reputation would be made.

The sound of the winery door creaking open surprised him and he looked up to see Alexis walking through the tasting room toward his small office. The late afternoon sun was weak, yet it still struggled through the windows as if determined to bathe her in shades of golden ocher. His body responded accordingly, again stirring to unwelcome life. His pulse beat just that bit faster, his gut clenched just that bit tighter.

She was alone, a fact that immediately put him on the offensive—the easiest way, he'd found, to cope with this unnerving awareness of her each time she was within a few meters of him.

"Where's Ruby?" he asked, his voice gruff.

"She's having a playdate with Jason over at Matt and Laura's. I'll pick her up in an hour."

"An hour?"

Raoul raised an eyebrow, his mind filling with all manner of things he could enjoy with Alexis in the space of sixty minutes. Just as quickly, he tamped those visions back where they belonged.

"Yes, the kids seem to get along in as much as they can socialize at this age. And, anyway, it's good for her to get out of the house. I said I'll do the same for Laura one day next week. I hope you don't mind. I'm sorry, I probably should have discussed it with you first."

Alexis seemed determined to justify herself to him. Was that what he'd reduced her to? Someone who constantly felt they had to make apology for their actions? He knew Matt and Laura well, he trusted them implicitly.

"If you think it's best for Ruby, it's fine. Did you want me for something?"

"I wanted to see if you're planning to have dinner with us tonight. If not, I'll put yours in the warmer."

"The warmer is fine."

She sighed, and the sound acted like a torch to touchpaper.

"What?" he demanded.

She shrugged. "Nothing."

"No, you sighed. There's something bothering you. What is it?"

"Well, if you must know, I'm sick of you avoiding me,

avoiding us. Is it because we slept together or is it something else I've done?"

He was about to refute her accusation but, in all honesty, he couldn't.

"I don't want you to get the wrong idea, that's all," he muttered.

"Wrong idea? Oh, like romance and candles?" Alexis laughed. It was a brittle sound that plucked at something deep inside him—made him feel unexpectedly ashamed for putting that sarcasm in her tone. She was the kind of woman who deserved both romance and candles— and more.

There was a cynical twist to her mouth as she continued. "Don't worry, Raoul. I know where I stand. I don't care so much for myself, but your withdrawal and your mood this week has been really bad for Ruby. Whether you like it or not, she's your daughter. When are you going to accept your responsibilities toward her?"

He bristled. "She's fed, isn't she? She's clothed and sheltered. What else does she want?"

"Love. *Your* love."

He got up from his chair and pushed a hand through his hair. "She doesn't need me. She has you, she has Catherine. I make sure she has what she needs, it's your job to provide it."

"It's not enough, Raoul."

"It has to be. That's all I have to offer her."

"I disagree."

"Really? You think you know me better than I know myself?"

"I think I know what you're capable of, and this iceman act isn't you. It isn't the real Raoul Benoit."

"Oh, and just who is?" he answered scathingly.

She stepped forward until she was directly in front

of him—so close he could feel the heat of her body. It was as if his own sought and craved it, as if deep down he longed for her warmth. He pushed the thought away. It would be a cold day in hell before he ever admitted to needing someone again. Alexis held his gaze as she lifted a hand and put it on his chest, over where his heart suddenly did a double beat at her touch.

"He's the man inside here. The one you won't let out. I don't know why you've felt the need to lock him away the way you have, but it's time to let him out. Don't you think he's done enough penance now? Don't you think you deserve to live your life?"

He pushed her hand away but the imprint of it had already seared through his clothes and into his skin. She had that effect on him. She could get beneath the layers and slide deep inside.

"Penance? You think that's what I'm doing?"

"Sure. What else would you call it? It's as if you're punishing yourself for something you had no control over. You didn't kill Bree. You weren't responsible for what happened to her."

He spun away from her, determined to make sure she wouldn't see the way that the anguish her words had wrought reflected on his face. She was wrong. So very wrong.

"Raoul?" she asked, putting a hand on his shoulder.

He shrugged her off. He didn't want her touch, her comfort.

"I *was* responsible," he said in a dark low voice. "My expectations killed Bree. I failed her."

"That's not true."

"If I hadn't been so determined to have a family, to fill the rooms of that house up the hill with our kids, she'd still be here today."

"You can't know that. Besides, that was her dream, too. In her letter she told me she was prepared to do anything, risk anything, to have a family with you. The aneurysm—"

"She died, Alexis, and it's all my fault!" he shouted, his words echoing around them.

Alexis looked at him in shock. He really truly blamed himself for Bree's death.

"It happened, Raoul. It wasn't something you or she could control or quantify. Not even the doctors could say if or when the aneurysm could bleed out."

"I know, it was a time bomb. But you know what the kicker is? I didn't even know it was there until it ruptured. She never told me about her condition or the risks to it from her pregnancy. She kept it a secret, hiding it away from me. If I'd have known, if I'd have had the slightest inkling that her health would be compromised by her pregnancy, I would have taken steps to make sure it never happened."

"But that would have been taking her choice to have a family away from her," Alexis protested. "She wanted your child."

"I wanted her."

His voice was bleak, so sad and empty and filled with loss. Alexis didn't know what to do. What he'd just told her explained so much—his withdrawal from society, his reluctance to have anything to do with Ruby. Which brought her full circle to why she'd come to talk to him today.

"You can't blame Ruby. She doesn't deserve that."

"I don't," he answered simply.

"How on earth can you expect me to believe you when

you can't even stay in a room with her for more than five minutes, let alone spend any time alone with her?"

Raoul rubbed a hand across his eyes and shook his head. "It's not what you think. I don't blame her. I just can't let myself love her."

His words struck her like an arrow through her heart. "How can you say that?" she gasped, shocked to her core.

"Because it's true. I can't love her, I won't love her. What if I lose her, too?"

"What if she lives to be a hundred years old?" Alexis countered.

"You don't understand, she was born prematurely, she was seriously ill for the first month of her life—"

"And she's overcome all that, she's a fighter. She's a strong, healthy growing girl and she needs her father—not some coward who's prepared to pay everyone to take over *his* obligations!"

Raoul stood up straighter at her accusation—anger flaring in his hazel eyes, making them seem more green than brown, standing out even more as his complexion paled. "You're calling me a coward?"

Alexis stood her ground. "If the cap fits." She shrugged with feigned nonchalance. Right now she was worried she may have stepped over the mark. But it was too late to back down. Besides, she wasn't about to break the momentum now that they were finally getting to the heart of his issues. "Let's face it, you can't even bring yourself to talk about what we shared last week, about our night together. Instead you've been snapping and snarling at me for days, when you haven't been avoiding me altogether. What's wrong, Raoul? Can't you admit that what we did, what we had together, was good? Do you not believe you even deserve even that?"

"No, I don't!" he shouted. "It's a betrayal."

"Of Bree? As hard as it is, as cruel as it is, she's dead, Raoul. You're living—although not as if you're alive. She wouldn't have wanted you to do this, to cut yourself away from everyone and everything that mattered to you both, especially the daughter you both wanted so badly."

"So what are you saying, that I should jump into bed with you at every opportunity, pretend I'm *alive?*"

"If that's what it takes," she said quietly.

He moved up to her, grabbing her upper arms in his strong hands. Even though he vibrated with anger, his hold was still gentle. She knew this was the real Raoul Benoit. This man with such passion in his eyes that even now, after her goading, she knew he wouldn't hurt her.

"And if I said to you that I want you now, what would you do?"

Alexis calmly looked at her watch and then back at him. "I'd say you have about forty minutes. Is that enough?"

"For now, maybe," he growled.

In the next breath he was kissing her and she thrilled to his touch. Their night together had only made her want more. His last words about taking her birth control had made her believe that he'd come to her again, but instead he'd been so aloof this week, so filled with latent anger. If releasing that anger was what it took to prize him out of his ice cave than that's what she'd do. She'd make him so mad he made love to her every single day. Anything to bring him, the real him, back again.

She shoved her hands under his sweater and scraped her nails across his belly. His skin reacted instantly, peppering with goose bumps. He backed her up until she felt the hard edge of his desk behind her thighs, and bent her backward onto its hard surface. Immediately, his hands were at the waistband of her jeans, tugging at the button and releasing the zipper. He yanked the denim down her legs and cupped her through her lace panties.

The instant he touched her she was on fire. Wet with longing and burning up for what would come next. His palm bore down on her clitoris, the firm pressure bringing her nerve endings to life. She tried to open her legs wider but was restricted by her jeans pooled at her ankles. Somehow, she toed off her shoes and kicked the offending garment away, spreading herself now for his invasion.

As he moved between her legs, she wasted no time unsnapping his jeans and pushing them down, her touch now hungry for the feel of him. She slid one hand under the waistband of his boxers, pushing the fabric away and freeing him, her fingers closing around the velvet coated steel of his erection. Already his tip was moist and he groaned against her as she firmed her grip on him, stroking him up and down, increasing and releasing her pressure as she did so.

Raoul slid a finger inside the leg of her panties and groaned again as he encountered her skin.

"So wet, so ready," he murmured before pulling her underwear down her legs and dropping them on the floor.

Then, his hands were back. He cupped her again, this time inserting a finger, then slowly withdrawing it, his thumb working the swollen nub of nerve endings at her core, stoking the intensity of the fire that burned so bright inside her.

With his other hand he pushed her sweatshirt up higher, exposing the plain cotton bra she'd worn today. For a second she wished she'd chosen something more beautiful, more enticing, but when he unsnapped the front clasp and lowered his mouth to her breast she went beyond caring.

His teeth grazed first one nipple, then the other. Her

skin was so sensitive to his ministrations she screamed softly, lost in the spirals of pleasure that radiated through her body.

More, she wanted more. She guided the blunt head of his penis to her opening and let go when he took over control, sliding his length within her so slowly she thought she might lose her mind. His thumb never stopped circling her clitoris and she knew she didn't have long before she'd come apart, but she wanted this to be about him, as well. About what they could share together.

She clenched her inner muscles and felt him shudder against her. Her hands coasted up his abdomen, stroking his chest and skimming his nipples before tracing back down again to his hips.

Raoul kissed a hot wet trail from her breasts to her throat, then along her jaw to her mouth, capturing her lips again with his caress. Subtly, he increased the pressure of his thumb and Alexis couldn't hold back another second. She gave herself over to the ever-increasing waves of pleasure that consumed her, that thrilled her to heights she'd never felt before with another man.

She clamped around him, again and again as her orgasm built in intensity until she lost awareness, was oblivious to the thrust of his hips and the ragged groan of completion that rent from his body as he climaxed inside her.

It could only have been minutes later, but it felt much longer, when Raoul stirred and withdrew from her.

"Stay there," he said, his breathing still ragged.

She didn't even want to open her eyes, she was so filled with the delicious lassitude that bound her in the aftermath. "I don't think I could move if I wanted to," she admitted, a note of wonder in her voice.

A rusty sound, almost like a laugh, came from where

Raoul was adjusting himself back into his clothing. He left the room and she heard the sound of running water from the small restroom off his office, then he was back with a warm, damp towel in his hands. He wiped her carefully, his touch sending off little shocks of sensation to remind her of what they'd just shared.

"You don't have to do that, I can take care of it," she protested, pushing herself up onto her elbows.

"All done already," he answered, leaving the room again.

She slid off the desk and reached for her panties, pulling them up legs that felt about as strong as overcooked spaghetti. But she felt compelled to move fast, to be dressed before he came back into the room.

His face was impossible to read when he returned and Alexis mentally braced herself, uncertain of what would come next.

"We need to talk," Raoul started, and he saw her pale before him, her eyes widen.

"Wasn't that what we were doing…before?"

He made a movement with his hand, brushing aside her words. "We need to discuss us."

"Us? What about us? Do you want to stop…?"

Her voice trailed away as if she couldn't quite find the words to define the exquisite pleasure they'd enjoyed together. But he had no such difficulty. It was what it was. Just sex. Period. It could never be anything else and she needed to know that.

"No. But I want to be clear going forward that it is only sex between us, Alexis. It will never be, and can never be, anything more than that. You want me to be alive. Fine, I'll be alive—with you—but it won't be anything more than this. I want us to be sexual partners, no strings attached. Can you accept that?"

He watched her carefully for her reaction. If she looked uncomfortable about this in any way, if the idea made her unhappy because she wanted more from a partner or because she secretly harbored feelings for him that she thought might be reciprocated, he hoped it would show on her expressive face. But for once she remained a closed book to him. A faint nod of her head the only acknowledgment of what he'd just said.

"Are you certain, Alexis? Because if you can't, we stop now. I don't want you to be under any illusion that we're going to fall in love and have a future. I'm never going down that road again. I did it once and I can't trust anyone that way again."

She caught her full lower lip between her teeth, the sheen in her eyes a telltale giveaway. A shaft of fear sliced through him. She wanted more. Of course she did. It was in her nature to love, to nurture. It was only natural she'd want the same in return. She was the kind of person who always put others first, the one others turned to when in need. But he didn't want all of that from her—couldn't accept it, couldn't give it to her in return.

"Can I have some time to think about it?"

"If you need time to think about it, you obviously have questions. If you have questions, or doubts, then we should probably forget the whole idea."

He could see her weighing his words. Before his eyes she changed. Her eyes cleared and the expression on her face hardened. She drew herself up to her full height and looked up at him. Then, to his surprise, she gave a brief nod and spoke.

"Yes, I accept."

"Yes?"

He barely dared to hope she was giving him the answer he desperately wanted to hear.

"Yes, I'll be your…" she hesitated just a barest moment "…your sexual partner."

"No strings attached."

The clarification was important. Vitally so.

"Agreed, no strings attached."

"And you'll keep taking your pill. I don't want there to be any mistakes. If you're not happy with that I'll take care of protection myself."

Maybe he should be using condoms as well anyway. You could never be too safe.

"I'm still taking my pill. I don't plan to stop, so don't worry. Is that everything you wanted to discuss?"

Hell, no, it wasn't.

"Just one more thing."

"And what might that be?"

"Our sleeping arrangements. I can't stay in your room."

"That's okay, I can sleep just as well in your bed—if you want me there all night, that is."

Did he? Of course he did. The idea alone had him hardening again.

"I do," he admitted, his voice roughening with mounting anticipation and desire.

She drew in a breath and then slowly released it. "Is that all?"

He nodded, suddenly unable to speak.

"Fine, I'll go and collect Ruby, then."

He watched her through the window as she left the winery and walked up the hill to the house, feeling as if something vital had changed between them and not for the better. But he didn't doubt that he'd made the right decision. He was just happy that she'd agreed. When he turned back to his work he didn't stop to question how right it had felt to hold her, or how desperately he needed to lose himself in her softness again. And again. All he wanted to think about was that, from tonight, he could.

Ten

No strings attached. God should have smote her for that lie. Her agreement had come back to haunt her virtually every day these past couple of weeks. There'd been strings attached to Raoul Benoit from the moment she first laid eyes on him—the very day Bree had excitedly introduced him as her fiancé. That instant attraction, that irresistible tug of physical awareness that happened every single time she saw him, only grew stronger.

He'd kick her out of here faster than she could imagine if he had any idea of how she felt about him. How each day, each hour, each second with him only made her love him more. She stayed with him every night. Falling deep into sleep after they made love, sometimes waking in the small hours to feel him reaching for her to make love all over again.

Last night, after he'd fallen asleep again, she'd committed a cardinal sin. She'd given in, against all her promises to herself to the contrary, and she'd whispered that she loved him. It had been a relief to get it out in the open, even if only for her ears alone.

She shifted her attention back to what she was doing and poured another jug of warm water over Ruby's head. Ruby squealed and splashed the bathwater vigorously, dragging Alexis's thoughts firmly into the present and her duties to her little charge. She laughed out loud at the child's sheer pleasure in bath time.

Strings, yeah, there were strings all right. Not least of which being the one that came from little Ruby and was now securely tied around Alexis's heart, as well.

It was impossible to refuse either of them anything but falling deeper in love with Raoul was starting to take a toll on her. Still, worrying about it wasn't going to solve anything. She just had to do what she did every day, and every night, and hope that the strength of her love could mend what was broken at Raoul's core.

She dragged a warmed towel from the rail and laid it on the floor before lifting a wriggling and squealing toddler from the bathwater. Now that Ruby was more confident walking, it was getting to be more and more of a challenge to keep her immobilized long enough to do simple things like dry her off and dress her. Since the baby had found her feet she'd been on the go all day every day. Of course, without the perception to realize what was risky and what wasn't, there'd been a few accidents—like the one at the coffee table in the main sitting room last week—which had left a small bruise on Ruby's ivory forehead.

Raoul had immediately removed the table and Alexis had been surprised when a local furniture maker had delivered a rounded edge oval one in its stead. Even though

Raoul tried not to care, it was obvious that he did, in spite of himself.

She patted Ruby dry, blowing raspberries on her tummy to make her giggle as she did so. As she righted herself, though, Alexis was assailed by a wave of dizziness. She put out a hand onto the edge of the bath to anchor herself. Ruby, not wasting a moment, rolled over and onto her knees, then gained her feet and headed straight for the door to the hallway as fast as she could go.

"Oh, no you don't, young lady!" Alexis called after the rapidly departing naked figure.

She shot to her feet, only to be hit by another dizzying wave. Black spots swam before her eyes and a roaring sound filled her ears. From what seemed like a great distance away, she heard Ruby's high-pitched squeal of delight. She forced herself to take a step, and then another. Her vision thankfully began to clear.

"I'm coming to get you," she called as she exited the bathroom just in time to see Raoul sweep the naked wriggling baby into his arms.

"Got a runaway, I see," he said, walking toward her and handing Ruby to her as soon as she was within distance.

"I just about need to tether her these days," Alexis said with a smile.

Raoul did a bit of a double take, looking at her more intently than a minute before.

"Are you okay?"

"I think I got up a little too quickly before. It left me a little dizzy but I'm fine now," she said, brushing off his concern.

"You look quite pale, are you sure you're all right?"

She nodded, and it was true. She was feeling fine now compared to earlier.

"Of course, I'm great. Really."

But there was a niggle there in the back of her mind, one she didn't want to consider right now if she could avoid it.

Later, after she'd settled Ruby for the night and had picked up the trail of toys that she had left through the house, she was surprised when Raoul sought her out. Usually he kept working in his study up until he was ready to retire for the night, often reading more about wine-making and blending techniques. He rarely joined her in the family room to watch television. But when they went to bed, it was a different story.

Usually, he came to find her wherever she was in the house and then took her by the hand back to his room. She cast a quick glance at the mantel clock above the family room fireplace. It was early, even for him.

"I've been thinking. It might be best if you sleep in your own room tonight," he said.

"Oh? Why?" *Sick of me already?* She clamped the words firmly behind her lips, not wanting them to possibly be heard in case they might be true.

"You need a decent night's rest and let's face it, I haven't exactly been letting you have one the past couple of weeks, have I?"

Disappointment crowded into her chest.

"It's okay. You haven't heard me complaining, have you?"

He gave her a crooked smile. One that made her heart lurch in that crazy way he always managed.

"No, I can't say I have but I'm worried about you. Get a good night, tonight, hmm? Situation normal again from tomorrow if you're feeling better."

He leaned forward and kissed her. Initially, his lips

were soft and undemanding but it was only a matter of seconds before their kiss deepened, before his mouth slanted across hers so he could kiss her more thoroughly. Heat snaked along her veins, priming her body in readiness for what usually came next. She looped her arms around his neck and gave back with everything she had in her.

She was so lost in the fog of desire that it came as a shock to realize that his hands had caught her at her wrists and were disentangling her so he could pull away.

"I'm fine, Raoul, honestly."

"Let me be the judge of that. One night. We can survive that, can't we? Now go. Get some sleep."

"Can't you just sleep next to me? We don't have to—"

He took a step back. "No, it doesn't work that way with us. You know that. No strings, remember?"

"Sure, I remember," she said, forcing a smile of acceptance to her face.

Just sex, she repeated in the back of her mind as she readied for bed. She continued repeating it for the next hour as she lay in the dark, staring at the ceiling, hoping against all hope that he missed having her in his bed just about as much as she missed being there.

The next morning Alexis felt a great deal more rested. Much as she hated to admit it, Raoul had apparently been right about the lack of sleep catching up to her. But then when she got Ruby out of her crib and was changing her diaper, the first wave of nausea hit her.

"Goodness," she said as she folded and bagged the offending diaper. "We might need to change your diet, young lady."

The second wave hit when she was preparing Ruby's breakfast cereal and stewed fruit—and with it came an overwhelming sense of dread. She was no idiot. She knew what her physical symptoms could mean. She hadn't been fully protected the first time she and Raoul had made love. Even though she'd made that trip to the local pharmacy and gotten the morning-after tablets, she'd been counseled that they were not always 100 percent effective.

"And ain't that the truth?" she muttered under her breath as she willed her stomach under control.

What had Raoul said, again, when he'd made his suggestion that they be sexual partners? He didn't want there to be any mistakes—yes, that was right. Well, it certainly looked as if she'd made a big one. But she needed to be sure. She already had plans to head out with Ruby today. Laura had suggested a playdate with little Jason again and Alexis had been looking forward to just having some time out alone in Akaroa, browsing the stores and stopping at one of the cafés for a triple-shot nonfat latte while browsing a tabloid magazine.

The thought of coffee completely turned her stomach. Alexis swallowed against the lump in her throat. Rather than indulging in her favorite vice, she knew exactly what she'd be doing at the local store instead—buying a pregnancy test kit.

Alexis stared at the indicator window on the stick. This wasn't how she'd imagined discovering she was going to become a mother—locked in the end cubicle of the public restrooms on the main street. Even though she'd known to the soles of her feet what the result would be, the strong positive that appeared was shockingly candid confirmation she really didn't need. One part of her was doing a crazy happy dance—shouting for joy that she was pregnant with Raoul's child. The rest of her quivered with anxiety.

The news that she was expecting his baby, after he'd

spelled it out perfectly clearly that pregnancy was an outcome to be avoided at all cost, would not be welcome.

She shoved the stick into its wrapper and back into the box—disposing of everything in the restroom trash can. Numb, she washed and dried her hands and walked outside, where everyone carried along on the pavement with their everyday lives, oblivious to the situation she now found herself in.

Alexis crossed the street to a park bench that sat on a grass berm, facing out to the harbor. Despite the cold day, she felt nothing. Not the sunshine on her face, nor the brisk wind that whipped along the shoreline, coaxing whitecaps on the water.

What on earth was she going to do?

She could only imagine Raoul's reaction. There was no room in his life, or his heart, for another baby. Hell, he fought against making room for the one he had.

But he was capable of love, Alexis knew that. She'd witnessed it for herself. He'd loved once and he could love again, she just knew it. His marriage to Bree had been happy, she'd seen that to her own cost. Somehow she had to convince him to take a risk on love again.

She understood that grief did strange things to a person—could blow normal emotions right out of proportion. She only had to look at her own family for proof of that.

Alexis's mother had had a first, unhappy marriage, and when she'd run away from it to marry for love, she'd been forced to leave her children behind. Years later, when her daughter from that marriage sought her out, Alexis's father had not reacted well. Her mother had been in the hospital by then, physically and mentally frail from the disease racking her body. Fear that seeing her long-lost daughter might upset her to the point of worsening her condition had made Lorenzo go so far as to enlist his business partner to actively steer her half sister, Tamsyn, away from discovering where their mother was. When Ellen Fabrini had died before Tamsyn could even see her again, Alexis had realized that nothing mattered more in this world than family. Nothing.

Maybe that was part of why she was so determined to break through the barriers with Raoul. To force him to learn to love again. To make him see how precious his daughter was—what a truly wonderful tribute she was to a marriage and a love that had sadly ended all too soon.

Unexpected tears sprang in her eyes. She blinked them furiously away. *Please don't let me become one of those overemotional wrecks with this pregnancy,* she silently begged. The last thing she needed was an exceptional change in her behavior that might tip Raoul off before she was ready to tell him her news.

An alarm on her phone chimed from the side pocket of her handbag, reminding her it was time to collect Ruby. She was no nearer to knowing what she needed to do about the baby she carried. Logically, there were steps to be taken. She needed to make an appointment with a local doctor, get her results confirmed, get checked out, etc. But, as to the rest—telling Raoul? She had no idea where to begin and, as much as it rankled to deliberately withhold the truth from him, she felt she had no other option right now. No other option at all.

She thought about the test kit in the restroom trash. Those things had a degree of inaccuracy, surely. She'd wait until she had official confirmation from the doctor. Then she'd decide what to do. Until then, everything would remain as it had been before.

Eleven

Raoul couldn't take his eyes off Alexis as she played with Ruby. The weather outside was miserable, cold and wet and blowing a gale. Alexis had lit the fire in the family room and put the guard around the fireplace. He'd wondered about the wisdom of the fire, even with the guard, but after watching Ruby he realized that she'd been schooled by Alexis to stay well clear of the hearth.

"Dad-dad!"

She'd spied him and ran toward him as fast as her little legs could carry her. He could hardly believe that an almost eleven-month-old baby could move so fast. Her hair was longer now and Alexis had tied it up into a little spout on the top of her head. Whoomph! Two little arms clamped around his legs as she came to a halt beneath him and gabbled off a rapid chain of baby babble.

"I think she's asking you to lift her up," Alexis said from her spot on the floor, her cheeks flushed with the heat of the fire.

"Asking, or telling me?" he said, bending down to un-peel her arms from his legs.

"Probably the latter." Alexis laughed. "Go on, pick her up."

"No, it's all right. I've got work to do."

"Oh, for goodness' sake! You won't drop her."

Alexis got to her feet and picked up Ruby and thrust her at him. Reflexively he took her. "Hold her! She's not made of glass. She's growing up before your very eyes, she's hale and hearty and everything's fine."

"Got out of the wrong side of the bed this morning, did we?" Raoul commented, awkwardly holding Ruby on his hip.

The baby reached for a pen he had in his shirt pocket and began playing with the clicker, eventually getting ink down his front. He extricated the pen from her in-creasingly deft fingers and waited for her to protest so he'd have an excuse to hand her back to Alexis. Instead, she lay her little head on his chest and gave a big sigh.

"You know exactly what side of the bed I got out of," Alexis responded, her voice softer now as she watched him and Ruby.

"She must be ready for a sleep," he said.

"No, I think she's happy to just sit with you for a bit. Why don't you read to her?"

"Read?"

"Yes. You know, pick up one of those paper things with the cardboard on the outside and words and pictures printed in the middle? I need to go and check on some washing in the dryer."

She was gone from the room before he could protest and he couldn't very well leave Ruby alone in here, es-pecially not with the fire going. It felt weird, but he sat down at the end of the sofa and picked up one of the baby books Alexis kept stashed in a basket on the floor beside it. He adjusted Ruby on his lap and opened the book, starting to read from it. It's not like it was rocket science. The words were simplistic and thankfully few, and the pictures were bright and colorful. He'd just finished the book and closed it, ready to put it back on the stack when Ruby grabbed it off him and opened it again, her little fingers struggling a bit to turn the pages. Giving in, he started to read it for a second, and then a third time.

By the time Alexis came back into the room, a basket of folded washing on her hip, he was on to his fourth attempt. Ruby had settled back against his tummy, her little head growing heavy against him.

"Oh, look at that. She's out for the count," Alexis said softly.

"Must have bored her to sleep," he commented, thankful he could at least stop reciting the story line, now committed to memory, over again.

"Actually, no. She obviously feels very secure with you. At her age she can be a bit off with some people. A baby's stranger awareness is honed around this age. Some kids start even earlier. I think it's lovely that she knows she's okay with you."

Raoul felt outrageously proud but hastened to downplay the situation.

"It's just because she's used to being here now. That'll all change when she goes back to Catherine and you go back home."

"You're still sending her back to Catherine?" Alexis sounded shocked.

"Of course, that was the plan all along. Here, take her and put her to bed."

"Sure thing, boss."

There was something about the tone of Alexis's voice that set his teeth on edge.

"Alexis, just because I read her a story doesn't mean we're going to play happy family."

"No, of course not. That would take far more heart than you're prepared to admit to."

With that, she deftly scooped the sleeping baby off his lap and disappeared out the room. Her comment rankled. It shouldn't, but it did. He hadn't asked for her to leave him alone with Ruby and he certainly hadn't asked for her opinion about his plans for Ruby's long-term care. Yet why had he experienced that absurd sense of pride that the baby had settled with him, and why did his arms feel ridiculously empty now that she was gone?

It was almost ten weeks since Catherine's surgery. Ten weeks since Alexis had come to look after Ruby. Catherine was walking steadily on her own now and, with regular physiotherapy sessions, was regaining her strength and independence day by day. She'd asked Alexis if she could have Ruby to visit for a couple of hours and Alexis took the opportunity to make an appointment to visit the doctor and get official confirmation about her condition.

She'd done the math, by her reckoning she was just over six weeks pregnant, thankfully still far too early to show. Luckily, so far, her only symptoms were that she felt queasy every now and then only if she was overtired.

Even if her symptoms had been more drastic, it was unlikely anyone would have noticed. Raoul was still incredibly busy conducting his one-man band of business in the winery. Alexis was in two minds about it. Half of her was hugely relieved he spent so many hours out of her sphere right now, especially as she struggled to deal with the mental ramifications of her pregnancy. The other half, well, that just saw the time he wasn't there as missed opportunities to keep building up the tenuously fragile link that was starting to develop between Ruby and her father.

Still, she reminded herself, progress was progress, even if the steps were tiny.

What scared her most was, what on earth would happen when her pregnancy started to be more obvious? She and Raoul shared a bed, shared one another's bodies, every night. He knew her body so well, eventually he'd feel the changes that she had begun to notice herself. Already her breasts were more tender and responsive than before and, as she'd noticed when she'd fastened her bra this morning, they were already slightly fuller, too.

Somehow she had to find the courage to tell him before he picked up on the physical cues that she had no control over. Picking the right time was going to be the challenging part.

The visit to the doctor went smoothly. The doctor congratulated her on her pregnancy and she tried her hardest to show the appropriate enthusiasm. Even though she knew everything was okay, that she was strong and healthy and that the pregnancy should continue to develop normally, she still felt an underlying anxiety. While termination was out of the question, how on earth would she cope with all this?

She'd already put her working life on hold to be there for Ruby and yes, granted, she was paid for her role here, but that was nothing compared to what she could potentially earn as her fashion clientele continued to grow. Having Tamsyn keep things running smoothly in her absence was one thing, but would she be able to continue to expand her business if she was busy with a new baby, as well?

Making the decision to come here had come from a position of guilt—from the fact that she'd owed Bree's daughter the support and love she'd failed to give the child's mother. When she'd started to withdraw from Bree, after meeting Raoul, she'd felt her friend's confusion, the hint of hurt in the background of her initial emails.

The lengthy, handwritten letter Bree had sent her before she died had been full of apology for some slight she had imagined was the only reason that could have caused a wedge between herself and Alexis. Bree was sad that they'd drifted apart the way they had but she'd felt, of all the people she knew, that she could still turn to Alexis in her hour of need.

And Alexis hadn't been there.

She and Raoul both lived with their own sense of guilt, and it pulled at each of them constantly—drove them to make the choices they did, feel what they felt. Alexis could only hope that, with its source being a common link for them both, that somehow they could find a solution together for the future.

Catherine looked tired but happy when Alexis arrived at her house to collect Ruby.

"Did you get done everything you wanted?" she asked after she invited Alexis in for a cup of tea.

"I did, thank you."

Alexis looked at the woman who had been one of her own mother's best friends and who had packed up her whole life in Blenheim to move to Banks Peninsula when it had become clear that Ruby needed a full-time carer other than her father. Catherine smiled back.

"I'm glad. So, how's it all going? We've hardly had any chance to talk since I've been back home. How's Raoul doing?"

Alexis bowed her head and studied the fine china cup in her hands. "I didn't realize just how determined he was to keep his distance from Ruby. Sure, I've got him to hold her a few times but overall I'm not making much headway. He cares about her, I know he does, he just won't show it or even admit it to himself. He's so inflexible."

"Bree used to say that, too. I think that's why she never told anyone about the aneurysm. She knew he would have refused to have a family if he'd known, and she so wanted one with him."

"Have you told him that?" Alexis asked, lifting her head to meet Catherine's understanding gaze.

"Oh, I've told him several times but, as you say, he's inflexible with a good dose of intractable thrown into the bargain. Once he makes up his mind, it's made up. He still thinks he's responsible somehow. I believe he finds it easier to accept that than to think he had no control over what happened. He's not the kind of man who likes to relinquish control, is he? After all, while he won't care for Ruby himself, he makes sure she's cared for—and to his expectations. He's still superprotective, isn't he?"

Alexis's lips twisted into a rueful smile. "Yes, that he most definitely is."

"Bree was always the one thing he could never control. She would exasperate him something terrible at times." Catherine laughed. "It used to puzzle me that they managed to work everything out between them—two people so different. I don't think he'll ever forgive her for keeping that information from him, though. He's still angry at her. He's not going to heal or move forward until he can let that go. Oh, I know he *thinks* he's moving forward, especially with the development of his wines, but he's just going through the motions. His heart's not really in it."

Alexis pondered her visit with Catherine later that

night as she lay in bed, the book she'd planned to read lying open in her lap. The older woman's words about Raoul's anger and his need for forgiveness weighed heavily on her heart. She understood what Catherine had said because, she'd painfully realized, it applied to her, too. She'd never thought about it until now but she'd been angry with Bree for a long time. Angry that she'd met Raoul first, angry that she found her happiness with him.

It was petty and infantile but there it was. And she'd stupidly let those feelings get in the way of a long-standing friendship, one that had seen them through so many things together as they were growing up. So another part of her was angry with Bree for dying while things were still unsolved between them—for not giving Alexis a chance to come to peace with Bree's marriage and renew their friendship.

It occurred to her that while Raoul had to forgive Bree for not telling him the truth about her health, she in turn had to forgive herself for allowing her attraction to him to come between her and Bree, and for not moving past her issues before it was too late. Could she do that?

It wasn't as if she could appeal to Bree herself anymore for her forgiveness. Instead, she was doing all she could to care for Ruby, to try to ignite a relationship between father and daughter as she knew Bree would want. Was that enough?

She was still turning the idea over in her head as Raoul came into the bedroom.

"You look deep in thought," Raoul said. "Problem?"

"No, just thinking about things," she hedged.

She wished she had the strength to tell him about her feelings, even tell him about her pregnancy now— to pour out how she felt and to have him take her in his arms and tell her everything would be all right. It was a futile hope. He'd so effectively compartmentalized his life and locked his feelings away that she didn't dare expose her vulnerability to him.

She had to believe that he could love her back before she could declare her heart to him and, she realized, before she could tell him about their baby. Attraction was there—every night together was evidence of that—surely there had to be more to this for him than just a release of physical tension.

"What are you thinking about?" he asked as he began tugging his clothes off, distracting her with his movements.

"Just something Catherine said," she answered lightly.

"Oh." He paused in the act of pulling his sweater off and Alexis's eyes were immediately drawn to the ridged plane of his stomach. "Is she ready to take Ruby back?"

"Hardly!" Alexis remonstrated. A knot formed in her stomach. "Are you in such a hurry to get rid of me?"

He finished shucking off his clothes and slid into bed beside her. "No," he said, reaching over her to put her book on the bedside cabinet and pulling her into his arms. "Does this feel like I want to get rid of you?"

His erection pressed demandingly against her and her body answered in kind, hunger for him spreading throughout in a slow, delicious wave. She forced a laugh, pressing her fears and doubts to the back of her mind and grabbing the moment, and him, with both hands.

Their lovemaking was a feverish joining of bodies, as it so often was. As if each sought something from the other that only they could give. And yet, there was still that lingering sense of incompletion for Alexis as she searched for the emotional connection she so needed with the man in her arms.

That it remained a one-way street struck home now more than ever before.

Raoul fell asleep almost immediately afterward, but Alexis continued to stare at the ceiling in the darkened room, wondering just how much longer she could keep this up before she broke completely. She'd thought she had the strength to do this, to fight past his barricades, to wear them down and to fill his heart with her love. Had it all been nothing more than a pipe dream? It certainly felt like it.

Twelve

Raoul looked up from his breakfast to see Alexis coming down the hall. He was getting a late start on his day, something that he found himself doing more and more often recently. Sharing a little extra time with Alexis at this stage of the day was something he'd discovered he enjoyed. And he had to admit, watching Ruby's antics as she ate her breakfast had been known to bring a smile or two to his face.

Alexis came into the kitchen with Ruby, looking a little paler than usual—a worry mark scoring a line between her brows. He was so used to seeing her smile and being her relaxed and easygoing self that the sight of her like this rattled him. Raoul felt an unfamiliar tightness in his chest. Was she all right?

"Good morning," she said, popping Ruby in her high chair and doing up the harness that prevented her from climbing straight back out again. "I'm glad I caught you. I need to ask you a favor."

"A favor?" he asked, absently passing Ruby a small square of his toast, something that had become a part of their morning ritual.

Aside from wanting him to spend more time with Ruby, Alexis didn't usually ask him anything. He wondered what was on her mind. "What is it?" he asked, getting up from the table to rinse his dishes and put them in the dishwasher—and to position himself with his back to her, so she couldn't see the worry he was certain was written all over his face.

Alexis hesitated a little before speaking. "Look, I need to head out to an appointment this morning. I tried to see if Laura could have Ruby for me, or Catherine, but Catherine's got plans for today already and Laura's just texted me to say their household is down with a tummy bug so I can't leave her there. Can you have Ruby for a couple of hours for me?"

A couple of hours without Alexis in calling distance? Without even Catherine to call upon if anything should go wrong? Icy water ran in his veins.

He shook his head immediately. "No, I can't. I'm sending out samples of last year's vintage to restaurants around the country and I've got couriers coming and going all morning. I won't be able to keep an eye on Ruby, as well."

It was true, he justified to himself. The risks to Ruby if she was down in the winery with him were untold. A moment's inattention and she could get into serious mischief and his day was already too busy and structured to accommodate an active baby. Add to that the additional traffic that would be on the lane and the whole exercise would be a nightmare.

Contrition stung at the back of his mind as he saw Alexis accept the news. The frown on her forehead deepened.

"Okay, I'll just work around her, then," she said flatly.

"Can you change your appointment? What is it, anyway?"

She looked at him and for a moment he thought she looked scared. The urge to protect her from whatever the problem was filled him but was beaten back by the self-reproach he felt at not being willing to take Ruby for her.

She gave him a shaky smile, one that didn't quite reach her eyes. "No, don't worry, it's nothing important. I'll work something out. Are you heading down to the winery office now?"

"I'll be in my study here for a short while, then I'll go down to the winery."

She gave a little sigh. "I'll see you later on today, then."

"Yeah, sure. I should be all done by three."

He left the kitchen and started down the hall but his steps slowed before he reached the study. Something wasn't right. Alexis hadn't been herself for days now. Possibly even a couple of weeks. At least since the day she'd been to see Catherine with Ruby. He cast his mind back. She'd been worried then about something Catherine had said. Obviously it was still playing on her. He made a mental note to pursue it with her this afternoon.

From his study window he saw Alexis leave the house about a half hour later. She put Ruby in her car seat in the back of the car and buckled her in, just as she always did. Something wasn't right, though. Alexis moved more slowly than usual, more carefully. He continued watching as she went around the back of the car and put the diaper bag in the trunk before walking around to the driver's door.

Something definitely wasn't right. She leaned against the car, her hand to her stomach, then her legs collapsed beneath her.

He was out of his chair and flying toward the front door before he saw her hit the driveway. She was already stirring when he reached her side.

"Are you all right? What happened?" he demanded, his eyes roaming her pale features as her eyelids fluttered open.

"I need to see the doctor, Raoul. Can you take me, please?"

"I'll call an ambulance."

He had his cell phone out in his hand, his thumb already poised over the emergency call button. A wave of sick fear swamped him, making his hand shake, along with an awful sense of déjà vu. The last time he'd felt this scared, this totally helpless, was when Bree had gone into labor with Ruby.

Alexis's hand closed over his. "No, the medical center in town. They're expecting me—it's the appointment I told you about. Please, just take me there."

"Are you sure?"

"Please, let's just go."

He helped her up to her feet and shepherded her into the back of the car, with Ruby who was now beginning to fret.

"Not now, Ruby," he said sternly as he helped Alexis with her safety belt. "I need you to be good for me."

To his surprise, the baby stopped and popped her thumb in her mouth. Her big blue eyes stared straight at him. A tickle of relief that he wouldn't have to deal with a crying baby on top of his concern for Alexis flickered on the periphery of his mind.

"That's a good girl," he said absently before giving his sole attention to Alexis again. "Are you comfortable?"

"Enough for now," she answered weakly. "Can we go?"

He closed her door and then got into the driver's seat,

adjusting the rearview mirror so he could keep an eye on her in back. Her face was still pale and her big brown eyes met his in the mirror. She looked frightened and identifying that look on her constantly cheerful and indomitable face terrified him.

The drive to the clinic was short and Alexis was already struggling out of her seat even as he flew out of his to come and assist her. She waved him away.

"Let me go, I'll be all right getting in there. Just see to Ruby."

"She can wait, she's safe where she is for now. Let me see you insi—"

"No, Raoul!" Alexis's voice was sharp. "You can't just leave her in the car. I can manage for now."

Without waiting for him to reply she began walking slowly toward the entrance, disappearing between the front sliding doors as he fiddled with the baby car-seat buckle—cursing its efficacy until he had it loose—and lifted Ruby from her restraint. He ran with her to the building and straight to reception.

"Alexis Fabrini, where is she?" he demanded when he reached the counter.

The receptionist stared at him over the edge of her glasses. "And you are?"

"Raoul Benoit," he replied automatically.

"Are you her next of kin?"

Inwardly he groaned. He could see where this was going. They weren't going to let him see her, or tell him anything. "No, I'm not. I'm her employer. She has no family locally."

"Then I'll ask you to wait over there," the receptionist said firmly, gesturing to the bank of chairs lined up in the waiting area.

"I'd like to see her, be with her—"

"She's with the medical staff. I'm sure they'll call you if necessary," the woman placated. "There's nothing you can do right now but be patient."

There was a sympathetic look in her eyes as if she understood his frustration, but he didn't want her sympathy. He wanted Alexis. He wanted her well, not pale and trembling. Not sliding unconscious down the side of her car. That she hadn't hit her head when she'd fallen was sheer luck, but why had she passed out in the first place? She must have known something was wrong to have made the appointment in the first place—had she expected this to happen? And, if she'd had a medical appointment today, why hadn't she just been upfront and told him about it? They were lovers. They'd shared more with one another than most people. Knew each other intimately.

But sitting here, confused and worried, he was struck with how little he truly knew. He didn't know that she was unwell, or what she thought was wrong. Didn't know how long she'd been worried about whatever it was, or why she hadn't told him. And the more he thought about it, the more he realized how little of her thoughts she really shared with him. What were her hopes, her dreams for the future? Had he ever bothered to find out what they were? Had he ever taken the time to learn about *her*? What made her happiest, what made her sad? He knew for a fact that he made her angry with his reluctance to be a part of Ruby's life.

Ruby squirmed in his arms, wanting to be let down to play with a toy in the waiting area. He eyed it suspiciously. The wooden base looked clean enough but who was to say the roller coaster of colorful wooden beads was hygienic? Who knew what she'd catch if she played with it?

"I don't think so," he murmured to the little girl, holding her firmly on his lap.

Ruby squawked a protest.

"It's okay," the receptionist said blandly from behind her desk. "I disinfected all the toys at the end of clinic last night. She'll be fine."

Raoul still felt uncomfortable with the idea, but he nodded his acknowledgment and gingerly set Ruby on her feet. He followed her to the toy and sat on a chair beside it as the little girl squatted down and reached for the beads, picking them up and dropping them on the brightly colored wires that threaded through them.

"Here," Raoul said, getting down to her level. "I think you're supposed to do this."

He demonstrated with one bead, guiding it along a wire as Ruby watched. But she was having none of it. She quite happily continued to do what she was doing. With a sigh, Raoul sat back on his chair, his eyes flicking every now and then to the corridor where he assumed Alexis had been taken. The waiting was interminable— the minutes stretching out to ten, twenty, thirty, then forty. The long wait was getting to Ruby also, it seemed, as she worked her way from interest in the bead roller coaster to every other toy in the waiting room. Finally, she brought a book to Raoul, making it clear what she wanted him to do.

"Not now, Ruby. You read the book," he stated, but the baby continued to vocalize her demand.

Mindful of the risk of her cries disturbing the other people that were now coming into the waiting room, he lifted her onto his lap where, to his surprise, she settled quite happily and banged her hand on the book. He opened the cover and started to quietly read. When that book was done she squirmed back down and got another.

And so passed the next painfully slow ten minutes until Ruby began to fidget and fuss again. Feeling at a total loss, he stood up with her and started to walk back and forward, rubbing her gently on her back as he'd seen Alexis do so many times before. But it seemed he didn't have quite the knack he needed.

He looked again down the corridor where the examination rooms were. Which one was Alexis in? he wondered. Was she okay? What on earth could be wrong with her that they had to keep her so long?

Ruby's fussing worked up a notch. Raoul felt helpless. He had no idea what to do.

"Maybe she needs a bottle or a drink?" an elderly lady suggested from her perch on a seat near the door.

Raoul remembered the diaper bag that Alexis had put in the trunk of the car. "Good idea," he said with a grateful smile to the woman and headed out quickly to the car park.

He unzipped the bag with a bit of difficulty and spied Ruby's drink bottle inside. The baby nearly tipped out of his arms as she reached for it. He grabbed her and secured her with one arm before passing her the bottle. He watched with relief as she jammed it into her mouth and began to drink. Slinging the bag over his shoulder, he closed the trunk and went back into the waiting room.

Settled with Ruby in his lap again he kept an eye on the corridor. People came and went but there was still no sign of Alexis. Ruby began to grow heavier in his arms and he realized she was drifting off to sleep. He took the bottle from her weakening grip and popped it back in the bag and adjusted her slightly so she could lie more comfortably across his lap.

He looked at her face as she slept, a face that was so familiar to him it made his heart ache to see Bree reflected there. But there was more than Bree in her features. There was Ruby's own growing personality beginning to show, too. She felt so small in his hands, so precious. How on earth could he keep her safe for the whole of her life? How could he keep the bad things from happening to her, the disappointments, the setbacks?

The responsibility was crushing. How did people cope? How did they balance love with care and obligation? He'd thought he and Bree had had the perfect mix of devotion and trust, until he'd found out that she'd kept the truth about her health from him. They'd promised one another to love and honor each other, to care for one another in sickness and in health. But she hadn't honored his love for her when she'd withheld the risks of pregnancy from him. She hadn't given him—them—a chance to face the obstacles together.

The all-too-familiar mix of rage and defeat pummeled his gut. She'd left him with the child he'd so wanted, yet was now too scared to love. The sense of betrayal cut as deep today as it had when the medical team had rushed him from the delivery suite and when they'd eventually informed him of Bree's death, despite all their efforts to prevent it. She'd taken a risk to have Ruby and she'd paid for it with her life. And he was angry. So very angry.

He lifted his head and looked around the waiting room, reminding himself of where he was and why he was here. Again that infuriating and painfully familiar sense of helplessness seeped through him. Alexis was in a room in here somewhere and he had no idea why. He'd been shut out because he had chosen to shut her out of that part of his life, as well. If he'd tried to be more open with her, become a true lover to her, he'd be in there with her—holding her hand, supporting her. Being her partner.

The idea resounded through his mind. Was he even

ready to take that step with someone again? He examined his feelings for Alexis. Feelings he had tried to keep at bay, had tried to mask with desire and the purely physical side of being together. But he couldn't deny it any longer. Alexis meant more to him than a convenient bed partner—way more.

A sound from the corridor to the examination rooms caught his attention and he saw Alexis walking toward reception with a nurse at her side. He got to his feet, carefully so as not to disturb the sleeping child in his arms, and started toward her—catching the tail end of what the nurse was saying as he drew nearer.

"The doctor will refer you through to Christchurch's maternity services and you'll need to take it easy for the next few days until the bleeding subsides. Oh, and no sex until it's stopped completely." The nurse put a comforting hand on Alexis's arm. "Don't worry too much, the ultrasound didn't show up any abnormalities, but take care and don't hesitate to call us if you have any concerns."

"Thank you, nurse," Alexis said weakly, her face suddenly growing even more pale as she realized that Raoul was standing right there.

He looked at her in shock, bile rising in his throat as he played the words he'd heard over in his mind. Bleeding? Ultrasound? Maternity services? Just what the hell were they talking about?

Thirteen

Alexis took one look at Raoul's face and knew he'd overheard the nurse's instructions. This was the last way she would have wanted for him to find out. She wished it could have been different. Wished he hadn't had to bring her here at all, or wait for her, no doubt with questions piling up upon themselves as he did so.

When she'd woken this morning and discovered she was bleeding, her first reaction had been complete panic. She'd rung the clinic and made an urgent appointment, then tried to find someone to care for Ruby. When that hadn't worked out she knew she'd been pushing it to expect Raoul to look after the baby.

Fainting at the side of the car hadn't been her finest moment but it had achieved one thing right today, she realized as she flicked her gaze over the sleeping child in his arms. Raoul had clearly had to spend some quality time with his daughter.

"Can we go?" she asked quietly. She wasn't looking forward to the demands for an explanation that were certain to come once they were alone, but she needed to go home. She couldn't avoid telling Raoul any longer and she certainly wasn't about to do that here with the entire waiting room packed and all eyes now fixed on her and Raoul.

Tension rolled off Raoul in waves as he negotiated the road back to the house. Alexis tried to make herself as small as possible in the passenger seat and focused her gaze out the side window but in her periphery she could see him turn his head and glance at her every now and then, as if he expected the answers to all the questions that no doubt rolled around in his head to suddenly appear neatly scripted on her face. She was glad he didn't start questioning her in the car but she dreaded the moment that he would.

At the house, she went to lift Ruby from her car seat—the wee tot was still out for it—but Raoul pushed her gently aside.

"I'll take her, you go and lie down," he said gruffly, then competently lifted the baby from her seat and carried her down to her room.

Alexis did as he'd told her, going back to the master suite and suddenly feeling very shaky on her feet—though she wasn't particularly tired. Still, maybe if she could feign sleep, Raoul would leave her alone for a bit longer. She was out of luck. He was in the room in minutes.

"Tell me," he demanded as he came to stand beside the bed, looking down at her.

She shrank into the bedcovers, hating what she had to say but knowing it would be useless to try to stall or evade. There was no putting this off any longer, no matter how much it hurt. Even forming the words in her head felt all wrong, but verbalizing them—putting them out there for Raoul to hear—that was crucifying.

Alexis drew in a deep breath. "I had a threatened miscarriage."

She watched his face for his reaction, but could only discern a tightening of his jaw and the flick of a pulse at the base of his throat.

"Threatened miscarriage. What exactly does that mean?"

"I woke up this morning and noticed I was bleeding. The clinic told me to come straight in. They think it'll stop, that..." She dragged in another breath. "That the baby will be okay."

"Baby."

His voice was cold and flat, much like the empty expression in his eyes.

"Yes," she acknowledged in a whisper.

"And I'm assuming that I'm the father of this baby?"

"Yes," she said again, this time a little more firmly.

Raoul huffed out a breath and dragged a hand through his hair. "Tell me, Alexis. At what point were you going to let me know about this?"

"I...I don't know."

"What? Did you think you could hide it from me?"

"Not for long," she admitted, curling up onto her side.

He started to pace, back and forth, and when he stopped she knew what was coming.

"You lied to me when you said you were protected even though you knew how I felt about something like this happening. Why?"

"I thought I'd be okay, I'd only missed a couple of pills. I went to the pharmacy the next morning and got a morning-after prescription. I did everything I could to make sure this didn't happen."

"And yet it did."

"Yes, it did."

"I shouldn't have trusted you. I shouldn't have touched you. God, what are we going to do?"

"Well, if the bleeding stops as it's supposed to and everything settles down okay, we're going to become parents together," she said softly, trying to infuse her voice with enthusiasm and encouragement in the vain hope it might sink past his shock.

He looked at her in horror.

"*If* everything settles down? What are you saying—are you going to be okay?" he asked, his face suddenly pale.

"The doctor wants to refer me to maternity services in Christchurch to be certain. I need to wait for an appointment."

"No, no waiting. I'll get you in to see someone privately."

"I can't afford that, Raoul," she protested. "I don't have full cover on my medical insurance."

"I'll pay for it. I need to know what's going on." He diverted from his pacing path, seeming to head to the door—most likely to make the necessary calls to doctors right away.

"Raoul, please, believe me when I say I didn't want this to happen," she whispered before he could leave.

He closed his eyes and shook his head and she saw his throat move as he swallowed.

"Neither did I, Alexis. Neither did I. Try to get some rest. I'll see to Ruby when she wakes."

He took the mobile monitor that Alexis kept at her bedside and clipped it to his belt.

"But what about the couriers? I thought you had a busy day ahead."

"I do, but I'll just have to work around it, won't I?"

Tears of frustration pricked at the back of her eyes but she refused to let them go.

"Raoul," she said as he moved once more to leave the room. "I'm so sorry."

"Me, too."

She stared at the door as he closed it behind him, her heart aching for what she was putting him through. She'd seen the abject terror in his eyes this morning, followed later by shock when he'd overheard the nurse talking to her at the clinic.

Alexis pressed a hand to her lower belly, hoping against hope that everything would be all right. For all of them. This wasn't the way she'd wanted him to find out. She'd wanted to tell him, in her own time, her own way. But nature had decided otherwise. And now it was Raoul's turn to decide how to respond.

Raoul paced back and forth in the family room, bound to stay at the house by his promise to take care of Ruby and to let Alexis rest, which meant staying within range of the baby monitor. He fought his instinct to flee, to head deep into the vineyard and walk and walk until he could walk no more.

Dark clouds scudded across the sky, heavy with rain that began to fall in steady droplets, battering against the glass stacking doors that looked out over the garden. He leaned his forehead against the glass, welcoming the cold, the numbness. Anything was better than the horror that played through his mind right now.

Alexis. Pregnant.

He braced his hands against a door frame and stared blindly out into the drenched garden as the two words echoed over and over in his head.

This couldn't be happening. Not again. Hadn't life

dealt him a hard enough blow with Bree, now it had to throw this at him, too? This wasn't something he could come to terms with. And tied in with the fear he felt at her condition was a strong sense of betrayal—again. He'd trusted Alexis, believed she was telling the truth after that first time they'd been together. She'd never mentioned the slightest doubt that she was safely protected from pregnancy.

His eyes burned as the wind picked up, blasting cold rain directly at the surface of the glass doors. Still he didn't move. Couldn't. He was frozen to this spot as much as he was frozen inside. He'd begun to thaw, he'd felt it, noticed it bit by bit as Alexis had worked her way under his skin and into his heart. Had stopped fighting against it, had even begun to trust that maybe, just maybe, the time was right to live again.

He was a damn fool. Hadn't he learned his lesson the hard way? People who professed to love you were also prepared to lie to you, as well. Bree had. He hadn't thought that Alexis ever would. She was so honest, so open and giving. He'd heard Alexis say she loved him one night as he'd fallen asleep. He *knew* how she felt. It was there in her every word, her every touch. When they made love he could feel her giving him a piece of her every single time. Making him feel again, making him want more, even making him begin to dream.

But she'd lied, too. And now worse, she, too, was at risk. The baby possibly already threatening her life as well as its own.

He'd always wanted a big family. That wish continued to come back to haunt him. He fought back the scream that struggled to be released from deep inside of him, too afraid to let it go in case he couldn't stop howling once it started.

He couldn't do this again. He simply couldn't. He'd already lost one woman he'd loved—a woman he'd pledged to spend the rest of his life with. The pain of that loss had been crushing. Discovering she'd kept her life-threatening condition from him even more so.

He wasn't prepared to lose another.

Oh, my God, he thought, *I love her. I love Alexis.*

Hard on the realization came fear. With love came loss, he knew that to his cost. Already Alexis's pregnancy was putting her at risk. If the worst should happen and Bree's experience be repeated, he knew he wouldn't survive that again. He had to put away those feelings for good. He thought he had achieved that already but Alexis's steady and constant undermining of his stance with Ruby had undone that.

Her gentle ways, her care and support, all of it had left him wide-open to hurt all over again. He hadn't wanted to love her—hadn't even wanted to *want* her the way he did. Even now he felt the urge to race back to her room, to make sure she was okay, but he couldn't trust himself around her. Couldn't trust her.

He needed to pull himself together, to shore up his defenses all over again. Only this time he needed to make them impenetrable. Nothing and no one would get past them ever again.

Feeling stronger, more in control, Raoul dragged his cell phone from his pocket and thumbed through his contacts list. There it was, the number for Bree's obstetrician. He hit Dial before he could change his mind. For all that had happened to Bree, the guy was one of the best in the country and Alexis deserved that. And he himself needed to know exactly what they were dealing with.

A few minutes later, an appointment made—thanks to a cancellation—for in a couple of days' time, he shoved his phone back in his pocket. Until then he had to keep his mind busy and his heart firmly locked down back where it belonged, where nothing and no one could reach it.

"I don't see why you weren't prepared to let me wait until my appointment came through from the hospital," Alexis grumbled as he drove her to Christchurch two days later. "I've stopped bleeding anyway."

"Don't you want to know why you started bleeding in the first place?"

"Raoul, sometimes these things happen. There might not be a why, sometimes things simply *are*."

He shook his head, dissatisfied with her answer. "No, there's always a reason and always a solution. There has to be."

He heard Alexis sigh and out the corner of his eye he saw her turn her head and look out the side window.

"Are you feeling okay?" he asked, the same question he asked of her several times each day.

"I'm fine, a bit queasy but that's normal. Unless I'm driving I often get a bit of motion sickness."

"Do you want to drive?" he offered.

"No, it's okay, I'll be all right."

"Let me know if you need me to stop."

"Sure." She sighed again. "Do you think Ruby will be okay with Catherine? She was pretty upset when we left."

"She'll settle. Call Catherine if you're worried."

"No, I'm sure she'll settle, like you say."

They traveled the rest of the hour-and-a-quarter journey in silence. When they reached the specialist's rooms, Raoul parked the Range Rover, assailed again by the awful reminder that he'd been through this before. Maybe coming to the appointment with her wasn't such a great idea after all, he thought, his stomach tying in knots as they got out the car and he guided Alexis toward the building and through to reception.

Alexis gave her name to the receptionist and joined Raoul in the waiting room. He could feel her nervousness wash over him in waves. If theirs had been a normal relationship, he'd be holding her hand right now, infusing her with his strength and lending her his support. Instead, she perched on the chair next to him, as tightly wound as a bale of grapevine trellis wire.

"I'm okay, you can stop looking at me," she said through tightly clenched teeth. "I'm not about to break apart."

"That's good to know," he said, and leaned back into his chair, feigning nonchalance by picking up a discarded magazine off the chair next to him.

"Ms. Fabrini?" a man's voice called.

"That's me," she said, getting to her feet.

Raoul got to his feet as well and started to move forward with her.

"Hi, I'm Peter Taylor, nice to meet you," the doctor said to Alexis, extending his hand.

As he did so, he looked over her shoulder and spied Raoul standing there.

"Raoul, good to see you. How's Ruby doing?"

"She's growing and getting into everything."

The obstetrician looked from Alexis to Raoul.

Alexis spoke up in the awkward silence that sprang between them. "I'm Alexis, Ruby's nanny."

"I see. Well, would you like to come through with me? And Raoul?"

"No, just me," Alexis said firmly.

Raoul wanted to object, to shout he had every right to be there in that room with her, but he knew he had none. He'd made no commitment to Alexis and it was clear she didn't want him there, either. He lowered himself back down onto his chair, that sense of history repeating itself hitting him all over again.

So, he was to be kept in the dark, just like he'd been with Bree. With her, she'd managed to time her appointments for days when he'd be busy and unable to accompany her, except for when she had her scans. Thinking back on it now, she must have requested that all information about her aneurysm be kept from him because he knew now that they'd monitored it carefully throughout her pregnancy.

Waiting was hell. Not knowing what was going on was even worse. He couldn't just sit here. It was doing his head in. He went to the receptionist and told her to let Alexis know he'd be waiting outside for her, then turned and left the building.

It was cold and crisp today, the sun a distant beacon in a washed-out blue sky striated with wispy streaks of cirrus cloud. Raoul waited by his vehicle, and tried to tell himself he didn't care that Alexis had shut him out. He should embrace the fact, be glad she didn't want him to be a part of this. He could offer her nothing but a man broken by the past. A man now too afraid to trust. Look what had happened when he'd trusted her!

And if he kept telling himself these things, surely eventually he'd convince himself he believed them.

He uttered a sharp expletive under his breath and shoved his hands into his jacket pockets. Leaning against the side of the Range Rover he lifted his face to the sun and closed his eyes. If only he hadn't given in, if only he had kept his distance. If only she'd never come at all.

Life was full of "if onlys," so much so that a man could drive himself crazy worrying over them all. Things had been simpler before she came, there was no denying it. In this case, it came down to just a handful of questions. Could he go through this all again? Could he watch her grow full with child, *his* child, and wait again in fear for what might happen?

The answer was swift coming. No. He couldn't.

Yes, it was cowardly. Yes, it was stepping back from his obligations. But he'd been down this road already, and he wasn't strong enough to do this again. But, the question remained, could he let her go?

Fourteen

Alexis was in the kitchen making herself a cup of tea when she heard the front door open and close. Raoul was back. Her heart jumped in her chest and she wondered what he would say or do next. Since her consultation with the obstetrician they'd barely said more than two sentences to one another at a time.

She had yet to tell him everything about her examination—but she had good reasons for holding back. Raoul had withdrawn from her, wholly and completely. It wasn't just that she now slept alone back in the master suite, it was apparent in every way he interacted with her—or didn't interact, which was more to the point.

This pregnancy was a major step in her life, one she was willing to take on alone if necessary, and especially if she couldn't be certain that she had the wholehearted and loving support of a man at her side. Raoul, to be precise.

His heavy footsteps sounded in the hall and she felt the usual prickle of awareness between her shoulder blades that warned her he'd come into the kitchen and was staring at her. Slowly, she faced him.

"I'm going for a shower. Are you okay? Should you be up?"

He sounded like the Raoul Benoit she'd fallen in love with, yet different at the same time. She looked at his face, met the flat emptiness that now dwelled in his eyes. Her heart sank. Any hope she'd had of possibly turning him around on this situation between them sank right along with it.

"I'll be all right. As I've already told you, I'm just not supposed to do anything too strenuous. That's all."

He nodded. "Don't go lifting Ruby from her crib," he reminded her for the umpteenth time since Monday's race to the clinic. "I'll get her up when she wakes."

With that, he left her. He did that a lot lately. Made sure he was home around the times that Ruby went down for her sleeps and was back in time for when she roused. On the rare occasions he wasn't, she'd seen the censure in his eyes afterward when he returned to find she'd been lifting and carrying the baby, but she knew exactly what she was and wasn't capable of. Caring for Ruby was high on her to-do list, with all it entailed.

Behind her, the kettle switched itself off, the water boiled and ready to pour onto her tea bag, but still she didn't move. So, this was how it was going to be between them now. A cold politeness that ignored everything except the medical concerns involved in what was happening inside her body, the life they'd created together?

Part of her wanted to march on down the hallway behind him, to confront him, to force him to talk to her. Force him to acknowledge her and what they'd shared before he'd found out about her pregnancy—to find out if there had ever been more between them than just the convenient release of no-strings-attached sex. But that look in his eyes just now, it had chilled her. It had told her far more than words could ever say.

What they'd had, as little as it was—everything they'd shared when they'd shared each other—was over. Gone. Except for getting Ruby out of bed in the morning and putting her down for her sleeps, Raoul stayed well out of the way. The stresses and joys of pregnancy were entirely her own, with no one but herself to marvel over the life growing inside her—or worry over possible problems.

To her huge relief, all the signs of the threatened miscarriage had eased off, just as Dr. Taylor had said they should. Further, slightly obsessive reading on the subject told Alexis that a high percentage of women experienced what she had in their first trimester. Trying to convince herself what she'd been through was normal was easier said than done.

She felt fragile, adrift, and the massive chasm that had opened up between her and Raoul prevented her having anyone to share her fears with. This wasn't news she was ready to spring on her own family just yet—not when she still hoped against hope for Raoul's support, even for his love. Still, at least she had a visit from Catherine to look forward to today. When the older woman arrived, though, she clearly knew something was up.

As the two of them watched Ruby playing in the family room Catherine broached what was clearly bothering her.

"Alexis, did you know that Raoul has asked me to look for a new nanny for Ruby until I'm able to take her back full-time again?"

If the other woman had slapped her, Alexis couldn't have been more shocked.

"He wants me to leave?"

"He didn't say as much—well, not in as many words—but he requested that I make it clear in the advertising that it's a live-in position."

Alexis's head reeled. "He hasn't said anything to me. Not at all."

Catherine fidgeted in her chair. The corners of her mouth pulled into a small frown.

"He told me you were pregnant. Is it true?"

"Yes, it's true."

"How far along are you?"

"Nearly nine weeks now," Alexis answered with a small sigh.

"And you're okay?"

"Did he tell you about Monday? About taking me down to the clinic? And then to the obstetrician when we left Ruby with you on Wednesday morning?"

"No, but I guessed something had happened. He acted different again. Like he did after Bree died."

Catherine got up from her chair and joined Alexis on the couch. She put a comforting arm around her shoulders.

"Tell me," she commanded gently.

So Alexis did. She pushed aside her fears about how Catherine would react to what she had to say—after all, hadn't Alexis just been sleeping with Catherine's dead daughter's husband? It was a relief to off-load to someone, especially someone who had known her as long as Catherine had, someone who had been as much of a mother figure as her own had been. Catherine just listened, her arm tightening around Alexis from time to time, lending her more comfort, more silent strength.

When Alexis finished she realized her cheeks were wet. Catherine pressed a freshly laundered handkerchief into her hands.

"You poor dear," she said after Alexis had blown her nose and wiped her tears away. "You love him, don't you?"

Alexis nodded, then gathered the threads of her fraying thoughts together. "You—you're not mad at me?"

"Why would I be?" Catherine asked in astonishment.

"Because of Bree. Because it hasn't even been a year and here I was throwing myself at him."

Catherine laughed. "Oh, my dear girl. You? *Throw* yourself at Raoul? Hardly. Besides, he's not the kind of man a woman throws herself at without expecting to slide straight off that granite exterior of his." She patted Alexis on the leg. "Look, I love my son-in-law dearly and I know that he and Bree were ecstatically happy together when they weren't at complete loggerheads. We've all suffered for her loss. But I'm a realist. She *is* gone. As hard as that has been to bear we've all had to go on with living. Raoul…well, he's just been existing. When you came, something sparked to life in him again. You gave him something to fight against."

"Fight against? I don't understand."

"He'd shut himself down, put his feelings where no one could touch them. Not even Ruby. I still remember seeing him standing in the neonatal intensive-care unit, staring at her in her incubator. No emotion on his face, not even a flicker. I knew then that she would need help— they both would.

"Looking after Ruby helped me come to terms with losing Bree. It would have helped him, too, but with her being sick for that first month of her life, it only served to push him further away."

"I still can't understand how he did that," Alexis said, shaking her head.

She'd seen photos of Ruby in the NICU. They'd raised every protective instinct in her body. She'd wanted to reach right into the pictures and cuddle the precious baby back to health. How could Raoul not have felt the same way about his own daughter?

"He's a strong man with powerful emotions. Sometimes emotions like that can get to be too much, even for someone like Raoul," Catherine said. "Bree's father was like that, too. I'm sure she was drawn to that strength the same way I was with her father. But we had our troubles through the years, just as I know Bree had fights with Raoul, over the way that both men thought being strong meant shutting out anything that might make them vulnerable."

Ruby had stopped playing and had gotten to her feet and walked over to her grandmother who happily lifted her onto her lap.

"The sad thing is, he doesn't even realize what he's been missing out on. Or maybe he didn't, until you came along."

"Whatever good I might have done has been destroyed now," Alexis said ruefully.

"Maybe, maybe not. I think he needs a bit of time to come to terms with things."

"Well, if, as you say, he's looking for a new nanny, then my time is definitely running out."

Catherine gave Ruby a kiss and popped her back on the floor. "Don't give up, Alexis. If he's worth fighting for, then you have to fight."

She left soon after that, promising to call by again the next day. As Alexis and Ruby waved her off at the front door Alexis weighed Catherine's words in her mind. Could she do it? Could she fight for Raoul? Would he even let her?

* * *

He hated to admit it, but he missed being with Alexis. That said, he'd made up his mind. She had to go.

Obviously that left him with a problem. Catherine wasn't fit enough yet to take Ruby back on full-time so he had to find someone who would fill in for the short term.

In the meantime, he kept a surreptitious eye on Alexis. Watching like a hawk for telltale signs that she was overdoing things. He hated the thought of her leaving and yet he couldn't wait for her to be gone—for things to go back to the way they were before she arrived here. He tried to tell himself, over and over, that he'd be able to forget her, to put her from his heart and his mind. He only hoped it was true. He never even let himself think about the child—his child. *Their* child.

Raoul walked into the house and braced himself. Today he would tell her that she had to go as soon as he'd found a replacement. He wasn't looking forward to it. He went to his bathroom and turned on the shower, then stripped off his clothes and dived under the hot stinging spray. It had been cold out in the vineyard today where he'd begun cane pruning the vines. The work was slow but methodical and had unfortunately allowed him far too much time to think.

He closed his eyes and dropped his head to take the full brunt of the shower stream, blindly reaching for a bottle of shampoo. The instant he opened it he knew he'd taken the wrong one—his senses immediately filled with that fresh floral scent he always identified with Alexis. His body felt an unwelcome stirring of desire, his flesh growing semihard. He snapped the lid closed and threw the bottle to the bottom of the shower with a clatter.

She was everywhere. In his thoughts, in his dreams, in his bathroom. He finished his shower as quickly as possible. Determined to get facing her and telling her what he'd done over with as quickly and as painlessly as possible.

He could hear her in the kitchen with Ruby as he made his way down the hall and through the house. Could hear the love in her voice as she coaxed the little girl into eating her vegetables. It made something twist inside him, but he forged on.

"Hi," she said matter-of-factly as he entered the kitchen.

Ruby squealed her delight at seeing him, banging on her tray with a spoon. From the look of her, she'd been attempting to feed herself, and not very successfully if the mush all over her face and hair was anything to go by.

"I need to talk to you tonight. When's a good time?"

"What? You need to make an appointment to speak with me now?" Alexis's eyes looked bruised underneath, as if she was sleeping just as poorly as he was himself.

"I'd prefer to have your full attention. It's important," he said stiffly.

"If it's about hiring a new nanny, don't worry. Catherine already told me yesterday. So, have you found someone?"

She caught him on a back foot. "There have already been a few applicants."

"That's good," she replied, rinsing a muslin cloth at the kitchen sink and then coming over to wipe Ruby's face and hands before giving her a couple of slices of apple to occupy herself with. "I've been thinking, out of fairness to Ruby, it might be best if we have a two-week transitional period with both me and the new nanny here."

"You do?"

"It makes sense, don't you think? It wouldn't be good for the new nanny or Ruby if my leaving disrupted her too much. She's more aware of strangers now than she was when I arrived, less open to trust them."

"Right."

"Ruby's going to need you more, too."

"More?" God, he needed to stop with the monosyllabic replies.

"Of course, you'll be her touchstone. Her constant. She needs stability."

"She's going back to Catherine's soon."

"Yes, I know. Catherine said. Are you seriously going to do that? Send her back to her grandmother?"

"Of course. She can't stay here."

Alexis looked at him fair and square. "Why not?"

"Because it's not feasible, that's why not."

Saying the words caused a sharp hitch in his breathing. He'd mulled it over time and time again. As much as he was bonding with Ruby every day, he had to take a giant step back. It was the only way to stop the chance of being hurt.

"If she has a nanny, or even a rotation of nannies together with Catherine, I don't see why you have to turf her out of her home."

"I…"

The words he was going to say dried on his tongue. He'd been about to refute that it was Ruby's home but as he looked around him and saw the detritus that she spread about the place every day, he found he couldn't bring himself to utter the words. Nor could he honestly say he didn't want her here anymore. Sure, the idea of being solely responsible for her care still scared him witless, but for as long as she had a reliable nanny, or rotation of nannies as Alexis had suggested, then maybe it could work out.

He tried to think of what it would be like not to see

her cherubic face each morning or hear her chant "Dad-dad" as she did whenever she saw him. Even the mere thought of it made him feel empty, lost.

"Raoul?" Alexis prompted.

"I'll think about it. We'll have to see what the job applicants are like first."

She gave him a weak smile. "Well, that's progress, I guess."

Raoul continued to stand there, feeling at a loose end as she competently moved around the kitchen, putting the finishing touches to their evening meal and tending to Ruby.

"How are you doing…since Monday?" he asked awkwardly.

"Everything's settled down," she replied, keeping her back to him, but he saw her face reflected in the kitchen window and noticed how she hesitated over her task.

"When do you see the doctor again?"

"I had an appointment in four weeks' time but if I'm leaving then I think I'll see someone when I get home."

"I'll pay for your medical expenses, Alexis, and for the…baby, when it comes."

"I'll call you if I need help," she said, her words clipped.

"I mean it. I will stand up to my responsibilities toward him or her."

She made a sound somewhere between a laugh and a snort. "Except for the ones that really matter, right?"

He felt a flush of humiliation stain his cheeks. "I said it before, Alexis. You ask too much."

"Do I? When I, Ruby, everyone in your life, basically, is prepared to give you everything in return? Is it too much to ask you to love us, to care?"

His hands clenched into fists at his sides. He felt his

short fingernails biting into his palms and he relished the pain. It was the distraction he needed to remind himself not to reach out for her, to drag her to him and to show her exactly how much he felt for her. A fine tremor rippled through him.

"I've said what I wanted to say. Don't wait dinner for me. I'll eat later."

Alexis watched him leave the room. A view she seemed to have a whole lot of lately. She'd been an idiot to think she could win this tug of love with him. It had been destined for failure from the beginning. She deserved more than that, and so did he—so why on earth couldn't he see that? Why wouldn't he grab what he was offered with both hands and run with it?

It made her heart ache to think he'd chosen to remove himself from love, that he was so broken that he couldn't try again. No, it was more that he *wouldn't* try again. It was a conscious choice. She just couldn't understand why anyone would choose loneliness and solitude over love.

Over the next few days she watched as a handful of selected applicants arrived at the house for interviews with Raoul. Each time, he'd ask Alexis to bring Ruby in to the meetings to introduce her to her potential carer. Some introductions had gone okay, some not so much. When Raoul told her at the end of the week that he'd made a suitable appointment and that the woman would be starting the following Monday, Alexis's heart sank. Her time here now was limited. Soon, she'd have to leave and the very idea just broke her heart.

The only bright light in the darkness was planning Ruby's first birthday party next week. Catherine had suggested they hold the celebration at the play center since it was already designed to cater to a big group of small children and everyone who she would have been inviting went there anyway.

Raoul, though, was adamant he wouldn't go.

"No," he said emphatically when Alexis invited him.

"But it's Ruby's birthday," she implored.

"She won't know the difference."

Alexis rolled her eyes. "That's not the point."

"It's also the anniversary of Bree's death, have you stopped to think about that?"

"Of course I have," she argued back. It seemed they always ended up arguing these days and it was taking a toll. "But you can't punish Ruby for that for the rest of her life. Are you going to deny her a celebration every year because you lost Bree that day, too? Can't you grasp what you have for once, rejoice in it instead of holding on to what you've lost?"

"I said no. That's the end of it."

It was like talking to a brick wall. He'd distanced himself so effectively she had no idea of how to get through to him anymore.

The following two weeks passed in a blur. The new nanny, Jenny, was wonderfully competent. She'd just returned to the area after working for a family up in Wellington who had a job transfer to overseas. She hadn't wanted to go with them, preferring to stay in New Zealand, so the position with Ruby was perfect timing for her.

Alexis hadn't wanted to like the other woman and had, in what she recognized as a ridiculously petty way, resented how easily she'd taken over Ruby's care and how quickly Ruby seemed to bond with her. Each day Jenny took over more and more of Alexis's duties, and Catherine, too, agreed the other woman seemed to be working out really well.

With less time with Ruby herself, Alexis had more time to think about nursery preparations for when she got home, and even time to get back to her designs. She'd played a little with some sketches in the past couple of weeks, a few ideas for herself mostly, and her hands itched to see how the ideas would come to life in her preferred range of hand-dyed natural fabrics. She'd never imagined designing a maternity range of clothes before, especially not for the high-end fashion boutiques her work usually showcased in. Now she was getting excited about the idea.

Besides, she reminded herself, she'd need something to distract her once she left. This was going to be one of the hardest things she'd ever had to do. The second hardest was going to be telling her dad about her pregnancy. He'd be disappointed in her, she knew it, but the prospect of new life would help lift him from his grief and give them something they could look forward to together.

Alexis had toyed with the idea of phoning him with the news, or sending him an email, but she knew this was the kind of thing she'd have to tell him face-to-face. At least, she consoled herself, moving back to her father's home meant that she'd be nearer to Tamsyn, her half sister, and Tamsyn's husband, Finn, her father's business partner and the man who'd been like a big brother to her growing up. She could almost begin to tell herself she was looking forward to it.

"Wow, are those your sketches?" Jenny asked as she came into the kitchen where Alexis was working at the table. "You're good."

"Thanks. I'm thinking of expanding into maternity wear. These drawings are just ideas for now."

"So, you're a designer, not a nanny?"

"Both, really. I trained and worked as a nanny after

I finished school. The designing has come in the past few years and I spent most of the previous year, before I came here to help out Raoul, in Europe, traveling and looking for inspiration."

Help out Raoul. The words sounded so simple, so uncomplicated. Nothing at all like the tangled web of unhappiness and adversity it had turned into.

Jenny picked up one sheet and then another. "So is that why you're leaving? To get back to your work?"

Alexis looked up as Raoul entered the kitchen and helped himself to a coffee from the carafe on the warmer.

"We've imposed on her for long enough," Raoul said before she could say a word. "It's time she returned to her own life."

But this was the life she wanted. This life, with him, with Ruby. She could work from anywhere when it came to her designing, and goodness knew there was plenty of space here for her to establish a workroom. But he didn't want her, not like that, not as a partner, not as a piece of his heart. And that was where her dreams began and ended.

Clearly sensing the undercurrent that crackled between Raoul and Alexis, Jenny made a vague excuse about checking on some laundry and left, leaving the two of them staring at one another. Expelling a breath of frustration, Alexis gathered up her things and got up from the table.

"So have you warned the new girl off falling for the boss?" she said, determined to provoke Raoul in one way or another.

"Low blow, Alexis."

"I'm sorry. I shouldn't have insulted her like that. I'm sure Jenny has far more sense. She's very well trained, and she is good with Ruby."

"Yes, I think Ruby will be quite safe with her."

"Safe, Raoul? Safe? Is that all you can think about? What about loved? Don't you think that's equally as important in her life? Weren't you loved as a child, weren't your parents there for you every step of the way? Of course they were because that's what real parents are. They're the people who are always there for you—not the ones who just pass the buck on to someone else."

"That's rich, coming from a nanny. Without parents 'passing the buck' as you call it, nannies wouldn't even be needed."

She groaned, fed up to her back teeth with his bullheadedness. "At least every family I've worked for before has openly loved their children. Has included them in their lives when they haven't been tied to work."

"Enough!" He made a slashing movement with his hand as if he could just cut her off as effectively as he'd cut off his own feelings. "Stop pushing me, Alexis. Ruby has settled with Jenny, who has proven she's competent and knows what to do. Catherine is at hand if she needs any advice or help. You can leave today. I'll pay you through to the end of this month and you will hear from my lawyers regarding support for you and—"

"Today? You want me to leave today? But I still have another week."

Alexis sat down abruptly in one of the kitchen chairs, feeling as if all the breath had been knocked out of her. She looked at him, taking in his features and committing them to memory. The curl in his brown hair that had begun to grow overlong since she'd been here. The flecks of gold in his hazel eyes. The breadth of his shoulders and the lean strength of his body. All of it so achingly familiar, all of it so completely out of bounds. It was impossible to reconcile the lover who had filled her nights with pleasure with this cold shell of a man who stood before her, seemingly determined to never see her again.

"I don't need you anymore," Raoul said.

"And that's the trouble," she whispered. "You never did."

Fifteen

He didn't need her anymore. The words echoed round and round in her head as she pulled herself to her feet, gathered her drawings and staggered from the room. Alexis tried not to hear them when she returned to the master suite and began haphazardly throwing her clothing onto the bed as she picked the drawers of the tallboy clean. Tears streamed unchecked down her cheeks.

Alexis had thought the pain of saying goodbye to her mother had been hard enough, followed soon after by discovering Bree had gone, too. But this was something else entirely. This was raw and sharp and jagged and sliced at her insides with unrelenting strikes. He didn't need her, didn't want her, didn't love her. Each fact hurt as much as the other.

She went to the walk-in wardrobe to retrieve her case. As soon as she opened the door she felt a sense of Bree, as if she'd only stepped out for a minute and would be back any moment. The soft hint of her floral fragrance teased at Alexis's nostrils, reminding her of the kind of woman Bree had been. A woman so loved, so missed, that her husband wouldn't take a chance on love again. She couldn't compete with that. It was an impossible task. Her love simply hadn't been enough to bridge that breach.

"I failed, Bree," she said softly through her tears. "I thought I could do it, that with enough time, enough patience and enough love that I could bring him back, but I failed. I'm sorry, my friend. Sorry for everything, but especially sorry for letting my feelings for Raoul get between you and me."

In the distance she heard Ruby wake from her nap and Raoul's deep tones murmuring to her as he tended to the little girl.

"But he's doing more with Ruby, getting closer to her and learning how to be a father—at least I achieved that much, if nothing else."

Her voice cracked on the last words and she wheeled her case from the wardrobe and closed the door behind her. Closing it on so much more than a half-empty closet. Lifting the suitcase onto the bed, she shoved her things inside together with her toiletries, reaching every now and then for a tissue to wipe her face and blow her nose with.

She had to pull herself together, even if only long enough to say her goodbyes to Ruby. Whether Raoul would be there when she left was something else she'd have to face with her backbone straight and her shoulders squared. Part of her wanted to see him one last time, to draw this entire episode to a natural close, but there was another part of her that hoped he'd make himself scarce so she wouldn't have to face the pain of looking into his eyes and seeing nothing reflected back at her but relief that she was leaving.

Logically she knew they'd have to have some sort of ongoing contact, especially after the birth. He'd already made it clear he would financially support her. While that was probably the least she ought to be expecting from him, for her that was the lowest denominator in this complicated equation. She simply wanted him. All of him. Not just a no-strings lover.

She drew in a shuddering breath and then another until she felt as if she had herself under control. Taking a last look around the room, she pulled the suitcase off the bed and stood it up on its wheels. Could she do this? Could she really walk away from Raoul and Ruby and never look back?

Only time would tell.

Feeling as if her heart was breaking a little more with each step, she slung her handbag over her shoulder and, wheeling her suitcase behind her, left the room.

Jenny was in the hallway with Ruby in her arms. The instant Ruby saw Alexis she clamored to be let down and raced toward Alexis the instant her feet touched the ground. Alexis bent down and scooped the little girl in her arms, burying her face in Ruby's neck and inhaling that special, fresh, soft baby smell that was so precious. Three months, she'd cared for her, but it had only taken about three seconds to fall in love.

The pain in Alexis's chest sharpened as she whispered a goodbye to Ruby and handed her back to Jenny.

"Well, I'd better be off, then. If I've left anything behind, perhaps you could send it on to me? Catherine has my address."

"Don't worry, Raoul told me family matters have

drawn you away. Thanks for helping so much this past week. It's made taking over that much easier."

"I aim to please," Alexis answered with a bitter twist to her mouth. She looked around but couldn't see Raoul anywhere. "I thought I'd better say goodbye to Raoul, is he around?"

"Oh, he had to go down to the winery. Something about a truck coming to pick up some cases of wine, I think."

So, it was to be like that between them.

"I see," she said.

But she didn't see at all. Had their time together meant so little to him that he couldn't even give her the courtesy of a farewell face-to-face? She swallowed against the lump in her throat and grabbed at the handle of her suitcase.

"Well, I'd better be on my way, then. I've got quite a drive ahead of me."

She wasn't kidding. From Akaroa all the way to her home was going to take at least five and a half hours of solid driving. She only hoped she had the energy to cope with it.

Jenny followed her out to the car and helped her lift her case into the trunk.

"Thanks," Alexis managed through lips that felt numb.

In fact her whole body had taken on an emptiness that made her feel as if this wasn't really happening to her. It was better, at least, than the pain she'd felt a short while ago, she told herself. She slipped into the driver's seat and tried to summon a cheerful smile and a wave for Jenny and Ruby who stood on the driveway, waving goodbye.

Alexis drove on autopilot, the numbness that had mercifully invaded her body fading away as each kilometer flew under her tires. By the time she reached the outskirts of Christchurch she was crying again, great hiccupping sobs that made it impossible to see, let alone drive safely. She pulled over to the side of the road and grabbed her cell phone, calling the only person who had ever been there constantly for her all her life. The one person she'd been putting off calling.

"Daddy?" she said, through tears that threatened to close her throat. "I'm coming home."

"I'll bloody destroy him," Finn Gallagher growled malevolently. "No one treats my baby sister that way."

He and Tamsyn had met Lorenzo all set to drive down to Christchurch to collect Alexis. As he was so upset himself, they had worried that it wouldn't be safe for him to drive and had offered instead to fly to Christchurch to drive Alexis home themselves. Their timing meant they'd missed the only direct flight of the day but even with the detour to Wellington it was still faster than driving. Now they were ensconced in a hotel room having something to eat before they hit the road together.

"It's not all his fault, Finn. I went into it with my eyes wide-open," Alexis said as rationally as she could manage.

"Don't you dare condone his behavior. What he's done to you is unspeakably wrong," Finn replied, seething with suppressed fury.

"Finn, ask yourself this, how would you feel if it was you and Tamsyn, if she'd kept something from you that meant the difference between living the rest of your lives together or losing her forever? And then the next person you trusted also kept something from you?"

Tamsyn rose from where she'd been sitting and curved an arm around her husband's waist. "This isn't helping, Finn. Alexis needs our support, not your censure."

"I'm not angry at *her*," he protested, but his wife's touch seemed to have a soothing effect on his temper. "I just can't stand to see Alexis hurt like this."

"I know," Tamsyn said gently. "Neither of us can. Our job is to be there for her as and when she needs us. She's a big girl and she's made her own choices."

"Yes, I have, and I'm strong enough to stand on my own two feet. Well, once I've got myself back together again, anyway," Alexis said ruefully, remembering only too well the wreck she'd been when Tamsyn and Finn had met her here in the hotel. "I'm so glad you came, thank you so much."

Her voice wobbled and her eyes filled with tears yet again. Instantly she felt the warmth of Tamsyn's arms close around her in a comforting hug.

"I'm s-sorry, I just can't seem to stop."

"Should we even travel tonight?" Finn asked. "Maybe it'd be better if we stayed the night and left in the morning."

"No, I want to go home. I need to."

"Sure you do," Tamsyn said, smoothing Alexis's hair from her face with a gentle hand. "And that's exactly what we'll do."

It was early evening when they finally got in Alexis's car to drive north. Exhausted, she lay down in the back and was soon asleep. By the time they arrived at her father's cottage it had been dark for hours. All the lights inside the cottage were blazing, their golden glow a flame of welcome. She sat up, rubbing at her bleary eyes, and was hit with a huge sense of relief when she saw her father's silhouette backlit by the veranda lights. Then, he was at her door and within seconds she was in his arms, listening to his voice murmuring endearments in his native Italian tongue.

Finally she was home, safe in her father's arms. As he led her into the house and to her bedroom, Tamsyn and Finn following with her suitcase, she wondered if Ruby would ever have the chance to feel that deep sense of security with Raoul.

Raoul flicked the collar of his jacket up and pulled his beanie down lower on his head. The weather had turned bitter cold. Or maybe it just seemed that way since Alexis had left four weeks, three days and two hours ago. He could count the minutes, too, but that had proven to be a fast track to Crazyville.

God, he missed her. It went beyond the physical. As much as he'd tried to ignore it and push her away, he missed what she'd come to mean to him. It had been difficult from the first to adjust to no longer sharing her bed after he found out about the pregnancy. He'd assumed that her permanent absence would make things more comfortable for him, ease the longing he felt for her touch. But the longing had become much worse, instead—now there was so much *more* of her to miss. Not just her body but her laugh, the sound of her voice. The warmth she brought to his life.

The house just didn't feel the same, didn't feel like a home. Ruby had become more irritable than she'd been under Alexis's care and he found himself watching over Jenny with the baby more and more often, hardly wanting to trust her with the child.

As a result, Ruby had begun to turn to him when he was in the house—complaining loudly if he didn't pay her the attention she obviously felt she was due. He felt the bond between him and his daughter growing stronger every day. And this time, he didn't try to fight it.

Somehow the little tyke had wrapped him right around

her little finger, and now she had a hold on his heart that terrified him and thrilled him in equal proportions. He found himself looking forward more and more to spending time with her each day, and to reading her bedtime stories at night—because one was never enough.

When she'd caught a cold from one of the other children at the play center, he'd been the one who'd sat up with her in a steam-filled bathroom at night as she'd coughed and spluttered herself back to sleep. He'd been the one to take her to the doctor every day until the doctor himself had told him—in the nicest way possible—that Ruby really, truly was going to be okay and to stop wasting their time.

He began to have a new appreciation for what Alexis had done in caring for her, and how she'd managed it all on her own. Realizing that had highlighted his own inadequacies as a father, and as a man. How he'd thought he could hide in his work and relegate his responsibilities to others—that it was enough to simply provide, but not to participate. How he'd made himself believe that if he stayed away, if he just threw enough money at a problem, that it would miraculously go away.

He'd been such a fool.

And that's what had led him here today, to Bree's final resting place. He laid the bunch of yellow roses, her favorite, at the base of her headstone and knelt beside her grave. The ground felt cold, so cold—as cold as his heart had been for far too long.

For quite a while he said nothing, remaining still, listening to the birds in the trees around him. He'd avoided coming here since the day they'd buried her. He'd told himself it didn't matter—that the Bree he'd known and loved had gone, she wasn't here anymore. But when he'd known he needed to talk to her, really talk, one last time, it had only been natural to do it here.

A cool wind worked its way around him, sliding under his collar and tickling around his ears. He shivered. He'd been compelled to come here—as if he couldn't move forward again until he'd done this. He took a deep breath and let it out slowly.

Any other time he'd have thought it verging on the ridiculous, needing to talk out loud to a headstone, but today nothing else had ever felt so right.

"Hi, Bree, it's me." He huffed a self-deprecatory laugh. As if it would be anyone else. "I know I should have been here more often, and probably brought Ruby, too, but I was so angry at you, Bree, so bloody mad I couldn't even think straight anymore."

Exasperation, fury, helplessness—they all flooded through him all over again. "What the hell were you thinking not telling me about the aneurysm? How could you have kept that from me? I wanted a family, but I wanted you more. Why couldn't you tell me about the risks?"

The cold air whipped around him more sharply and he pulled the collar of his jacket closed around his throat. He stayed like that for a while, not daring to speak for the emotion that built up inside him like a volcano about to blow. He closed his eyes and when he opened his mouth again, he talked instead about the first thing that came to mind. Ruby. Bit by bit, he felt the roiling emotions inside him begin to subside.

"Our daughter's beautiful, Bree. You would love her. She's just like you. From her hair to her eyes—all the way through to her ability to get her own way."

He felt a reluctant smile pull at his lips and he opened his eyes again. "Especially the latter," he added.

"I've let you both down, though. I've been so wrapped in my own anger at you, at the whole damn world, and in my fear of getting hurt again that I failed Ruby as a father. But you should know that she's fine. She's wonderful. Catherine's done a great job with her so far, and Alexis. Certainly a far better job than me.

"I felt so bad when Alexis arrived. She awakened something in me that I didn't want to feel again. That I'd *promised* myself I would never feel again." His voice trailed off as a thought occurred to him. "But you sent her to me, didn't you? And me, the fool that I am, I sent her away.

"She tried, Bree, she tried to break me out—to make me be myself again, to live my life again, but the anger and the fear held me back."

He dragged in another breath and let it go, noticing as he did so that his heart began to feel lighter. The darkness that had held him in its grip for so long was receding and with it came acceptance for Bree's decision. She'd been willing to risk everything for him and for the dreams they'd woven together, come what may. He'd thought he'd known love, understood it, but he'd known and understood nothing at all. Somewhere, he had to find the courage Bree had had. The courage to risk everything, to love absolutely, all over again.

"I'm sorry I never understood you well enough, Bree, and I'm sorry I've been so stupidly angry with you for all this time—especially because I let it rob so much of your love from me. Thank you for our daughter," he said roughly, bowing his head and closing his eyes. "Thank you for the all-too-few years you and I had together. I will always love you and you will always have a special piece of my heart."

He got to his feet again, his movements stiff, and

paused a moment to reflect on the woman his late wife had been before turning away from her grave and, he hoped, toward his future.

Sixteen

You're doing the right thing.

The memory of Catherine's words when he'd told her his plans was gently encouraging to Raoul as his car ate up the kilometers. Oh, of course he still had doubts. All he knew for sure was that he had to find out. There was something missing from his life. More particularly, someone. When he'd told Catherine he was going after Alexis, her first comment had been a simple "About time." But it was the hug she'd given him when he'd left Ruby with her this morning, on Jenny's day off, that had given him the most comfort. That and her words that he was doing what was right.

For so long he'd done the wrong thing, so long it had become habit, easier to slide into that than doing what he ought to have done all along. It didn't negate the seriousness of how he'd treated Alexis, or how he'd summarily dismissed her. He hadn't even had the courage to face her as she'd left, instead hiding in his work as he'd hidden from everything else this past year. Digging himself into things he could quantify and control, knowns versus unknowns.

But he was diving into the unknown now, in a headlong free fall. She was worth the risk.

As he left Christchurch and drove north, cruising through Kaiapoi and Rangiora and then further afield to Kaikoura he wondered what the hell he'd been thinking to send Alexis on this journey on her own. He hadn't been thinking, though, that was the problem. Certainly not about anyone but his selfish and self-centered self.

That was all going to change. If Alexis let him.

As he passed through Kaikoura he realized he had about an hour and a half to his destination. Logically he knew he should take a break but now that he was on the road, nearing Alexis with every revolution of his tires, he couldn't bring himself to stop.

He wondered how Ruby was doing. She'd been distraught when he'd left, almost moving him to tears over the way she'd kept reaching for him from her perch in Catherine's arms. He'd had to pull over after ten minutes on the road and call Catherine to make sure she was okay—which, of course, she was.

On the phone Catherine had assured him it was perfectly normal behavior for a one-year-old, in fact for any child who was attached to their parent, and that he should take heart from the fact that Ruby so obviously loved him. Even so, it had done little to alleviate the feelings of guilt he bore for putting his daughter through such a harrowing scene. It made him think about the things Alexis had said to him, about him needing to be a constant in Ruby's life. Well, she had that now, but he owed it to her to give her more. With any luck, after this journey, she'd have what she deserved. A father and a mother—and a brother or sister soon, too.

A weariness that can only come from long-distance driving pulled at his muscles as he drove slowly along the road Catherine had given him as Alexis's address. She'd warned him the driveway was hard to find and she hadn't been wrong; he was almost past the shrub-surrounded entrance before he realized it. Braking heavily, he turned off the road and into the driveway.

His heart began to hammer in his chest and nerves clutched at his stomach. Should he have called ahead? What if she refused to see him?

"A fine time to be thinking about this now," he said under his breath as he traveled up the lane and pulled to a halt outside a quaint turn-of-the-twentieth-century cottage. The skies opened as Raoul got out of the car, releasing a deluge of bone-chilling rain that forced him to run toward the wide covered veranda out front.

Even though he'd run, he was wet through when he got to the front door. He dragged a hand through his hair, skimming off the excess of water that threatened to drip in his eyes and down his face. He caught sight of his reflection in one of the front windows. Drowned rat. Not exactly the best foot to be putting forward when hoping to appeal to the woman you loved, he thought. Still, there was nothing else for it but to push forward.

He stepped up to the door and knocked. Inside, he heard steps coming toward him and he braced himself, both fearing seeing Alexis again and yet yearning for her so strongly that it was almost his undoing. His throat clogged with all the words he wanted to say but he was forced to swallow them back as the door swung open to reveal an older man with gray hair and the type of tan and deep lines on his face that spoke of a lifetime in the outdoors.

"What can I do for you?" the man asked in lightly accented English.

"I was wondering if Alexis was home," Raoul said awkwardly.

In all the ways he'd imagined this, he hadn't pictured seeing her father first. He felt about as nervous as he had as a teenager going to pick up his new girlfriend on their first date.

"I am her father, Lorenzo Fabrini," the man said, his dark eyes full of questions as they narrowed at him from under grizzled brows.

"Raoul Benoit," Raoul said, putting his hand out in greeting.

Alexis's father flatly ignored it and Raoul let his hand drop. His stomach clenched up another notch. This was not going well.

"So, now you come to see my daughter?"

"Mr. Fabrini, I apologize it's taken me this long, but yes. May I see her?"

The older man shook his head. "That is not up to me. If it were up to me you'd be back on the road and back to your miserable existence, where you belong."

He was right. Raoul's existence had been miserable—until Alexis had come along. And even then he'd been too trapped in his cycle of unhappiness to see how much better his life was with her in it.

"Please, sir, I beg of you. I know I was wrong, I know I hurt her badly—"

"Hurt her?" Anger flashed in Lorenzo's eyes. Eyes that reminded Raoul so much of Alexis. "You didn't just hurt her. You broke her. When she left here she was full of hope, full of purpose. When she returned she was empty, dead inside. Destroyed by you!"

He punctuated the air with his finger, making his point and with it, making Raoul awfully glad Lorenzo hadn't answered the door with a shotgun in his hand.

"I was wrong."

"Wrong! Pah! Wrong is denying your child your time and affection. Wrong is taking my daughter's love for you and belittling its worth. Wrong is using her for your own satisfaction and then sending her away when things got too hard. You call yourself a man?" Lorenzo muttered a curse in Italian. "I call you a worm. You're a disgrace."

"I know, you're not telling me anything I haven't learned already. I'm deeply ashamed of what I've done, of how I've hurt Alexis. Please, let me talk to her. Let me explain—"

"No, let me explain," Lorenzo interrupted, his finger once again pointing in Raoul's direction. "I am a humble man, a man who has worked hard all his life. I didn't finish school, I don't have all the fancy letters after my name that you all find so important these days. But I know what is important—that above all else, you honor life, you honor family, you honor love—and most of all, you honor the woman who brings them all into your life. You don't hide from her like a sniveling child."

"Sir, I respect how you feel, and I agree. I'm sorry for hurting her, truly sorry."

"Your apology is nothing to me and it is not my place to forgive you. It is Alexis you should apologize to."

"Please, then, let me see her. Let me talk to her."

"No."

Raoul felt his heart drop into his boots. "No? She won't see me?"

"No, she's not here—yet. If you are serious about making amends to my daughter you may wait here until she returns but you must promise me one thing."

"Anything, what is it?"

"That if she asks you to leave that you will go. Just go, and never bother her again."

The thought of never seeing Alexis again, never watching the way her face lit up when she was happy or never again seeing that fierce look of concentration in her eyes when she was working on her designs struck fear into Raoul. It was entirely possible that she would tell him to get lost. Hadn't he, essentially, done as much to her? Expected her to walk away, carrying his baby, and never look back? To be satisfied with some financial arrangement brokered by a pair of lawyers in separate parts of the country? If her state of mind was anything like her father's, she might tell him to do exactly that.

It was a risk he had to take.

"If that is what Alexis wants, then that is what I'll do."

Lorenzo nodded. "You may wait here," he said, gesturing to the sagging rattan chairs on the porch. "I will not have you here in our home, until I know she welcomes you also."

Without waiting for a response, Lorenzo closed the door in Raoul's face. It was no less than he deserved, Raoul thought as he lowered himself into one of the chairs. Despite being sheltered against the front of the house, the cushions still felt damp. Combined with his already cold, wet clothing, it proved to be an uncomfortable wait ahead. He didn't care. He'd do whatever it took to have his chance again with Alexis. And this time, if she was willing, he wouldn't mess up again.

Alexis drove carefully on the rain-slicked roads. At nearly sixteen weeks pregnant she was already finding it was getting uncomfortable to spend long periods in her car. Her tummy jiggled a little as a tiny occupant moved within her. She smiled. As exhausted as she felt after today's journey and meetings, those little movements still made her feel as if she was the luckiest woman in the world. Well, almost the luckiest.

She had a father who loved her and stood by her, no matter what. She had a half sister and foster brother who had pledged to support her in any way they could. She had new life growing inside her—a fact that never ceased to awe and amaze her. Her business was picking up again and, in reality, she lacked for nothing. Nothing except the love of the man she'd lost her heart to. Still, she consoled herself as she approached the driveway to her father's house, she had more than many others. Far, far more.

Through the rain, she caught a glimpse of the rear end of a vehicle standing near the front of the house. She was surprised to see her father had a visitor. He hadn't mentioned anything about expecting anyone when she'd phoned him to say she was on the road and heading home. As she drew nearer to the vehicle, though, recognition poured through her. The big black Range Rover was painfully familiar, especially with its VINTNR registration plate.

Her belly fluttered and she rested a hand on the movement. "It's okay," she murmured. "Looks like your daddy has come to pay a visit."

She gathered up her things and her collapsible umbrella and prepared to get out of the car. Before she could, however, her driver's door swung open and there he was. Alexis froze in her seat, halfway through the action of starting to put her umbrella up, torn between leaping from the car to demand an explanation for why he was there, and wanting to pull the car door closed and take a few extra minutes for herself.

"Let me take that," Raoul said, not bothering with the niceties of "hello" or "how are you."

He reached for her umbrella and held it above the driver's door, then extended a hand to help her out. She really had to get something a little less low-slung, she told herself as she was forced to accept his help to get out from behind the wheel. It wasn't as if her sedan was supersporty or anything but by the time she was full-term, getting out of here would require a crane.

"Thank you. How convenient that you were here. Just passing by, were you?" she asked as he shut the door behind her.

Her attempt at flippancy fell about as flat as her hair in this weather.

"No, I've been waiting for you," he answered as they half walked, half ran to the veranda where Raoul shook out the umbrella.

Standing in the shelter, her eyes drank in the sight of him. He was just as beautiful to her as he'd ever been and her heart did a little flip-flop of recognition. She ruthlessly quashed it. She'd had plenty of time to think in the past month and while she was inwardly overjoyed to see Raoul here, she was determined to hold firm to her decision to move forward with her life, without him. She wouldn't settle for half measures in anything anymore, especially now when there was not only herself to consider.

It didn't stop her concern when she saw him shiver and realized that he was soaking wet.

"Come inside," she said brusquely. "You need to get dried off."

"Thank you."

There was a strange note to his voice and she looked at him sharply, noting his attention was now very firmly on the bulge of her tummy.

"Have you been here long?" she asked as she wrestled her things to find her front door key.

"About an hour," he answered.

"Outside? You're soaking wet and must be freezing cold. Is my father not home?"

"Oh, yeah, he's home," Raoul said with a rueful smile.

"Oh," she said, suddenly flustered.

If he'd already talked to her father she had no doubt that there'd been more than a few terse words exchanged. Finally, thank goodness, she found her key and inserted it in the door.

"Hello? Dad? I'm home," she called as she pushed the door open and gestured for Raoul to follow her inside.

"So, you're letting him in?" her father asked as he came through from the kitchen into the sitting room of the compact cottage.

"He's traveled a long way, Dad, and it's pouring rain outside."

"I will give you your privacy," he said stiffly, his dark eyes fixed on Raoul as if in challenge. "But I will just be up the hill with Finn and Tamsyn. You will call me if you need me, yes?"

"Sure I will," Alexis answered, and crossed the room to give her father a hug. "Thank you," she whispered.

"Ti amo," he said, holding her close before releasing her. Then, with another silent glare at Raoul, he shrugged on a coat and stomped out the front door.

Silence grew uncomfortably around them. Finally, realizing she had to say or do something, Alexis put her things down on the coffee table between them.

"I'll get you something to dry off with."

"Thanks."

She was back in seconds, handing a towel to Raoul and stood there watching him as he toweled excess moisture off his hair. His shirt, however, was soaked through.

"You can't stay in that," she said. "Would you like a shirt of Dad's?"

"No, I'll be fine, I'll dry out soon. Besides, I don't think he'd—"

"Don't be silly, you'll catch your death that way. At least take your shirt off and let me put it through the dryer."

Raoul stepped up closer to her and took her by the hands. "Alexis, stop trying to find reasons not to talk to me."

"Is that what I'm doing?" she said, looking up into his hazel eyes and wondering exactly what it was that she read there.

Even now, after the way he'd summarily dismissed her, her pulse betrayed her by leaping at his touch. Some things, it seemed, would never change.

"Yes. Please, sit down. Let's talk."

"Sure, do you want a tea or coffee?"

"Sit," he commanded gently, and guided her to the sofa and sat down beside her. "I owe you an explanation and an apology."

Alexis fidgeted on the chair, unsure of what he expected of her. Did he think that just because he was about to say sorry that she'd forgive him everything? He was in for a sad surprise if that was the case.

"Go on," she urged him. "I'm listening."

She forced herself to calm down and pushed back into the seat, absently rubbing her belly. Raoul's eyes tracked from her face down to where her hand moved in slow, gentle circles.

"You're looking well," he said.

"You came here to tell me that?" she asked, her tone bordering on acerbic.

"No, what I came here to say is I am deeply sorry for the way I treated you. You deserved more."

"Raoul, I made my own choice when I accepted less," she pointed out.

"I know, but you, of all people—with your loving heart and your giving nature—you should never have been asked to settle for so little. I knew that and I took what you were prepared to give without thinking about the damage it might do. All I was concerned about was me. I just wanted… Hell, I don't even know what I really wanted. All I knew was that you offered me a light in the darkness, warmth in the cold. You made me feel again, but then I felt too much. I didn't know what to do, so I ended up pushing you away.

"I didn't want to be vulnerable again. When Bree died it hurt so much. It left me feeling so empty inside that every breath was agony. The idea of loving anyone again scared me into telling myself I *couldn't* love again—that I didn't deserve to."

"Everyone deserves love," Alexis said softly.

"I know that now." He drew in a shuddering breath. "For so long I was angry—felt so helpless. I hated having choice taken from me the way Bree did when she didn't tell me about her aneurysm. I'll never know whether, knowing the risks, she believed she'd get through Ruby's birth okay or whether she had some kind of premonition that she'd die and thought it would be worth it regardless, but either way she made choices that should have involved me and instead she shut me out. Doing that went against everything we'd promised one another, and if I couldn't trust her anymore, how could I trust anyone?"

Raoul leaned forward, his elbows on his knees and lifted one hand to his face, rubbing at his eyes.

"When Ruby was born I was too afraid to let myself love her. At first she was so ill that the doctors said her survival was touch and go, especially in the first few days. Even after she battled past that, I wouldn't let myself feel anything for her. She was so vulnerable, so dependent. I knew nothing about babies, nothing about being a father. We were supposed to have done all that together, Bree and me. The very idea of taking Ruby home and caring for her, alone, made me sick with fear."

"You would have had Catherine, your friends, your extended family," Alexis reminded him.

"I know that now, but I couldn't think rationally then. And there was something else, too." He made a sound of disgust. "I resented her. Can you believe it? I resented my tiny newborn daughter because her mother had chosen Ruby's life over her own. Rather than see her birth as a gift, I saw it only as a burden. So, instead of stepping up to my responsibilities I ignored them. I let Catherine take over Ruby's care, telling myself it was okay because I was grieving. But then it became easier to simply let things keep on going the way they always had. The more distance I had from Ruby, the closer she grew to her grandmother, the less I needed to worry that I might have to assume my obligations toward her as her father, any opportunities to fail her, hurt her or lose her."

"Ruby's lucky to have Catherine in her life," Alexis said, not minimizing in any way Raoul's desertion of his daughter. "She could have done worse."

"Yeah, she could have been forced to spend all of her first nine months with a father who saw her as a constant reminder of his failures as a husband and as a father. Every minute I spent with her, and Catherine would insist on bringing her around from time to time, she just forced me to remember that my big dreams for a family had taken her mother from us both. That, ultimately, I was responsible for everything that happened."

Alexis shook her head. "You're taking rather a lot on yourself. You weren't the only one involved here."

"It seemed like it at the time. Unreasonable, I know. Self-centered, definitely. I put myself in a loop where every day would be the same with work as my panacea, my catharsis. Even so, until you arrived, I was just going through the motions. Living only half a life."

"Until I arrived?"

"You made me remember what happened the first time I saw you, the way you made me feel. For months I'd imprisoned anything remotely like sensation. I thought I'd finally purged that from my existence, and then, there you were. A golden light just pulsing with warmth. And you wouldn't take no for an answer."

Alexis frowned, remembering their meeting when she arrived at the winery. "The first time you saw me...you mean back in April?"

"No, I mean the very first time. There were sparks between us the day that we met, when Bree introduced us. I know you felt them, too. It's why you pulled away from Bree, wasn't it?"

"Yes," she whispered.

Alexis closed her eyes in shame. He'd seen the way she'd felt about him even then? Did that mean Bree had seen it, too?

"I loved my wife, but for some reason I couldn't help but be attracted to you, too. When you came back, that all came rushing back with you. It left me not only hating that you'd roused emotions from deep inside of me again but also hating myself for what I saw as a betrayal of Bree."

His voice cracked on his words, making Alexis's heart squeeze in empathy. She searched in vain for the right words to say. Raoul turned to her, his face a tortured mask of pain.

"But I betrayed you, too. I betrayed your trust, your faith in me that I could be a better man and I betrayed your love. I'm so sorry, Alexis. More sorry than you could ever understand. You offered me a gift, a lifeline, and I threw it back in your face. I can see why you hesitated to tell me about our baby, but at the time I only saw it as history repeating itself, with you keeping a secret from me that involved me at its basest level."

"I would have told you, in my own time," she hastened to assure him.

"And, I'm ashamed to admit, I probably wouldn't have reacted any differently. I've been an absolute fool. I tried to ignore what you mean to me and I drove you away. Can you ever forgive me for that? Could you ever begin to want to give us another chance?"

Alexis drew in a deep breath. Could she?

"Raoul, you really hurt me. Making me leave you, leave Ruby—I…I don't know if I could put myself through that again. I could barely function for days afterward. I couldn't even drive any further than Christchurch the day you sent me away. I had to have help to get home. The first week I was back here I was like a zombie, barely functioning, barely speaking. It frightened the people who love me and it terrified me.

"I've only just started to put myself back together. To plan for the future. I know you said you'd always provide support for me before and after this pregnancy but I need to stand on my own two feet, too. There've been times recently when I needed to talk to you, needed to share something with you that's vitally important, but I've been too afraid because I couldn't be certain what your reaction would be. Will you hurt me again? Reject me? Reject what it is that I have to tell you?" She shook her head. "I just don't know and I don't know if I can trust you to be there."

Raoul felt his whole body quake at her words. All his old fears threatened to choke him. His throat seized and he couldn't find words to push past the obstruction. What was she saying? Was there some problem, some abnormality with the baby? Or with her—was she all right? Was the pregnancy putting her at risk, as it had with Bree? If she didn't tell him, how could he move heaven and earth to make things right for her? How could he keep her, and their baby, safe? Was he doomed to failure yet again?

Blood pounded in his ears and he fought to clear his mind from the daze of dread that had so quickly risen to consume him. He could do this. He was being given another chance, which was more than most people had in their lifetimes. He had to prove to Alexis he could be that man she needed, the man he believed that deep down, at the core of his heart, he still really was.

"I'm sorry I made you feel that way," he said, his voice sounding strained. "I want you to trust me. I want you to know you need never hide anything from me, ever again. I love you, Alexis, so much that it hurts to know that I've damaged what we started to have together, that I've risked your love and the right to be in your life and by your side. I will do whatever it takes, for as long as it takes, to be worthy of you. Please, give me another chance. Let me love you like you deserve to be loved.

Let me show you how much you mean to me, how much our baby means to me."

"Babies," Alexis said quietly.

His breath caught in his throat. Had he heard her right?

"Two of them, to be exact," she continued, her eyes watching him carefully, almost as if she expected him to get to his feet and run to the door and keep running.

He had to admit, she'd floored him. Panic threatened to overwhelm him. Pregnancy in itself carried risk, ergo a multiple pregnancy had to carry more. Could he do this? He reached beyond the panic and the shock at her words and let the idea play around in his mind.

Twins.

His heart swelled with hope and he reached for her hands, his own brushing against her swollen belly as he did so. His babies. A rush of pride and anticipation built up inside and he felt a smile spread widely across his face.

"Two of them," he repeated. "My God, are you okay? I thought you looked bigger than I'd expected but, wow, twins?"

"I'm doing fine. *We're* doing fine," she amended.

"How long have you known?"

"Since that first appointment with Dr. Taylor. His equipment was more accurate than that at the clinic."

He was stricken with remorse. He'd made her life so difficult, made the situation between them so uncomfortable that she hadn't felt able to reveal that news to him. News like that should have been a delight to be shared, not a burden to be borne alone.

"Alexis," he said, moving closer to her and drawing her into his arms. "I will spend the rest of my life making up to you and our children for what I've done if you'll only let me be a part of your future, yours and our babies'. You've taught me so much—how to be a real father to Ruby but most important, how to love again, to love you and Ruby *and* our unborn children. I owe you everything."

"You owe me nothing but your love, Raoul. I deserve that at the very least. Unencumbered and whole. Can you do that?"

Alexis drew back, searching his face for something he only hoped she could see.

"It's yours. Everything I am, everything I'm yet to be."

She didn't answer him immediately. Instead, she regarded him carefully for a few minutes. Time stretched out interminably.

"I'm not just answering for myself," she said eventually. "I'm answering for these children, too. They deserve unconditional love, no matter what happens now or in the future. I've loved you a long time, Raoul, at first from afar and then close up. I won't lie to you. All along it's hurt like hell and I'm only just beginning to recover. I'd all but come to terms with the fact that you would never be mine to love the way I wanted to love you. If I commit to you, I'm committing on behalf of the babies, as well. I need to be able to trust you, for all our sakes."

"I'm only human, I can't promise that I'll never let you down again someday in the future, Alexis. But I am prepared to pledge the rest of my days to being the best man I can be, the best husband, the best father."

"Husband?"

"I want to commit to you, Alexis. I want to wake up with you beside me every day for the rest of my life. I want to fight with you, I want to make up with you. I want to spend every minute of every day making sure you know I love you with everything I am and everything you've made me see I can be." He slid off the sofa and onto one knee in front of her. "Will you be my wife?

Will you come back to me, marry me and help me raise Ruby and our children together?"

"Oh, Raoul. I want that with all my heart. Yes. Yes, I will marry you and fight with you and make up with you and all those things. You're all I ever wanted from the first time I saw you. I never believed, in my wildest dreams, that we would have a chance together and I'm not going to let that go now. I love you, Raoul, so very, very much."

She slid down to her knees in front of him and wrapped her arms around him. As they drew close he was filled with unspeakable joy, as if things were right again in his world for the first time in a very long time.

"You won't regret it, Alexis. I promise. I will be a good and loving husband and father for as long as you'll have me."

"Forever will never be long enough," she whispered, lifting her face for his kiss and, as his lips touched hers, he knew she was right.

* * * * *

"Tell me why you're leaving. Is it because of me?"

He couldn't seem to help himself, and lifted his finger to trace her lips. Her breath caught, and his face darkened as he watched.

Kiss him, tell him it's him and that he's going to be a father!

But while all these impulses rampaged through her, she drew back an inch, considering it a good moment to retreat before she truly lost her senses. She'd lost them once. Now she was pregnant. She didn't want to castigate him for that night, a night she had been wishing and praying someday happened. But she didn't want him to pay his whole life.

She simply loved him too much.

ONCE PREGNANT, TWICE SHY

BY
RED GARNIER

Published in Great Britain 2014
by Mills & Boon, an imprint of Harlequin (UK) Limited,
Eton House, 18-24 Paradise Road, Richmond, Surrey, TW9 1SR

© 2014 Red Garnier

ISBN: 978 0 263 91464 1

51-0414

Harlequin (UK) Limited's policy is to use papers that are natural, renewable and recyclable products and made from wood grown in sustainable forests. The logging and manufacturing processes conform to the legal environmental regulations of the country of origin.

Printed and bound in Spain
by Blackprint CPI, Barcelona

Red Garnier is a fan of books, chocolate and happily-ever-afters. What better way to spend the day than combining all three? Traveling frequently between the United States and Mexico, Red likes to call Texas home. She'd love to hear from her readers at redgarnier@gmail.com. For more on upcoming books and current contests, please visit her website, www.redgarnier.com.

As always, with my deepest thanks to everyone at Harlequin Desire—who make the best team of editors I've ever come across! Thank you for making this book shine.

This book is once again dedicated to my flesh-and-blood hero and our two little ones, who, it turns out, are not so little anymore.

Prologue

He was the sexiest best man the maid of honor had ever seen, and he wouldn't stop looking at her.

Stomach clenched tight with longing, she stared into his gorgeous obsidian eyes and wondered how she was going to have the courage to tell him that their one incredible night together, that night that should have never happened but *did,* had resulted in a little surprise on the way.

That the stork would be paying them a visit in eight months or so.

The thought alone made her legs tremble. Clutching her white orchid bouquet with trembling hands, Kate Devaney forced herself to focus on her sister, Molly, and how stunning she looked up on the altar in her snow-white wedding gown next to the drop-dead-gorgeous groom.

The fresh noon sun lit her lovely pink-cheeked face, its warm rays illuminating the couple as they stood before the priest. They were surrounded by an explosion of white casablancas, orchids, tulips and roses. The train of the bride's wedding gown reached almost to the end of the red velvet carpet, where the guests sat in rapt attention on rows and rows of elegant white benches. Molly's voice trembled with emotion as she spoke her vows to Julian, her best friend for forever, and the man she'd always loved.

"I, Molly, take you, Julian John, to be my husband…"

Kate's heart constricted with emotion for her little sister, but no matter how much she fought the impulse, her eyes kept straying to the right side of the groom…to where the best man stood towering and silent.

Garrett Gage.

Her tummy quivered when their eyes met again. His eyes were hot and tumultuous, his jaw set tight and square as a cutting board.

He'd been looking at her for every second of the ceremony, his palpable gaze boring pinprick holes through the top of her head.

What a pity that his fiancée wasn't at the wedding, so that he could go and stare at that blonde and leave Kate alone, she thought angrily.

But no, he haunted her. This man. Day and night she thought of him, wanted him, ached for him, while every second of the day, she tried futilely to forget him.

For the past month, it had been a struggle to ignore the enticing memories of the things he'd said to her, a struggle not to remember the way he'd held her in his strong, hard arms like she was more precious than platinum.

She'd told herself, every night for the past thirty nights, that they would never work, and when she'd finally heard of his upcoming marriage, she'd had no other choice but to believe herself.

It was fine. Really. She hadn't wanted to marry him. She would never marry unless she could have what Molly and Julian had; if Kate couldn't have a little piece of real love for herself, then she'd rather be alone.

So tomorrow she was leaving. She had a one-way ticket to Florida. Miami, to be precise. Where she could begin a new life and never have to see the man she loved with another woman again. But before she left, she must let him know the truth. A truth she had been carefully keeping to herself for a month, not wanting to detract from the joy of Molly's big day.

Molly was her only sister; Kate had practically raised her they had both been orphaned as little girls. She wanted Molly's wedding day to be perfect.

Yes, Kate was pregnant, but there was still plenty of time to find the right moment to tell Garrett about it. If only he'd stop looking at her like he wanted her for lunch, making her insides twist and clench with yearning.

"You may now kiss the bride!"

Startled, Kate couldn't believe she'd missed so much of the ceremony, and then she watched as the handsome, blond-haired Julian lifted Molly in his arms as if she weighed no more than a feather and kissed the breath out of her.

Arms twining around him, Molly squeaked in delight as Julian swung her full circle, still kissing her. But he pulled back with a frown and murmured, "Oh, crap!" when he realized Molly's train had gone round and round both their bodies.

When they looked down to the coil around them, they both burst out laughing, then they started kissing again, Julian's open hands almost engulfing all of Molly's petite face as he cradled it.

"I got it," Kate said, laughing as she easily detached the train from her sister's dress. With Molly in his arms, Julian hopped out of the tulle and carried her down the aisle to the cheers and claps of their guests and the blaring sound of the "Wedding March."

They looked so happy, so in love, as they headed for the beautifully decorated gardens where their outdoor wedding celebration was to take place, leaving Kate behind with a pair of stinging eyes, the train and the best man.

As Kate began gathering what felt like a hundred miles of tulle, Garrett came over, bringing her the other end of the train. She couldn't seem to look up at him. "Thanks," she said, and felt her cheeks burn. God, why was she even blushing? They'd grown up together. He should be a man she was comfortable with and instead she was a wreck just wondering how she was going to tell him.

Despite how much it hurt her to know he was marrying someone else, she didn't want to ruin his life, because he'd always protected and cared for her. Always.

And she feared this news was going to be a whopper for him.

Suddenly his tan, long-fingered hands captured and stilled hers, and she held her breath as the warmth of his palms seeped into her skin. She looked up and into those riveting onyx eyes, her lungs straining for air.

"Tell me if I'm mistaken—" his voice was low, his eyes so unbearably intimate she could die "—but did my brother just marry your sister?"

She wouldn't stare at his beautifully shaped lips as he spoke. She wouldn't. But, oh, God, he was so handsome she could burst from it. "It only took a full hour, Garrett. You couldn't have missed it," she said, trying to keep her voice level.

And yet, maybe she was hallucinating, but…was he staring at *her* lips? "Apparently I did."

"You were standing right there. Where were you? Mars?" She straightened and rolled her eyes, ready to leave, but his voice, the intensity in his words, stopped her.

"I was in my bedroom, Kate. With you in my arms."

She went utterly still, her back to him, while every inch of her body fought to suppress a tremor of heat that fluttered enticingly down her spine. His words seduced her body and soul in ways she couldn't even believe were possible. Her legs felt watery, and every pore in her body quivered with wanting of him. His words transported her to his bedroom. To his arms. To that night.

No, no, no, she couldn't do this here. She just couldn't.

Shaking her head almost to herself, she started down the beautiful red path that led to the Gage mansion, painfully aware that he followed.

"Kay, I need to talk to you," he said thickly.

That low, coarse timbre managed to do sexy things to her skin, and her physical response to him irritated her beyond measure.

"If it's to tell me about your wedding, I already know. Congratulations," she said in a voice as flat as the bottom of her shoe.

"Then maybe you can tell me the details, since apparently you know more about it than I do? Dammit, I need to talk to you somewhere *private*."

He grabbed her elbow to halt her, but she immediately yanked it free. "I need to talk to you, too, but I'm not doing it here. Nor am I doing it *today*."

He followed her again with long, easy strides, the determination in his voice nearly undoing her. "Well, I *am*. So just listen to me." He stopped her again, forced her to turn and stared heatedly into her eyes. "I don't know what happened to me the other day, Katie.... What you told me left me so damn winded, I swear I didn't know where to begin...."

She covered her ears. "Not here, please, *please not here!*"

He seized her wrists and forced her hands down. "I know I hurt you, I know you don't want me to apologize, but I need to say I am sorry. I am sorry for how things have gone down and for hurting you. I'm sorry how it happened, Katie. I wish I'd done it differently. If I could take it back, I would, if only to get you to stop looking at me like you are just now."

His apology was the last straw. It really was. The last. Straw. "You wish to take the night back, that's what you wish?" The pitch of her voice was rising, but she couldn't control the hysteria bubbling up inside her chest, couldn't stop herself from incredulously thinking, *How can I take back the baby you gave me, you ass!* "Oh, you're something special, do you know that? You're something else. I can't even believe I let you put your filthy paws on me, you no-good—"

"Goddammit, I really didn't want to do it this way, Kay. But you're giving me no choice!" Teeth gritted, he scooped her up into his arms and stalked across the gardens toward the house.

"Wha—" The tulle train fell inch by inch from her grasp and trailed a path behind them as she kicked and squirmed and hit his chest. "Garrett, stop! Put me down! What are you *doing?*"

He kicked the front doors open and carried her up the stairs, his jaw like steel, his hands blatantly gripping her buttocks. "Something I should've done a long, long time ago."

One

Two months earlier...

This was hell.

The Gage family mansion was lit up with light and music and flowers tonight. All the movers and shakers in San Antonio seemed to be having a good time, a good wine and a good laugh. But Kate had gone well past purgatory an hour ago and was now sure that this night, this endless night, was nothing other than hell.

With a sinking feeling in the pit of her stomach, she watched the striking couple across the glittering marble floor.

"Garrett," the slight, sensual blonde gushed to the tall dark man, "you're just like fine wine, better and better with age."

Garrett Gage, the sexiest man on the planet, and the

devil in Kate's hell, ducked his head and whispered something into the woman's ear with a wicked gleam in his dark eyes.

How many nights had she dreamed Garrett would look at her like that? Not like a little girl, but like a woman?

In a black suit and blood-red tie, with his dark hair slicked back to reveal his chiseled features, standing proud and imposing like the media baron he'd become, Garrett Gage could cause lightning to strike. He could make butterflies rise in your stomach. Make the earth stop. Make your heart thump. He could make you do *anything* just for a chance to be the one woman at his side.

For years, Kate had thought that feeding him, seeing him enjoy and praise her creations, was good enough. The next best thing to having sex with him, she supposed. But now it just pained her to cook and cater for a man who didn't even notice that *she,* Kate Devaney, the woman who made the chocolate croissants he so loved, was on the menu, too.

If only one of her waiters hadn't failed her at the party tonight, Kate might have showcased her new dress with just the right amount of hip sway to finally draw Garrett's discerning eye. But with a tray fixed permanently to her shoulder, no one spared a glance at the glossy satin dress she wore; she was just passing the food.

"Darling, be a dear and bring over some of those cute little shrimp skewers with the pineapple tips," a woman said as she swept up a crab-and-spinach roll and guided it to her lips.

"Orange-pineapple shrimp? It'll be right over," Kate said.

Grateful for the distraction, she swept back into the kitchen to load up a new tray. Usually the sight of her workers milling about the three-tiered cake and pulling out mouthwatering snacks and hors d'oeuvres from the oven would fill her with satisfaction. But even that didn't lift her spirits tonight. *Eight more weeks, Kate. Just two months. And then you never have to see him with another woman again.*

As she carried a new tray into the busy living room, it struck her that she was going to leave behind this house with so many good memories, and this family who'd practically raised her as one of their own. She'd been so happy here; she'd honestly never imagined leaving until her feelings for Garrett had become so...painful. Moving to Florida was the best thing to do—the healthiest. For her. To be away from that hardheaded *idiot!*

"Mother tells me you're leaving." Julian John fell into step beside her as she navigated past a large group. Kate had been so deep in thought that she started at the low, sensual voice.

She glanced up and into the gold-green eyes of the youngest Gage brother, a beautiful man with a heartbreaking smile who was known to be guarded and quiet—except with Molly. He was only two months away from marrying Kate's perky and passionate younger sister and officially becoming her brother-in-law. But if Julian already knew about her departure—*who else did?* Her stomach cramped in dread.

"I can't believe she's told you. I asked her not to tell."

Julian plucked a shrimp skewer from the tray and popped it into his mouth. Like all Gage men, he had massively broad shoulders, and his symmetrical, masculine face looked as if it had been cast in bronze. "Knowing my mother, she probably thought you meant not to tell the press—and that would exclude its owners."

Kate smiled. At seventy, still stout and active, the Gage matron was a force to be reckoned with. She was the proud mother of three strong, successful media magnates—not that Landon, Garrett and Julian John were powerful enough to keep the sassy woman from having her say.

She glittered tonight in a high-end ruby-colored dress, which was completely undermined by the plain black bed slippers she wore. Comfort, to her, was everything. She didn't care what others thought and had enough money to ensure that everyone would at least *pretend* they thought the best of her.

She'd been the closest thing to a mother to Kate, who'd grown up without one. At the tender age of seven, she and her bodyguard dad had moved in to this very house where Garrett's birthday celebration was being held. Her father had died shortly after, leaving Kate and Molly orphans, but this house had remained their home.

"Nothing Molly and I can do to change your mind?" Julian asked, gold-green eyes flicking across the room toward Molly.

Kate could melt when she saw the glimmer of pride and satisfaction in his eyes when he looked at her sister.

It only reminded her of what she herself wanted in her future.

A family of her own.

Which was why she had to leave and rebuild her life, find other interests, and find herself an actual love life with a man who *wanted* her.

"I really have to do this, Jules," she told him as she shook her head and extended the tray to the people standing opposite him. Within seconds, the shrimp skewers started to disappear, one by one.

She had to get away, before she ended up watching the man she loved marry another, form a family. Before she became the dreaded "Aunt Kate" to children she'd always wished would be hers.

"But don't tell Garrett yet, okay? I don't want him on my back already."

"Hell, nobody wants that man on their back. Of course I won't tell him."

Smiling at that, she stole a glance in his direction, and yes, he was still there, as gorgeous as he'd been a minute ago, the blonde looking completely absorbed in him.

The woman was some sort of business associate of his who clearly enjoyed raising men's temperatures. Kate didn't know her, but already she abhorred her.

Seeming distracted, Garrett glanced around the room, and his liquid coal eyes stopped on Kate. Her heart stuttered when his gaze seemed to trail down the length of her silky form-fitting dress—the first male eyes to take in her attire tonight—then came back up to meet her startled stare.

Suddenly the look in his eyes was so dark and unfathomable, she almost thought that he—

No.

Whatever emotion lurked in his eyes, it was swiftly concealed. He raised his wineglass in the air in a mock toast, and added a smile that, although brief and friendly, went straight to her toes.

But that smile had nothing on the one he gave his companion when he turned away from Kate. His lips curled wide, with a flash of white teeth, and Kate just knew the poor woman was done for.

So was Kate.

Damn it, why hadn't she gotten one of those wolf-ish smiles?

Garrett had been there for her for as long as she could remember. A permanent fixture in her life. Steady and strong as a mountain. Her father had died for him. And Garrett had taken the promise he'd made to the dying man to heart.

Now Garrett protected Kate from raindrops and hail, from snow and heat, from kittens with claws and barking dogs. He even protected her from bankruptcy by ensuring the family always had a catering "event" around the corner. But Kate did not want a father.

She'd had one, the best one, and he was gone.

Garrett couldn't replace him; nobody could.

"He's not going to be pleased when he learns, Kate," Julian warned her.

Kate nodded in silence, watching Garrett's mother walk up to him. The elderly woman said something he didn't seem to find particularly pleasant to hear, and a frown settled on his handsome face as he listened.

If only she didn't love that stubborn moron so very, very much...

"Lately he's not pleased about anything," Kate absently said. She remembered the times she'd caught him looking at her with a black scowl during the family events, and just couldn't see why he seemed so bothered with her. "And I don't want him to stop me."

Her father's job had been to protect the Gages. And he had. But somehow, with his death, the family had ended up feeling like they should protect Kate.

They'd made her feel welcome and appreciated for almost two decades. But after receiving so much for so long and giving back so little, Kate felt indebted to the family in a way that made her desperate to prove to them, to all of them, that she was an independent woman now. Especially to Garrett.

"Fair enough. Sunny Florida it is," Julian agreed.

He had always been the easiest to talk to. There was a reason everyone, possibly every female at this party other than Kate, had a little crush on Julian John.

He seized her hand and kissed her knuckles, his eyes sparkling. "I guess this means we'll be buying a beach house next door."

She laughed at that, but then sobered. "Julian. You will take care of Molly for me, won't you?"

His eyes warmed at the mention of his soon-to-be wife. "Ah, Kate, I'd die for my girl. You know that."

Kate gave him a smile that told him silently but plainly how much she adored him for that. Witnessing their love for each other and how it had started out of friendship had been surprising and inspiring, and yet also heartbreaking for Kate. She loved seeing her sister so happy, but couldn't help wish…

Wish Garrett would look at her in the way Julian looked at Molly.

Stupid, blind Garrett.

Blind to the fact that the little girl who'd grown up with him had become a woman.

Blind to the fact that she would gladly be *his* woman.

And even blinder to the fact that before he could say *yay* or *nay,* Kate Devaney was moving to Florida.

"What do you mean, Katie's moving to Florida?"

Stunned, Garrett stared in disbelief at his mother,

his date and business associate completely forgotten at his side.

"Only what I meant. Little Katie's moving to Florida. And no, there's nothing we can do about it. I already tried. And hi there," she said to the blonde pouting at his side. "What did you say your name was?"

"Cassandra Clarks." The woman extended a hand that sparkled with almost as many jewels as his mother's.

But Garrett was too preoccupied to pay attention to their sudden conversation, a conversation that was no doubt about the promising possibility of merging Clarks Communications into the Gage conglomerate. He spotted Kate across the room, and a horrible sensation wrenched through him. *She was leaving?*

When her gaze collided with his, the grip in his stomach tightened a notch. God, she looked cute as a ladybug tonight, too cute to be waltzing around in that dress without making a man sweat.

Then there were her eyes. Every time she looked up at him with those sky-blue eyes, pain sliced through his chest as though that bullet had actually hit Garrett, instead of her father. He'd never forget that he was living now, breathing now, because Kate's father had stepped into the line of fire to save him.

He'd tried to make it up to her. The entire family had. A good education, a roof over her head, help with securing her own place and encouragement so she'd open her catering business. But lately Kate seemed sad and discontent, and Garrett just didn't know how to resolve that.

He felt sad and discontent, too.

"But...she can't go," he said.

Eleanor Gage halted her conversation with Cassandra and turned her unapologetic expression up to his. "She says she can."

"To do what? Her whole *life* is here."

His mother raised a perfectly plucked brow that dared him to wonder *why,* exactly, she would want to leave, and a sudden thought occurred to him. He frowned as he considered it. Kate's distance would be good for him. He might even finally be able to get some sleep. But no. Hell, no.

He'd made a promise to her father, years ago, the tragic night of his death. Kate and her little sister, Molly, had become orphans because of Garrett. They would always belong here, with the Gages. This was their home, and Garrett had done everything in his power so that they would feel comfortable, protected and cared for.

Molly was marrying his younger brother now. But Kate?

Garrett had always had a weakness for her. He respected her. Protected her. Even from things he himself sometimes felt.

His whole life he'd ignored the way Kate's hair fell over her eyes. The way she said *Garrett* an octave lower than any other word she spoke. He'd ignored the way his chest cramped when she spoke of having a date, and he'd even done his best to try not to count all the freckles on the bridge of her pretty nose.

It wasn't easy to force himself to be so damned ignorant. Of that. But he'd done it by force and that was exactly how it would remain.

Kate was like his sister and best friend. Except she was truly neither....

No matter.

He would still do all kinds of things to protect her—

and this included making her see that moving to Florida was not a good option. Not an option, period.

Scowling, he snagged his mother by the elbow and pulled her closer, so that Cassandra didn't overhear. But the woman took the cue and easily began to mingle— leaving him to talk to his mother in peace. "When did she say she was leaving?"

"The day after the wedding."

"Eight weeks?" His brain almost ached as he tried to think of ways to keep her here. "Long enough to change her mind then."

"My darling, if you manage to—" his mother gently patted him on the chest "—you'll make me a very happy woman. I don't want Katie anywhere in the world but *here*."

Garrett bleakly agreed and snatched a wine goblet from a passing server. He almost downed the liquid in one gulp, wondering how in the hell one could change the mind of a stubborn little handful like Kate. She could teach old, grumpy men a thing or two about sticking to their guns, and Garrett wasn't looking forward to being on the opposite end of the field from her. Or then again, maybe he was.

It was always fun to pick a fight with Kate.

It seemed the only way he could vent his frustrations sometimes.

Frustrations that seemed to grow by the minute as he stalked over to Cassandra, who was engaged in a conversation with two other women Garrett knew but couldn't remember the names of.

He was interested in securing her family's company to consolidate the Gages' grip on Texas media, but he couldn't even think about that now.

Kate was packing her bags and flying out of his life in eight weeks, and he was so determined to stop that from happening that, if he had to, he would run to Florida after her on his own two feet, and come back carrying her like a sack of potatoes on his back.

Which might even be more fun than fighting with her now.

"Something's come up," he apologized as he brought the blonde around to look at him. "I'm afraid I'll need a rain check on our talk."

He smiled down at her to ease the blow, marveling that he could, and he was glad to find there was no hostility in her eyes. She didn't tell him to go take his apology and shove it where it hurt, but instead she said, sounding alarmed, "When can I see you again?"

"Soon," he said with a nod, his mind already on Kate.

Two

He spotted her out on the terrace, and his insides twisted painfully tight. Tall and slender, Kate leaned against the balcony railing outside of the French doors, peacefully gazing out at the gardens. Her dress dipped seductively in the back, exposing inches and inches of flawless bare flesh and the small, delicate little rises of her spine. Something feral and dangerous pummeled through him. *She's leaving me....*

She'd been avoiding him tonight. And now he knew why.

He clenched his hands, hauled in a breath, then yanked the doors open and stepped outside.

A warm breeze flitted by as he approached her. A slice of moon hung in the sky above her, bathing her with its silvery light. It was the kind of night lovers waited for. A night for whispers, for promising forever...

"Why?"

She spun around in a whirl of silk and red hair, her lips slightly parted, her eyes wide and bright. "Don't tell me," she said with a disappointed shake of her head. "Your mother told you."

"Why, Kate? Why am I always the last to know?"

For a moment, she didn't seem to have an answer. *She's leaving you. She's leaving you and won't tell you. Won't look at you.*

Restlessly, she pulled at her small earring as she gazed out at the majestically lit lawns. "I…uh, planned to tell you."

"From where? *Florida?*" he scoffed, unsure whether he was wounded, angry, amused or just plain damn confused.

"Okay, maybe yes, from Florida," she admitted. "But you've been grumpy lately, Garrett. I can't handle you right now. I'm too busy."

His lips twisted into a cynical smile as he leaned on the balustrade next to her. He eyed the length of her glossy hair, wondering what it would smell like up close. Raspberries in the summer…? Peaches and cream? And why in the hell did he need to know? And what did she mean, he was grumpy? "I don't *need* to be *handled.*"

With a pointed stare that told him that he really *did,* Kate studied him with mischievous blue eyes. "You haven't exactly been easy to be around lately."

"Come on, I can't be that bad!"

She shot him a wry smile, and Garrett found himself responding to that captivating grin. He nudged her elbow up on the railing. "Kate. What did you think I'd do? Tie you to your kitchen to keep you here? Steal your damn plane ticket?"

"The fact that you've already thought of that makes me wonder about your sanity."

"The fact that you're leaving makes me want to check your head, too. You belong here."

He sensed—rather than saw—the smile on her lips, but when she refused to look at him, Garrett wondered why Kate seemed so absorbed by the dark gardens it was as if she'd never seen them before—as if she'd never played outside in that yard when she was growing up. His heart jerked as an awful suspicion struck him.

"This is because of a man, isn't it?"

"Excuse me?"

"You don't just dump a life like yours and go away for nothing. So why are you running? Is it a man?"

"Does it matter?" she asked, thrusting her chin up a notch. "I'm leaving, Garrett, and I'm certain."

The rebellious note that crept into her voice only confirmed to him that it was a man.

A toad Garrett wanted to kill with his own two hands.

Pushing away from the railing with sudden force, he plunged his hands into his pants pockets and paced in a circle on the terrace, lowering his voice when he stopped at her side again. "Who's going to protect you?"

She scrunched her pretty nose with a little scoff. "I don't need protecting anymore. I'm grown up, in case you missed it."

He was struck by a memory of holding his jacket over Kate's head while they rushed into the house, soaked and laughing. They'd both been just teens. His chest turned to lead as he wondered if he'd never do that again. Laugh with her again. Laugh, period.

"Adult or baby, you still need to know that someone's got your back," he grumbled.

She glanced down at the limestone terrace floor, and for a nanosecond, he detected a flash of pain in her expression. "I know you've got my back," she said softly.

She sounded as sad as he felt, and suddenly he wanted to punch his fist into something.

Because *nothing* in his life felt right anymore.

Everything he did felt pointless. He felt restless. Angry. So angry at himself.

He imagined her all alone in a new place, with no one to help her with anything. Not if she got lost. Not if she was lonely. Not to unload her stuff. Not if there was thunder outside—she hated thunder. He clamped his jaw, loath to think of how many Florida men would be out there just ready to use and discard her, and then continued his attempt at persuasion. "What about Molly? You two are close."

"And we still will be. But Molly has Julian now. Plus she's promised to visit, and so will I."

"Then what about your catering business?"

"What about it?"

"It's taken off during the past couple of years. You worked your butt off to make it happen, Kate."

She lifted her shoulders in a casual shrug, as if leaving her entire life behind were just an everyday occurrence to her, as if she couldn't wait to leave the shadow of the Gages behind. "Beth's my associate now. Trust me, if Landon married her, it means she's very capable of handling things by herself. We'll hire a couple more helpers, and I can start a new branch in Miami."

Frustrated at her responses, he ground his molars as he thought of a thousand arguments, but he predicted she'd have a retort for each one. How in the hell was he going to change her mind?

Her smile lacked its usual playfulness as her pretty blue eyes held his. "So that's it? Those are your arguments for me staying?"

Her lips…they looked redder tonight, plumper. He wanted to touch them with his thumb and take off her lipstick. See her all fresh and pure like he was used to seeing her. Not all made up. Just pink, fresh-skinned, with those seven freckles on her nose, and that soft coral mouth that he—

Damn.

He stiffened against the heat building in his loins.

But Kate… She made him feel so damned protective it wasn't even funny. Her smiles, her personality, her alertness… There was no part of Kate he would ever change. No part of her he wouldn't miss when she left for Florida.

Luckily, she wouldn't be going anywhere.

"What am I going to do to change your mind?" he asked, more to himself than to her.

"Nothing. Honestly. My mind's completely made up."

He noticed the tray of wineglasses she'd set down nearby. She was taking a short break from making the rounds, he supposed. So he seized one and offered her another.

"Here's to me changing your mind," he said with an arrogant smile. He would find out what she was running away from, and he would eliminate it from the face of the planet.

She laughed, and the sound did magical things to him even as she declined the wine he offered her. "Oh, no, I don't drink when I'm working."

He snorted. "I should've stopped seven glasses ago, and yet here I am. Still going strong. Drink with me, Freckles."

"Well it *is* your birthday. You might as well enjoy."

"Come on. Join me on this toast. I relieve you of your duties." He pressed the glass against the back of her fingers, glad when she finally took it. He felt cocky and arrogant as he lifted his glass. "Here's to me changing your mind," he repeated.

Kate's eyes gained a new sparkle as she did the same. "And to me, and my new life in *Florida*."

They knocked glasses in toast, and it was on.

It was *on*.

Like when they were kids playing Battleship…hell, yeah. Garrett was going to sink Kate's Florida ship to the bottom of the ocean.

As though mentally plotting, too, Kate quietly sipped, watching him over the rim with a little glimmer in her eyes. A glimmer that told him she was definitely onto his plan.

Think what you want, Freckles. But you won't be going anywhere.

"I'm not backing out until I get my way, Kate. You know this, correct?" Garrett warned with a smile

Kate shook her head, but was smiling, too. "See? And you asked me why I didn't tell you? There's your answer. I can't *deal* with you right now, Garrett. I need to pack and make plans, help Molly with preparations so I can leave after the wedding."

"You don't need to *deal* with me. I will be the one dealing with *you*," he countered as he finished his glass. He snatched another and then gazed out at the gardens, the alcohol already slowing his usually sharp brain. Oh, yes, he was determined.

He just couldn't imagine his life without Kate in it. Every family celebration—hell, every family dinner, gathering or festivity—she would be there. Every morning in his office, her delectable croissants would be there. In his mind, his very dark soul, every second of the day, she was *there*....

"Will you be spending the night here?"

The lights in her eyes vanished at his question, and she nodded sadly. "Your mother said I could use my old room. She doesn't want me driving alone so late. You know what happened..."

To our fathers, he thought. They'd taken Garrett to watch a rock concert.

Neither had returned.

The reminder made his stomach twist and turn until he thought he'd puke.

He wanted to discuss Florida, take back control, make her promise she would stay and settle this here and now. But he didn't feel like he was in control of all five senses anymore; he'd drained the second glass already, which brought tonight's drink count to almost a dozen, so perhaps he could save this for another day.

Setting down the empty glass on the tray, he said, "All right, Kate. Sleep tight. I'll see you in the morning."

"Garrett." Her voice stopped him, and he turned from the terrace door. There was regret in her eyes, and he worried she'd see the truth of his torment in his. Then she sadly shook her head. "Happy birthday."

"You know what I want from you for my birthday, don't you?" he asked, his voice so low she'd probably barely heard it.

For a long, charged moment, their gazes held. The wind rustled the bottom of her dress and pulled tendrils of hair out of her bun. Watching the way the breeze caressed her, he felt unraveled on the inside with crazy thoughts about tucking that hair behind her ear, feeling the material of her silky dress under his fingers.

"What?" she asked, sounding breathless. "What is it that you want for your birthday?"

Her eyes had glazed over. Now her chest heaved as though his answer made her nervous and, at the same time, excited, and for a moment, Garrett felt equally nervous, and equally excited. For that fraction of a second, he just wanted to say one word, just one word, that would change their lives unequivocally in some way. But he forced himself to say the rest.

"You," he whispered, barely able to continue when he noticed the way her cheeks flushed, the way she licked her lips. "Here. I want you here on my next birthday. I want you here every day of the year. That's all I want, Kate."

You...

Kate felt strangely melancholy, lying in her old bed, in her old room, with its decorations still left over from her childhood. She didn't want to think that this was the last time she'd be sleeping here, a door away from Garrett. She didn't want to think it'd be the last birthday she spent with him and that some other guy she'd meet in Florida, a cabana boy or whatever, would be the one she'd settle down with.

She'd been barely seven when she buried her dad, and in that strange reflective moment when a grieving child gains the maturity of an old person, Kate had realized that her chance to be loved, to belong to something and someone, was now buried six feet under, in a smooth wood coffin.

She'd never blamed Garrett for anything, at least not at first.

She hadn't been told what had happened in the beginning. She'd only learned that two men had been murdered and the killers had been caught and would spend their lives behind bars. Which had seemed like such an easy punishment, compared to how her father and Garrett's had lost their lives. Garrett and his brothers had grieved their father, and Kate and Molly had quietly grieved their own. But then she had overheard a conversation Garrett's mother had had with the police, and Kate had found out what really happened. She had felt betrayed, kept from the truth by their whispers. Garrett's betrayal had hurt most of all.

She'd always had a soft spot for that dark-haired boy, and she'd felt like he hadn't even cared enough for her to tell her the truth. That her father had not died to save his dad. He had died to save Garrett. She'd rushed up to him one day and told him he should be ashamed of himself. She'd asked him how he could stand there with that poker face, and laugh, and try to pretend nothing had happened, when it had been his fault! Her father had died protecting Garrett from the gunshots. All because Garrett hadn't run for cover when he should have. She'd been angry because they'd all lied to her, to her and poor innocent Molly, who was merely three and lonely. But she had been especially angry at Garrett.

She'd regretted the words instantly, though, when she'd seen the way his neck had gone red, and his fisted hands had trembled at his sides, and his eyes had gone dead like she'd just delivered the last blow that he'd needed to join the two men down under.

The death wish the boy had developed afterward

had alarmed the family to such an extent that the Gage matron had asked Kate to please talk to him. Horribly remorseful, Kate had approached him one day and apologized. She'd realized that her father would have done that for anyone, which was true. No matter how painful it had been to speak, she'd said that it had been his job, and he had done it well. He was a hero. Her hero, and now he was gone.

Garrett had listened gravely, said nothing for long moments, and Kate had felt a new, piercing sense of loss when she realized in fear that she and Garrett would never be friends again. They would never be able to cope with this huge loss and guilt again.

"I wish it had been me."

"No! No!" She'd suddenly hated herself for having planted this in his head, for not coping well with this strange anger and neediness inside her. Maybe she'd been so angry because all she'd wanted was for someone to put his arms around her and Molly and say it would be okay, even if it was a lie and it would never be okay.

But Garrett had tossed a small twig aside, and gazed down at her hand like he'd wanted to take it. She hadn't known if she wanted him to hold it or not, but when he had, a current had rushed up her arm as if the tips of her fingers where he touched her had been struck by lightning.

"I'm gonna be your hero now," he'd said.

And he was.

He'd protected her his entire life, from anything and everything. He'd become not only her hero...but the only man she'd ever wanted.

He could feel Kate in the house somehow.

Of course his mother wouldn't let her drive so late

back to her apartment alone. Garrett also had an apartment of his own in a newer neighborhood, but tonight he'd also planned to stay in his old room so he could get blissfully inebriated without having to drive. And yet even after all the wine he'd drunk, he didn't feel so high.

The news of Kate's plans to move had sobered him.

Now he lay in bed with just a little buzz to scramble his brain, not enough to numb his thoughts. He couldn't stop thinking about her.

He might as well have been eighteen again, staring at the ceiling, sleepless with the knowledge that Kate slept nearby. Except now, Molly no longer slept in Kate's same room, and Kate wasn't a teenager anymore. Neither was Garrett.

With the vivid imagination of a man, he imagined her red hair fanning out against the white pillow, and the mere thought of her in bed caused his muscles to tighten.

His chest became heavy as he grappled with the same feelings of guilt and solitude that he always did when he thought of her.

Garrett had also denied little Molly of a father. But Molly had never looked at him with resentment. She had never really looked at him like she *wanted* something from him, like Kate did.

Sometimes, when he got drunk and reflective, he wondered if that night had never happened, would things have been different for him? He might have been happier, like his younger brother. He could have also waited until Kate was the right age, and then, if there had been any hint of her having any special feelings for him, he might have let himself feel them back for her. But it was pointless to imagine it. Pointless torture and torment.

Because that night *had happened,* and Garrett could still feel the dank air, hear the gunshots and remember it as if it had happened less than twenty-four hours ago.

Yeah, he remembered exactly how those gunshots had exploded so close to him, how they'd burst between the buildings of downtown San Antonio like an echo. He remembered his father's grip—which had been firm on Garrett as he guided him into the concert entrance— and how suddenly he'd jerked at his side and his fingers had let go. His father had crashed like a deadweight to the asphalt.

"Dad?" Garrett had said, paralyzed in confusion for a second, only to be instantly shoved aside by Dave Devaney, whose expression clearly told Garrett he'd already figured out what was going on.

"Get down—run!" the man had shouted, reaching for the weapon Garrett knew he carried inside his jacket. But Garrett could hear his father sputtering, struggling to breathe, and he had been paralyzed for a stunned moment. The world could have been crashing over him. As far as he'd known, it had been. But all he had been conscious of was his father. In the middle of the street, clutching his chest, where blood spurted through his open fingers like a fountain.

Instead of running away, Garrett had run back to him. He hadn't known what he planned to do. He'd only known his father was covered in blood, choking on his own breath, and that his eyes—dark as coal like Garrett's—looked wild and frightened. As wild and frightened as Garrett felt.

He'd dived back for the figure on the ground and gripped him by one arm, trying to drag him aside, when he'd heard Devaney's "No, boy! Dammit, no!" A half dozen more gunshots had exploded, and in that instant, the weight of a man had crushed him to the ground.

Garrett had cursed in front of his father for the first time in his life and squirmed between both men. Something hot and sticky had oozed across both his chest and back as he'd tried to push free, which had proved immensely difficult being he was only ten, and Dave Devaney had been a big man. His father had sputtered one last time beneath him, and when Garrett swung his head around, Jonathan Gage's eyes had been lifeless.

Garrett had gone cold, listening to sirens in the distance, footsteps, chaos around them.

Suddenly he'd heard Dave's voice, saying, "Garrett," as he rolled to the side to spare Garrett his weight. He'd blinked up at the man, shocked, mute when he realized the man had stepped into the line of fire to save him. Him. Who hadn't run when he'd been told to.

The man had reached out to pat his jaw, and Garrett had grabbed the man's hand and attempted a reassuring squeeze. He'd shaken uncontrollably, felt sticky and startlingly cold. "My daughters… They have no one but me. No one but me. Do you understand me, boy?"

He'd nodded wildly.

The man had seemed to struggle to swallow. To speak and breathe. But his eyes had had that wild desperation Garrett's father had worn, except his gaze had also been pleading. Pleading with Garrett. "Help me…. Be there…for them…"

He'd nodded wildly again.

"So that they are not alone…taken care of…safe. Tell 'em…I l-love…"

Garrett had nodded, his face wet and his eyes scalding hot as he tried to reassure the dying man. His chest had hurt so much he'd thought he'd been shot, as well. "Yes, sir," he'd said low, with the conviction of a ten-year-old who'd suddenly aged to eighty. "I'll take care of them both."

But how *could* he take care of Kate now, if they would be miles and states apart?

Kate was jolted from her thoughts when the door of her bedroom crashed open. She sat upright on the bed, her heart hammering in her chest. A huge shadow loomed at the threshold.

Garrett.

"I don't want you to leave," he said gruffly.

Shock widened her eyes. His voice was slurred, and she wondered how many more drinks he'd had after they'd last seen each other.

From the light of the hall, she could see he was still partly dressed in his black slacks and button-up shirt. His tie was loose around his collar. His hair rumpled. His sleeves rolled up. Oh, God, he looked adorable.

"I've made up my mind," she told him.

"Then unmake it."

He shut the door behind him and strode into the darkness, and her heart beat faster in response.

"I can't unmake it," she said, her voice raspy. Her throat was aching and she thought that the night of no sleep yesterday and the marathon to get everything set up today had just set her up to fall ill. "Look, I made up my mind. I can't stay here."

"Why?"

"Because I'm unhappy, Garrett. I've got everything I ever wanted, and yet don't. I make money for myself,

I've got great friends, and Molly, and I've got you and your family…and I'm so unhappy."

The mattress squeaked as he sat down, and suddenly she felt his hand patting the bed as though to find her. "Why are you unhappy?" he asked. He found her thigh over the covers, and when he squeezed, her stomach tightened, too.

She couldn't remember ever being in a dark room with him, or maybe she could, decades ago, when he had been sick and she would help Eleanor nurse him and feed him soup. But now she was no longer a girl. Her body was a woman's, and her responses to this man were purely feminine and decidedly discomforting. Her blood raced hot through her veins as her body turned the same consistency of her pillow behind her. Soft. Feathery. Weightless.

"Why are you unhappy?" he murmured. She felt the mattress squeak again when he edged closer. He seemed to be palpating the air until he felt her shoulder; then he slid his hand up her face. The touch of his fingers melted her, and she closed her eyes as he cupped her jaw and bent to her ear. "Tell me what makes you unhappy and I'll fix it for you."

He smelled of alcohol. And his unique scent.

She shook her head at his impossible proposition, almost amused, but not quite. More like unsettled. By his nearness, his touch.

She had promised herself, when she'd decided she had to move away, that she would forget this man. And now all she could think of was reaching up to touch his hair and draw his lips to hers. She couldn't see him in the darkness, but she knew his face by memory. The sleek line of his dark eyebrows. The beautiful tips of his sooty eyelashes. The strikingly beautiful espresso shade of his eyes, dark brown from up close and coal-black from afar.

She knew his strong face, with that strong, proud forehead, as strong as his cheekbones and jaw, and she knew the perfect shape of his mouth. She might not have touched his face with her fingers in her life, but her eyes had run over those features more than they had touched any other thing on this earth.

"You can't fix it. You're not God," she sadly whispered. Her throat now ached with emotion, too.

"You're right. I'm a devil." He cupped her face in both hands and stroked his thumb across the flesh of her lips, triggering a strange reaction in her body. "Why did you wear lipstick tonight? You look prettier bare."

Her breath caught as she realized he was stroking her lips with his thumb like he wanted to kiss her. He'd called her pretty. When had he ever called her pretty? Decades ago, maybe by accident, he'd blurted it out. But it had been years since he'd ever complimented her. Or touched her.

He'd just done both.

And suddenly the only thing moving in the room was her heaving chest, and his thumb as it moved side to side, caressing her lips, filling her body with an ocean of longing. She swallowed back a moan.

"You're right to want to leave here, Kate." His voice thickened as he bent his head, and he smelled so good and exuded such body warmth and strength, she went light-headed. "You should run from here."

It took every ounce of willpower for her to push at his hard shoulders. "You're drunk, Garrett. Go away and get out of my bed."

His hands tightened on her face as he nuzzled her

nose with his, the timbre of his voice rough with torment. "Kate, there's not a day I don't remember what I took from you—"

"Garrett, we can talk about all this tomorrow."

"There's nothing to discuss. You're staying here. *Here,* Kate. Where I can take care of you and I know you're safe. All right, Freckles?"

"Even if I'm miserable?"

He dropped his hands to her shoulders and squeezed. "Tell me what makes you miserable, Kate. I'll take care of it. I'll make it better for you."

Kate wanted to push him away, *needed* to push him away. He was drunk and she didn't have the energy to deal with him tonight, not like this. But the instant she flattened her palms on his shirt, they stayed there. On his chest. Feeling his hard muscles through the fabric, his heart beating under her hands. Between her legs, she grew moist and hot.

When she was little, she'd wanted him because he was strong and protective, and her favorite boy of all the boys she'd ever met. But now she was older and a new kind of wanting tangled up inside her. Her breasts went heavy from the mere act of touching his chest through his shirt, and her nipples puckered against her nightshirt.

"Do me a favor, Kate?"

His voice slurring even more, Garrett sounded drunker by the second as he stroked her face with unsteady fingertips. Every pore in her body became aware of that whispery touch, causing shivers down her nerve endings.

"Stay with us. My mother loves you. Beth loves you, and so does her son." He seemed to wrack his brain for more to say. "And Molly. Molly loves you, Kate. She needs you. Julian, Landon, hell, everyone."

But not him?

She didn't know if she wanted to laugh or cry or hit him for excluding himself, but she already knew that she was a weight on him, a responsibility to him. That's what she'd always been. Forcing her arms to return to her sides, she sighed. "Garrett…"

"What will that obsessed client of yours, Missy Something, do without your currant muffins? What will I do? Hmm, Kate? It's a tragedy to think about it."

"I don't want to argue about this now, Garrett." She rubbed her temple.

"All right, Katie."

She blinked.

"All right?" she repeated.

Confused by his easy concession, which was not like Garrett at all, she suddenly heard him shift on the bed and spread his big body down the length beside her.

Eyes widening in horror, she heard him plump one of the two pillows.

"All right, Katie. We'll talk about it in the morning," he said in that deep, slurred voice.

She heard him shift once more, as if to get more comfortable. Sitting on the bed, frozen in disbelief, she managed to sputter, "You're not planning to *stay* here the night, are you?"

He made a move with his head that she couldn't see but rustled the pillow.

"Garrett, you moron, go to your *room*," she said, shoving at his arm a little.

He caught her hand and squeezed it. "Relax, you little witch. I'll go back to my room when I stop spinning. Come here and brace me down." He draped his arm around her shoulders and drew her to his side, and Kate was too stunned to do anything but play rag doll.

Minutes passed as she remained utterly still, every part of her body excruciatingly aware of his powerful arm. Garrett was not the touchy-feely brother; that was Julian. In fact, Garrett seemed to do his best not to touch her. But his guard was down and he seemed not to want to let *go* this time.

She frowned when he tightened his hold and slid his fingers up beneath the fall of her hair. Cupping her scalp, he pressed her face down to his chest.

"Garrett," Kate said, poking on his abs. They were hard as rocks under his shirt.

He breathed heavily. Oh, no. Seriously. Was he asleep?

"Garrett?"

She groaned when there was no response and wondered if she should move into Garrett's room and leave him to sleep here, because she was certainly not dragging him to his own room. He must weigh double what she did, even if he was all muscle, judging from the hardness of the arm around her and the abs she'd just poked.

Instead, she grumbled and complained under her breath, and ended up using her pillow as a barrier between them. She eased his arm from around her, setting it on the pillow. His hand was enormous between her fingers, and for a moment, she seemed to be unable to let go, kept her hand over his just to feel that he was not a figment of her imagination. Then she realized what she was doing and that it was stupid and foolish, and she yanked her hand away.

Damn him.

He was going to do everything possible to keep her in Texas, she knew.

But he wasn't going to take Florida away from her.

Oh, no, her life had stopped revolving around Garrett Gage ever since she'd decided she didn't want him anymore, and now she'd be damned before she let him screw up her perfect plans, too.

Three

Monday morning, business at the *San Antonio Daily* was more intense than normal.

Usually Landon, the eldest Gage brother, would bark about the grammar mistakes in that day's print edition. Julian John, the youngest, was no longer working at headquarters since he'd started his own PR firm, but he still occasionally dropped in and offered his services in weekly status meetings. Lately, Garrett had been focused on maneuvering their assets to make one of their greatest takeovers, one that would absorb Clarks Communications into the *Daily* and the rest of their holdings.

Which was why Cassandra Clarks was visiting today. She sat in Garrett's office, quietly eating the remaining muffin from the batch Kate had sent to the office this morning.

It made Garrett grumpy to see that muffin go.

But he feigned indifference as he flipped to the next page of the current stock statistics for Clarks Communications. Still, he wasn't really paying attention to their impressive growth numbers. Instead, he kept going back to Saturday night and Sunday morning.

He'd woken up alone, dressed in the most uncomfortable way possible, with a stiff back and the scent of Kate in bed, which had made him hard as marble.

Then he'd realized he was lying on Kate's old, frilly pink bed. Which he'd apparently decided to take over during the night while on a semidrunken spree.

Damn.

He'd immediately texted her Sunday morning, and even now, he kept glancing at his phone, replaying their conversation.

Sorry for crashing in last night.

You mean that was you? That's all right, at least u didn't break anything.

But my pride. And my back.

Ouch. Ok, but it's nothing my muffins won't cure.

Holy hell. Was she flirting with him?

I'm going to savor every bite.

He wasn't sure if he'd been flirting, too. *Savor every bite.* The alcohol had still been running through his system, clearly messing up his head. Thank God Kate hadn't replied after that last one. But she'd sent a dozen muffins this morning and he had gobbled three up with barely a drink of coffee. His experience with Kate's food was almost sexual.

He couldn't help it; it had always been like this since the beginning.

The first time she'd made chocolate-chip cookies on her own, Garrett had been fresh out of bed on a Sunday in his randy teen years. He'd been scouring the kitchen for breakfast and had shoved a warm cookie into his mouth, nodding when she'd asked if it was good. Then Kate had laughingly stepped up and brushed a crumb from the side of his mouth, and he'd almost swallowed the cookie whole.

Sometimes he waited until he was alone to eat her stuff. And he imagined he was licking her fingers when he wrapped his tongue around her sugary frostings. And when they had little sprinkles, he pictured her freckles.

He really should look into therapy.

Suddenly he heard Landon sigh and slap his copy of the report shut, and he was jerked back to the present.

"So if your brother is still not aware of our plans," he asked Cassandra, "why are you chickening out on selling?" The chair creaked as he leaned back, folding his arms over his chest.

Cassandra Clarks may have had the appearance of a blonde bombshell, but behind that "bimbo" facade, Garrett had learned, there was actually a brain. The woman was not only smart, but about as flexible on her terms as a damned wall.

Today she exuded casual confidence, slowly shaking her head as Landon explained his position.

"We're supposed to keep buying the stock until we get over twenty percent," Landon told her. "In a week, two at most, your brother's company will be ours before he even realizes we're in bed with him. No pun intended."

"None taken," Cassandra said, eyeing Landon judiciously as she finally stopped shaking her head and allowed him to continue.

"Once we secure your remaining thirty-two percent, it puts us in control, and it leaves you a very wealthy woman, Cassie."

"That's the problem. My brother will know I sold to you. He will destroy me and anything else I have," she said, her entire countenance clouded with worry. "What I wanted to propose to Garrett on Saturday before he cut me short was a marriage of convenience. My brother has control of my stake in the company now, but if I marry, he won't have control over financial decisions regarding my stake anymore. My husband can take over the shares and compensate me discreetly. It would be an easy arrangement, and over in six months, where we'll both happily walk away with what we want. Me with my money, you with the stock."

Garrett remained silent as he absorbed the proposal.

He met Cassandra's gaze unflinchingly, the ambitious businessman in him wanting to say yes. But in his mind, he went back to waking up to Kate's scent on the pillow, to the memory of somehow holding her in his arms.

He tugged at the collar of his shirt several times, aware that his frown was pinching into his face. "I'm afraid that's not an option, Cassandra," he said, signaling for his assistant to refill all their coffees.

Hell, he might even start drinking whiskey at this hour. Because *marriage*?

"Like Landon said, we're willing to buy those shares up front. No need to get dramatic about it."

"I'm afraid selling out front is not an option. My brother is… You don't know him. Marriage is the only way I can free myself of his control. You take the shares, transfer the money to me, and then we walk six months later with irreconcilable differences. It's a marriage in name only and we have nothing to lose. That's the only way it's happening: you marry me and by right take my thirty-two percent."

Landon's and Garrett's eyes met across the conference table. Landon's gray gaze almost looked silver in his concern.

"Look, Cassandra," he started. "We're almost at twenty percent already. We'll buy your position outright at way above market price. At fifty-two percent, we'll be in control and can get your brother out of there. He won't have a say in the matter anymore."

She shook her head, her eyes tearing up. "You don't know him. He has a say in a lot of things in my life. I don't get real financial independence until I marry—can't you understand?"

She reached across the table and squeezed Garrett's hand as if she were falling from a precipice and he'd been appointed the task of hauling her up.

"It'll be a marriage in name only, but I can make it sweet for you. I can. I know I'm pretty. I think you're an incredibly sexy man."

His stomach turned, and he was amazed at how calmly he looked back at her. Several years ago, he'd probably have done it without thinking. He was a businessman, after all. She was an attractive woman offering something and he had nothing to lose. People got married and divorced for other reasons; why not for business?

He just didn't have the energy for it right now. What

he'd told Kate at his party had been the truth. All he wanted was for Kate to be home. He would dedicate every waking moment to making that happen. Life without Kate to him was…unimaginable.

He was selfish when it came to her.

He was stupid, unreasonable and stubborn when it came to her.

But Cassandra Clarks didn't know this. She didn't know that as he sat in this chair, and let her squeeze his hand, every cell in his body was burning with yearning for another woman. He'd burned for so many years, it was a miracle he hadn't turned to ashes by now.

"We'll talk about this during the week, see what we can come up with," Landon finally said. In silence, the Gage brothers both stood up to dismiss her.

Cassandra went over to shake Landon's hand, and then returned to Garrett, giving him a hug that crushed all of her assets against his chest. He could see she was trying very hard to look seductive, but he saw fear and frustration glowing in the depths of her eyes as she eased back.

Cassandra was blonde and beautiful, and she also appeared desperate. If Garrett had an ounce of mercy in him at all, he'd find a way to help her. "You'll let me know?" she asked hopefully.

He nodded. "You'll hear from us in a week or two."

"Marriage," Garrett grumbled as the door closed behind her. He fell back on his chair and rubbed his temples as he tried to think of a way they could free Cassandra from her brother's grip and get their hands on Clarks Communications.

"In name only," Landon said, gazing out the window with a thoughtful frown.

"I'm not interested in a fake marriage, Lan."

Landon sighed and spun around, coming back to the table. "Do you have any other ideas?"

Garrett lifted his shoulders. "We find another fish in the pond, let go of Clarks," he said bitterly, glaring down at his coffee.

The silence that followed made it clear that neither Landon nor he was ecstatic at the possibility. Clarks was the biggest fish in their pond, and if they were smart— which the Gage brothers were—they would secure it at all costs.

When evaluating the big picture, six months wasn't a lot of time, if it meant getting Clarks into their pocket. And Garrett had everything riding on this project. Currently, Clarks posed a threat. But once they'd acquired the company, it would be a huge asset for the Gage conglomerate.

But at the cost of a fake wedding?

Hell, it's not like you plan to ever marry. Why not at least do some business?

The two large doors of the conference room knocked open, and in strode Julian John, casual as could be, blond and Hollywoodesque, an hour after the scheduled meeting time. Behind him, one of the secretaries rushed to close the doors.

Jules never said good-morning, but then they were brothers. They didn't have to.

He regarded the pair of somber men seated at the conference table and remained standing. "I had something to do, so drop the long faces, both of you."

Landon arched a challenging brow and leaned back in his chair. "I hope it was business and not you playing around while we try to take over Clarks Communications."

"Do you even remember I no longer work here? I'm here to offer my assistance, that's all. Molls needed me this morning."

"Tell Molly to leave the baby-making for the evening," said Landon with a devilish smile.

Heading to his chair, Julian rolled his eyes at his brother. "I picked up some medicine for Kate, idiot, after Molly took her to the doctor. And if I want to make babies in the morning with my Molls, I sure as hell will make them without your permi—"

"What the hell is wrong with Kate? Is she sick?"

Julian's attention swung back to Garrett, and his blond eyebrows flew upward. "Why? Are you a doctor?"

"Is Kate," Garrett slowly enunciated, "sick? Ill? Feeling badly?"

Julian's eyes twinkled like they did when he was up to no good. "Don't you think it's about time you did something about how you feel for her, Dr. Garrett?"

"I feel responsible for her, that's how I feel," he gritted out. "And right now I'm going to punch your face if you don't tell me what's wrong with her."

Plopping into his chair, Julian grabbed his folder and started scanning the contents. "She's running a fever. A high fever. Molly took her home to stay with her, and I was the guy who picked up the prescription and dropped it off."

Garrett's overwhelming protectiveness surged with a vengeance. Kate was never sick. Ever. He didn't like knowing she was sick at all, and now, he felt sick inside. "I could've picked it up for her."

"And tear you away from Cassandra Clarks and our

plans for world domination?" Julian said. "No, bro. If that girl is selling anything, she'll sell it to you. I saw her with you at your party. I think she digs you even if you don't dig her."

"She digs him enough to marry him." Landon filled his brother in, then broached the topic currently setting Garrett's brain on overdrive. "Is Kate still planning to move to Miami?"

"As far as I know, nothing has changed her mind. But Molly's privately freaking out about it," Julian said, his expression going somber. Garrett knew his younger brother was intensely territorial and protective of Molly, and even if he was usually cool as a cucumber, it must irk him not to be able to do anything to spare her any pain.

"So is Beth," Landon murmured sadly.

Garrett looked down at the conference table and scowled. Nobody in this goddamned world could be as freaked out about it as he was.

He pictured Kate in Miami, sick and alone. Who would take her to the doctor? Who would even know that she was sick? The thought was so disturbing he pulled at his tie, feeling choked to death.

But as much as he loathed that she was sick today, maybe this would provide an opportunity to make Kate see how indispensable family that protected and cared for you was. Also, her stubbornness might be at a low point because of the fever, and he might be able to talk to her without putting her on the defensive.

"You guys don't mind if I take the rest of the day off? If there's even a chance of making her stay, I need to filter through her defenses and find out why the hell she wants to *leave*."

"You mean you want to bulldoze through her walls,

without any tact whatsoever, and screw everything?" Julian teased.

"Jules, I happen to think Kate is the one who's bull-dozed through Garrett's defenses with her imminent departure," Landon said.

Both his brothers looked terribly amused.

Garrett shoved his arms into his jacket and grabbed his iPhone. "Screw you. You guys know how hotheaded Kate is when she gets something in her mind—at least today she won't have all the energy to fight me. Hell, you took two months off for your honeymoon, Landon, and you don't even work here anymore. Jules. I'm taking a day off, no matter what you both have to say."

Julian answered, with a laugh, "We have a lot to say about it, bro. We just won't be saying it to you."

"So I know you're going to find all sorts of things wrong with my stupid soup, but it's still chicken and broth and I'm not the baker here, okay, Kate?"

Molly set the tray with the steaming bowl on a chair by the window and parted the drapes.

Kate almost hissed as she raised her hand to shield herself from the sunlight.

"Wow. You look so bad, Kate."

Molly's blue eyes brimmed with sisterly pity as Kate sat up in bed and tried to peel her sweaty T-shirt off her skin. The cotton was soaked from when the fever had started dropping during her nap. Her hair was plastered to the sides of her face as if with glue.

"I feel worse than I look, I guarantee," Kate rasped out, her throat raw.

She had strep throat. Which meant she had nausea, a

throat that ached like hell and a fever that was kicking her fanny. *Wonderful.*

"Let me run a bath for you."

Molly disappeared into the bathroom, and Kate groaned when she heard the loud chime of the doorbell.

"I'll get that, Kate. Don't even move a finger. I'll be back in a bit. In the meantime, you can eat my sucky soup," Molly said, poking her head back into the bedroom. Kate smiled weakly and nodded.

As her little sister went down the hall to the front door, Kate marveled at how sharp and efficient she was being.

Molly had always been a red-hot mess, but today Kate truly felt Molly's motherly instincts surge to the forefront as she tried to pamper her big sis.

It was a rare event when Kate succumbed to being sick. She just didn't have time for it. What the hell was wrong with her?

The stress of her move had her sleepless and anxious and now, apparently, had left her with no defenses against strep.

Sighing and plopping back on her pillow, she heard voices in the living room. Then she heard footsteps approaching. Kate opened her eyes, and her stomach dropped when she saw him.

The last man she wanted to see.

Or to be more precise, the last man she wanted to see *her* like this.

She flew upright to a sitting position, her cheeks warming in an awful blush when Garrett stopped at the threshold. Her blood bubbled in her veins, and the feeling was unbidden and unwanted. He looked positively beautiful, his shoulders about a yard wide, his patterned tie slightly undone. His dark hair stood up on end as if he'd been pulling at it on his drive over.

He was honestly the most beautiful thing she'd seen all day.

She indulged in a small moment of grief as she realized that while he looked so excellent, she'd never looked worse.

"Did you lose your GPS? Your office is the other way," she said, merely because attitude was the only thing she had left now.

"I followed another compass today." A tender look warmed his eyes as he stepped inside and shut the door behind him.

He removed his jacket, and her pulse jumped at each flex of his muscles under his snowy shirt.

"How do you feel, Freckles?" He draped his jacket on the back of her desk chair and rolled his sleeves to his elbows. "We should've made you drink tequila Saturday. That would've killed anything off."

All the grogginess fled from her when he seized the tray with the soup and brought it to the bed.

"Molly suggests you eat her sucky soup."

Kate grimaced. "I'm not hungry, Garrett," she said in her slightly raspy strep-throat voice. "There's no need to check up on me."

He settled down on the edge of the bed and lifted the spoon, his eyes glimmering in pure devil-like mischief. "Starve the virus, feed the fever."

"And that means, Confucius…?"

"You need to feed your immune system. Come on. Open your mouth."

After a brief hesitation, she parted her lips and Garrett offered her the soup. Her stomach was warmed by the intent look on Garrett's face as she curled her lips around the spoon. He tipped it back, and she swallowed. Then he lowered the spoon, watching her.

"It's not that bad," she said. The soup slid down her throat and coated her sore spots. "But it's still a little too hot."

He immediately set the tray at the foot of the bed. "Molls said you're about to take a bath? Would you like to hop in there now?"

Before she could even nod, he disappeared into the bathroom, where she heard the water stop, and then he returned. He looked so sexy but at the same time, so domesticated; she almost felt giddy at all this sweet male attention.

"While you relax in your bath, I'll go get my laptop and briefcase, all right?" He signaled toward the window at his Audi parked outside. "Since she's having such success as an artist, I told Molly I'd stay here so she could go to her studio and finish up her pending works before the wedding."

"Wh-what? No! No! I don't need a babysitter!"

"Good because I didn't hire one." The smile he shot her was rather wolfish, and he looked very damned pleased about himself. "It's just you and me now. I can see you're excited about it."

"As I am about having strep!" she countered.

He burst out laughing, and once again she felt things she didn't really want to feel. Kate was going to kill her sister. Kill her. But of course Molly must've been thrilled about this turn of events. She kept insisting that Kate should stay in town until some miracle happened and Kate and Garrett finally became an item. *Ha*. She was clearly still such an innocent.

And right now, especially, not even a miracle would make someone want Kate. Only a thing called strep throat wanted her.

And just then, she remembered the exquisite feel of Garrett, big and warm, in bed with her Saturday night.

As the thought rushed through her, Kate ducked her head to hide her blush, never wanting Garrett to know the effect he had on her. On the night of his birthday, she'd been so angry and frustrated. She'd felt all kinds of unwanted arousal while he'd slept soundly next to her. So she'd promised herself she would get over him. And she would. No matter what. She merely wished that he, of all the men in the world, hadn't seen her in this state.

"You want help getting to the tub?" He gestured toward the bathroom. She was still in bed, holding the sheets to the top of her neck like a shield.

"I can walk," she answered the moment she realized how silly she must look. Frowning in annoyance at her own prudish attitude, she kicked the sheets aside, then realized that her T-shirt had ridden up to her hips. As she struggled out of bed, Garrett got a perfect view of her pink panties.

He whipped his eyes away, but not before she saw that he *saw*. Her pink panties. And her toned thighs.

Garrett's face hardened instantly, and he rubbed the nape of his neck as Kate felt a red-hot flush creep up her body.

"So, you have strep?" he asked, looking away quickly.

"It's very contagious. You should leave." In fact, she'd probably even had it incubating when he'd slept in her bed the other night. The thought of giving him strep made her insides twist in foreboding. "You should really leave, Garrett."

"I'll leave when your fever's gone, Katie."

Groaning in disgust at his stubbornness, she went into the bathroom and locked the door behind her. Oddly, she felt acutely aware of her nakedness when she stripped. Aware, also, of only one measly door separating her from him.

After double-checking the lock, she settled in the tub. The water felt so warm. She closed her eyes and sighed as she dunked her head and slowly surfaced, starting to relax.

As the minutes passed, she couldn't stop wondering what Garrett was doing out in her room. She definitely heard noises, and she figured he must be setting up a miniature office. The thought both annoyed her and… didn't. He looked extremely good today. But she couldn't help but wonder what the purpose of this sudden attention was. Of course something sneaky was going on. She had no doubt this all had to do with her leaving for Florida—and Garrett intending to convince her not to.

No way are you going to stop me, Garrett Gage.

She scowled at the thought. She hadn't even had boyfriends because of him. Directly or indirectly, he'd been responsible for Kate waiting to lose her virginity until she was over twenty-one and then she'd lost it to someone she didn't even like all that much. Even then, though, she'd kept expecting him to one day realize they were meant for each other. Now she was determined to stop waiting for anything Garrett-related.

Fiercely resolved, she came out minutes later, wrapped in a towel, bathed, refreshed and wet.

She found, not to her surprise, that Garrett was already settled in her room. He lounged back in a chair with his laptop open on her small desk before him. He'd also turned the chair so that it was facing the bed, rather than the window. He looked as out of place in her feminine bedroom as a bear would.

He glanced up when she padded barefoot toward her dresser, and an irresistibly devastating grin appeared on his face. "You already look better."

"Actually, I feel tons better." Clutching the towel to her chest, she rummaged through her drawers and was about to try to get dressed under the towel when she remembered to say, "Look away for a second, please."

As she selected her new panties, purple this time, she asked, "Are you looking away?"

"What do you think, Kate?" he asked, annoyed.

She took that as a yes and quickly let the towel drop and slipped into her panties. Even though he was looking away, her cheeks flushed red at the thought of him being so close when she was naked. She quickly slipped on her bra, still feeling hot inside, but then she realized he would probably be as moved by her nakedness as a sofa. The man was completely immune to her.

Then again, her butt was quite nice thanks to her Pilates classes. As she was thinking these thoughts and smoothing her panties over the curves in question, a strange silence settled in the room.

Garrett's voice was deceptively calm when she reached into her drawer again.

"Did you really think I'd look away, Kate?"

Kate's stomach clenched, but she went about the task of selecting a T-shirt.

And now she could feel his eyes were definitely on her.

Boring holes into her bottom, actually.

And suddenly she really prayed that it was, indeed, a very nice bottom.

"Please don't tell me you were looking," she threatened, starting to panic. She broke out into a fresh sweat as the fever continued dropping after her bath.

As she grabbed a T-shirt with a Minnie Mouse image on the front and pulled it on, she heard a deep male groan.

"Freckles, I'm not made of stone you know."

Garrett sounded grumpy, as if he was in danger of getting strep, too.

"Really? I thought you were." Instead of being embarrassed, she was suddenly amused as she pulled the T-shirt as low as possible and turned around. But her smile froze on her face.

Garrett sat like a marble statue on the chair, his muscled arms crossed, his forearms corded with veins, his lips hard and completely unsmiling. His face was harsh with intensity, and his eyes were the blackest she'd ever seen them. There was such an unearthly sheen in them, Kate stopped breathing.

They stared at each other for a heart-stopping moment, and the atmosphere seemed to morph, becoming heavy and thick with something inexplicable. There was a deeper significance to their stare that she couldn't quite pinpoint, but it felt like a delicate thread between them was pulling tight.

It hurt. This strange link. It felt threatening.

It hurt, and ached in all kinds of places inside her.

Garrett put his forehead in his hand for a moment, then sighed and ran a big, tanned hand down his face in pure frustration. "Look, Katie."

"Look, Garrett, you need to stop this now."

"Stop what?"

They stared once more, and the atmosphere in the room continued feeling heavy and odd. Kate's nerves could barely handle it.

"I know what you're trying to do, and it's not going to work," she finally said.

His eyes remained almost predatory in their intensity. Finally he raised one sleek black eyebrow. "My plot to save the world, to keep Kate in Texas, won't work, even if I put in some good hours of doctoring time?"

"It won't work."

"So you didn't mean it the night of my birthday when you said that we would talk about it later?"

"We'd both been drinking. Whatever we said that night was the alcohol talking."

"All right, so today the strep is talking. When is Kate going to talk to me?"

"I'm talking to you now."

His eyebrows fell low over his eyes. His shirt stretched over his square shoulders as he sat back, his muscled arms still crossed over his chest. "Then tell me if you're leaving because of a man. First. And second, you're going to tell me who."

"Ha. This is my house. I run it. So I say who has firsts and seconds here, not you."

She bent to put on some socks. A rivulet of water slid along her toned legs, and when she straightened, she saw his eyes had darkened even more. He continued to stare at her legs for a wildly erotic moment.

Her pulse jumped at the thought of him touching her—of him even *wanting* to touch her—and her hands trembled as she bent her head and slowly wrapped the discarded towel around her wet hair.

When she straightened, Garrett's expression had turned bleak as a funeral, and he pushed to his feet, stalking over like a pissed-off predator. "What do you need so you can get back in the damned bed, Kate?"

"I don't want to get into bed. I've been there all day. My fever is dropping and I'm sweating. I feel hot."

"Then put something on, would you!" He signaled at her long legs, and a wash of feminine awareness swept through her when his eyes raked her up and down as if he couldn't help himself.

She laughed nervously and glanced away so that he wouldn't notice his effect on her; then she hopped into a comfortable pair of white cotton shorts she used for yoga sometimes.

Garrett seemed completely disturbed and grumpy... but more than that, he seemed alert. Did this mean she'd finally gotten past one of Garrett's walls?

She almost laughed. She'd always tried many subtle ways to get his male attention. Who would have thought she just needed to do a little striptease?

It's too late, Kate. You don't want him anymore. You want a new start—without him.

Turning in sudden annoyance, she shoved at his chest so he stepped out of her personal space. "Just go home, Garrett. You don't have to do this. Aren't you working on that big deal all your brothers are talking about?"

He looked agitated and started pacing around, scowling down at the carpet. "There's nothing I can do about it today. We're ironing out the details."

"Well, go iron them out somewhere else."

"On the bed, Freckles! Unless you like your soup cold!"

With a complaining sound, Kate plopped down on the

bed and crossed her legs under her body. He expelled a breath, as if finally appeased; he was just so handsome her heart ached. She propped her head back on the headboard as he brought back the tray, and she quietly studied him as he fed her.

Garrett Gage was one of the least emotionally accessible men Kate had ever met, and to see him do something so honestly sweet for her triggered a wealth of unreasonable emotions in her chest.

She didn't want to feel giddy and protected and cared for. But she did. She felt safe. And fiercely achy for so much more. His dark espresso eyes wouldn't stop watching her mouth as he guided the spoon inside, and out, and it made every time she wrapped her lips around the spoon unbearably…intimate.

Suddenly all she could hear was the sound of their breathing in the bedroom. Hers was not all that steady. His was inexplicably slow and deep, his chest extending slowly under his shirt as those dark, thick-lashed, half-mast eyes remained on her face.

"Poor Jules. I swear Molly doesn't cook for anything," Kate whispered, anxious to break the silence.

Now that she was able to taste the soup better, she definitely knew her little sister could use a little cooking advice from her.

Garrett chuckled. The sound was rich and male as he set down the spoon. "He's in love with her, Katie. She can feed him cotton balls and he'll be content."

"I love how they love each other."

Suddenly feeling drained, she shook her head when Garrett offered more soup. She slid down the bed a little so that the back of her head could rest on her pillow.

The thought of Julian and Molly made the ache in her chest multiply tenfold.

"They're not afraid to," she added.

Garrett didn't respond. He merely set the tray aside and turned thoughtfully back to her. "I wouldn't let fear keep me from someone," he said then, his voice a low murmur.

"No? Then what would?"

His powerful shoulders lifted in a noncommittal shrug, and then he said, "If you love someone, you want what's best for them. Even if it means it's not you."

Something in his words caused a little ribbon of pain to unravel within her. Had he ever felt anything for her, and thought that he wasn't good enough for her?

No. How could he not be good enough for anyone? He was honorable and dedicated, fiercely passionate about those he loved, as protective as an angry panther.

"Garrett, you don't have to stay. I know you told Molly you would but I'd rather you go," she said, getting sleepier by the second. "The antibiotics and steroids make me dizzy anyway, so I'll probably sleep all afternoon. And if you stay here I'm going to give you strep."

The tenderness that liquefied his gaze suddenly made her feel even more soft and languid. "You're not giving me anything. Relax and I'll be here when you wake up."

His voice was so soothing and gentle she couldn't help but nod and close her eyes. As she heard him take the tray to the kitchen, she snuggled into her pillow, her stomach warmed with Molly's sucky soup, which, even if tasteless, had served its purpose well. Ever since Molly had moved in with Julian, the house had seemed so quiet. Just knowing Garrett was around right now made her feel safe and protected.

The steroids were kicking in as well as the antibiotics, and her fever seemed to be breaking.

New beads of perspiration popped onto her brow, and a new, unexpected heaviness settled in her chest as she thought of her move to Florida and how she wouldn't see Garrett and Molly and all her loved ones as frequently as she did now.

She sighed when she felt something cool and damp slide along her forehead. Her pulse skittered when she realized Garrett was stroking her face with a cool towel, and she felt out of breath as she murmured, "That feels good."

He dragged the damp cloth along her cheek, and the cool mist on her skin made her nipples bead under her T-shirt. His voice was low and sensually hypnotic. "So of all the states, why Florida?" He ran the towel along the length of her bare arms, and her nipples turned hard as stones.

With a delicious shiver, she sighed and leaned her cheek to her right, into his chest. "Some of my college friends live in Miami Beach. And I'm a sun person."

She hadn't realized she was grabbing onto his arm, but she knew that she didn't want to let go. He smelled so good and felt warm and substantial, so she kept her arms curled around his elbow. God, she'd done the impossible to get this man to notice her. The impossible. She'd dated men she hadn't even liked. She'd said she'd marry other men. Ignored Garrett and paid attention to everyone else. It had made him scowl, but that had been the whole extent of his reactions to her efforts.

It had been infuriating and disheartening.

He really did see her as some sort of friendly sister, while Kate had fantasized about him for decades. She

hated that she never could really enjoy sex with her partners because a part of her heart had always belonged to
this man.

This man who now caressed her neck with that cloth,
and made her new purple panties damp with wanting.
Even if she'd convinced herself she didn't love him anymore, her body was still hazardously attracted to his.
Hell, if she weren't sick, she would open her eyes and
kiss him even if he didn't want her to. She'd just go crazy
and kiss him, because that was the only thing she'd never
tried, of all the crazy stunts she'd pulled to get him to
notice her. She had his attention with Florida. But this
was no longer a stunt.

She had to leave. And she had to leave now.

So that when she came for a visit, she would have a
new life, a steady boyfriend and an equally great catering business in Miami, and when she saw Garrett, she
would see what she had been meant to see all along. A
friend and a brother figure.

"Do you want me to bring my laptop here?" he whispered in her ear, his voice strangely husky. "Kate?"

She nodded, not opening her eyes as she released
him and waited, with a new kind of fever, for him to
come back.

Garrett was hard as granite and hated that he was,
but he was trying his damnedest to ignore it as he set
his laptop on the nightstand. He kept the computer shut,
and instead kicked off his shoes and plopped down on
the bed next to Kate, stretching his legs out as he put his
arm around her shoulders, sensing her need for comfort.

She'd been holding his arm so hard, he hadn't wanted
to move.

Hell, his back had gone stiff as a board as soon as her fingers had curled around him. He'd desperately wanted her touch and at the same time, he'd been distressed over the way his body responded to it. In the end, he'd wanted it more than he'd disliked it, and he'd come back. For more. Like a needy dog wanting a bone.

When she'd been getting dressed, he had thought he'd have a heart attack at the sight of that beautiful bare bottom. Kate was willowy and slim, and her wet hair had so temptingly caressed her shoulders. In a fraction of a second, he'd visualized about a dozen things he wanted to do to her, a dozen ways he wanted to kiss and feel her.

Now she was cuddling against his side, with that cute little T-shirt, and that soft, almost dreamlike smile on her lips.

He put his arm around her shoulders, and she sighed in contentment and snuggled into his chest, clutching a piece of his collar. The gesture was so possessive and sweet his chest knotted with emotion as he set his head back on the headboard and held her to him.

What would it be like to marry someone like Kate? Someone he cared for. He wanted. Not for any other purpose but because he needed her by his side.

Flooded with tenderness, he felt her squirm to get closer, and her T-shirt rode up to reveal…those purple panties that made his mouth water.

Just give me something to think about other than those long legs. Those sweet purple panties…

Her hair was still wrapped in a white towel, and Garrett gently unwound it and ran it slowly over her scalp, seeing her lashes resting on her cheekbones as she let him dry her hair, her skin pale in the sunlight.

He wanted to kiss those soft lips, which were natural and bare today, peachy in color. He wanted to slide his hands up her arms, touch her bare skin and memorize its texture, its color, its temperature. He wanted her eyelashes to flutter apart, so he could stare into her eyes and say something about the things roiling inside of him.

Instead, he finished drying her hair and tossed the towel onto the chair by the window. He shifted back to her side, noticing how she stiffened and tightened her hold on his collar until he wrapped his arm tightly around her again, and she relaxed.

He yanked off his tie and set it on the nightstand, and then wrapped his other arm around her waist and set his jaw on the top of her head. Her hair smelled of raspberries. He'd wanted to know? Yeah. He had his answer. And now his blood heated with one whiff. He grabbed the bed sheet and pulled it up over them both, not wanting her to notice his painfully pulsing erection if she opened her eyes.

She sighed and turned to him, snuggling closer. Her breasts brushed his ribs, and his body went crazy. He dragged his fingers down her shoulder and to her waist and stroked the little bit of skin exposed from her raised T-shirt.

He kissed her forehead. She didn't stir. Sweet baby, she looked so vulnerable today. He knew she was strong, but he still wanted to coddle her. He looked at her lips and ran a hand down her damp hair. He'd never wanted anything more than to make this woman happy. And right now, he wanted to kiss her.

"You awake, Kate?" he asked, his voice barely recognizable, it was so gruff.

She was breathing evenly, which confirmed she'd fallen asleep. Garrett slid his hand up and down her arm, his heart pounding. He bent his head and kissed her freckles, a light, dry kiss, and then he stole a kiss from her soft, marshmallow mouth.

Intoxicating. Soft. Female. *Perfect*.

Coming undone, he drank in her expression. Her eyes remained shut, her lashes forming titian-colored half-moons against her cheekbones.

He stroked the back of one finger down her jaw. She was everything he'd wanted and never allowed himself to have, and she was breathing like a baby, sleeping like one. He heard his own haggard exhale as he tried to draw back. He bent down again, softly brushing his lips over her forehead, then her nose, her cheekbones, her jaw…until he fitted his mouth back over her lips and whispered, "Kate."

She remained asleep, but sighed at her name and opened her mouth under his, her breath blending with his. Desire exploded in the pit of his stomach. The urge to splay his body over hers, open her lips wider, search her tongue with his, bury himself inside her, was so acute, he had to drag his jaw up her temple as he fought for control, completely infuriated with himself.

What was he doing?

Since when had he become a masochist?

He'd always known he couldn't have Kate. He'd done everything in his power to stay away from her. He'd hurt her enough, and he didn't truly feel he could ever make a woman happy when he had so many regrets on his shoulders.

It was hard to believe you were ever worthy when someone had died to give you your life.

But the thought of Kate leaving had set a beast loose inside him. He wanted to protect her and look after her, and just imagining that she could meet a man in Florida, a man she could have powerful feelings for, made him feel rabid to stake a claim.

Even now, when there were no states separating them and he was holding her snug in his arms, it just didn't seem like he could get close enough to her. He'd spent years pushing her away, and now it felt like she wouldn't ever let him back in.

And if she did, he didn't even know what he'd do with himself or this wanting.

Four

More than a week later, Kate's wood-paneled kitchen was a mess of cooking utensils as she, Beth and Molly fiddled around on the kitchen island. Kate and Beth had a looming deadline to cater a baby shower this afternoon. Worse, now only Beth would be going to set up, since Kate had had a last-minute change of plans.

Molly had been the one to deliver the plan-altering news less than an hour ago, when she'd casually mentioned that Julian had been asked to fill in for Garrett at the *San Antonio Daily* this morning. Garrett had come down with strep.

Kate had been floored. How could she not go and take care of him?

"You love that man like crazy, Kay. Just look at how you're running to his side at the first sign of trouble! I just can't see why you're so determined to leave Texas,"

Molly complained as she licked the remaining vanilla topping off a discarded spatula. Her cheek was smeared with a streak of red.

Since she was an artist, Kate's little sister always had smudges on her clothes, hair or face, but it only enhanced her bohemian style and made her look even cuter—especially to Julian, who would always tickle and poke her whenever she was "messy."

"You know, I thought you guys would bond over your strep throat," Molly continued with a frown. "You still could now that you gave it to him. Did he kiss you?"

Kate clicked the oven light on and peered through the window to check on Garrett's muffins. "Molly, please start supporting me a little more in my decision. I've told you I'll fly over here to see you as much as I can. We can talk on Skype all the time, too. And of course we didn't kiss. I'm not stupid! Who kisses a sick person?" Kate said in disgust.

"Someone who loves them."

She snorted. "We're not you and Julian."

"Kate, the day Julian and I got back together, he and Garrett had a talk. Julian tells me that the man is severely and painfully in love with you and doesn't even know it."

Kate's heart stuttered, and at that moment, her chest felt as spongy as the muffins she was watching through the oven window. She remembered the way Garrett had taken care of her the day she'd come home with strep.

He'd checked in on her every afternoon afterward, but that first day, he'd spent the night with her. A quiver raced down her skin when she remembered how they'd cuddled all night. He'd stayed dressed, like he had when he'd been drunk and crashed in her bedroom the night of his birthday, but he'd held her as if she was precious.

When she'd woken up in the middle of the night to realize he was holding her, she had been engulfed with such a feeling of happiness beyond what she'd ever felt before. On impulse, she'd stroked her fingers along his stubbled jaw, and he'd made a strange, groaning noise as he'd turned his face into her touch, his voice deliciously groggy. "You feel all right? Do you need anything?"

"Sorry. I'm perfect. Go to sleep."

She'd cuddled back down to hear his heart beat under her ear, and she'd wanted to stay awake just to memorize its rhythm. She'd never, ever, felt so whole. Which only made her feel sorry for herself now. Because they hadn't even kissed. Had he made her melt over some snuggles?

It wasn't just the snuggling. It was also that they'd known each other for so long they didn't even need to talk. When she'd woken up, he'd been awake and watching her with a smile on his handsome face, and his eyes had seemed to turn liquid as he'd run a finger down her cheek. "Fever's gone," he'd whispered.

And she'd almost swallowed her tongue and nodded. Because she'd known there was nothing she could do for the other kind of fever inside her. She'd had to remind herself that this was Garrett, a very stubborn, hardheaded Gage man, and that he wasn't her lover or a Prince Charming. Garrett had some serious baggage to deal with, and Kate had once loved him—too hard, and for too long, and too painfully—to allow so much as a little flicker of hope to linger.

Julian might think that Garrett had feelings for Kate, but all he surely felt was the same thing he'd always felt. Guilt and responsibility.

Beth spoke up from her corner of the island, where she busily worked her artistic skills on a tray of cookies for the shower. "You're shaking your head at me now, Kate, but now that I think about it, I also suspect Garrett has always had a thing for you."

"No, he doesn't. And I'm sick and tired of chasing after him like some tramp," Kate countered as she dumped the egg shells in the trash and wiped the granite counter clean.

Molly laughed. "Kate, you've never chased after Garrett, at least not blatantly. Men are sometimes stupid about those things—you need to be frank with them."

Frank?

All right, so let's be frank.

Kate had stripped in front of him. She had almost kissed him in her bed when he'd dragged that cool cloth around her body. Hell, she was pretty sure if she hadn't been sick, she would have thrown herself at him. And she'd done this with her plane ticket to Florida already sitting in her night drawer. That just couldn't be good. Could it?

She'd lain there with her eyes closed as he ran that cloth over her, and she'd been shaking in her bones as she'd imagined what it would feel like to be kissed by him. She'd even had dreams about it all during the week. Heat had spread through her at one particularly erotic one, when she'd felt him touch her aching nipples, then kiss them....

That night in her bed, she'd wanted to dissolve into his strong arms when he'd held her, and when he'd dried her hair, she'd been so affected and felt such desire pool between her thighs, she'd almost released an embarrassing sound that only her raw throat—abused by the strep—had been able to stop.

No. If she stayed here, she wouldn't be able to stay

away from Garrett, and seeing him while not having him would be torment. It had always been so, but after the night of his birthday, when he'd cradled her face and tried to tell her he'd do anything to fix her "dilemma," and after he'd nursed her when she was sick, it felt doubly so.

It.

Hurt.

The man might not love her as his mate, but he cared about her, and Kate knew this was exactly why she'd never be able to ever come clean with her feelings. He'd either feel awful about not responding, or feel pity for her and do something gallant like keep on sacrificing himself for her to make up for what he "took."

She. Had. To. Leave!

And start fresh, without Garrett's shadow torment-ing and taunting her.

She knew it would be difficult. But she still had to leave. She had to give herself the chance, and Garrett his freedom.

Thinking about him, sick and bedridden today, made her stomach knot as she put on a floral-print oven mitt and bent over to pull the tray of muffins out of the oven. She'd made this particular recipe because it had lately become her favorite. The muffins were healthy and yummy, made of almond flour, with orange zest and black currants and walnuts. She set them on the cool-ing grill and prepared a small basket while the chicken soup finished.

"Food. That's how you guys make love, I swear. Those sounds he makes when he eats your cookies."

"Whoa!" Beth said from the corner, where she was now adding the decorations to the pacifier-shaped choc-olate lollipops. "You're getting wicked, Molls!"

Molly laughed, fairly radiating mischief.

Beth laughed and shook her head, but then turned sober as she watched Kate stir the chicken soup. "Kate, it's not a bad idea. If you're taking that over to his apartment, you could totally seduce him. I mean, clearly the man wants you. Every time you're not looking, he's staring in your direction. Maybe if you guys work it out, you wouldn't be so determined to leave?"

"You're confusing him with Landon looking at you, Beth," Kate countered, turning off the stove. "Plus, I won't begin with the way Julian looks at you, Molly—oh, Lord, that man loves you."

"Does he?" Molly said with a cheeky grin, twirling the tip of her ponytail in one finger. "I don't ever tire of him telling me he does. God, I can't wait to marry him and make him all mine."

Looking thoughtful, Beth followed Kate to the cupboard as she pulled out a glass container.

"Kate, if Garrett didn't want you he wouldn't spend all day taking care of you when you look like leftovers."

Kate rolled her eyes. "Thanks, Beth. With friends like you, who needs an enemy?"

"Kate! Come on, listen to us. We're dishing out good advice here."

"Even if he 'wanted me' for one crazy night and I managed to get him to drop his guard," Kate said, facing them, "I want love. If I can't have what you guys have, I'd rather be alone."

Molly sighed. For the first time since her Florida announcement, Kate could tell that the possibility of her moving to another state was truly sinking in. It hurt, too. To hurt them. She knew they didn't want her to leave, but she also knew that deep down, they understood.

"I still think you could find love here in Texas." Despite her words, Molly sounded more dejected now. "Garrett would make a *great* husband once he realizes everything that happened is *not his fault*."

"Molly, please, I can't talk about this anymore. I don't love him anymore, and he's not interested in me. When will you guys understand? Garrett always gets what he wants. He's not a subtle man. If he wanted me, don't you think he'd go for me?"

When Beth and Molly exchanged sad looks and fell silent, Kate's stomach sank. Well, what had she expected? Had she wanted one of them to lie and contradict her? Maybe so, but the truth was the truth, and they couldn't change it.

Molly attempted to lighten up the suddenly somber ambience. "I still think it's sweet, you going over with soup and muffins."

"Well, he's obviously sick because of me. I have to repay the favor. I was thinking of doing something nice for him to say thank-you for taking care of me, anyway."

For holding me and watching my fever break and just making me feel like he cares at least a little bit.

Even if the devil's ultimate plan had probably been to remove Miami from Kate's agenda.

She sighed as she glanced at the muffins. Without further hesitation, she put them in a small basket, then poured the soup in a large glass container. This might be the last time in her life she nursed Garrett back to health, so she had to make it count.

The doorman recognized Kate as she walked into the marble lobby with her goodies in her arms. She told him that she was here to drop the stuff off for Garrett, and he allowed her to go up to the penthouse.

Trying not to make noise, she entered the palatial bachelor pad. It was simple and modern, with dark leather furniture with chrome accents, glass tables and dark walnut flooring. But what she most loved was the stainless-steel, state-of-the-art kitchen. It almost seemed to be merely decorative, since she knew Garrett rarely ate at home, but it was still worthy of a five-star restaurant.

Heating up the hot drawer, Kate slid the chicken soup container inside, and then set the muffins on a covered cake stand. Satisfied with her work, she resisted the urge to go primp herself, but did take a peek at her appearance in the mirror over the entry console.

She looked…quite nice, actually.

Now that she was no longer sick, the color had returned to her cheeks. Her eyes had a nice shine, as though she were excited about something, and the soft cotton sundress with blue-and-white stripes almost made it seem like she was ready for the beach. She'd bought it specifically with Florida in mind, but, oh well, today she'd felt like wearing something he hadn't seen her in before.

And she wasn't even going to dwell on her reasoning either.

It was only that he'd looked extra good when he'd come to see her and she'd felt and looked like crapola, and now she wanted him to…well, to think she looked like a fresh piece of sunshine.

"Garrett?" She called his name softly down the hall, her stomach turning leaden at each tentative footstep she took toward his bedroom. She didn't know what she'd do if she found him in bed with someone. Nothing, probably, but she would definitely cry about it later.

She knew he slept with women. A man like him had his choice of girls all the time. But Garrett had always been discreet about it and he'd never really paraded a lot of women in front of Kate. She couldn't begin to imagine how much it would hurt if she saw him kissing someone, or lying in bed with someone, or putting his arm around someone....

She paused at his open bedroom door, holding her breath. The drapes were wide open, letting the sun inside. His bedroom was done in different shades of gray and black, the nightstands made of ebony wood with chrome accessories. It was all so manly, she couldn't imagine any design more fitting to Garrett's dark good looks.

Something warm flitted through her when she spotted his prone figure on the bed. Her heart almost stopped when she realized he was only wearing a pair of black boxer briefs, the rest of his body covered in his natural golden tan and nothing else. Suddenly he looked very large, very dark and very powerful.

"Garrett?"

He stiffened almost imperceptibly, but Kate couldn't miss the tensing of the muscles in his back. "I'm going to kill my mother," he growled into his folded arm.

"She didn't tell me. Molly did."

"Then I'm going to kill Julian."

He rolled to his side and pulled the satiny gray bedspread up to his waist.

It was hard not to notice how beautiful his muscled torso was, and how sexy he looked with his dark hair all rumpled.

It was also hard not to notice his scowl.

Kate bit back a smile and stepped in with her arms up in feigned innocence. "Me. Come. In. Peace. Bring food. For. Grumpy. Man. May I pass?"

"Freckles, get away or you will get strep again."

"I will not."

"Get out of here, Katie."

She shook her head. "Katie. No. Understand. What. Grumpy. Man. Says."

"Grumpy man says *leave*," Garrett said, but all of Kate's maternal instincts had flared to life with just one look at him, and she couldn't suppress the need to coddle this man like she had when they were younger and she'd helped Eleanor take care of him.

She kicked off her shoes, and before thinking about it, jumped onto the bed next to him, taking care not to touch any part of his body. "You're not the only bed crasher, you know. I have full authority to crash your bed now that you've crashed mine twice."

He sighed and closed his eyes, banging his head on the headboard. "Get out of my bed."

"Not until you let me feed you. Starve the virus, feed the fever? Sound familiar? My part-time doc told it to me."

"Docs are renowned for failing to take their own advice."

"This one is special. Hey, have they medicated you?"

"I'm already drugged as hell. I don't want to eat, Freckles. Just get out of here."

Now Kate scowled, too.

"Garrett, why won't you look at me? Are you in pain? You look like you are."

"Yeah, I'm in pain."

"What is it? Is it your head?" She felt his forehead and he was definitely hot. And she noticed he'd stiffened.

"Don't," he murmured, seizing her wrist and returning her hand to her lap.

Eyes widening at the lines of agony carved in his face, she curled her fingers into her palm because they tingled after his touch.

He inhaled long and deep before his lids finally lifted open, and her heart melted when he looked at her with that dark, tired gaze. His glassy look killed her, but something there, something she couldn't decipher, made her stomach constrict. His pupils were fully dilated and his eyes held a strange awareness.

"Please just leave," he said, and there was something very desperate in his voice that almost made her hesitate.

"Come here, Garrett." She slid closer until her back was against the gray suede headboard, and she urged his dark head to rest against her chest and ran her fingers through his hair. "If you don't want to eat, just let me keep you company."

He groaned on contact, and wrapped his arms around her waist. "Kate, I don't have the energy to do this with you today."

"This what? I'm not planning to fight you."

"This… Damn." He made another deep noise when she lightly massaged his scalp. As her fingers twined in his hair and he pressed closer and tightened his hold around her, her body experienced all sorts of chemical reactions. He was adorable. She wanted to hug him. To tuck him into her suitcase and take him with her.

Crazy girl. The point was to get away from him, wasn't it?

She continued caressing his hair until he relaxed

against her, and her body also turned mushy. When his voice reached her ears minutes later, she started, for she'd almost been falling asleep with him.

"You used to bring me soup when I was sick." He spoke in a murmur against her chest, and his warm breath slipped seductively into her cleavage. "I liked getting sick because of you."

She laughed. "You're a very troubled man, Garrett."

"I was a very troubled young boy."

He angled his face so he could peer up at her, then raised his hand and absently ran his thumb down the bridge of her nose. "And you? You weren't Little Miss Perfect. When you heard the thunder and lightning and that huge storm one night, you lost your marbles completely. Do you remember?"

She dropped her hands as he sat up.

"I'm not sure, since I lose my marbles with all the storms."

"The one that made both you girls run into the boys' room. Before we knew it, Molly had jumped into Julian's bed and you were in mine. But Jules tried to hide her under the covers, and you and I immediately went all around the house looking for Molly, thinking she was somewhere else."

"Okay. Now I remember."

He sat back with his temple propped against the headboard, his eyes suddenly warm with the memory. "You and I ended up splitting up to find Molly, and I found you asleep in the living room after I found out Julian had hijacked her and was hiding her in his bed. Do you remember what you said?"

Kate was so riveted by his retelling, by the way his

smile flashed as he remembered, she'd lost all power of speech. He looked...happy. And also sad?

And devastating.

When she didn't answer, he tipped her head back by the chin, and his voice acquired a strange note. It was deeper. Especially with that strep-throat rasp. "You asked me why I hadn't hijacked you, too."

A strange tingle was growing in the pit of Kate's stomach, and she couldn't stop it, couldn't control it.

"I was probably more asleep than awake."

The atmosphere around them felt heavy with something unnameable and untamable. She became fiercely aware of every point of contact of their bodies. Her knee against his thigh. Her shoulder against the side of his arm.

"Do you want me to hijack you now, Kate?"

Her stomach tightened at the question. "What do you mean?" She narrowed her eyes and told herself his husky tone was due to the strep throat, but it was too thick, too heavy, as heavy as those coal-black eyes.

He cupped her cheek in one huge, dry palm. "You always took care of Molly until she found Julian. You always put her first, before anything else. Didn't you?"

When Kate could only nod, he continued.

"This is how I am with you, Kate. It's instinctive in me. Putting you first. I'd never take advantage of you, that's my number-one priority. But if I knew you might want something from me, I would like to give it to you. So..."

Suddenly he looked as hungry as he did when he ate her food.

"Do you want me to hijack you?" he asked. "Want

me to come after you? Is that why you're leaving for Florida? Do you want me to give chase?"

His stare was so piercing and primal, he didn't look weak or sick at all.

He looked predatory and male, and she felt fragile and female. Inside her, a dozen words rippled with the need to come forth.

I want you. Please give me your love. Yourself.

But how could she tie him up this way? Was this really the answer he wanted? Or was he seeking for her to appease him by saying that she didn't need anything else from him? He'd given her so much already. For his whole life.

A sound of protest tore from her chest, and it sounded so sexual, Kate swallowed it back in horror.

He smiled slowly, almost seductively, as his thumb trailed down the curve of her jaw. "Cat got your tongue?"

Kate couldn't think. Speak. Breathe.

His thumb went lower, and now slowly brushed over the sleeve of her dress. Then it trailed down her bare arm, the touch a shivery, silken whisper that made her insides quiver with yearning. Her heart galloped as pure need kicked in. His other fingers joined his thumb to caress the inside of her left arm, and her skin broke out in goose bumps as her lungs strained for air.

Garrett was quiet as he watched her reactions. She realized she hadn't pulled away from his touch, but instead had leaned closer.

He slid the fingers of his other hand into her hair, softly tangling them inside the loose mass. He watched her with somber expectation, as though wondering if she would stop him.

She didn't.

Oh, why didn't she?

What on earth was he doing?

What was she doing?

Intense sexual thoughts began to flicker through her mind. Garrett's lips, his beautiful body naked against hers...

Their gazes held, both of them silent, their eyes almost questioning but also on fire with desire. His breath, slow and deep and slightly uneven, bathed her face.

Suddenly, he tugged her dress up her thighs and then slid his hand under the fabric, up her panty-clad bottom, then up her back, his fingers slowly tracing the little dents of her spine.

Kate sucked in a mouthful of air.

She probably should stop him. She probably should. Instead, she trembled and bent to brush a kiss across his lightly stubbled jaw. Then she drew back and noticed that his eyes were closed, his face almost in an expression of pain. She cupped his jaw and kissed his forehead, her insides melting when he groaned, encouraging her, so that she kissed the tip of his nose.

His hands were suddenly on her hips. Pushing her away? No. He drew her over his lap, guiding her so that she straddled him, and suddenly his fingers stole under her panties to caress her buttocks as his nose slid down the length of hers. She should pull away, but she was breathless, waiting for something, anything, as he buzzed her lips with his. "Kate, stop me," he said softly.

Five

Holy hell, what was he doing?

He blamed the seven freckles on her nose. They made him do stupid stuff.

He blamed the strep, the fact that he was on steroids, antibiotics and some strange tea his mother had made him this morning. He blamed the fact that Kate smelled like spring and raspberries. He'd never been so hungry, and he didn't know if a thousand men could tear her away from his arms today.

He was fixated on her lips. It was surreal, so surreal, having Kate in his bed. "Stop me, Katie," he found himself saying, as he continued to run his hands up and down her thighs, and grip her lovely bottom.

He wanted to squeeze her so tight he feared he'd break her bones. He shouldn't be touching her buttocks, but he was too tired to fight the urge and too sick to care. They felt too good. *She* felt too good.

He'd wanted to do this since he'd seen her slide into those purple panties and he'd been haunted ever since. Why had she done that little striptease? He couldn't stop thinking she'd wanted him to see her. She'd wanted him to want her.

And he did, he really did.

"You think I'm blind? That I don't know?" he murmured against the top of her head. He drew back and stared into her face, noticing how soft her lips looked parted. "What you want is right here—and you'll want it whether you're in this room with me or all the way in Florida. You'll want *me*."

He didn't know why he was testing her like this. But he wanted to see…

If she feels anything for me.

Anything even remotely resembling this madness that I feel.

He caught her closer when she squirmed and tried to push herself away. "You have no idea what I want!" she angrily spat.

"I know exactly what you want! I notice it every time you look at me, like I'm everything you've ever wanted. But I'm not, Kate. We both know I'm not. There's not a day I don't remember what I took from you—"

"Shut up, Garrett! You're sick and…medicated and clearly out of your mind."

He caught her back against him and stroked her cheeks as tenderly as he could, but knew his hands were shaking. "I know you'll probably hate me for this, but I still won't let you go to Florida. I want you close to me, where I know you're safe."

"I'm not asking for your permission!"

He frowned and stared into her beautiful shining eyes, wondering why he couldn't have this girl, why he felt like he was poison for this girl.

"So you'll make me follow you? Hmm? Is that what you want, Kate?"

She glared at him, and he couldn't stand that little glare. He set a kiss on her forehead and rubbed her back under her dress, and she shuddered and pressed closer. Her need seeped into him, warming him to the core, until he felt like a torch was blazing inside of him. Blazing for her. He could feel her need of him like you'd feel rain pelting your back or the sun on your face. There were days when he could successfully ignore the pull between them, the undeniable chemistry. But tonight, his heart beat like a crazed drum for her. His muscles strained with aching desire. He could hardly stand not to touch her, felt dizzy with temptation, weak from fighting it.

"Do me a favor and say you'll stay?" He nuzzled her face with his own. "Stay with your family. With me."

His chest cramped as he thought about what he felt for her. What he felt for Kate was like a storm, and it was always there, consuming him from the inside, tormenting his every living moment.

Her voice sounded resentful. "Why? So I can keep on playing my Oscar-worthy role of the good little—"

He lost it. It was the anger and need in her voice, the closeness of her body. It was Kate. Driving him past the point of obsession, past the point of reason. He curled his hands around the back of her head and growled, "Damn you, the only one playing the role of a freaking wallflower, pretending not to want you like this, is *me*," and his mouth pressed, scorching and hungry, against hers.

He hadn't meant to kiss her. He hadn't planned to crush her body against his and part her lips with his own. He hadn't planned to hungrily push his tongue into her soft mouth, but he did all that, because he needed to. And when she responded by twining her arms around his neck and releasing a soft moan that nearly drove him to his knees, he did more.

He wanted her, wanted her more than air, more than food, water, anything.

Blood boiling in his veins, he grabbed her curvy buttocks and molded her body tighter against his as he twirled his tongue around hers, wildly tasting every inch of her warm, giving mouth. The kiss was fire, lightning, electrifying to him, surpassing his every dream and fantasy about her. Surpassing any other kiss he'd ever had.

He was thirty already, and he had never felt so out of control, gotten so carried away with a woman before. His arms, his legs, his every muscle shook uncontrollably with pure, raw lust, as if one mere taste of Kate alone was enough to make him addicted to her. And he was, he *was* addicted.

Her luscious flavor, the erotic little moans she poured into his mouth, stimulated his thirst to levels far beyond quenching. He wanted her so much he could eat her up alive and still not be satiated. He could lick every inch of her creamy skin and be still ravenous for more. Because she was everything he wanted and everything he couldn't have. *Dammit.*

It took an inhuman effort for him to draw back, and he did it with a pained sound from deep within his throat.

"Kate, do you know what's happening here?" He

panted hard for his breath, and dropped his head, unable to resist her.

His hungry mouth opened wide around the fabric of her dress and he sucked hard, mindlessly, as his hand cupped her breast from beneath and squeezed the tip even farther out for him to suck.

"Garrett," she gasped as he drew her nipple, fabric and all, deeper into his mouth.

He groaned in ecstasy, turning his head to nuzzle the tip of her second breast. "Kate, if you don't want this—stop me...stop me now...."

She palmed his jaw and drew his mouth up to hers, searing him with her eager kiss, her lips trembling with desire.

He groaned and shut his eyes when she dragged her mouth up to kiss his nose, then his eyelids, and an out-of-control shudder wracked his large body.

He knew he was losing himself in the fragrant scent of her arousal, in the feel of her small body trembling against his, in the sound of tears in her voice. He should make her leave, so he could go back to hell. But some demon was shouting at him that he was losing her, that she would be out of his life in weeks, and suddenly he couldn't take it.

"Three seconds," he rasped as he opened his eyes, his hands unsteady as he cupped her breasts and used his thumbs to circle the budded peaks. "You have three seconds to tell me to stop."

To emphasize his words, he gave her another branding kiss, praying that she would resist him.

And that somebody would just whack his head from behind, tie up his hands and gag his mouth, so that he didn't use them all over her body like he was aching to.

Because he just couldn't withhold his desire any longer. He didn't care if he was going to hell. As far as he was concerned, he'd been living there for years, and every one of those years, he'd wanted her.

Yeah, he must be a devil to be here with this angel in bed, ready to have the best sex of his life with her. Ready to make the fantasies he'd had for hours and days and weeks and months and years come true for him. For both of them.

I'm going to hell and it will damn well be worth it....
"One," he warned.

Kate only watched him, as though waiting for him to get to three to kiss him again. The thought made him grind out, "Two."

She looked thoroughly kissed and ready to be taken. He'd never in his life wanted anything so much.

"Three."

When she sighed in outward relief and never made so much as a move to stop him, he went crazy. He pulled her dress over her head and tossed it to the floor, then trailed his lips down her flushed face as his hands coasted down the sides of his newly revealed treasure. She was smooth, slim and curvy, and she made him want to kneel at her feet and revere her. Adore her. Make love to her until they died from it.

With a little sound of frustration, Kate reached to the waistband of his underwear and tugged down his boxer briefs.

He helped her, and once he was naked, rolled around immediately, almost crushing her with his weight as he flattened her back on the bed and held her by the hair. His tongue plunged into her mouth, flooding him with her essence, feeding his reckless thirst.

Her bare skin slid against his as she suckled his tongue, and the unexpected act triggered ripples of pleasure through his system. She rubbed her breasts against his chest while he slanted his head for deeper access to her. Crazy good. She tasted crazy, crazy good.

Warnings shot across his mind as he pulled open her bra. This was the time to stop, but he was past stopping.

He did not care about anything else except branding her, taking her to a place where there would be no talk of Florida, no talk of leaving; there would be nothing but the two of them. Together.

He shoved the fabric aside and exposed her nipples. Perfect and pink.

He cupped one in his big hand and licked his way down her throat, down to the pebbled nipple. He groaned at her taste, then slid his fingers between her parted thighs and easily yanked down her panties. Squirming restlessly, she pulled him up by the hair, to her lips, and kissed him while she breathlessly murmured, "Hurry."

He cradled her head and angled her back for his devouring kiss. Murmuring her name softly, he blanketed her body with his, his erection nestling between her legs.

He ducked his head to nibble hungrily on her lips and reached between her legs again, stroking his fingers along her slick folds. She was so hot and wet. He groaned, then stuck his finger into her channel only to bring it up and stick that finger into his mouth, tasting her before he stroked and penetrated her again. "How long has it been for you?" he asked, her tightness closing around him.

"A long time," she gasped.

"How long?" he pressed.

"Years."

He closed his eyes as his chest swelled with emotion. *Mine, mine, mine,* he thought, noting how tight she was, how hot she was, as she rocked her hips to his caress.

The fact that she had also not been with anyone for a long time made him wild. He already felt dangerously close to orgasm as he added his thumb to caress her tender spot. He watched her toss and turn in pleasure, his erection throbbing painfully between his legs.

She's going to be just yours from now on....

He couldn't think beyond sinking himself inside her, taking something no one would ever take from her. Her sex was slick against his fingers as she curled her legs around him and locked her ankles at the small of his back, urging him on with a sensual rock and a breathless, "Please. Garrett, please, I hurt."

She wants me so much she's hurting for me....

Groaning softly out of pure sheer overwhelming need, he slid his hands up her arms and intertwined their fingers as he pinned her hands at her sides.

"Are you ready, Katie?"

Her voice got strangled in her throat, thick with need and desire. "Please, yes."

His body tensed in anticipation as he teased his hardness along her entrance. She was slick and wet and swollen—so damned perfect. He closed his eyes and savored her body as he gently prodded her entry, inch by inch, slow and deep, releasing a growl of pure animal need. "Ahh, Kate."

"Garrett," she cried out and stiffened. A killer wave of red-hot ecstasy whipped through him, tensing his muscles that already strained for release.

He groaned when he realized he wasn't wearing any protection.

"Kate...damn..."

She cried out when he dragged out, grabbing his shoulders and saying, "Don't stop, don't stop!"

He groaned in torment and eased back in, totally lost in her heat. The sound she released was slow and dark, as if the pain were morphing into pleasure. "Better?" he rasped.

He took her answering whimper in his mouth and kissed deeper until her body was writhing wildly underneath his.

He drove inside her once more.

Kate gasped, moaning out his name, and it was the sexiest thing he'd ever heard her say. And when she said, "More," he snapped and began a frantic pace.

They kissed like crazy for several minutes, and then she clutched his hard shoulders and gazed up at him with cloudy blue eyes.

She was so damned beautiful like this—this was how he wanted to have her every night in his bed. Red hair. Coral lips. Rosy cheeks. Thickened, recently kissed nipples.

He didn't even remember that his body hurt, that his throat was raw. All he knew was that Kate watched him, her breath rippling from between his lips as they moved together. All he knew was that he was shattering with pleasure as he gripped her waist and increased the pace. He thrust deeper, harder, lost in her grip, her heat, in *her*.

A knot of ecstasy pulled inside him and shot him off to outer space, and with three more thrusts, he pushed her past the precipice into an explosion that made her shout his name as he sank all the way home, spilling himself inside her.

For minutes they lay there, entangled and sweaty. He was breathless, sated and frankly, awed as hell.

He'd never felt so whole. He'd never made love like this. He shifted to look at her, then groaned at the sight of her languid body and dewy face, so beautiful and so taken.

"I'm sorry I lost control, Katie," he murmured, kissing her cheek, loving how warm and loose she felt as she snuggled closer. "I should've worn protection. What day are you in your cycle?"

"I don't know. Eight maybe," she said, tucking her face in his neck, as if hiding from his prying eyes. "Please don't worry, Garrett."

"Eight. Is that even safe…?" Man. He'd been as careless and excited as an adolescent to touch her. Not using protection had been inexcusable, made his chest churn with disgust at himself. "Freckles, damn…"

She sat up and pushed his hands away, shaking her head. "Please just…please stop apologizing for it, Garrett. I wanted this to happen, so did you. We had fun, it was great, it's done. There's no need to get all serious about it, and there's certainly no need for you to add it to your guilt bag."

Garrett sat back, so stunned at her words, his mind came up blank. Guilt bag? So she thought he had a guilt bag?

"What the hell is that supposed to mean?" he demanded.

"It means it was no big deal! It was just sex. You've had it with millions of women and I plan to do the same with other men in the future. I don't want you to apologize and I definitely don't want you considering…thinking that it could possibly…everything is all right here, okay?"

"I'm trying to be responsible. If there are repercussions—"

"Stop! Just stop! Even if there *were*…"

"If there were, I need to fricking *know* before I enter into any sort of agreement with Cassandra Clarks!" he angrily barked.

Kate stiffened. "What do you mean? What agreement?"

His lips formed a thin, angry line.

"What agreement, Garrett?"

He groaned and raked a hand through his hair, then let his hand fall. "She wants to marry me as a condition for selling us her share of Clarks."

"Marry…*you?*"

A thousand expressions crossed her face, until hurt ended up on the forefront, and Garrett felt like an ass.

"You! How dare you touch me when you're thinking of…I would *never* marry for anything other than love!"

He winced as she angrily jumped out of bed and searched for her dress.

He'd just had sex without a condom and honestly? He didn't even care.

He wanted her. He just wanted her. If it meant taking responsibility and doing something about it now, he would. But now it felt like the last thing she wanted was to be tied to him.

She'd basically told him that she thought the worst of him, that she wouldn't marry him if he were the last man on earth. Of course she didn't want him. He'd mucked up her entire life, and if she got pregnant, he'd muck it up again, taking her dream of Florida away from her.

The realization hurt him so much, he could only watch her from the bed, wondering if he'd actually stayed away from her all these years out of duty, or because he was a coward and knew, deep down, that he just didn't deserve her.

"Do you want some of the food I brought over, or should I just go home now?" she asked, and as if she'd already decided on the latter, she slipped back into her dress. Then she resumed searching on the floor for her panties.

He held them out to her with a scowl. "You were trembling in this bed with me, Kate. You. *Begged.* For me."

"You're right." She covered her face with shaking hands, then plunged her legs into her panties. "I even started it."

He was baffled. She looked very perturbed by the fact that she'd slept with him. He didn't know what to make of it when he'd just felt her writhe beneath him, wet and wanton.

"No. *I* did, Kate. I started it," he said, gentling his voice, standing up to embrace her. "Hell, I've been thinking about doing this with you since…"

Her eyes widened as though he'd just divulged something completely damning. "Since when? Since I said I was going to Florida? Ohmigod, are you trying to use sex to get me to bend to your will and stay here? Why else would you touch me when you haven't your whole life!"

She suddenly looked enlightened, while he stared blankly at her, puzzled and confused. Her cheeks were reddening by the second, but Garrett was growing too angry at her accusation to care. "Kate, do you seriously believe I'm that cold and calculating?"

Did she think anything even remotely redeeming about him, and was there any chance in hell she could ever love him when she was holding their past against him?

"Of course I do! You're a man who just confessed to be considering some sort of weird business marriage with some bimbo you barely even know!"

"She's not a bimbo, Kate," he said, just to be fair to Cassandra.

Kate's cheeks went redder. "You still haven't told me why you went behind your beloved's back and slept with me."

"Why don't you first tell me why the hell you slept with *me?* Were you just horny or did you just pity me tonight, or were you apologizing for giving me strep?"

"Who do you think you are to judge? Garrett, you *slept* with me even while thinking of marrying some stranger in the name of…business. I swear that's the most disgusting thing anyone's ever done to me!"

"You're just goddamned playing with me! You've teased me your whole life, parading around with other men! You just gave me a little taste of what I want, and once you got what you wanted, you're ditching me!"

She glared and stomped to the door. "Go to hell!"

"I'm already there, Kate. It's been my damned zip code since I was ten!"

As she stormed out of the room and slammed the door behind her, Garrett punched his fist into the pillow and yelled, "Goddammit!"

Six

"We're sitting at twenty-eight percent today…" Landon said. As usual, the man droned on and on about business.

Garrett made it a point to occasionally nod as if he were listening while he scrolled through his last text conversation with Kate. He'd texted her in the middle of the night after the debacle of their argument four nights ago. He'd been lying awake at midnight feeling medicated and as low as a dog. All he'd needed was for someone to put a bowl of Alpo out for him. Instead he'd found her food in the kitchen, cursed himself over and over again, heated up his soup and chowed down on several muffins, then grabbed his phone and texted her. Despite the fact that it had been past one in the morning, she'd replied. Which meant she'd been lying awake, too, as sleepless as he was.

Thanks for my food. When can I see you? I want to talk.

Everything is fine. I've already forgotten about it.

Garrett wasn't so stupid as to believe this, but had answered.

K. So I hear you're getting your dresses fitted Wednesday. I'll drive you.

Won't your girlfriend get jealous?

I'd like to explain to you about her.

It's fine. The fitting is at five so I'll see you before then.

"Are you even listening, Garrett?"

He lifted his head to Landon's confused gray gaze. "Hmm? What?"

Landon scowled and then continued, raising his voice as though to be clearer. "Clarks...new strategy..."

So, Kate thought Garrett had planned it all?

How could she believe that he'd planned to get sick, so that he could get her to bring over some food for him, get her into bed, seduce her like some out-of-control adolescent and conveniently forget a condom so she might have to stay? Well, hell, it sounded so brilliant, he felt like an idiot for not thinking of it before.

"Garrett, dammit, did you hear?"

"Yes. Clarks. A new strategy." He set his phone aside, but putting thoughts about Kate aside wasn't that easy.

"You're the last single Gage. Will you or won't you go through with this?" Landon asked.

With a major wrench of mental muscles, Garrett

pulled his scrambled brain together and tried to focus on the topic today.

"All three of us know that I'm not really the last single Gage, Lan." Garrett leaned back to survey both his brothers' expressions across the conference table.

Landon's eyebrows shot up. "Don't go there."

"Why not?" He shrugged. "He's still a Gage."

"Mother wanted nothing to do with him. Hell, we paid him millions to get out of our lives for good, and you want to bring him back?"

"How badly do you want Clarks?" Garrett countered.

"As badly as you want it," Landon returned.

Garrett scraped a hand along the tense muscles at the back of his neck. He wanted Clarks, but not as bad as he wanted something else.

"Plus who's to say that selfish bastard will want to help us?" Landon rose to pace by the wall of windows. "He will want a big piece of the pie, and he'll want even more than that. Do you remember Father refused to recognize him?"

"But we know he was Father's son, no matter how many times he denied it to Mother," Garrett countered. He'd been wracking his brain for other options and this was, fortunately or unfortunately, the only one he'd been able to come with.

To bring their illegitimate half brother, Emerson Wells, back into the fold.

Julian chewed on the back of a pen before he lowered it and spoke. "We could entice him with money. Stock. Something. Maybe we should call just him."

"He's trouble," Landon said pointedly, his face furrowed in thought. "What does he do now anyway?"

"Last I heard he was in the personal security business here in San Antonio. Started as a bodyguard."

"Seriously?"

"What can I say? He likes beating people up."

"All right then." Crossing the room, Landon clicked the phone intercom and rang his assistant. "If you'd please get me Emerson Wells on the line. You should be able to do a Google search and find his number. He owns some sort of personal security business here in town."

Hanging up, Landon rubbed his chin thoughtfully, his gray eyes on Garrett. "If he denies us…would you still go through with it?"

Kate's face and words surfaced in his mind with a vengeance, and his chest cramped. *I would never marry for anything other than love!*

For one painful moment, he wondered if she'd even care whether he married someone else, for whatever reason. But although her words had cut through him, her body had spoken another language. He'd lost control, and so had she. They'd both been so needy he hadn't even been able to stop to put on a condom.

What had he done?

Perhaps Garrett hadn't technically broken his promise to her father, but he felt like he had. There was probably no man more undeserving of Kate's affection than he.

Clearly, you blew it, Gage.

But she had wanted him. Hell, she'd not only wanted him, she'd melted under his touch. Was he supposed to turn his mind blank and forget about a moment like that?

"Molls said they have a fitting this afternoon that you insisted on driving them to?"

He glanced up at Julian in confusion. "Molly? I told Kate I'd drive her. I didn't know it included Molly."

"And Beth," Landon added with a grin. "They're all going together."

Garrett almost groaned. So much for talking to Kate one-on-one.

"Fine, then. I'll drive the three of them," Garrett reluctantly conceded. An infuriating hunch told him that Kate was doing this on purpose. Clearly, she had no desire to discuss anything with him.

Julian dropped his pencil on the table and angled his head, his eyes sparkling in amusement.

"You know, bro, I can't help you here. Molls would strangle me if I see her in *the* dress."

"That's fine." He plunged a hand through his hair. He'd wanted to spend some time with Kate and talk, but he would manage somehow. "I'll drop Kate off last and see if she'll do dinner with me."

"So I take it this means whatever Emerson says, you're not keen on the marriage of convenience?" Julian queried.

"Would you be?" Garrett countered. "Keen to marry a stranger? When your every thought is consumed by someone else?"

"Why don't you just tell Kate how you feel and get it all out there?"

Garrett shook his head.

Because he didn't deserve her.

Hell, the way things stood, even if he were to tell Kate how she made him feel, she'd probably tell him to stick his declaration where it hurts. She resented him for having taken her father from her, no matter how much she tried to pretend she didn't. He still couldn't forget those words she'd lashed out at him with when they were young: *How dare you!*

He'd never forget the hurt betrayal in her eyes when she'd found out her father had died because Garrett hadn't run as he'd been told to. And now, to top it off, she believed he'd deliberately slept with her just to make sure she stayed in San Antonio. True, it might have been the catalyst, but that was so not the reason.

"You know, Garrett," Landon said, coming over to pat his back, "we all get the love we think we deserve...and you *deserve* it, man. No matter what you think. You both do. So you better own it before she leaves for Florida, brother. Neither Julian nor I, nor for that matter, Mother, has any desire to watch what her departure does to you."

Seven

Kate checked herself in the mirror for the tenth time. She wore a plain khaki skirt and sleeveless halter top. She knew that it would be silly to try on another top, so she grabbed her purse and her phone, then glanced down on impulse at Garrett's last texts.

He'd said he wanted to talk and tell her about the "bimbo," but just thinking about the way he'd defended her made Kate's blood boil. Worse was that every time she went back a little further, to his kisses, little bubbles of remembrance shot through her system. She didn't want the bubbles. Or the tingles. Or any of the gut-churning jealousy she felt when she thought about him and Cassandra Clarks.

She hadn't slept a wink last night; she could still feel his touch on her traitorously sensitive skin. Now, Beth and Molly were waiting in her living room for him to pick them up, and Kate was grateful for the buffer they would provide.

Coward. That's why you asked them to come over.

Yes, yes, so fine, she was a coward. She just didn't trust herself to be alone with him. She feared she'd either do something sexual, which she had to put a stop to, or say some other cruel things that she didn't mean. She regretted getting so defensive when he'd started apologizing. Garrett was actually the most unselfish man she knew. He'd always thought ahead to how he would protect her if something unexpected happened. But the last thing Kate had wanted was to add to his burdens when it came to her. She hadn't ever imagined they'd end up naked and entangled. But he'd been there. So available. So sexy, tan and bare-chested. How could she resist? And the bastard had broken remorselessly through her walls, all in his stupid attempt to bend her to his will and liking!

But then he'd pretended to be hurt by her accusation, and accused her of being a tease. The reminder made her frown. She'd never considered that she was. Did she tease him? She'd tried to make him jealous for years, but she'd never known it had even had an effect.

Maybe it had more than he'd let on.

"Landon thinks he's going to do it," Beth was telling Molly.

"Do what?" Kate asked as she came back into the living room.

Molly turned to her with a sad, moping face. "Marry Cassandra Clarks. Jules told me yesterday. I just didn't know how to bring it up."

Kate's stomach clenched.

"It's got something to do with acquiring Clarks Communications," Beth said, shaking her head. "Kate, I'm sorry."

Once again, Kate felt the painful stab of jealousy inside her. "All the more reason I should leave," she whispered.

"You'd let the man you love marry another woman?" Beth asked uncertainly.

"If he wants her, yes. And I don't love him. I might have had a crush, but I'm over that. I'm in love with the idea of Florida now."

"Kate, I think it's hard for him to let himself want something, with what happened to your father, but I've always seen that he's got it bad for you," Beth said.

"No. *I* had it bad for *him*. And now I've promised myself to forget him. I should find a man with no baggage who actually makes me feel loved, Beth."

Both women quietly watched her pace to the window and then back.

"So there's nothing going on between the two of you? The boys say he's distracted. And so are you," Beth insisted.

Her best friend's eyes twinkled all of a sudden, and Kate wanted to groan when she saw Molly's mischievous smile also appear. Did they suspect Kate had totally gone sex-crazed at Garrett's place several days ago?

"There's nothing going on. We're…normal. Friends." *Who slipped up once,* she mentally added. Through the window, she watched his silver Audi pull over to the curb. Little bugs tickled the insides of her stomach. "He's here."

"I guess I'll just slide into the back with Molly," Beth offered as they went outside, and Kate locked up behind her.

She hated how her heart pounded when she walked up to the shiny silver car. Garrett stood holding the door open, his eyes sweet and liquid chocolate as he smiled. "Hi, Katie."

Her bones went mushy every time he called her Katie. "Hey, Garrett." His broad shoulder brushed hers as she got in, and her pulse sped with his nearness as he bent to kiss her on the cheek.

Oh, God, please don't be nice today, she thought miserably.

She could handle fighting with him. But this?

The thought of him marrying anyone, touching anyone like he'd touched her, tortured her.

He settled behind the steering wheel. She watched his hands on the gearshift as they sped off, and her core warmed and boiled hot as she remembered the ways he'd caressed her. Every part of her body wanted to do it again except her mind, where warning bells were ringing at full volume.

She couldn't let it happen again.

He was talking *marriage* to another woman.

She was only too glad she wouldn't be here to watch it.

After forty-five minutes at the dress shop, Garrett could now totally understand his brothers' amused grins from only hours ago.

He'd never gone to a dress fitting before.

Torture.

He sat on a chair outside a line of dressing rooms and watched as the ladies came out to stand before a huge mirror, where a busy little woman picked and poked and stabbed the material until she'd shaped it to her liking.

He'd been doing fine, answering emails on his iPhone, until Kate came out and took his breath away.

He watched her hop onto the platform and model the dress, exposing her slim, creamy ankles as she discussed the length with the short, busy-bee shop attendant. He felt as if a grenade had just exploded in his chest. His blood heated as he remembered the hell of watching her grow up, grow breasts, wear her hair longer, develop those curves. He'd seen her in her prom dress, in a barely there black bikini that hugged her silken curves in all the right places and made Garrett hurt in all the wrong ones.

He'd seen her naked in his bed...writhing in his arms....

And once he got her back there, he never wanted to see her dressed again.

He wanted to touch her, hold her.

He wanted to hear her breathe next to him at night. He just knew if she slept at his side, the mere feel of her would make all his nightmares vanish.

He suddenly saw, clearly, how he'd be complete and whole with her. How he'd feel worthy and needed in a way he had never, ever felt before. But at the same time, he'd be vulnerable. Because, holy God, he needed this woman so much.

He saw her eyes go bright when the girls came over, squealing in delight.

"That blue looks so good on you," Molly gushed.

"Oh, your date is going to be so thrilled!"

Garrett cocked a brow as he pushed himself off the chair and came over, listening to her ask if they were sure.

He stood next to her and caught her gaze in the mirror. "Date?"

She spun around to face him and her lips trembled in a smile. "I don't know. We won't be catering so I'll have some time to spare."

"Exactly. Flirt around with a man. Have a little fun," Molly said from nearby. Garrett couldn't miss the mischievous glint in Molly's eyes as she surveyed Garrett for a reaction.

He gave her none.

"Do we want this fitted...?" The saleslady maneuvered Kate's skirt, and Garrett watched in rapture as the woman tucked the fabric around her waist to enhance Kate's luscious curves even more.

He studied her breasts, how lush they were, tightly constrained by the corsetlike bodice. His mouth watered and his hands ached. He was in hell and heaven at the same time, and it was the most puzzling feeling he'd ever experienced.

Kate stared at his reflection, her blue eyes shining in concern and somehow pleading for a compliment. "Do you like it?"

They both stared at one another, and for that one moment, nothing mattered but her. She held his gaze, and he held hers. His world centered around this one woman he'd always tried not to want.

His eyes trailed along her body, taking her in, and he heard the soft, amusing sound of her breath catching. The gown was sapphire-colored, consisting of a tight corset top clinging to her body like second skin, then flaring into a wide skirt. He wanted to toss it up in the air and bury himself between her legs. Her arms were toned and slim, her breasts perky and tightly constricted, making him want to free them. Her glossy hair, too long and beautiful to keep restrained, hung down her shoulders.

She was gazing at him nervously, wetting her lips. "Garrett…do you like it?" she repeated.

He nodded while his body burned under his skin.

Smiling tremulously, she hopped off the platform and started toward the changing rooms, but within three steps, he caught her wrist and spun her around. As if shocked, she looked down at his fingers curled around her flesh, then watched him, wide-eyed, as he lifted her hand in his and kissed her knuckles, one by one. "Speaking of dates," he whispered when he was done, "do you have one?"

Surprise and excitement flickered in her gaze, and his smile widened as he watched her struggle for a reply. He should probably ask Cassandra out on a date, start playing up appearances, but the hope he saw in Kate's pretty eyes… He wanted to kiss her eyelids, and track her jaw with his tongue. Then go to the shell of her ear, where he would whisper all sort of things to her, naughty and nice. He wanted to have what his brothers had; he wanted all of that, with Kate.

This talk of marriages of convenience and business mergers…

Did any of it matter to him? If he didn't have Kate?

He didn't deserve her, but he was damned ready to work to get her. He wanted to stop punishing himself, stop blaming himself for people dying, and just dream of all that life and love he felt when he looked at Kate.

"I…" She hesitated, then shook her head, her cheeks coloring pink. "It's best I go on my own."

She quickly pried her hand free and disappeared behind a velvet curtain to change once more.

* * *

Garrett Gage asking her out on a date?

No. Not a date. Garrett Gage asking her out to the wedding.

And he hadn't really asked her. He seemed to be checking whether she already knew whom she'd go with, which was different.

Still. In her heart, her gut, in the way he'd looked at her...*oooh,* how it had felt when he'd asked her that question.

Kate was still reeling at the possibilities as they dropped off Beth and Molly and then rode in silence back to her place. Rain caught up with them by the time he pulled over in front of her one-story house. The drops were so big, they made huge splattering sounds on the windshield and the top of the car.

"Oh, no," Kate groaned.

Garrett reached into the backseat and grabbed his suit jacket. "Remember this? Something like this has saved your pretty head from getting wet before."

The memories surfaced, and when his teeth flashed wide in a white smile, there was no future in Florida, no painful past, only Garrett and his coat, and the rain outside.

He grabbed the door handle. "All right, Kate, here we go."

Heart pounding with emotion as she remembered other times he'd saved her just like this, she watched him sprint around the car and jerk the door open, holding his jacket over both their heads as he pulled her up against his side and onto the sidewalk. As her flats began getting soaked, she pressed close to his massive chest and suddenly his arm slid around her waist, his eyes glinting. "Ready? On three."

She nodded breathlessly, a gasp already poised in her throat.

"One, two, three!"

They ran for cover to the door, the fresh puddles at their feet splashing at each step as they both burst out laughing. Kate knew this wouldn't have happened if her catering van hadn't been parked in the middle of her driveway, but rain in Texas was truly rare and she hadn't expected it at all.

Once at the door, she struggled to fit the key into the doorknob, and she could hear Garrett breathing at her back as he hunched his shoulders over her, the jacket covering them both.

"Katie, be any slower, and we could just shampoo here already."

"I'm getting it!" she cried, laughing at her own awkwardness as the angle of the rain managed to get them both wet from the sides. The door clicked open at last, and she hurried inside, turning to see him standing just outside the door, getting wetter by the second. She couldn't bear to leave him there like that, so she motioned him inside and slammed the door after him. His white shirt clung damply to his back and right side.

She squeezed a couple of raindrops out of the tips of her hair as Garrett shook his jacket in the air and hooked it on the coat stand. When Kate kicked off her shoes, their shoulders touched, and she realized Garrett smelled of fresh rain.

She couldn't miss the way his broad chest jerked and stretched his white dress shirt with each breath. And she knew her nipples were poking into her dampened blouse;

she caught his dazzlingly sexy white smile as he stared down at her. "Someone looks wet," he said laughingly.

"You should see yourself."

"I'm perfectly aware that I'm wet."

"Take your shirt off, and I'll dry it for you. I'd do the same for your jacket, but I assume it's dry-clean?"

"So is the damn shirt."

"Then at least let me hang it." Without thinking, her hands flew up to start unbuttoning him, and by the time she started to undo the last button, she realized that he'd gone utterly still. His eyes had darkened completely, and emotion clogged Kate's throat as their love-making vividly came back to her mind.

"Katie, if you don't want this—stop me...stop me now...."

He seemed to notice that something had made her hands fall still, for he angled his head downward and peered mischievously into her eyes. "Just say you want me naked and I'll take it all off."

"You're so easy," she scoffed, but she dropped her hands when she realized the danger, and his shirt fell open to reveal his beautiful tan abs. She shouldn't be talking to him. She shouldn't even want to, need to, be close to him. She could have almost kicked herself when she asked, "Do you want some dinner?"

He didn't hesitate, even when the tension between them as palpable.

He followed her through the living room. "I don't want to put you to work."

"It's not work to me. I'll cook us something easy. I hate eating alone and miss Molly terribly," she said.

But was that really why she'd asked him to dinner? Or was it because she knew that as soon as she left San

Antonio, she would never be able to enjoy his company like this again?

"I'm sorry, Kate."

For a moment, she didn't know what he was sorry about. *He's sorry about you missing Molly, Kate. Get your head in the game.* "But she's so happy," she finally answered. She smiled as she eased into the adjoining kitchen, quietly slipping on an apron.

"Aren't you a cute one," Garrett murmured.

His gaze was so openly admiring that Kate's stomach squeezed. She grabbed a knife and gestured dramatically with it. "Flattery will get you equal portions, so don't waste your breath."

"I'm not wasting it. I'm holding it."

Ignoring the butterflies in her stomach, Kate rummaged through the fridge and pulled out her almond flour, eggs, milk and a bunch of vegetables. She set the veggies on a cutting board and transferred them to the kitchen island. "Help me with these while I work on the dough?"

"Of course. Just tell me what to do."

"Cut the mushrooms, red peppers, onions and zucchini into small but pretty slices."

"I can do small, but I don't guarantee pretty." His lips curled upward as he grasped the knife that she offered and his fingers closed warmly over hers.

Shivers of delight shot from the place he touched, and she couldn't suppress the shudder that ran down her limbs. "They're not going to a beauty pageant. Just small will do," she whispered, impulsively pressing in behind him and leaning to watch as she showed him how. She shifted her hands so that he held the knife, and she held *him,* and then she slowly guided him to cut in the size she wanted.

Garrett stood utterly still and compliant, letting her guide him, and suddenly her nipples pressed painfully into his hard back as she realized how intimately her arms were going around his narrow waist.

"What are we making?"

She swallowed when he turned slightly and glanced directly at her. His voice was smooth and calm, but when she spoke, Kate's wasn't. "Vegetable goat-cheese pizza."

He turned back to watch her cut a slice of pepper. "Kate, you're going to kill me."

"Why? I thought you liked it?"

"Exactly. My mouth is watering."

Her cheeks flamed up as she thought of his mouth, and she instantly released him and went back to her spot to prepare the dough. Moments later, she lifted her head when the rhythmical sounds of Garrett's chopping stopped. He was watching her massage the dough. A lock of his dark hair fell over one eye. Her legs weakened at the sexy look, and her heart grew wings in her chest. Garrett looked incredibly beautiful in her kitchen. As beautiful as he did in bed with her.

She opened her mouth to say something, then closed it when her cheeks burned at the memory. She really shouldn't have slept with him. Now she couldn't even look at him without becoming hyperaware of the electricity between them.

A smile slowly formed on his lips as if he could read her thoughts. Then he turned his attention back to his chopping, his profile hard and square, but the expression on his face also thoughtful. Kate swallowed and mixed her dough, then slammed her fists into it and rolled it a couple of more times.

"Bring the veggies once they're cut so you can help me arrange them."

He didn't answer, but soon, he brought over the cutting board. He set it on the counter, and as Kate began to arrange all the little pieces on the flattened pizza crust, his hands gripped her waist from behind. Her breath was knocked out of her when his fingers squeezed her and his lips brushed against her ear.

"Why'd you sleep with me, Kate?" he murmured.

Heat arrowed from her ear straight to her toes, and she stiffened against the dissolving sensation in her bones.

He didn't sound angry. He sounded confused, but patient, much as he did when he wanted to get to the bottom of something.

He surprised her by pressing into her body, trapping her between the counter and himself. Kate had nowhere to go, her spine arching up against his chest as she closed her eyes and tried to still her racing heartbeat.

His voice sounded in her ear as his fingers started a trail up her rib cage. "Did you feel pity for me because I was sick—?"

"No." She could barely utter the word.

"Then why?"

His breath was warm, and damp, and it made her shiver. "It was a mistake. We weren't thinking clearly." Trying to gather her wits, she nervously turned in the cage of his arms, gripped the tray and slid the pizza into the oven, forcing him to step back as she bent forward.

When she shut the door and turned, Garrett had stepped back and merely stood watching her. His snowy-white dress shirt was still parted at the middle, and her saliva glands went crazy at the sight of his bare chest, his flat, hard abs and his belly button.

"Maybe it was a mistake, Kate, one I've spent all my life avoiding. But what if it isn't a mistake?"

Her blood started heating in her veins as she remembered the delicious way he'd moved in her. Kissed her. Gripped her.

She knew they had to talk about this, no matter how much she wished they would pretend nothing had gone on that day. And now that he'd brought up the topic, she could barely think straight. The look in his eyes was beyond intimate. It was downright proprietary, and she almost drowned in the darkness of those eyes that haunted her dreams. With an inhuman effort, she made her way around the kitchen island, putting some distance between them.

His voice stopped her as he followed her around.

"Kate. Answer me. What if it wasn't a mistake?"

Her breath caught in disbelief, and suddenly, she did a one-eighty to face him. "You just want to keep me here, Garrett. You'd do anything to win—that's how you are. And you want to keep me from going to Florida."

"You know me better than that, Freckles."

"I know you're the most stubborn man I know."

He lifted one lone eyebrow. "And you aren't stubborn? You're stubborn *and* proud, Katie. The combo makes for a very difficult lady."

She shook her head but couldn't help smiling. Then she signaled at his damp shirt; it was still driving her crazy how it stuck damply to his beautiful brown nipples. It was about as sexy as him being naked or, strangely, even more so. "Are you taking that shirt off? I can still dry it for you."

He whipped it off, and it gave her something to do as she hooked it on a high kitchen cabinet close to the oven heat. "So that's how you get men naked," he roughly teased.

"Of course. I make it rain, then I strip them." She smoothed her hands down the sleeves to unwrinkle them.

"What do you do after you strip them?"

She stopped fussing over his shirt and realized he was coming closer. His smile was overtly sexual, his dark eyes glimmering in liquid mischief. "Do you kiss them?"

"Maybe," she said and slid past him to go back around the kitchen island. There was something very predatory in his eyes, and she began backing away more quickly as her heart kicked wildly in her rib cage.

"Do you caress them with those hands of yours? Look up at them with those pretty eyes?"

She blinked for a moment, then burst out laughing. "*What* do you mean? These are the only eyes I have. Which others should I use?"

"It's the look in those eyes I refer to. Do you use that doe look on them, too? The one that makes me want to chase you?"

When she laughingly shook her head and backed away farther, he charged and she squealed and sped around the kitchen island, managing two rounds until he caught her and spun her around, both their smiles a mile long. His grin faded before she could even bask in the beauty of it, and his expression fell deathly somber. "I want to kiss you very badly," he whispered, bending his head, his chest heaving.

"Garrett, no," she murmured, struggling to pull free. She spun around and went to check on the pizza, her pulse throbbing in her temples as she pretended to be busy watching the cheese melt.

He came up behind her again and stroked a hand down her hair. "What if I asked you for what you wanted, and you told me exactly what it is that you *want*?"

"Florida."

His stare almost bored holes into her profile, and through the corner of her eye, she noticed his jaw clamped, hard as granite. "Be real with me, Kate. For once in our lives, let's stop playing games."

She shook her head, feeling panicked and afraid of opening up to him. "Whatever it is, you can't give it to me."

"Just try me."

Gnawing on her lower lip, she studied his face, his features carved fiercely in determination, as if he truly did care for her. Well…did he? Had he seen her like a woman all along and had she not noticed because she'd been too busy pretending she didn't love him? She wanted him. All of him. A family of her own. She knew it was too much to want of him, to *ask* from him. Especially after what she'd heard.

"Everyone knows about you and…that heiress you're planning a wedding with."

His eyebrows lifted in mock interest. "Like it's a fact now?"

Ignoring the dangerous purr in his voice, Kate put on an oven mitt, pulled the pizza out and set it on the stove top. "I can't believe you'd marry for business." She couldn't look at him while saying that, so she occupied herself with preparing the food.

He was silent as she used her cutter to slice the pizza into perfect pieces.

Then he murmured, "I wasn't going to marry at all. So why would it matter if I just used it as means to an end, if it's what Cassandra's asking for and it will all be over in six months anyway?"

"You're better than that, Garrett," she whispered.

"But not good enough for you," he mumbled, watching her closely.

Her throat tightened on a reply that she just refused to give as she put a slice on a plate for him, and another on one for herself, staying quiet. What was the point? Flirting with him? Playing with fire? He never wanted to marry, he'd just said, and if he did, it was purely for business. She had to believe she deserved a family of her own. Especially since she'd had her own family torn apart when she was so young.

Quietly, she carried both plates to the kitchen island. He sat down on the stool beside her, then took a large bite, munching.

"Freckles, this is so good." He shook his head and took another bite, making a groaning noise that made her remember...sex. With him.

"It is, isn't it?" The sweet vegetable flavors combined with the toasted-almond flour and goat cheese melted in her mouth, but her insides melted more at the sounds he made. She squirmed on her stool and watched him get up to pour two glasses of water from the pitcher in the fridge.

He set hers down next to her plate, then continued eating. When he licked up a crumb from the corner of his lips, her heart raced in a strange mix of fear and anticipation. He'd asked if she wanted him to give chase... and suddenly she couldn't imagine anything more exhilarating than being hunted, chased and claimed by him.

Shaking her head, she washed down her pizza with the water. She was surprised when he spoke again; he'd already finished his slice. Now his attention seemed fixed solely on her again.

He stroked a finger down her jaw.

"What about me?" he asked.

She frowned and set her half-eaten pizza down. "What do you mean, what about you?"

"You say you'd only marry for love. Do you feel nothing for me? If I go through with this marriage to Cassandra, how would you feel about it?"

The meal suddenly wasn't sitting too well in her stomach. "If she's what you want…"

"I'm very interested in something that she has, but I want to make it clear that I don't want her." There was no mistaking the steel in his voice as he set a hand on her thigh as if it belonged there. "What I want to know is if there's even a chance that I can have what I most want on this earth."

Her pulse skyrocketed when she saw the stark hunger in his gaze, a gaze that ping-ponged from her eyes to her mouth and made her pulse race erratically. But when he began to get close, she stood up for some reason. Garrett laughed darkly, quietly, as if to himself. Then he followed her up and began to back her into a corner with purpose, his eyes blazing.

"Where are you going, Kate?"

She quickened her steps, but he followed closely until she stopped when the back of her knees hit a wall.

He smiled delightedly. "You do want me to catch you, don't you?"

With painstaking slowness, as though to torture her, he raised his hand and set it on her hair, and it was as if she could feel his fingers tangling inside her, tangling around her heart. "Do you want to be with me again?" he rasped, using his fist in her hair to tip her head back.

Every instinct of self-preservation warned her against reaching out to him, giving him this power over her again, but there was no pulling away from him as his hand wound deeper into the fall of hair at her nape, his piercing onyx eyes drowning her in their depths.

"I've been inside you once—and it wasn't enough. I wanted to wake up and look into your eyes and see you smile at me. I didn't want you to leave. Not like that. Not like it was a mistake."

Her breasts rose and fell with each strained breath. "It wasn't a mistake to me. I loved every moment of it."

"Then why don't you put your arms around me now? Why don't you touch me? Was I too rough?" His voice dropped even lower as he tightened his fist, his eyes holding a sexy, primal shine as he drank in her face. "Katie, I promise you that next time I'll take it so much slower. I'll kiss you from the tip of your toes to the top of your lovely head. I'll move slowly inside you…"

He bent his head, tipped up her face with a crooked finger and kissed her parted lips. The gasps stealing out of her were impossible to hold back. He opened his mouth as though to breathe them into his body, drag them into his lungs.

"I'll prepare you for me again. Prepare you for hours, Kate. Hours. I don't regret it happened, Kate, only that I didn't do it right."

He grasped her hands and placed them on his shoulders, and Kate didn't take them away. Her nails gouged into his skin as she pressed against him, her eyes drifting shut. "Please don't do this."

"How long will you hold out, Kate? If I do this…"

Expert fingers traced the tips of her sensitive breasts through her damp shirt, and Kate gasped as sensations stormed through her.

"Will you say no? If I do this…?"

He undid her halter top and let the fabric pool at her waist, and then eased one breast out of the material of her bra. He bent his head and kissed one straining nipple, laving it expertly with his tongue, priming it before he latched on and suckled her with his warm mouth.

Moisture pooled between her legs, red-hot desire rocking to her very core.

She clasped his head, thinking to pull him back, but instead she just clutched his silky hair as he turned his head and performed the same expert torture on the other puckered tip.

She struggled weakly, halfheartedly, until he pressed her arms down at her sides, their fingers linking in a tight grip as he took her mouth in a wild, stormy kiss. Her lips opened, allowing him entrance with a soft, welcoming moan, and she was undone by his taste. "Garrett."

Not even thinking what she was doing, Kate clung to him and curled one leg around his hips, her skirt hiking up as she nestled his hardness between her open thighs.

He curled a hand around the back of her knee to keep her leg up, and he rocked his hips and pulled back to stare into her wide, sparkling eyes. He bent down to take her lips softly. "You want that, Katie? You want that from me?"

The feel of him, the reminder of what it felt like to have him, hot and hard, inside her, made her feverish.

She wanted to nod, to say yes, to tell him not to ask

and just take her, but instead she wedged a hand between their burning bodies and palmed his erection. He hissed out a breath and nipped her earlobe, the closest thing to his mouth, then swept down to devour one aching nipple again.

She moaned feebly and began to pant. Arching her back, she pushed her breast up, as if craving a deeper kiss, so he opened wide around her flesh and sucked hard. "Garrett!" she cried.

A groan rumbled up in his chest as he seized her hands and pinned them over her head, trapping her as he looked at her with wild, hungry eyes.

"I want this so much." He ducked his head and his lips brushed the tip of her breast, his hand tightening on her wrists.

She felt a new surge of dampness in her panties, her breasts weighing heavily with the need to be cupped by his palms. Kate couldn't believe how many times she'd dreamed of this, wanted it. She moaned softly and arched her back in invitation once more.

"Garrett..." She pressed herself up to his mouth, and his lips returned to her nipple. Fire swept through her.

Fisting her flowing, flaming hair in his hands, he pulled her face back to look at him. "Tell me you want me." He spoke in a dangerous tone as his hands slid downward to unzip her skirt.

"I want you," she gasped.

He kissed her hard, blindingly, as he shoved the material down her hips, then slid her clinging halter top off, as well.

His lips softened on a groan as he cupped her sex in his big palm. His voice was but a breath in her ear, shaking her world like a cannon blast. "I want you, too. I can't stop wanting you."

He pressed the heel of his palm to the bundle of nerves hidden at her core, and she released a soft cry.

He dipped his hand into her panties, then watched her as he parted her folds with his fingers and pushed the middle one inside. Her hips rolled while her eyes searched his face and he pushed her arousal even higher.

"Does one feel good? Or would you rather have two?" he rasped.

He watched her expression dissolve as he added a second finger into her snug grip. A surge of moisture drenched his hand, and he bent his head and prodded a taut nipple with his tongue.

That's when he heard voices out in the living room.

Kate snapped out of her daze and stiffened when she heard the front door slam shut. She practically flew away from Garrett, jumping as the voices became clear and the two figures appeared in the living room—which adjoined the kitchen.

"—so just be quiet and let me get it real qui…"

Molly and Julian froze in their tracks.

Molly's eyes flared in mute shock as Kate struggled to right her bra and panties and used the vegetable chopping block to cover what she could. Julian's eyes widened like saucers as he took in Garrett's bare-chested state and Kate trying her damnedest to hide behind one miserable little cutting board.

"Okay, I'd rather not have seen that. What about you, Molls?" Julian smirked.

Molly blinked, her cheeks about as red as her hair, but Kate was sure she wasn't nearly as red as Kate. "Seen what? I didn't see anything. I think I'll come visit with Kate another day."

They shuffled backward through the living room, and even after the front door slammed shut behind them, Kate just couldn't look at Garrett. Her face burned in embarrassment. They were panting, the sounds of their haggard breaths echoing in the silence. Slowly, he reached out, but she stepped back and shook her head.

"What is it you want from me, Garrett?" she asked brokenly.

His voice was low and textured with wanting. "I want you to stay in the city, Kate."

"Is that all?"

"For now, yes." His face tightened with emotion as he watched her slip back into her skirt, and his eyes flashed as he saw her reach for her discarded clothing. "Fine, no."

"Then what?" Her arms shook as she shoved them back into the arm holes.

"I want you in bed with me." His eyes raked down her body almost desperately, and she hated how easily her blood bubbled again when he grabbed her hands to stop her from dressing. "Please. Kate. Don't."

"So this is about sex," she said. She pushed his hands away.

"You make it sound like that's a bad thing. Katie, I know you want me, too. You were just trembling in my arms."

"For how long do you want me in bed? A week? Two?" she dared, her heart twisting in her chest when she tried to recall if Garrett had ever really even been with anyone for that long. "What about Cassandra? Don't you think she'd like to know about your little side plan here?"

His mouth dipped into an even deeper scowl than usual, then he restlessly raked his fingers through his hair. "Damn, Katie, I keep feeling like I'm falling short here. What the hell is it that you *want* from me?"

"You're talking about marriage with another woman, Garrett! And you stand here telling me you fall short? You damned well do fall short! If I'd wanted an affair, I'd have it with someone other than you. I want a shot at having the family I've never had, that's what I want!"

In the instant she spoke those last words, Kate wished she could take them back. It was as though she'd slapped him; Garrett suddenly looked like that young boy, that dark, tormented young boy, so forlorn after what had happened the night of the murders.

"Well, then you were right about one thing," he said, a tinge of angry frustration in his voice. "I can definitely not give you back what you want."

"Garrett, you misunderstood me—"

But he was gone, the bang of the door that followed his departure making her wince.

Eight

Garrett knew that their half brother, Emerson Wells, harbored no love for the Gages. Even though the Gage patriarch had apparently been screwing Emerson's mother for years, he'd refused to recognize Emerson as his son and bought the woman off to stay quiet and away from them—something the family had discovered when their father's lawyer, upon his death, disclosed the existence of another heir who could contest part of the inheritance.

He never did, though Eleanor Gage had thought it wise to pay him a few million dollars to go away for good.

Naturally, if Emerson had half the clout and pride of a Gage—which he apparently did—he would have no intention of ever catering to a Gage's wishes. So he'd denied Landon's summons six times during the past several weeks, something that didn't surprise Garrett. But now, they were running out of time to make concrete decisions about the Clarks Communications deal, and Garrett finally had it with begging the imbecile for a meeting. This limbo was putting everyone on edge, especially him, since not only his two brothers, but Cassandra herself, seemed to believe Garrett was the only one who could make the deal possible now.

He'd been so close to just saying, "To hell with it, I'll do it."

Kate would never have him anyway.

And yet a little part of him knew that he could never stop trying. Not now. Not when he knew that she wanted him, knew the delicate feel of her body against his, knew the fragrance of that devilishly sexy red hair. Kate might not know it yet, and hell, Garrett might have spent his entire life fighting it, but they belonged to one another.

The recent times they'd seen one another at his mother's Sunday brunches, they'd spoken of trivial things, their last argument forgotten—or at least, not mentioned. But the air crackled between them. Her eyes seemed bluer when they rested on him. They softened when she saw him. He wasn't blind to it, couldn't be blind to those looks anymore. He had to do something, and fast.

So that's how he'd found himself sitting in his office yesterday, dialing Emerson's mother. He was surprised that she'd picked up after a few rings.

"This is Garrett Gage, and I realize Emerson doesn't want to hear from us, but it's imperative we talk to him. I assure you he'll be happy to hear us out, if you could—"

The woman had hung up.

But Garrett hadn't given up. He'd then punched in some numbers and got Emerson's secretary on the line.

After a moment of silence, she'd put him on hold. When she finally came back, she'd reluctantly conceded, "He'll give you ten minutes tomorrow morning."

Now, as he presented himself at his half brother's office downtown, he marveled at how well his brother seemed to be doing for himself. Garrett strolled through the floor containing the executive offices and found his brother's secretary waiting for him. "Mr. Wells will be here shortly, Mr. Gage. You can go right in."

He grabbed a mint from the plate on her desk as she continued typing on her keyboard, and instead of taking a seat, he paced around while the woman continued typing. After taking a phone call, she hung up and left her desk, and Garrett knew exactly where he would wait for his brother. He strolled directly into the sumptuous office with the plaque EMERSON WELLS, PRESIDENT on the door. He took the seat in front of Emerson's desk and laced his fingers behind his head as he waited, taking in his surroundings with an admiring eye. Apparently his half brother appreciated art—he had a vitrine full of pre-Columbian artifacts that stretched across an entire wall. There were no photographs on his desk; in fact, there were hardly any personal effects at all.

After a few more minutes the man arrived, and his murderous expression told Garrett he didn't like seeing him one bit.

But he *had* agreed to the appointment, at last.

Emerson sighed and crossed his arms. "Which one of the three brothers are you?"

"The middle one," Garrett said.

Emerson's expression softened somewhat at the news, and for a moment, Garrett even sensed that he'd dropped his guard a little. His voice was still wary, though. "So you're the one who was there when Father died."

Garrett's insides went icy cold at the reminder, but he still managed a curt nod, though Emerson hadn't seemed to phrase it as a question anyway.

"He say anything about me?" Emerson asked, and Garrett flashed back to the sidewalk, the street, the concert they'd just come from that night.

Chest knotting up painfully, Garrett dragged in a long, steadying breath. "He tried to speak, but he couldn't get much out."

The talk about his father made the memory so goddamned fresh now, his stomach roiled. He thought back to Dave Devaney's last breath, and to Kate. The way her face had crumpled when the police had brought Garrett home and he'd told everyone that both men were dead.

Kate wanted a family. A family she'd never had, because of *him*.

There hadn't been a night since she'd said that when he hadn't recalled her words. He hadn't been able to face her a moment longer. She'd torn him open and apart, and for weeks he'd been grappling for ways in which he could ever make it up to her. Would he never be able to put it behind him? Was she leaving because Garrett reminded her too much of what she couldn't have? Or because she'd never forgive him for repeatedly screwing up her life?

Shaking the disturbing thought aside, he stood up and stuck his hands into his pants pockets, assuming a casual stance as they faced each other. "I can tell you want me gone, so I'll happily drop the chitchat. My brothers and I want to make a deal with you. We're not interested in making friends, and we know you aren't either. What we're interested in is business, and judging by the luxurious surroundings and the Picasso on the wall, you're a man who thinks of business just as we do. Am I right?"

Though he was dark-haired like Garrett, Emerson's eyes weren't the same. He had Landon's silver eyes instead, and they glowed eerily with warning. "My father ran me over like a goddamned mongrel without a tail. I won't allow the same from you."

"I'm sorry that he felt he had to," Garrett said, but he understood what his father was trying to protect. He hadn't wanted his wife to ever find out he'd strayed. So he'd cut off his illegitimate son and lover from his life, only to die so soon afterward that his lawyers had still been paying off the woman for her silence when it happened.

It had been tragic, to watch his mother find out she'd been betrayed. When she could do nothing about it.

She'd been broken at the funeral—crying nonstop at first, already having found out from the accounts, and the lawyers, her husband had not been the faithful, loving man she'd always imagined. Garrett had had his own grief on his shoulders, and he'd blamed himself for the pain he saw on her mother's face. His mother would have never found out about Emerson, or another woman, if her husband hadn't died so abruptly and she hadn't been forced to take over the financials of the family. The records of money sent to another woman's account, regularly, sparked alarm, confusion, until finally, the truth had sunk in.

"He freaking ruined my life. He broke my mother's heart and mine, too," Emerson grated, his teeth tightly clamped as he curled his fingers into fists.

Garrett was taken aback by the hard anger in his half

brother's eyes. Would Cassandra Clarks be able to handle being married to this guy for six months? He appeared only half-civilized, and dangerous, to boot.

"Emerson, I'm sorry if the measures he took were not to your liking, but your mother liked them very well," Garrett said. He was referring to the three million-dollar payments she'd received for her silence—after his father died. Not to mention that he'd already been providing for her to have quite a healthy living while he was still alive. Emerson couldn't have been more than twelve at the time. Julian had barely been ten. Garrett had been fifteen and Landon eighteen.

If their father hadn't died, Emerson would be walking the streets without the Gage brothers ever knowing he existed.

Maybe they should have tried to contact him. Maybe Emerson resented that, too. But just seeing the grief on their mother's face had been enough to make them want to keep him as far away from the family as they could.

Maybe, all hell would break loose when Mother once again realized they were dealing with him. But Landon had said that he'd take care of Mother. Enough time had passed that hopefully she'd look beyond her dead husband's transgressions at this point. And their mother was shrewd when it came to business, too.

"Will you meet with me and my brothers to discuss our business proposition? We really need your help."

Impatient, Garrett waited for Emerson's answer, but his half brother only glared at him as he slowly headed over to resume his place behind his desk.

Emerson was more rugged than all his brothers, and even with his well-groomed appearance in that gray suit, there was an air of isolation around his tall figure that made Garrett somehow relate to him. He knew that Emerson was somewhere between Julian and Garrett in age, so that put him around twenty-eight or twenty-nine. His hair was dark as Garrett's, his face as square and tan, but personality-wise, he seemed to be a wild card.

"I'll give you a half hour," Emerson finally conceded, his expression unreadable as he dropped into his chair and powered on his computer. "But not today. I have too much to do."

"Fine," he agreed. "Tomorrow then. Be at the *Daily* at nine a.m."

"No can do. I'm afraid I can only do it Friday."

Friday wasn't ideal. It was three days from now and only a day before the wedding. But Garrett ground his molars, shut the hell up and took the offer. Something in Emerson's angry expression when he looked up and gestured at the door to signal the conservation was over told Garrett this offer was the best he'd get from him.

"Don't be late," Garrett growled as he left.

"Kate, I'm calling and calling and no answer, then I come to get the things for the shower and they're not even baked! What is wrong with you? It's ten in the morning and we have work to do. This is our last gig before we're swept away with all this wedding stuff. You didn't talk to anyone all weekend. What's the matter? It's Tuesday. A new day awaits!"

Kate groaned when a chirpy Beth yanked open her bedroom curtains and a shaft of sunlight sliced between Kate's eyelids. She waved a weak hand in the air and rolled onto her stomach.

"Go away, Beth."

"No, I'm not going away. You, my sleepy little chef, will stand up, take a shower and—"

"I'm pregnant," Kate groaned.

"—get to work. What did you just say?"

Kate covered her face with the pillow and screamed into its feathery depths while kicking off the sheets tangled around her ankles. "I'm pregnant. *God!* I'm such a fool. Fool, fool, *fool.*"

"You're pregnant as in...you're with *child?*"

Kate sat up and cracked open her puffy eyes. "Three tests, Beth. Three. And they all agree on the fact that I'm preggo. What am I going to do?"

Sighing in misery, she covered her face with her hands, refusing to answer the string of startled, quick-fire questions Beth bombarded her with next. *"Well, whose is it? When did this happen? Why didn't you tell me? When did you find out, damn it? Are you sure?"*

Oh, Beth. She was like a bright little shooting star today—a bright little shooting star in Kate's dark gray world.

Was Kate sure? Yes, she was sure. The test stick couldn't get any pinker! The two lines, almost neon in their brightness, had been clear enough to spin Kate into a whirlwind of despair all through the night.

While miserably pondering what to do, Kate heard Beth shuffle around the room, no doubt in search of the pregnancy tests. Beth was big on evidence and that sort of thing. This came from being married to a douche bag before she'd fallen in love with Landon.

When her friend couldn't seem to find them, Kate muttered, "They're in the trash, Beth."

"Oh."

Beth disappeared into the bathroom. Kate glumly

wondered what Garrett would do when he eventually found out she was carrying his baby. She remembered how handsome he'd looked two Sundays ago at brunch. He had been thoughtful and dark as sin, and staring at her so intently and so intimately, Kate had barely been able to eat anything. She'd felt eaten by *him*. He'd stood to follow her when she'd gone to pretend to fill her plate at the buffet, and she'd felt his hand at the small of her back. "You all right?" he'd murmured.

"Of course. Why wouldn't I be?"

"You've been so busy with work, I keep wondering if you're avoiding me."

"I'm sorry. We can talk at the rehearsal dinner…that is, if you don't…if you're not bringing…"

"I won't bring anyone if you won't," he said, staring at her intently.

"I won't," she assured him.

"Then I won't," he said back.

And oh, how she wished she had the courage to say she was sorry for what she'd said to him that day in her apartment, but the continued talk she heard from Molly and Beth regarding the Clarks and Gage wedding was driving her insane with jealousy and anger.

It killed her. How could he? How dare he tell her he wanted her in his bed while he was planning his brilliant and very convenient wedding? The desire that had whipped them up like tornadoes had now dropped them hard on land, and the whirlwind and the emotions in the air had been reduced to nothing.

Nothing but a one-night stand, that's what it had been.

But of course, good ol' Murphy's law had come for a visit and made *sure* Kate got pregnant.

And now they were going to have a child together.

"Yes. You're pregnant," Beth agreed when she came back out of the bathroom.

A silence settled bleakly in the room.

You're pregnant....

Her chest gripped with yearning. Along with the inexplicable fear of dying alone, without a family or anyone to love her, Kate had harbored another kind of fear for years. It was one of those little fears that took root in you and you never really knew why you had them— only that you did.

She'd feared she'd prove infertile when she grew up, and that she'd never be able to have the family she'd always longed for. She'd imagined, on her best days, that if she ever got pregnant, the thrill she'd feel would obliterate anything else.

Now, maybe a little kernel of thrill had taken up residence somewhere, in some quiet, motherly part of her, but it was too hidden to recognize.

Kate had proven fertile, yes. Physically capable of having a family, yes.

But she had conceived this baby with Garrett Gage.

And her considerable pride already smarted like *hell* since she knew she would have to tell him. Especially after this past month, when they'd both pretended at the family Sunday brunches that they were still just friends.

Kate saw that Beth had her cell phone in her hand and leaped out of bed. "No! What are you doing?"

Beth held the phone out of Kate's reach, her expression stern as a concerned mother's. "I'm calling a doctor. Unless you want me to call Garrett, Kate. It's his, isn't it? You look pale, Kate. I think—"

"Call anyone and die. Do you hear me?"

The thought of Garrett knowing this so soon, before

she had time to build up her emotional walls against him…the thought of him finding out that just the thought of carrying his baby inside her made her queasy and restless…and the thought of him demanding to *marry* her out of duty and honor and all he held dearer than Kate…

No. God, it was worse than she could imagine.

Her worst nightmare come true.

Beth paused when she noticed the angry flush spreading up Kate's neck. Lips pursed, she hung up, and started dialing again.

"No! Beth, don't you *dare*."

"I'm calling Molly, okay? We need to figure out how we're handling this with the family. Don't even try to stop me this time."

Kate groaned. "Molly's getting her paintings shipped to New York, and she's got enough on her plate with a wedding in five days!"

"Fine, then Julian. Julian will help us with this, Kate, you know he will."

An image of hunky, easygoing Julian, never judgmental, always one for cool-headed thoughts, flitted through her mind. Julian had always been the perfect coconspirator. Not only did he know how to stay quiet, it was his nature to.

But Kate still shook her head. "Beth, the wedding is in five days. Let's just…drop this for now. Please. Please don't tell anyone until I'm ready."

Beth met her eyes dubiously. "But what are you going to do when you see Garrett at the rehearsal dinner? At the wedding? When are you going to tell him?"

"After the wedding. I can't do it before. I want Molly to enjoy her day," she said miserably.

"No, no, no, that's not a good plan. It might be too

late, Kate. He might be engaged by then to another woman!"

Pain wrenched through Kate's insides. "I don't expect him to stop his plans for me. Honestly. We could be better parents if we weren't together than if we are forced to be together."

"You're afraid, Kate, and that's okay. But you're turning into a coward. Where's the girl I know? The Kate I know would fight for him. Stop being afraid that he will break your heart. You're breaking it yourself without even letting him know that he has it."

Kate couldn't reply.

But the words replayed in her head like an echo of a truth she wasn't sure she was prepared to listen to when she had a pregnancy to deal with.

Was Beth right?

Was Kate so afraid of letting him in that she was running away, not from being hurt by him, but from *loving* him?

Oh, God. And now what was she going to do about Miami?

Nine

Kate was turning out to be one of those pregnant women who had nausea every morning, and it wasn't fun at all. But at least by Thursday evening at Molly and Julian's rehearsal dinner at the Gage mansion, she felt better. The wedding was to be held this upcoming Saturday at noon, and the gardens had been bursting with activity all day as contractors had started delivering tables, chairs…the works. Through the windows on the other side of the living room, Kate could see the beautiful white trellis that would serve as the chapel, halfway to being fully erected.

It was going to be a beautiful wedding.

Her heart soared as she watched Molly and Julian laugh while talking to the minister. Julian towered behind Molly, who seemed to be leaning back against him as if he were a pillar. His arms were loosely around her, his chin resting on the top of her head.

There was no doubt in Kate's mind when she saw them that they belonged together. Molly had always loved Julian, but Kate hadn't realized that Julian had loved her sister back until a couple of months ago.

She'd always believed in having one soul mate…until, at eighteen, she'd realized that the man she thought might be her soul mate didn't seem to agree. He'd never openly touched her like Julian had touched Molly, but now she kept remembering the way he'd made love to her.

Did he *care* about her? Or was this all about her leaving?

"There you are!" Kate heard the booming voice of Eleanor Gage from nearby, and in the same instant, spotted the person she was speaking to as he came into the room.

Dressed in a black suit and gleaming silver tie, Garrett made such a striking figure that the atmosphere altered dramatically with him near. His beautiful face looked thoughtful and intense as he kissed his mother on the cheek, then lifted his head and seemed to be scanning the area for something. His gaze stopped roaming when he saw her, and she couldn't breathe.

With an expression almost of relief, he came over. He had such purpose in his step, and her heart almost stopped when she saw the way his eyes glimmered with…happiness?

Oh, God, she was going to die when she had to tell him.

"We should've driven over together."

His liquid black eyes raked her figure, and her pulse skyrocketed as though he could suddenly see with some sort of X-ray vision the little baby growing inside her.

For a moment she thought he knew. He knew her secret and it would all be out in the open.

Drawing in a deep breath, she blew a loose strand of hair out of her face. "I hitched a ride with Beth and Landon." The thought of being alone with him in the close confinement of his car again both terrified and excited her.

The more distance she kept from him, the smoother her plans would run.

He seized her elbow and pulled her along the room, leading her to the terrace doors. "Come with me outside."

"Why?"

"Because I want to talk to you, Kate."

She let him lead her to the exact spot they'd visited on his birthday, when he'd found out she was leaving. Rather than release her, his hand stayed on her elbow as he smiled and took in her dress with the thirsty eyes of a man who intimately knew her.

The situation worsened when he bent his head and his voice caressed her ear, its texture a seductive black velvet. "So what have you been up to? Besides avoiding me?"

She ducked, not wanting him to know he still made her knees weak, her insides mushy. She wished—goodness, she wished—that Garrett wasn't considering marriage to another woman, so that Kate wouldn't dread the moment she'd have to mention a child was on the way so much.

"Working and…packing."

"Packing," he repeated without any inflection whatsoever.

The fact that his hand was on her elbow, causing all sorts of ripples of want inside her, made her drop her gaze to take in the contrast of his tan skin with her fair complexion. As though that were an instruction for him to let go, he dropped his hold.

His eyebrows pulled low over his eyes—eyes that were hard with frustration.

"Kate, honestly, what the hell are you running from?"

Anger flared inside her. What else would she be running away from but him? "What do you care if I leave? Why are you so hell-bent on stopping me? Go and worry about your heiress!"

"I will, but you come first, Kate. You've always come first for me. Before anything in the world. And I happen to be responsible for you, Kate."

"Oh puhleeze! Responsible, my fanny. I'm a grown woman, Garrett, a fact that you can attest to yourself. Why do insist on continuing to treat me like your sister?"

"Sister? Kate, I freaking *slept with you!*"

Her eyes widened in shock. Her throat clogged with emotion, and she spun around toward the glass doors. "I can't do this right now. Not here. Not now."

He stopped her with one hand. "I'm sorry, I didn't mean to upset you. But it would be very damn simple for me to marry an heiress right now if it weren't for the fact that you and I made love, Kate."

"We had se—"

"We made love."

His eyes glowed down at her fiercely. Crazily, she even thought she saw longing there. But if he longed for her, why would he even consider marrying anyone else?

"I told you it was a mistake. Please just carry on with your plans, and I'll carry on with mine."

"God, you're so stubborn, Kate." He propped his elbows next to hers on the balustrade and gazed outside, his expression pained. "You'll never be able to forget your father died because of me, will you?"

She swallowed and shook her head. "No. That's not true. I don't blame you, Garrett. You were just a boy, and you wanted to help your father. Like you always want to help everyone. You misunderstood what I said. I might have blamed you for a time because I needed someone to blame. I was so angry."

"Me, too." He leaned forward and stared at the cluttered tables and chairs out on the lawn, and Kate watched his profile as the urge to touch him began to consume her.

"But my anger isn't about that now. It's about me. It angers me to want something that I can't have."

He glanced at her curiously, his head cocked to the side as he patiently waited for her to explain.

"Having a family is something I've wanted my whole life," she admitted, softly.

He dragged her into his arms, and she was so exhausted from learning she was pregnant, she closed her eyes and let him. His thumb stroked her arm, causing goose bumps to jump along her bare flesh.

"I never thought I'd have one of my own, and now I can't stop thinking about it," he whispered.

Fighting to ignore the sensual stirring inside her, Kate closed her eyes, her connection with him too great to ignore. She suddenly wanted to cry, right here in his arms, at his confession. Because she was sure he was imagining having a family with someone else, with a woman he might marry for convenience. Not with Kate. Still, she loved him so much she couldn't hate him for wanting the same thing that she did.

"You deserve to be happy, Garrett. You've tried to take care of all of us for so long. Even Julian and Molly."

He rubbed her back and she rubbed his. "They hate me for making them keep their hands to themselves until now." His whisper stirred the top of her hair.

His scent made her light-headed but instead of drawing away, she drew closer and inhaled, happy that he had an arm around her. "You've always tried to do the right thing."

His lips twitched against her scalp, and he edged back and glanced down at her, searching her expression. "You've always trusted me, Katie. To do the right thing. But you don't trust I'll make the right choice with Cassandra?"

Her stomach twisted uncomfortably, and when she attempted to pry free, Garrett kept her pinned to him. Even his eyes held her trapped. "Relax. Let's not fight, all right? Let me just hold you like this."

His body emanated heat, and her every cell perfectly recalled the night she had belonged to him. Kate's throat closed so tight she couldn't talk, especially when she settled down against him once more. He ran a hand tenderly down the back of her head, and she relaxed her muscles despite herself.

"Katie, let me make it better for you," he whispered against the top of her head.

Kate closed her eyes. She knew he felt compelled to watch over her, but Garrett had been tied to his promise and had looked at her as a *duty* his whole life.

Kate would rue the day she ever trapped him any further.

But now she was carrying his baby.

"If you leave—" he tipped her chin back to look at

her "—who's to tell me it isn't your way of making me come get you?"

She edged back, wide-eyed, then scowled. "I would never do that! I don't want you to…do anything. Plus, it would be hard for you to follow me with a new wife attached to your arm."

"A wife I will not have if I choose not to," he said. "Why don't you tell me why you're so interested in her if you're not interested in staying here?"

She glared, and suddenly it was just too painful to look at him.

She shook her head, and turned to walk away but he wasn't letting her go just yet.

"Where are you going, Katie?" he taunted. "Do I frighten you? Is it me you're running away from?"

She was struggling, but he caught her and looked fiercely into her eyes. His breath fanned her face, slow and steady, warm and unexpectedly sweet.

"Garrett…" she whispered, dying with want as she clutched his shoulders.

He squeezed her. "Kate, I've known you all my life. I've been there for you all my life—I have to be there for the rest of it. You have to let me. We need to talk about what happened. We can't just pretend that it didn't when I'm consumed with knowing that it *did*."

Her eyes were fastened to his mouth, and all she could think of was that his mouth was *there* for her. His lips were there to sear her again, brand her again. Kate trembled with the need to wrap herself around his shoulders and neck and never let go. She wanted to crush his mouth with hers and do all the things she hadn't done with anyone else because she'd been waiting for the boy she secretly loved to *look* at her.

Now he was looking at her. His gaze hungry, missing no detail of her features. Almost seeing into her soul, discovering her secret, aching love for him.

"Tell me why you're leaving. Is it because of me?" He couldn't seem to help himself as he lifted his finger to trace her lips. Her breath caught, and his face darkened as he watched.

Kiss him. Tell him it's him and that he's going to be a father! But while all these impulses rampaged through her, she drew back an inch and considered it a good moment to retreat before she truly lost her senses. She'd lost them once. Now she was pregnant. She didn't want to castigate him for that night, a night she had been wishing and praying would someday happen. She didn't want him to pay with his whole life. She simply loved him too much.

Kate shook her head and glanced away. "No, it's not you."

Spinning away before she could lose her head, she hugged herself and stared into the house, where there was light and music and smiles everywhere.

"You could be carrying my—" Garrett cleared his throat behind her "—you could be pregnant, Kate."

The air felt static as she turned back to him in alarm. "Excuse me?"

The intensity in his eyes terrified her. "We didn't use protection, Freckles."

She shook her head. Fast. Almost too fast.

"You'd tell me if there were consequences, right?" he asked meaningfully.

Her world tilted on its axis. What if she went ahead and told him that she was having his child? Her stomach cramped at the thought.

She was loath to worry Molly a day before her wedding. Kate was the eldest and had cared for her like a mother, had always set a good example. How could she bear detracting from her sister's joy right now?

She had to wait until after the wedding.

She bit her lip, glancing away. "Whatever happens, I meant what I said. I'm not marrying ever without love."

"Why? Do you love another man?"

Swallowing, Kate met his stormy black gaze. "No, Garrett. It would have been hard for me to love anyone, when my whole life I've been in love with you."

He blinked at her words.

God.

She couldn't believe she'd said them.

But she had.

She had to come clean.

She glanced away, blushing. "That's why I slept with you that night, Garrett. And that's why I'm leaving. I want to be loved back."

He stared at her as though flabbergasted, motionless and unmoving.

"We need to go. Dinner is about to be served," she murmured and went inside.

He didn't follow her for minutes, and from inside, she saw him leaning on the balustrade with his face in his hands, breathing hard.

Her insides knotted with pain for him. Maybe she shouldn't have confessed it. But Beth was right. Kate was a coward, afraid he'd hurt her. She'd had to at least let him know that all the time they'd spent together had meant everything to Kate, even when she knew he had not ever been emotionally available to love her like she wanted him to.

Garrett was a fair man. He was a man who recognized his own flaws, maybe even to the extreme extent that he saw flaws where none existed. She knew he felt...unworthy. That he believed a man had died because of him. But he was also generous and giving, and he wouldn't be able to stand the idea of causing Kate any pain.

He'd let her go so she could find what she was looking for, especially once he recognized that he wouldn't be able to give it to her himself. And he'd marry his heiress, for whom he wouldn't need to feel anything. But at least Kate had stopped lying to him and to herself about not loving him anymore. At least she'd told him her real reasons for leaving.

Baby or not, she would still go.

Once they were seated at the tables in the formal dining room, she felt him stare at her as intently as ever from across the floral centerpiece.

Waiters brought over the salads first—arugula, organic pear, goat cheese and candied pecans, topped with a soft vinaigrette dressing with a hint of pomegranate. That was followed by an assortment of lamb, duck, beef tenderloins and chicken medallions, accompanied by the most deliciously spiced vegetables Kate had ever tasted.

She ate whatever she was served and almost still felt a little hungry. But most of all, she was conscious of everything Garrett did on the opposite side of the table. Under the table, she held her hands over her stomach, where she could feel and sense her baby, feeling almost nostalgic that the father was so close, and didn't even know what he'd just given her.

She stole peeks at him throughout the night as idle conversation abounded. When their eyes met, emotions and confusion flooded her.

Once they were enjoying a variety of sorbet, cheese, and sweet desserts, Landon pushed his chair back and stood. "Cheers! To Julian and Molly," Landon said, and glanced at Garrett.

Kate saw the manner in which Garrett nodded somberly at Landon, almost as though saying, "You're next," and Kate jerked her eyes down at her plate, the nausea suddenly coming back with a vengeance.

But no matter how fervently she wished it, there was no taking back her *I love you*.

The next morning, all three Gage brothers sat across the conference table from their half brother. Garrett noticed how Landon and Julian were taking stock of their brother. Emerson was beastly in size, very large and muscled. As president of his personal security business, it seemed fitting, but today Emerson was also proving to be a very moody man. He'd seemed impatient to leave from the moment he arrived.

It seemed truly unjust to Garrett that his father had treated Emerson and his mother the way he had. And when he'd died, he'd ended up hurting everyone, for the truth easily had come to light. Their lawyers had had to explain to the Gages, once they took over all the financial accounts, why there were so many transfers and payments made to an unknown woman.

When they'd learned it was because this woman had borne a Gage son, Garrett's mother had entered a wild depression for years, and he didn't even want to think of how it had been for Emerson and his mother. It had hurt the Gages to lose their father to death, but the pain of losing him while he was living might possibly be even worse.

Now every bit of pain and resentment marked Emerson's hard, unyielding features. Garrett couldn't know the true extent of his resentments, but he'd bet they ran deeper than the man let on. His energy was too controlled, and his eyes were too ruthless and sharp to reveal his emotions.

Garrett knew it would hardly matter to Cassandra which man she married as long as she got out of her brother's clutches, and he and his brothers would be happy to compensate Emerson for the task.

If, that was, they could convince the stubborn man to agree to this whole scenario.

With a bleak, tight-lipped smile, Emerson finally spoke after Landon explained the situation. "If this chick is as hot as you all say, why don't *you* marry her?" he asked, silver eyes trained on Garrett.

"Garrett's not inclined to marry," Landon answered. He sat calmly in his leather chair on the opposite side of the conference table.

"Well, that makes two of us," Emerson said with a growl. "I'm never marrying, especially no damn heiress."

"You might like to reconsider with what we're offering," Landon said, signaling at the open folder sitting before him on the table. "You'll be a very rich man, Emerson, if you agree to this."

"I'm already very rich without needing to deal with any of you."

"Emerson, we're talking fifty million for your take *alone*. That's almost ten million a month for just marrying her."

"Why don't *you* do it?" he persisted, glaring at Garrett.

Garrett wasn't going to tell him why.

But he still remembered Kate in his arms on the terrace last night. He'd been so damned excited to have her in his arms. He'd wanted to make love to her again, had been more than ready to physically. He could have moved back so that she wouldn't notice, and perhaps she hadn't, but instead he'd remained in place, his every sense attuned to her, to the contact of their bodies—the press of her belly against his erection. He'd wanted to press harder into her, to devour her and break her every resistance until she gave him everything he wanted, and admitted to everything he needed to know. At the same time, he wanted to protect her from everything and everyone.

He hadn't pushed, but he knew the thought of leaving was killing her. He knew Molly's wedding had to get to her. Kate was a woman. And she was the older sister, almost like a mother to Molly.

He wanted her. Needed her with a force he'd never needed anyone in his life. Physically, he wanted to be with her again, but it was more. It had always been more with her. *She loved him*....

But he wasn't going to tear his guts open in front of Emerson, not even in front of his other brothers, so when silence reigned, Emerson sighed and rose.

"Sit down, Emerson. I'm planning to marry someone else," Garrett snapped, scowling because he'd had to let the cat out of the bag.

Emerson plopped back down and cocked a brow. "Should I start renting a tux?" he asked, his cockiness reminding Garrett of his younger brother, Julian, somehow.

"Rent it for your own wedding. You won't be coming to mine."

"*My* own wedding is tomorrow and we need this engagement settled. So are you in, or are you out, Emerson?" Julian demanded.

Emerson eyed Julian, then Landon, then Garrett, then Landon again. "There's only one thing that would ever tempt me to agree to this farce."

"Name it and it's yours," said Landon with his business voice.

"I want the Gage name. I'm as much his son as you are. My mother provided a paternity test, and he refused to acknowledge me. I want it acknowledged today. If I get my rightful name, you have a deal."

Garrett crossed his arms and eyed Landon, who seemed to be the one most reluctant to grant Emerson's wish. Garrett wasn't against it. The Gage brothers had no right to withhold something their own father should have granted his kid in the first place, but they would need to talk to their mother first. She was a just woman, but she might need some time to get used to the idea of a fourth Gage in town.

In a terse but quiet voice, Landon spoke at last. "When you go through with the marriage and quietly walk away from Cassandra without trouble, we'll amend our former agreement so you can become a Gage."

Emerson rose to his feet. "I'll need to get it in writing."

"Of course," Landon assured him.

"So do we arrange for them to meet?" Julian queried, rising, too, probably eager to leave to get his other business in order before his wedding and honeymoon.

"Do whatever the hell you want," Emerson snarled. "Just tell me when and where I get to meet my wife."

"So, it's done then," Landon concluded, still keeping

up his cool facade. But once Emerson stalked out of the conference room, Landon sighed wearily and scraped a hand along his face.

"Mother's going to throw a fit."

"Let's not tell her yet. He's not a Gage until he carries through…and he might fail," Jules said. Then he swung his full attention to Garrett. "So do you have something to tell us, bro?"

Garrett knew what he was referring to, of course.

It would have been hard for me to love anyone, when my whole life I've been in love with you.

She'd killed him with those words. He'd been replaying them in his head all night, dying in his bed, aroused and pained when he relived them. He wanted her by his side. He wanted every inch of her. Now, his chest swelled with emotion as he reached into his jacket pocket and pulled out a small blue velvet box. He opened it and extended it so that both his brothers could see the ring nestled at its center.

Julian chuckled and swung his head up with a look of incredulousness. "That ring is obscene, man. I've never seen anything as obscene in my life."

Garrett scowled at him. "Tiffany and Company doesn't do obscene."

"But *you* do."

Ignoring the jibe, Garrett studied the brilliant rock. It was the whitest, the purest and yes, the biggest he could find in seventy-six hours. An 8.39 carat, D, internally flawless round brilliant, in a solitaire platinum band. And he had every intention of putting it on Kate's ring finger.

"I need to make a statement," he murmured at Julian,

who seemed to be amused by the fact that Garrett had gotten himself in this mess in the first place.

"Statement. You mean like 'I'm a jerk and I had to make up for it with a big rock'?"

"Go to hell."

"Tsk, more respect, old man. You're marrying my fiancée's sister."

"If she'll have me," he grumbled.

"A little drastic of you to do this just so she doesn't move to Florida, don't you think?"

Garrett snorted.

He just wouldn't let her leave.

For years, he had seen that need in her, calling to him like a siren song. He had needed to summon more self-control every year not to cave in. He had prayed she would one day realize she was too good for him and move on. Now, he needed to prove to her the opposite. He needed to remind her what that night had meant to him, how it could have been between them all along if two deaths and a lot of regret hadn't stood between them.

He freaking *loved* her, too. More than anything or anyone.

He wasn't letting her go.

He was ready to chase her to Florida if he needed to.

He held the ring between his fingers and watched it catch the light. The man at the store said it was guaranteed to make a statement, and when Garrett had said, "Guaranteed to make her say yes?" he'd nodded amiably. If only the man knew half of it. That she could be pregnant with his child.

His stomach roiled once more at the thought, and he snapped the velvet Tiffany box closed.

If she wasn't pregnant, he couldn't wait for her to be.

She wanted a family. He hadn't realized how much he wanted one, too, until now.

He imagined being a father in eight months.

She didn't seem to want to consider the possibility, but he did. Hell, he even hoped she was pregnant. *Because she'd have to take me no matter what.*

It had been years since he'd had a father. Kate herself probably no longer remembered what her father had smelled like, felt like. Garrett barely remembered his own. But he could remember how good it had felt to have him around, and he burned with the desire to be one himself. Protective and just, but he wanted something their fathers hadn't given them.

He'd once thought he'd never marry. For Kate was out of his reach.

Now he would marry no one else. And he wanted a litter of little kids for them. Girls and boys.

He would bond with his boys over cars and planes, money and business….

As for girls, a picture of a red-haired little girl like Kate popped into his mind, and his toes almost curled with the love he already felt for that little thing he'd pamper like a princess.

Then he thought of Kate when she was young, the age when her father died. His chest constricted at the reminder. Garrett still dreamed about that night, and woke up drenched in sweat, hearing the sounds of gunshots. Sometimes in his dreams they were shooting at Kate and Molly. Sometimes at his brothers. And the worst part was that Garrett survived every time.

And somehow it was always Garrett's fault.

Would he never do things right? Would his actions always hurt the people he cared about?

He breathed out through his nose as he shoved the ring box into his suit pocket. It wasn't time yet. But it would be. And once he put that ring on her finger, it would never be undone. She would be his.

And he'd spend his life making things right for her. For them both.

Ten

Molly was freaking out in the bathroom of Eleanor Gage's master bedroom, waving her hands in front of her face as her cheeks turned crimson. "It's too tight, it's too tight. Kate, it's too tight."

"Molly, you just had it altered."

"Kate, I'm pregnant."

Kate's eyes widened with joy and disbelief. "You are? Molly!" Kate squealed and hugged her, and Molly crushed her in her arms. "Does Jules know?" Kate demanded.

"No! I'm saving it for tonight. I'm almost bursting with excitement and bursting out of this damn dress! I wish I'd just married him in my boho skirt. I know he'd love it because it's more me."

"Yes, but you've already bought this beautiful designer dress, and now we want you to wear it," Kate said, shushing her and trying to see where she could loosen the material to give her some air while Molly hyperventilated.

The dress had a lovely bell skirt and a tight top—very much like the bridesmaids' dresses that Kate and Beth wore, except the bridesmaids' dresses were blue.

"Molly, relax, you look stunning," Kate assured her. Molly nodded, and their gazes locked in the mirror. Kate's eyes began to tear up. "I love you, you know that?" Kate said softly, patting Molly's bun, which needed only the veil to be perfect.

Molly turned and squeezed Kate's hand, then placed it over her stomach—where she carried Julian's baby. "I want to beg you not to go, Kate. Especially now."

Kate could almost feel the connection between both their babies as she touched her sister's belly. Her throat constricted with the need to tell her sister she was pregnant, too. She imagined sharing all things pregnancy-related with Molly and her heart swelled. "I don't want to go, Molly. The thought of not seeing my niece or nephew and not being here for you…" *And of my child not being close to people who would offer so much love.* "I'm just afraid."

Sympathy flooded Molly's blue eyes. "Kate, I know… I know you don't want to see him, especially with him getting ready to marry someone else."

The reminder that the man she loved would marry someone else while she would be alone with his beautiful baby, somewhere else, set a new world of pain crashing down on her. Her eyes stung.

It might be her pregnancy hormones. Or the fact that time was galloping closer, ready to slam into her. It would be time to leave soon. It was time for her sister to marry. This morning Beth had told her she'd heard that Garrett had proposed to Cassandra already, and she'd wanted to warn Kate to be strong during the wedding in case he appeared with her.

He'd told her he wouldn't bring anyone. But if they were engaged, he'd bring her, of course.

Yes. Soon, it would be time for Garrett to let her know that it was done, that he was engaged to another woman. But then, she already knew from Beth.

She helped Molly with the veil, all the while blinking back the tears, and then she softly kissed her cheek. "You're the most beautiful bride I've ever seen."

"Kate, I want this for you," Molly said, gesturing at her wedding dress.

Kate nodded. "That's why I might just go after all, Moo. To find love and hopefully a family of my own."

They shared a forlorn smile, until Eleanor's shout from the bedroom snapped them out of it.

"It's time, my little Molly dear!"

Molly's eyes widened in excitement and she immediately puckered her lips into an O and drew in a series of little panting breaths that made Kate laugh. Poor Molly would probably be anxious for Julian to get her out of that dress tonight.

Molly smacked Kate's derriere. "Come on, sis. Let's go make that man mine," she said cheekily, and Kate adjusted her train around her arm and told her she'd be right out.

It was definitely the hormones. Or maybe a broken heart. Or the sentiment of watching her baby sister in a wedding gown.

Whatever it was, Kate sobbed quietly in the bathroom stall for a quick minute, and then wiped her tears and patted her makeup dry. Once her eyes didn't look so swollen, she went out into the gardens.

It was a perfect day for a wedding.

A breeze rustled through the oak trees. The sun blazed high in the sky, and it seemed the entire elite from Houston, Dallas, Austin and San Antonio was congregated at the Gage estate, all sumptuously dressed, many of the ladies wearing high-fashion hats on their heads.

Flowers framed the beautiful arched trellis, and the orchestra began softly with their violins while Kate quickly lined up behind Molly. She hadn't even thought she'd have the courage to see Garrett today, but he stood at the other end of the red-carpeted aisle next to Julian, whose smile was mesmerizing, his green eyes staring possessively at Molly.

Kate's gaze was magnetically drawn to Garrett, so stunning in his black tuxedo that her heart almost cracked with emotion when the "Bridal Chorus" began and Molly took the first step forward. Because this would never be her, walking up to him, like this.

Garrett's mouth was watering like crazy. He was supposed to watch Molly make her grand entrance but he could focus only on one redhead, and even from afar, he could see that Kate's eyes were full of tears, which just worried him and made him feel an insane need to go to her and embrace her and offer her support.

His thoughts filtered back to the day he'd met her. She and Molly had been brought up to the house by their father, the Gages' new bodyguard. Molly had been a little bitty thing, toddling over to give her lollipop to Julian. Kate had been just a tad older, but she'd been as open and chatty as a teenager, immediately warming up to his mother, asking why this? Why that?

She'd made him scowl, and when she'd turned to talk to Julian and warn him not to take Molly's lollipop, Garrett had immediately wanted her to pay attention to him, too. It had been the story of his life. Wanting her attention, her eyes on him, wanting everything from her and hating that he wanted it. He'd wanted to be the apple of her eye, and instead, he'd been the idiot who took away her father.

He'd promised himself he'd be her hero, and he'd tried like hell to protect her from everything he could—especially himself. When all he'd wanted was her. He'd withdrawn with ruthless self-discipline, telling himself that he'd never deserve Kate like Julian deserved Molly.

Today Garrett's eyes were wide open. True, the past was loaded with regrets, but when he thought of the future, one without Kate at the center of it was unfathomable. No man on this earth would ever love and care for Kate and fight for her happiness more than Garrett would. Chest bursting with emotion, he watched the woman he loved walk behind her sister. He saw how her soft smile trembled with emotion, and God, he wanted to hug her and kiss those tears away, telling her whatever changed in her life, he'd always be her constant.

He couldn't take his eyes off her as she came up the aisle. He imagined her walking up to him and his heart stuttered in his chest, he loved her so much.

Now she took her place across from Garrett as her sister tied the knot with the love of her life, and all Garrett knew was that he wanted to do this with Kate. He'd have Kate. Or he'd have no one.

"Dearly beloved, we are gathered here today…" The

priest began the ceremony, and for several minutes, Garrett waited for Kate's gaze to turn to him. Finally, her eyes flicked over to his, and his gut seized with need. She looked so beautiful. Her lips shone in a coral color, her blue eyes highlighted by the sapphire fabric of her dress. A silent plea brimmed in the depths of those eyes, and whatever it was she wanted, Garrett wanted to give it to her.

Not because he'd promised her father that he would. But because he was selfish and he got high on her smiles, got completely drugged and deliciously drunk with her happiness.

"I, Molly, take you, Julian John, to be my husband..."

As soon as he heard Molly speak, Garrett imagined Kate speaking that same vow to him. His chest squeezed as their gazes held across the altar, Kate's blue eyes continuing to tear him to pieces.

She still wanted to leave, didn't she?

But he wouldn't let her.

Not after he'd had her trembling in his arms and whispering his name and giving him everything he'd always wanted.

He'd told himself every night for the past thirty nights that she might have felt pity for him, or that they were just a man and a woman in bed together, getting caught in the moment. It was bull. What they'd been caught up in had been years and years of denied attraction. Burning chemistry. Heated glances. And he was sick and tired of denying himself *her*.

The day she'd made love to him had been the best day of his existence. And he wanted to have her in his arms, where she belonged, every day and night in his future.

"You may now kiss the bride!"

Kate blinked and tore her eyes from his, looking startled as Julian grabbed Molly and twirled her around.

"Oh, crap!"

They ended up tangled in the train, and Kate came instantly to the rescue. Kate. Always taking care of Molly.

"I got it," she said, laughing as she detached the train and Julian proceeded to carry a laughing Molly away, the blaring sound of the "Wedding March" following them.

Watching Kate struggle, Garrett stalked down the aisle, grabbed the other end of the tulle fabric and brought it over, watching her duck her head to avoid his gaze.

"Thanks," she said, and he wanted to kiss her. God, why was this so difficult? They'd grown up together. She was the only woman who knew him, truly knew him. What he liked and loathed. That he would never truly feel like he deserved a life of his own.

If he was going to open up with someone, it should be easy to do it with her.

But the way she was acting skittish and defensive filled him with dread. And he knew that this was going to be one of the hardest things he'd ever done.

She struggled with the tulle. When he reached out and captured her small hands, she sucked in an audible breath. His heart pounded as she looked up at him, those blue eyes wide and concerned.

"Tell me if I'm mistaken—" his voice was low "—but did my brother just marry your sister?"

She didn't smile, but looked intently into his eyes as if she was as entranced as he was. "It only took a full hour, Garrett. You couldn't have missed it," she said.

Her mouth, the way it moved, drove him insane. "Apparently I did."

"You were standing right there. Where were you? Mars?" She straightened and rolled her eyes as she started walking away, the tulle clutched against her chest, and he had to raise his voice a bit to be heard.

"I was in my bedroom, Kate. With you in my arms."

She went utterly still, her back to him, and he knew she remembered. He could feel it in the air, burning between them.

But she didn't turn. Instead, she started down the path that led to the Gage mansion. Garrett fell into step beside her.

"Kay, I need to talk to you," he said.

"If it's to tell me about your wedding, I already know. Congratulations," she said.

He cocked a brow. "Then maybe you can tell me the details, since apparently you know more about it than I do? Dammit, I need to talk to you somewhere *private*."

He grabbed her elbow to halt her, but she immediately yanked it free. "I need to talk to you, too, but I'm not doing it here. Nor am I doing it *today*."

Simmering with frustration, he followed her again,. "Well, I *am*. So just listen to me."

Stopping her, he forced her to turn and gazed into those accusing blue eyes, trying to find the words to begin the wrenching of his damned black soul. "I don't know what happened to me the other day, Katie.…What you told me left me so damn winded, I swear I didn't know where to begin.…"

Her hands flew to her ears. "Not here, please, *please, not here!*"

He pulled her arms down, scowling. "I know I hurt you, I know you don't want me to apologize, but I need to say I am sorry. I am sorry for how things have gone down and for hurting you. I'm sorry for how it happened, Katie. I wish I'd done it differently. If I could take it back, I would, if only to get you to stop looking at me like you are just now."

She whipped around to face him, her eyes flashing in fury. "You wish to take the night back, that's what you wish? Oh, you're something special, do you know that? You're something else. I can't even believe I let you put your filthy paws on me, you no-good—"

"Goddamn it, I really didn't want to do it this way, Kay. But you're giving me no choice!" Jaw clamped, he grabbed her and swept her into his arms and stalked across the gardens toward the house.

"Wha—" The tulle train fell inch by inch from her grasp and trailed a path behind them as she kicked and squirmed and hit his chest. "Garrett, stop! Put me down! What are you *doing*?"

He kicked the front doors open and carried her up the stairs, his jaw like steel, his hands blatantly gripping her buttocks. "Something I should've done a long, long time ago."

Kate froze for a second, and then struggled with more effort. "Put me down!" she screeched.

He squeezed her bottom as he charged down the hall and into his old bedroom, kicking the door shut behind him. "I'm not apologizing for the night I made love to you. Dammit, Kate, I'm apologizing for being responsible for your father's *death!*"

He put her down on the bench at the foot of his old bed and stepped back so she didn't kick him in the groin.

She went utterly still, but her chest heaved up and down, and damned if that wasn't an attractive sight.

He expelled a long breath and continued. "Kate, I'm not going to apologize for the time you were mine. I won't. I apologized once, but I didn't mean it. I don't regret a second of that time with you. Except not being more careful with you and more than anything, for not doing it sooner."

She sat there, stunned and panting, and Garrett was only just beginning. His necktie was almost choking him as all his emotions surfaced like a hurricane gathering force.

"I apologize for not listening to your father that night, Kate. For being stupid and not listening—"

"Don't!" she pleaded, raising her palms. "Garrett, please don't apologize for that. Or for anything. Please stop apologizing to me. It was an accident. And it was his duty. My father would have…gladly died for you, for any Gage, for any reason. He was passionate about his job, and he was as passionate about you boys as if you were his children. He'd have done it over and over for you, Garrett. He loved you and I love you. I've always loved you."

Her words were like a salve. They might never absolve him, but they appeased him, tamed the dark regret inside him. And stoked the little flickering flame of new hope there.

"You do love me, don't you, Freckles?"

She met his gaze in silence. My God, *her face*. The blush spread everywhere, it seemed, and Garrett trembled with the urge to undress her and see that flush crawl along her skin.

When she didn't say a word, neither affirming nor denying it, he knelt.

* * *

Kate's eyes almost popped out of their sockets as Garrett Gage knelt at her feet.

"You asked me what I wanted from you—Kate, I want everything. The works. Yes, I want kids, I want to be your husband. I know I robbed you of a real family, and I want to give you one. I want to be the father of your children...not because I promised I would take care of you. Because I'm crazy-sick in love with you."

His words sucked the wind out of her.

She sat there, clutching her stomach, not even remembering where the tulle had ended up falling on their way here. Runaway tears streamed down her cheeks as the things Molly and Beth had told her about a Clarks-Gage wedding vanished from her head and she realized with a fluttering heart that Garrett Gage was proposing to her.

"Kate, I've never felt like this before. I can't think clearly when it comes to you. I've been trying to make you stay and at the same time that has driven you away. Don't go, baby. Stay with me. Here. Be my wife. Let me love you like you deserve."

She cried even harder, not believing this was happening. She had dreamed about this. For years. To the point that now her entire life and all her decisions revolved around forgetting it. Around trying not to want what she could *never* have.

And now Garrett Gage knelt, dark and beautiful at her feet, his face somber in its intensity, his gaze like liquid fire.

"If you think this has to do with the promise I made to your father, it doesn't," he murmured as he took her smaller hand within both of his. "I made that promise a long time ago and I've tried to keep it as best as I could.

No, this is about me wanting to promise you, the woman I love, my future."

She wiped her eyes, and squeezed one of his hands with hers. "What about C-Cassandra…?"

"She's marrying Emerson. Our half brother."

"Wh-what do you mean h-half—?"

A movement in the doorway made them both look up in surprise.

"Kate! What…?" Beth blinked. "I'm sorry…uh. This is a bad time, isn't it?"

Garrett nodded, but Kate shook her head and wiped the rest of her tears away. "What is it, Beth?"

Beth pointed in the direction of the stairs behind her. "They're all seated at the tables. And the maid of honor and best man need to speak before the toast."

Garrett dropped his head and cursed under his breath.

"We'll be right there, Beth," Kate said, trembling from head to toe as she rose to her feet.

Garrett held her up and stroked his thumb along her jawline. "You can answer me later," he said softly.

She nodded and rushed to the bathroom to pat her face dry with a tissue, making sure her mascara wasn't dripping all over her face. Garrett waited outside in the hall for her, and every cell in her body screamed at her to fling herself into his arms when she realized he was still there. But she didn't.

In silence, they went downstairs and into the gardens, and halfway there, after the backs of their hands bumped several times, he took her hand within his and led her across to their table.

Her throat closed, and she tried very hard not to think about the gesture and how many times she'd wanted it. It screamed "boyfriend" in her mind. Lover. Love.

Feeling as though five hundred pairs of eyes were on them as they made their way through the tables to the far end of the room, Kate held her gaze on the bride and groom.

Her fingers tingled when her hand unlatched from Garrett's and they each headed to their places on opposite sides of the long table, where Molly and Julian sat watching them with wide smiles. Garrett went to stand at Julian's side, and Kate stood next to Molly. Eleanor had indicated that she didn't want to speak, and she seemed to be hiding behind a tissue right now, but Kate remembered how the groom's mother always thought it proper that ladies go first. So Kate was the first to speak.

Regrettably.

She cleared her throat several times and shakily grabbed a small microphone, struggling to keep her voice level as she tried to quiet her racing mind. "Molly had a favorite story she liked for me to read," she said into the microphone, keeping her eyes on Molly to keep herself focused. "There was a part she loved to hear, when Piglet asked Winnie the Pooh, 'How do you spell love?' And Pooh answered 'You don't spell it.... You feel it.'"

She blinked back her tears as she studied the delightful little bundle by the name of Molly, the only blood family Kate had known for over two decades. Seeing her sister so happy as she started a family of her own with Julian, while Kate herself had a baby in her tummy from the man she loved and a proposal she had always dreamed of, made her suddenly feel weightless with joy. Laughing to herself, she lifted her glass with her free hand.

"Molly and Julian, you guys felt that love for each

other before you could spell it. And I'm just glad you didn't listen to me, Moo, when I filled your head with warnings and my own fears. I'm glad you listened to your heart."

People clapped and drank, and Kate sat down only to hear Garrett's sexy voice coming through the microphone next. "For the better part of my life I've thought it my duty to protect Molly from your claws, little bro."

Julian threw back his head and let out a great peal of laughter, soon joined by all the other guests, and Garrett winked at Molly. "I got to be the ogre separating you two for years, for which I hope you won't always hate me, Molly."

"I forgive you if you finally kiss my sister!" Molly shot back, throwing him a white rose she'd plucked from the centerpiece.

Garrett caught it and laughed, then glanced at Kate and held it in the air, as if promising to give it to her. Tucking it into his pocket, he glanced back at the groom.

"There's no denying that I got to be the voice of reason when Kate and Molly came into our lives, Jules. Because I knew better than you that we were both done for."

He turned his attention to his new sister-in-law next. "Molly, my brother loves you more than anything in the world," he told her, lifting his glass now. "And if you take care of my brother, I promise I will not only kiss your sister, but I will not rest until I make her my wife."

The guests whooped and cheered, as Julian stood to slap him on the back and everyone seemed to glance at Kate for a moment. Their smiles almost pleaded with her not to be stupid and just snatch up this man for herself.

And she would.

Of course she would.

She knew Garrett would want an answer, but before she could give him anything, he would need to know that she was pregnant.

Oh, God. She was having his child, and he loved her. He. Loved. Her.

The hours sped by. Soon, they were served the artichoke hearts with a special tangy mustard sauce, a variety of meats, an assortment of vegetables and desserts to spare.

By the time Molly and Julian were ready for the first dance, Garrett made his way to Kate, and she rose to her feet, anticipation making her heart race. She didn't know if she could postpone her answer until she had a chance to talk to him about the pregnancy. There was impatience etched across his features, as though he'd been waiting too long already to hear her acceptance and he wouldn't wait anymore.

He would want an answer now—she could see it in his eyes. Eyes that wouldn't stop staring at her.

Garrett's heart crashed into his rib cage as he approached Kate, who looked so warm and inviting as she waited for him to get close.

He let his gaze drift down her body, taking in the perky breasts encased in that corset dress he'd seen her try on, the form-fitting fabric that hugged her shapely hips and the skirt that flared over her legs. She wore her hair loose. Long and wavy and so damned glossy it looked like satin, it tumbled past her shoulders. Feather earrings clung to her little ears. And her eyes…

When he looked up at her eyes and found them staring at him with shy vulnerability, he almost couldn't take it, he wanted her so much.

He wanted these people gone, wanted her intimately, in his arms.

"Dance with me," he said quietly as he gently pulled her into his arms. She hooked her arms underneath his, and her hands curved over his shoulders from behind as she pressed her body to him and tucked her face under his chin.

He closed his eyes and savored the feel of her as she drew an invisible pattern with her fingertips along his back. She moved fluidly against him, like she belonged in his arms.

His insides thrummed with impatience as he held one arm around her waist, then slowly reached into his jacket pocket and pulled out the velvet Tiffany box. He clasped her left hand and slid the ring onto her finger, then lifted her hand so that she noticed the jewel as he kissed her knuckles, one by one.

He'd never been so impatient in his life.

He couldn't understand how he'd waited to claim her for so long, for he couldn't handle another second of wondering if she was still planning to move some-where else.

"I need to hear you say yes," he murmured, tucking her hand under his arm as he kissed her ear softly. Her hair caressed her shoulders as she angled her head back-wards an inch or two, and she looked at him with those blue eyes, shining with tears and emotion.

I love you, she'd said.

He was burning to hear it again.

"Say it, Kate," he pressed her, cupping the back of her head in one hand. Impatiently he fitted his lips to hers and hungrily searched inside her mouth for her response. When her tongue pushed back thirstily against him, she set him on fire. He splayed his hand at the small of her back and pressed her tightly to him as he dragged his mouth up to her ear. "Tell me yes."

She grabbed his jaw and turned his head so she could whisper, "I need to tell you something first."

He groaned, already burning with desire, needing to be with her. "Tell me after you've said yes."

She smiled. "You'd take me anyway? Whatever I have to say?"

He shot her a solemn gaze. "Yes, Kate. I would. Tell me yes, and then tell me what you want to say to me."

"Yes, I'll marry you. We're having a baby."

He drew back, staring wordlessly. His astonishment was so complete, his disbelief so overwhelming, he wasn't even breathing. "What baby?"

"Our baby, Garrett. We're having a baby."

"You're pregnant," he said, as if in a daze.

She bit her lower lip, her eyes shining with wariness and excitement and concern.

He shook his head to clear it, but it was full of one thought. Baby. Father. Parents. *She'll give me a child.... She loves me.... She'll give me a baby....*

"Kate...when were you going to tell me this? When?"

"I'm telling you now."

"And you were still going to Florida *without me?*"

Kate wiped away her tears.

"Were you?" he demanded.

"No," she admitted. "I'm not going anywhere. This is my home."

He was shocked. Suddenly he bent and kissed her stomach. "You're not joking me?"

"No. Molly's pregnant, too, but don't say anything."

He straightened again and seized her by the shoulders. "Holy hell, you have to say yes now."

"It was yes before, Garrett. It's…always yes. I've dreamed this. I've wanted it for so long."

He was reeling.

He looked at her and felt that same hot punch to his solar plexus. Then he pulled her back against him, infinitely closer.

He raised a languid hand to stroke the shell of her ear with the back of one curled finger. "Kate…" he murmured adoringly.

She gave him a smile, her eyes glowing. "Yes, Garrett?"

Jamming his fingers into her hair, he tipped her head back so she held his gaze. "God, we've wasted so much time, Kate."

"You said you weren't afraid. To love somebody." She cupped his jaw. "I am. I *was*. I won't be anymore. I'm going to love you like crazy if you let me."

"I'll not only let you, I'll encourage you. I'll do anything possible to make it true." He stroked her belly with one hand, and her scalp with the other. "Have you gone to the doctor?"

"I was going to. I kept hoping Beth and Molly were wrong. That you wouldn't marry Cassandra. And maybe… I'd try one more time to make you love me. Be honest with you this time. No more sneaky tactics to get your attention."

"Kate, you couldn't be sneaky if you tried."

"Garrett, I didn't want to trap you into marriage, please know that."

"I know, Freckles. You don't need to tell me this. But didn't you know? You trapped me with these ages ago…."

He stroked her seven freckles that he adored, then let his finger drift down to the flesh of her lips. "Trapped. Caught. I hardly ever got to chase you and I know you wanted me to."

"I didn't."

"You did."

"All right then, I did." She started running across the gardens, and for a stunned moment, he didn't realize she was heading back to the bedroom where he'd just proposed. Then everything in him burst to action and he chased after her.

Eleven

Garrett drove them over to his apartment, and their excitement made the air crackle between them.

She loved how he'd chased her, and caught her. The crazy man had *tickled* her. They'd danced together, laughed, enjoyed each other. Kate had never felt so free or happy. Garrett had never looked so content, his face never faltering from the dazzling white smile that curled her toes and warmed her tummy.

Now he led her down the hall of his apartment, and her body was going crazy from wanting him.

Their footsteps were rushed as she tried unfastening her dress and Garrett tossed his tux jacket on the floor, then left a trail of clothing to his room—bowtie, shoes, socks, vest.

"I can't wait," he said as he jerked off his snowy-white shirt.

Kate was breathing in little pants at the sight of him bare-chested. He watched her struggle to unlace her dress from the back for a moment, then said, "Turn around, let me get that."

His voice was gruff with desire, and her legs trembled as he got her dress undone. He eased the top half of her dress down to her waist, and then she caught her breath when his thumbs caressed her back in slow circles. She shuddered when he set a kiss at the nape of her neck as he started easing the dress off her hips, then splayed his hands over her rib cage and pressed her back against him before turning her around.

She wasn't wearing a bra and she mewed softly when his hands covered her aching breasts. Then she tilted her face upward as his mouth searched for and found hers.

He teased her with his tongue and rubbed her nipples with his thumbs. His body rocked against her, and Kate couldn't stand the agony.

"Garrett…"

All her emotions had spun and churned for days and weeks, and now she needed him inside her.

With her dress pooled at her ankles, he caressed his hands along the sides of her stockinged thighs. "Do you want me?" His low, erotically textured voice drove her insane.

"So much," she gasped, pushing against him so she could feel how much he wanted her, the proof in the erection straining against his dress slacks.

"Do you love me?" He palmed her between her legs, where a pool of heat had already gathered at the apex.

"Like nothing in my life."

He squeezed her sex in his palm. "I love you, Kate." He dragged his tongue along her neck and down her shoulders as he hooked his fingers around the waist-band of her stockings and tugged off the clinging material. He urged her onto the bench at the end of the bed as he removed them, and she sat and watched his dark head as he bent to tongue a wet path down her bare legs. Tingles of pleasure raced through her body. He tossed the stockings aside, and Kate edged back onto the bed, tossing away some of the decorative pillows as he unfastened his slacks and got naked.

He was beautifully masculine, tanned and hard, and swollen with desire for her.

"The last time I was with you has haunted me," he whispered as he started lowering his body over hers, his arm muscles flexing. Swallowing with a little sound of need, she spread her thighs to welcome him and he settled between them, his urgency matching hers as their tongues tangled heatedly.

"I haven't stopped thinking about it for a second, either," she admitted, nipping his mouth, then kissing his jaw, anxious to claim him like he was claiming her.

He teased her breasts with his thumbs, then grazed the straining peaks with his teeth. She moaned, and he lapped her with his tongue to make her delirious.

"You like that, Freckles? You like my mouth all over you?"

"I love everything you do to me."

He chuckled softly, his breath bathing her nipple tips as he mouthed her breasts, alternating from one to the other. He caressed them until she couldn't wait and was pumping her body eagerly for his penetration.

He primed her with one finger, then two. "I'll be careful with you," he vowed, and kissed her lips. "And you." He kissed her stomach, and Kate's heart unwound like a ribbon when she realized he was talking to their unborn child. "Freckles, I wanted this. You. I wanted something of ours."

"Then make me yours," she whispered.

He gripped her hips and meshed his mouth to hers as he entered her. She arched up for his thrust, clutching him. "Garrett."

He grabbed the sides of her thighs and kept them slightly raised as he inched deeper into her body. She tossed her head back with a grimace of pain that became absolute, exquisite pleasure when he was fully inside.

She was so turned on that every time he pulled out, her sex muscles clung to him, preventing him from leaving her. She wanted more of him, all of him, inside her.

She cried out when he started thrusting harder and deeper, and an explosion of colors rushed through her mind, stretching her nerve endings until they snapped and released. He growled and strained above her, and they rode out the pleasure together.

"That was amazing," she gasped when Garrett rolled over to the side and pulled her up against him. "You're so amazing." She hugged him, and he returned her hug, his arms hot and tight around her.

He clasped the back of her head and stared meaningfully into her eyes. "Every night from now on I want you sleeping in my arms."

"I'm not complaining."

He adjusted her against him so that he was embracing her from behind and his hands were splayed on her stomach. He spoke close to her temple. "If he's a boy, we'll name him after our fathers. Jonathan David Gage. And a girl...you'll drive me crazy if you give me a girl."

"You're the one giving it to me," she laughingly answered, and he turned her face by the chin and brushed her freckles with his lips.

"Always so contrary, my Kate."

"Garrett? Pinch me." He pinched her bottom, and she squealed.

He chuckled, clearly liking it. "Ask me to pinch you again."

"One's enough. I'm convinced I'm not dreaming now."

"You have a lovely bottom. If you let me pinch it again, I'll kiss it afterward."

She laughed. Feeling little tingles in her body, she nodded, and she felt the pinch that made her squeak, and then she felt his kiss, with tongue. It made her moan softly and cuddle back to him, wondering when she could have him again.

"Convinced it's no dream?" he murmured, brushing her hair behind her forehead.

With a smile that almost hurt, she turned over and pressed her face into his chest and stroked her fingers absently across his nipples, growing thoughtful. "Now what was it you were saying about a half brother?"

"You'll meet him soon," he told her. "He looks like me, actually."

"Wow, that good?"

He laughed. "Don't even think about staring for a moment longer than necessary."

"Why would I when I have you?" She tucked her head under his chin. "Why didn't we know about him?"

"Mother didn't want to know about him. But I think it's time we set the past behind us, don't you, Kate?"

"Yes, Garrett. I agree wholeheartedly."

Twelve

Sitting on her front stoop, Kate spotted Garrett's silver Audi turning around the corner and her smile widened. As soon as the car came to a stop, she started for the passenger door.

He couldn't even get out, she got in so fast. "Hey," she said.

His car smelled of him, of leather and spices, deliciously male, and it almost made her dizzy.

"Hey." He reached out and squeezed her hand, bending over and kissing her lips softly. "You look good."

She smiled. "So do you."

Once they arrived at the clinic, Kate filled out the paperwork while Garrett sat, enormous in the little chair out in the waiting room, pulling and pulling at his tie. There were pictures of babies and pregnant women hanging on the walls, but he only had eyes for Kate as she walked back toward him.

Soon, they were led inside to the ultrasound room.

Kate was lying down patiently as the doctor came inside, greeted them and pulled up her robe. After the doctor smeared a cold gel on her stomach, a little blob appeared on the screen.

Garrett had been standing back, but now he approached, his eyes on the screen.

"There we go," Dr. Lowry said.

Garrett peered at the screen, and Kate reached for his hand and squeezed, suddenly extremely excited. He squeezed back even harder, and smiled down at the screen.

"That noise you hear is the heartbeat," the doctor explained.

They were both silent as they registered this. Then the doctor took some measurements, and estimated the date of conception to be...of course, the night she accosted Garrett in his bedroom when he was sick.

"Thank God for strep," he said to himself, and his eyes glittered when he looked at her, as though that was the best thing that could have ever happened to him.

Sharing this with him was incredible. Irrevocable. She could feel the connection as they watched their child on that screen together.

The doctor gave them the estimated delivery date. "So we will be seeing you in two months to find out what you're having."

"Do we really want to know?" Kate asked Garrett.

"Hell, yes, we do."

She smiled and nodded.

The doctor slapped the folder shut. "In the meantime, everything looks fine, Mr. and Mrs. Devaney. You have yourselves a good rest of the day."

"It's *Gage*."

The doctor turned to Garrett. "Oh?" He quickly checked his folder, flustered and confused.

"I filled my name in as Devaney," Kate whispered to Garrett as she wiped the gel off her stomach. His eyes homed in on her bare skin like he wanted to lick the gel up and bury his face in her belly button.

"You're a Gage, too, starting tomorrow," he said flatly.

She rolled her eyes. "Of course I am. I just felt odd using the name before we go to city hall and church."

He helped her down from the examining table and kissed her softly but quickly. "You've always been a Gage, Kate. You've been mine from the start. I didn't need to sleep with you to show you that."

"Maybe you did." She smirked, patting her stomach, and he laughed.

Outside the clinic, he pulled her up against him when they got to his car. "Thank you, Freckles."

"For what?"

"For that night you spent in my arms," he whispered, framing her face in his hands and kissing her. "For agreeing to spend a lifetime of nights with me."

"No, Garrett," she said, cupping his face right back. "Thank *you* for asking."

* * * * *

A sneaky peek at next month...

PASSIONATE AND DRAMATIC LOVE STORIES

My wish list for next month's titles...

In stores from 18th April 2014:

☐ The Sarantos Baby Bargain – Olivia Gates

& The Last Cowboy Standing – Barbara Dunlop

☐ From Single Mum to Secret Heiress
   – Kristi Gold

2 stories in each book - only £5.49!

& Your Ranch...Or Mine? – Kathie DeNosky

☐ A Merger by Marriage – Cat Schield

& Caroselli's Accidental Heir – Michelle Celmer

Available at WHSmith, Tesco, Asda, Eason, Amazon and Apple

Just can't wait?

Visit us Online

You can buy our books online a month before they hit the shops!

0414/51

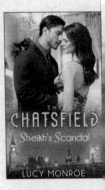

When five o'clock hits, what happens after hours...?

Feel the sizzle and anticipation of falling in love across the boardroom table with these seductive workplace romances!

Now available at
www.millsandboon.co.uk

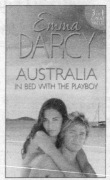

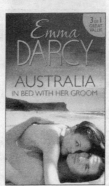
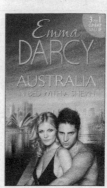

Join the Mills & Boon Book Club

Want to read more **Desire**™ books?
We're offering you **2 more** absolutely **FREE!**

We'll also treat you to these fabulous extras:

- Exclusive offers and much more!
- FREE home delivery
- FREE books and gifts with our special rewards scheme

Get your free books now!

visit www.millsandboon.co.uk/bookclub
or call Customer Relations on 020 8288 2888

The World of
Mills & Boon®

There's a Mills & Boon® series that's perfect for you. We publish ten series and, with new titles every month, you never have to wait long for your favourite to come along.

By Request

Relive the romance with the best of the best
12 stories every month

Cherish™

Experience the ultimate rush of falling in love
12 new stories every month

Desire™

Passionate and dramatic love stories
6 new stories every month

nocturne™

An exhilarating underworld of dark desires
Up to 3 new stories every mo